The LAST SEASON

a novel

JENNY JUDSON &
DANIELLE MAHFOOD

Relax. Read. Repeat.

THE LAST SEASON
By Jenny Judson and Danielle Mahfood
Published by TouchPoint Press
Brookland, AR 72417
www.touchpointpress.com

ISBN-13: 978-1-952816-63-5

Editor: Jenn Haskin
Cover Design: David Ter-Avanesyan, TER33DESIGN

Visit the authors' website at www.daniandjenny.com

First Edition

Library of Congress Control Number (LCCN): 2021941187

Printed in the United States of America.

To our high school girlfriends:
Romance isn't dead.

PART I

CHAPTER 1

Drayton Manor
October 1863

Inside the library, Miss Cassandra Drayton's Latin lesson dragged on. Words swam across the page like minnows in a stream. Outside, birds chirped, and the afternoon breeze chased the clouds across the sky. Unable to concentrate, Cassandra scanned the room, the rich oriental carpet, the heavy silk curtains, the overflowing bookshelves, the standing atlas, and the little marble statue of Artemis. She dismissed them all with a sigh. She was beginning to feel claustrophobic and restless in the face of this confining opulence. If asked, she couldn't have said why, but she wanted to kick off her silken slippers and sweep the Latin books off the desk.

Resting her chin in her hands, Cassandra gazed glumly out the big bay window at the manicured garden with its perfectly trimmed topiaries and softly bubbling fountains. There, behind the hedgerow was a boy she had never seen. She strained to take a closer look. He wasn't a boy really, rather a gangly lad about Cassandra's age, though much taller. He was angular, like a young colt, with an untamed, honey-colored mane. Their eyes met. Caught staring at her, the lad dropped with a jerk to the ground acting as though he were searching for something that had fallen in the grass.

Cassandra pushed her book away.

"Miss Fairfax, who is that?" Cassandra pointed to the spot where, moments before, the lad had stood.

"Who?" answered the governess. Miss Fairfax had attentively guarded and coddled Cassandra for the better part of a year. She was pretty and young, a little over twenty, so most of the time Cassandra regarded her as a companionable ally rather than a stern disciplinarian. But from time to time, Miss Fairfax retreated into her own thoughts and erected an invisible wall that Cassandra couldn't broach.

"That boy. In the garden. There."

He popped up like a jack-in-the-box and scurried away from the window.

"He's the new stable boy I suppose. Now, back to your lesson, my dear," Miss Fairfax answered in a distant sort of way—aloof and closed off, as if Cassandra was bothersome, which annoyed her to no end.

"What's his name?" She pressed Miss Fairfax.

"Whose?"

"The stable boy's."

"Shush, Miss Cassandra. Try to focus. Concentrate on your verbs. Conjugate fugere, please." When she said "please" like that she meant business.

"Fugio, fugis, fugit," Cassandra grumbled. Well, if Miss Fairfax wasn't going to tell her, she would go down to the stable and ask Jones herself. The head coachman had been with the family for as long as Cassandra could remember. He was a jolly, loquacious man with cheeks like roasted apples. He would tell her. Impatient and used to getting her way, the only thing holding Cassandra back was that she wanted to see her father first. He was returning from London that morning, bearing gifts, as always. Of course, the best gift of all would have been his taking her to London with him.

When he got home, she was determined to extract a promise from him that next time he would take her rather than leave her to sulk around Drayton Manor. She was sure she could convince him. The house felt so empty when he was gone, oddly quiet and lonely. Everyone—upstairs and downstairs—tiptoed around the labyrinthine hallways and spoke in hushed voices.

"Redeo, Redire, Redii."

Finally, Cassandra heard the wheels of the carriage on the drive and closed her Latin book with a clap. She ran out of the library and down a flight of stairs to the front door, which Baxter, the butler, held open, and launched herself toward the just-stopped carriage. Behind her, Miss Fairfax followed, moving at a more ladylike pace.

Lord James Drayton climbed out, a big smile across his face and two packages in his arms. His thick sandy curls fell across his forehead rakishly.

"My love!" He planted a kiss on his daughter's cheek and handed her one of the parcels. "Here you go! I've missed you so."

"Thank you." She inspected the package, a rectangular box wrapped in brown paper, the size of two or three stacked dictionaries. Probably a neatly folded petticoat or brocade jacket, or a fur capelet like the one she had seen in a copy of *The Queen* she had taken from her aunt, Lady Eugenia Gray—her father's sister—who visited too often and stayed too long in Cassandra's opinion.

"But you know what I really want?" She sighed and said in her most pathetic voice, "Papa, why won't you take me with you? It is so dull here when you are gone."

"You have Miss Fairfax and your lessons," he replied with gentle resolve. "Now, don't roll your eyes at me. You'll see plenty of London soon enough for your debut and the season. Why rush things?"

Yet, at thirteen, Cassandra knew that was a few years off, a span of time that seemed an eternity. The prospect of entering society was an event that thrilled her to no end. She had envisioned every minute and every detail of her first ball down the exact shade of pale-blush of her silk gown, and the tight, gold ringlets in her hair, pinned to perfection with diamond-encrusted combs. But for the time being, Cassandra was sheltered and closely guarded. It seemed as if her father feared the world would crush her like a porcelain doll under the heel of its boot.

Cassandra fumed, though she knew she should be grateful and in truth was dying to see what was in the package. Her father always surprised her with lavish gifts—embroidered slippers, bejeweled broaches and hair combs, and strings of pearls. Any other girl would have been pleased with the gift. But embers of frustration smoldered in her stomach.

Her cheeks flushed with anger. While she was left floating restlessly through the echoing hallways of Drayton Manor, she imagined her father was gallivanting around London, attending balls and dinner parties, dining at his club with acquaintances and associates. The tidbits of gossip her Aunt Eugenia read aloud from society columns shed light on that other, twinkling world outside of Cassandra's grasp. Cassandra would sneak sections of the paper up to her room and read and reread them voraciously, imagining herself taking walks in Hyde Park, sipping afternoon tea, and eavesdropping on the hushed chatter that fueled her aunt's beloved Ladies Pages. Cassandra sucked in her lips.

"My dear, are you alright? Miss Fairfax is she well?" He turned to Fairfax who answered with a perplexed shrug.

"She was this morning, My Lord."

Lord Drayton's gaze lingered on Miss Fairfax, whose flawless complexion blushed to a dusty rose. His face was strong and angular, but still a bit boyish. A flirtatious light danced across his eyes. Cassandra saw for a moment that she was not the center of her father's, or Miss Fairfax's, attention, which amplified the sting.

"I'm fine," she grumbled. "You just, you just . . . . you always leave me here. You seem to think that gifts and trinkets are all I want. I don't! I don't want any of them."

"Cassandra, dear, what has you so upset?"

Perhaps it was his mild, condescending tone or the befuddled pity in his eyes, Cassandra couldn't say for sure, but hot tears started to well up in the corner of her eyes. She willed them to dry, but they bubbled up and erupted like a geyser. She knew that she was being irrational, but she could not help it.

"It's awful. And lonely. I'm tired of living here and having no one to talk to. All the time I am by myself!"

"You have me, and Miss Fairfax . . . and Aunt Eugenia."

That was the last straw. Citing Aunt Eugenia as if she were a substitute for companionship and the attractions of London. Aunt Eugenia, who watched over Cassandra like a hawk and whose irksome presence filled every room. It did not seem to matter where Cassandra was in the house, somehow, she could always hear the exasperating rustle of her aunt's voluminous skirts just around the corner. Cassandra's mind reeled.

"I hate Aunt Eugenia. She's a fat fussbudget."

His voice turned brittle. "Do not speak of your aunt that way. Perhaps she's right—I've spoiled you too much." She knew her aunt often inserted her unwanted commentary on his childrearing and his defense of her galled Cassandra even more.

"Perhaps you have. Here. Take your gift." She threw it at him. "I don't want it." She regretted it almost immediately, but she was not going to apologize.

Her father looked at her silently for a moment longer, the package sitting on the ground between them. Then the corners of his lips rose as if he were about to laugh. He shook his head and bent to pick up the box. "Silly girl."

Filled with shame and anger, Cassandra did not stay to hear what else he had to say. She began to run toward the garden, her usual refuge, but she would be too easy to find there, so she passed the garden gate and crossed the gravel drive toward the stable. The barn door was wide open, and the stable looked dark and slightly scary. A musty, woodsy scent hung around the building. She had never spent time there and had never learned to ride. Her mother had died in a riding accident, so her father had forbidden it. No one would look for her there.

The backside of the barn was dotted with wooden mounting boxes, two steps high. Cassandra slumped down on one of them and put her head in her hands and cried. Soon, the tears grew cold on her cheeks, and she sniffed indelicately, wiping her nose with the back of her hand. When she had done this as a child, Aunt Eugenia would chastise her, "That is not at all ladylike, Cassandra! Your dance card will never be full if you do that." But Cassandra didn't care, and she wasn't sorry about what she said. Aunt Eugenia *was* a fat fussbudget and an old, infernal nag. She had no children of her own, so she hung around Lord Drayton and Cassandra like a head cold that couldn't be shaken.

As with all unchecked adolescent malaise, one melodramatic emotion tumbled into the next. Cassandra thought about how different her life would have been if her beautiful mother were alive, all the things she would have done. She craved stories about her mother, ones her father never regaled her with, and wanted to know about her. It was one of the only reasons she tolerated her aunt's presence. Aunt Eugenia would often happily recount tales about Lord Drayton and his spirited young bride. She was sure her mother would have taken her to London and introduced her to friends. She would have been a companion, and Cassandra would likely have had brothers and sisters. She squeezed her eyes tightly shut and imagined chasing siblings around in the garden, making funny faces and giggling behind Miss Fairfax's back during lessons, and playing duets on the piano, the house full of noise and laughter.

Just then a loud splash broke her reverie, and dirty water started to pool around the hem of her dress.

"Oh no! My Lady. I am so sorry. I didn't see you there." The shaggy-haired stable boy stood before Cassandra, white as a sheet, empty bucket dangling from his hand.

She stood abruptly almost as surprised as he, and for a moment they stared at each other stone still in mutual astonishment. Then, in a flash, he was on the ground pushing the muddy water away from her skirt as fast as he could.

"What are you doing? Stop that!"

"I'm sorry, My Lady." He shot up, his arms coated with clay-like dirt.

"I'm not My Lady. I'm Miss. Miss Cassandra Drayton."

"I know. I mean, yes, Miss. I know. I did not think anyone was back here behind the barn, or I never would have tossed that water out." He paused in confusion, bucket clutched like a hazardous object.

"What, may I ask, are you doing here?"

"I was . . ." What was she doing there? How could she explain to a stable hand that she had been crying because her father gave her a gift? So, she opted for an attack.

"What am *I* doing here! How dare you! I live here. This is my home. My father is Lord Drayton. I might ask the same of you, what are *you* doing here, boy?"

Rather than chasten him, her anger seemed to restore the lad's composure. He cocked his head with a measure of sympathy and contrition.

"Sorry Miss, I meant . . . well it's just a surprise that's all. I've never seen you around the stables before." Despite his ridiculous, mud-smeared appearance, Cassandra saw he was good-looking, tall with shoulders broadening past the seams of his shirt. His cheeks were ruddy and already more chiseled and square than round and childish. She flushed in embarrassment and redoubled her indignation.

"Well, mind your own business. I was taking a walk, not that you deserve an explanation, and I . . . I stopped to think. I wanted to be by myself, which thanks to you, I am not," Cassandra said, despite the pangs of regret that were already stirring in her. She knew she wasn't acting ladylike, and she had been raised better.

"I did not mean to disturb." He bowed his head and moved as if to resume his work, but then seemed to change his mind. He turned to face her, his bright blue eyes taking her in.

"Miss, do you want a handkerchief?"

"No. Why?"

"You look like you've been crying."

"I have not." Her cheeks brightened.

"Here." He handed Cassandra a dirty rag, which he'd pulled from his pocket. She examined it suspiciously but took it anyway and dabbed the corners of her eyes. "I'm Crispin."

"Oh."

"The new stable boy."

"I thought as much." She sucked in her breath and straightened her shoulders, determined to be more of a lady.

"I guess I'd better be getting back to work. Good day to you."

Before Cassandra had a chance to respond, he walked hastily away and disappeared into the barn. The sun was low in the sky, and the trees cast long shadows over the stable and garden. She felt awkward standing there in the fading light, and a chilly autumn breeze made her shiver, so she started up the hill toward home with Crispin's handkerchief still in her hand.

CHAPTER 2

November 1863

The guns cracked off in the distance. A storm of wings beat and clapped through the brush as the dogs flushed the grouse out of the undergrowth. Another rifle blast, and in the hollow aftermath of the shot, leaves and a few feathers floated to the ground.

"Crispin!" The barrel-chested Sloane shouted. "Here, boy."

Crispin ran toward the man, trudging as quickly as his necklace of grouse would allow, cursing all of Lord Drayton's friends. "Calling me like I'm a dog," he muttered under his breath which was becoming increasingly labored. Even during his dismal childhood years in the Queen's Bench Debtor's Prison, where his father had been forced to raise him after falling on hard times—a victim of bad decisions, poor horse bets, and gambling blunders—Crispin had not felt as lowly as he did in this moment.

His aunt Emma, Miss Drayton's governess, had secured him a position as a stable boy several months prior. She had written to his father: *It isn't much, but a fresh start perhaps, for Crispin.*

While he had hoped to establish a connection with this conscientious aunt, she kept her distance, and, instead of a newfound kinship, he found himself lonely and friendless. Until today, he had spent most of his time in the stables, including his slumbering hours for he had been given a small room in the quarters behind the barn.

Now, a country party had the house in an uproar. Three additional cooks had been brought in from the Kings Arms, along with extra footmen and ladies' maids. They had even taken on a local Blandford Forum boy as an extra stable hand. Crispin was exhausted, receiving orders from all sides and sharing his bed with the boy who snored through the night with the gusto of a man twice his size.

"Boy! A hand with my rifle before you go off. Blasted thing is stuck." Anthony Forsythe, the only one in the party who hadn't had success in the hunt, foisted his Spence into Crispin's chest. He was a priggish sort of man, a bit shorter than the rest with a large forehead and beady eyes, but handsome enough, in a manicured way. He engaged in the same backslapping and "old manning" that the others did, yet he seemed ill at ease, continually looking over his shoulder and giving the other men the once over as if he were studying their dress and mannerisms. Occasionally, Crispin noted, he would copy a phrase or a stance—legs akimbo and arms crossed as if he were as big as that man Sloane. "Hurry up!" he huffed impatiently, revealing that he had none of the gentlemanly nonchalance of the rest of the party.

Crispin fumbled a moment with the rifle, checking the lever to see if the shell from Forsythe's last shot was stuck. All the while sweat dripped down his brow, laden as he was with their prizes. There didn't appear to be anything wrong with the rifle, and Crispin was tempted to tell Forsythe the problem was his poor aim. It was abundantly clear that the man hadn't the seasoned skill of his companions, but they didn't seem to notice or mind. He served a purpose as part of their festivities. What that purpose was, Crispin could not imagine.

Sloane shouted again and pointed toward the small stream that wound through Drayton's' property.

"Boy, damn thing's over there. In the brush." His finger circled around in the general vicinity of a stream and copse of trees, giving Crispin little indication of where one might find the bird. Crispin nodded politely and whistled for one of the dogs. The two trotted obediently toward the invisible bird. The smell of grouse enveloped Crispin. Their cold feathers tickled the back of his neck and their hard bodies flopped against his chest as he ran. His father would be mortified to see his son in such a position. Despite his disastrous wagers and debts, George St. John was a gentleman, and Crispin the last in a long line of gentlemen. According to family lore, the St. Johns had been landowners and horse breeders since King Charles was restored to the throne. These stories were poor comfort when Crispin's young stomach ached with hunger pains, or when he woke in the dead of night to find his father's face pressed against the barred window, tears silently filling the permanent gullies chiseled beneath his eyes, wracked with guilt that he had broken the family legacy and gambled away his son's future. Though he was only thirteen, Crispin knew that if he was to help his father, he needed to find paying work, even low-laboring work, and become a man. And so, he had traded the dirty, gray prison landscape for a foreign, green world. *But is my lot in life any better?* he wondered as hair stuck to his brow and sweat ran down his back.

Crispin's thoughts turned to his aunt. He only met her once since his arrival at Drayton Manor. She had invited him to her rooms for tea in a beautifully penned note on thick parchment. He had anticipated enveloping embraces at a reunion with her long-lost nephew, but instead, he found her unapproachable. She was not uncaring, and she fed him a piece of poppy seed cake from a silver tray, sending him back to the barn with triangles of cake in each pocket, yet she let him know without words that they were to stay in their separate spheres. He left her quarters saddened by the visit, which had fallen so short of his daydreams of newly discovered kinship.

Now at the hunt, up to his ears in the field grass, it was clear to Crispin why she kept her distance from her stable boy nephew. She existed in the realm of pretty, indoor things—lace and silks, books, and oriental rugs. She would dine with Lord Drayton and Miss Cassandra and the rest of the party at their hunting picnic, wrapped in furs like the rest of the women, while Crispin routed around at the edge of the stream, hopelessly searching for another dead bird. Not so hopeless for the dog, however, who pranced proudly back to Crispin with the grouse in his mouth.

Finally, the Master of the Hunt blew the all-clear. The men moved in little conversational clumps toward each other. Off on the crest of a nearby hill, two carriages rolled slowly toward the red-faced men. The ladies were arriving. Lord Drayton headed straight to the carriages, moving like a peacock stretching his feathers.

Lady Eugenia Gray was the first to struggle out. Her voluminous furs and immense tartan skirt seemed to catch on every corner, hinge, and step. While the pinnacle of fashion, her attire had the accidental effect of making her already substantial frame seem expansive. In the end, both Lord Drayton and the driver had to grab her indelicately by the arm and waist and heave her out of the carriage.

"Eugenia, so glad you've come. Our rough and tumble group needs a little refinement." There was no hint of irony in his voice. He kissed her gloved hand, which was dangling in the air for just that purpose.

Lady Gray was followed by Mrs. Saunders, a rosy-cheeked, but graceless woman. Jones had given Crispin a run-down of the whole hunting party, and, according to him, Mrs. Saunders was a merchant's daughter who'd had the good sense to marry the prudent but ambitious Nathaniel Saunders. He was born nothing better than a gentleman farmer, yet he had become the county's wealthiest landowner through calculated risk and careful counting.

Saunders' good fortune had far exceeded Mrs. Saunders' expectations, and she now found herself in relatively uncharted waters, a girl from the city, who until recently knew nothing of hunting parties at colossal estates. She forged ahead mimicking Lady Gray's airs and dress, but even Crispin could see that she wasn't quite able to achieve a genuine aristocratic aura. Her accent, for one, gave her away. Crispin had heard that accent when he was a little boy running around the courtyard of Queen's Prison. It belonged to a country farmer or shopkeeper, who, mortgaged to the hilt, had succumbed to his creditors. Yes, her accent gave her away, and Crispin liked her for it and also felt a little sorry for her.

"Mrs. Saunders. A delight!" Lord Drayton bowed. Then Cassandra burst forth from the second carriage.

"Papa." She leaped into her father's arms and kissed him on the cheek. There was no pretense or reserve with her. Lord Drayton caught her as if she were a little girl, even though she was dressed quite as elegantly as her older companions.

With a slight toss of her head, she flipped her hair—golden in the autumn light—over her shoulder. Crispin couldn't help but stare at her. To him she was a golden girl and, though he'd only seen her a few times since their awkward meeting behind the barn, he'd thought of her quite often. Her initial hostility had faded quickly, and now when their eyes met, she gave him a quick, conspiratorial smile. She was his own age but moved with the ease and confidence that marked her father's every step. She was different from every girl or woman he had ever encountered—and not just because of her impeccable clothing, or the bows and ribbons in her hair, or her trim waist or fine posture. It was something else that Crispin couldn't quite name. Wherever she was, it was as if a spotlight shone on her, and everyone and everything else fell into shadow.

"Hello, Mr. Sloane, Mr. Forsythe . . ." Crispin's eyes followed Cassandra as she greeted each of her father's guests with familiar warmth, but she never once turned toward the stable boy or gave any indication that she was aware of his presence, let alone his too-intense gaze. His cheeks, already glowing with embarrassment, burned an even deeper red knowing that she didn't give him a second thought.

Cassandra was followed by his aunt, who, unlike her charge, observed Crispin's stare almost the moment she descended the last step. She gave him a quick nod and blinked in disapproval. Crispin lowered his head in return, wondering how such a small gesture could be so cutting.

"Miss Fairfax," Lord Drayton offered her his arm, "you will sit next to me, won't you?"

The luncheon was bountiful: plover's eggs and oysters, shepherd's pie and fresh quail, sherry and champagne, and baskets overflowing with fruit.

"What a party, old man!" Sloane raised his glass in their host's direction.

"Hear, hear," echoed the men as they settled into their seats.

Though he did not have the proper livery, Crispin was filling in as a footman during the picnic and stood straight-backed at the railing of the pavilion. From his post there, he could observe the entirety of the table. Forsythe slid with deliberation into the seat next to Cassandra with a silky greeting. "It's a pleasure, Miss Drayton. You look lovely."

She smiled coyly. She couldn't possibly find his slick manners and creamy voice appealing, but as a lady in training she made no gesture to indicate repulsion. Instead, she asked him about the hunt, pressing him to tell her taller and taller tales about his successes. Crispin attributed this line of inquiry and her animated responses to years of practice.

Lord Drayton looked over at her and Forsythe. His expression was a mixture of consternation and gratification, perhaps even newfound respect for his daughter. He must have been somewhat surprised, Crispin supposed, to find she had shed the skin of a spoiled child and slipped rather seamlessly into the role of hostess.

"Ehm, boy," Forsythe wagged a finger at Crispin. "Do you think you could stop gaping at the little lady and get me another glass of sherry?"

Crispin's insides turned liquid and eggy, but rather than move for the sherry, he stood stone-still as Forsythe leaned in to whisper something to Cassandra. His lips brushed the edge of her ear, and they snickered conspiratorially.

"You deaf?" Forsythe snapped his fingers, as Cassandra looked sheepishly in Crispin's direction. The imperative commands, the insults toward his host's servants, it was not done; even Crispin knew enough of refined society to recognize that. But the others politely ignored Forsythe's appalling gaffs. Crispin wondered what Forsythe was to them that they overlooked his poor pedigree and even poorer manners. What did he offer that they were willing to soil the lily-white doily of their dining table with his presence? It must be quite the prize.

Jones grabbed Crispin's shoulder, disrupting his paralyzing study. Jones, firm but patient in his instruction, had taken Crispin under his wing. He was an avuncular figure, quick with a joke and a friendly ribbing, and luckily, he was in good humor today.

"Crispin. 'ead up. You're needed in the stables. Better fetch those birds before you go and 'and 'em off to Mrs. C. She'll be wantin' 'em for dinner."

C rispin shouldn't have been in the barn, but he was desperate to escape the chaos of the hunting party and the anger and disgust it had ignited in him.

The stable loft was quiet and still, a welcome relief. The warm smell of hay made Crispin tired, and so he drifted off, while the breeze lifted and turned the pages of his book, *Nicholas Nickleby*—which he was reading for the umpteenth time, feeling very much like poor, lame Smike. His breath grew steady and slow, and his limbs rested like dead weights on the hay. Sweet sleep enveloped him.

By the time he heard them, it was too late. Crispin couldn't leave his perch or let his presence be known.

The first voice was his aunt's.

"My Lord, don't you think we should return to the house?" Her silhouette appeared in the doorframe. Miss Fairfax's thick auburn hair was pulled back in a loose bun framed by cascading ringlets that caught the afternoon light. She had high cheekbones and a refined face that looked as if it were drawn by a master draftsman, and porcelain skin the color of a dusty rose. Crispin was surprised by how young she looked.

There was no answer, but Drayton stepped into the light and leaned toward Emma seductively. Crispin's brain, slow with sleep, tried to comprehend what he saw. He didn't know what to do. Should he jump in to protect his aunt or hide under a bale of hay? The answer soon revealed itself. Emma did not shrink away as he would have expected. Instead, Lord Drayton and Emma stood like statues, staring at each other for what seemed like several minutes. Finally, Drayton broke the silence.

"Call me James," he commanded.

"Yes, My Lord."

"James." It was a quiet challenge.

"James," she breathed softly. Her voice was gentle and smooth. Crispin had never been touched by a woman, and yet, in that whisper, he knew exactly how it would feel.

"James, we should go back," she said, but she made no move to look away or leave the barn, rather she stepped toward him and raised a hand to his chin.

Lord Drayton clasped Miss Fairfax's hand and drew her toward him.

"Not yet." He lowered his head to her ear, burying himself in the cradle of her neck.

"Not here. It's too indiscrete."

"I know." His hands slid across her back, enveloping her narrow frame. He pushed his fingers through her hair, which came tumbling out of its neat bun in a tumult of auburn locks.

Crispin couldn't move or breathe. His heart beat so loudly he thought it would give him away. He wanted to run, but could not, mesmerized as he was by the scene.

Lord Drayton moved his hand from her hair to her face, and cradling it in his palms, he paused as if looking at a work of art. But the kiss that followed was hard and hungry. Their breathing grew louder like the gusts of autumn wind that churned up the trees. He pulled at the neckline of Emma's gown and pushed down the billowy sleeves revealing a milky white shoulder and the rounded mold of her breasts which he smothered in kisses.

"James," she gasped in a throaty whisper that was barely audible.

He grasped her fiercely and her back arched, giving him better access to her body, which he rained with kisses until she pulled his face to hers and pressed her lips to his as if she had done so a hundred times before. Back and forth they pressed into each other as if drawn by magnetic force.

Then, he seemed to lift her up, embrace her, and carry her all at once. They moved as one into an empty stall that was beyond Crispin's vision. He knew which one it was though, the one piled with bales of hay.

Crispin tried hard not to imagine what was going on below him, but he could hear the rustle of silk and crinoline, the clink of a belt buckle, waves of sighs, and a high-pitched gasp. Even the animals started to shift and hoof in their stalls with increasing intensity. Crispin bit the inside of his cheeks.

Questions ran through his brain: how long would this go on? Should he sneak away while they were distracted? Could he get out without discovery? And, worse, why didn't he want to?

Then there was silence. Crispin did not count the minutes of quiet, but it could not have been long. Night was coming; Miss Fairfax and Lord Drayton would be missed.

"We must go," said Lord Drayton with regret.

Crispin heard Lord Drayton kiss her again, a long, lingering kiss. "Minx." He sighed. "Emma, you turn me into an idiot. Promise me you'll never leave, never become governess elsewhere."

"I promise." Her disembodied response drifted up. She sounded serious yet worried too. The word "governess" erected a wall in their intimacy. In her voice, Crispin sensed uncertainty. Though he was not much more than a boy, he understood the predicament she was in. She had given over to Lord Drayton's pressures and now she was at his mercy. Even in light of his declarations of adoration, she could not be confident. Crispin shook his head in disbelief. He wondered at his aunt—the stiff, distant woman who kept him at arm's length. How little he knew her.

CHAPTER 3

November 1863

When Cassandra first walked into the drawing room, everything seemed so exciting. She had never before been allowed to participate in a hunting party dinner. The shaded lamps cast rosy shadows on the guests, who circled each other as though taking part in some choreographed dance. The gentlemen stood smart in their trim black suits and crisp white gloves. Their eyes were the only things that moved, darting up and down, stealthily tallying up everything they saw—the rugs, the mounted lion's head, the chandeliers, the rigid footmen with their silver trays. Meanwhile, their wives flitted around, bird-like, engaged in pecking conversations. They wore sumptuous gowns dotted with riots of embroidery, feathers, and buttons, stretching their necks long to accentuate their strands of pearls.

Cassandra stood, as instructed, with Aunt Eugenia, who was not to leave her side. That was the deal her father had struck with her: she could come to the dinner as long as Aunt Eugenia was her chaperone. While this was better than nothing, it jeopardized Cassandra's hope for the evening. She longed to talk to young Lord Bedford, who among friends went by Henry.

At eighteen, Henry was the guest closest to her age. His father, the Duke of Westmoor, was an old friend of Lord Drayton. They had gone to Cambridge together, where they played cricket, punted the River Cam, pulled tricks on the masters of Trinity College, skipped class, and generally lived like kings—according to her father's accounts. Lord Drayton often included Westie, which is what he affectionately called the Duke, in hunting parties as he was a sort of convivial oil that greased the gears of any social event.

Home for half term from his own seemingly riotous first year at Cambridge, Lord Bedford had inherited his father's gregarious, carefree nature and his easy way of making friends. Cassandra had known him for years. As children, they had been flung together at various gatherings, sent to play while the adults did adult things and had adult conversations. But the difference in their ages, a full five years, had been an unbridgeable chasm then. Yet Cassandra had spied on Henry with fascination, observing his every adolescent gesture, while he took little to no notice of her.

Now, on the brink of manhood, Lord Bedford was tall, with strong shoulders and wild, curly blond hair that was barely tamed by Macassar Oil. He looked the way Cassandra imagined Perseus would, floating over the Mediterranean Sea on his way to rescue Andromeda. Her imagination would have gotten the better of her if it weren't for two things. For one, oily Anthony Forsythe was fast approaching. He had cornered her during the entire luncheon, and she had tried her best to be polite for her father's sake. Though young, Cassandra was a keen observer of her father's interactions and had internalized his motivations. She knew that Mr. Forsythe had a sizable fortune, a part of which Lord Drayton was hoping he'd deposit into his latest investment. But entertaining him, Cassandra admitted to herself, was hard to do—she found Forsythe dreadfully fawning and fake.

And secondly, for better or worse, Aunt Eugenia had the idea that Cassandra would talk to no unmarried man that evening and so, at the sight of Lord Bedford, Cassandra could feel her aunt's sharp fingertips boring holes into her skin. With a turn of her rounded hips, Eugenia trotted her young charge off to greet Lord and Lady Winthrop, who had just arrived.

Miss Fairfax was right—dinner was an endless bore. Cassandra was seated between the most appallingly dull men. To her left was Mr. Sloane, who had a great mop of salt and pepper hair that fell into his antenna-like eyebrows. On her right was her uncle by marriage, Lord Gray, a fossil of a man. He had no idea how to engage anyone under the age of twenty, and even then, his conversation was not so scintillating. Perhaps that was why

Aunt Eugenia spent so much time at Drayton Manor, often leaving her husband at their home in Bath for weeks on end. This was one of the rare occasions Lord Gray had accompanied his wife to the country. Cassandra stared intently at the painted vines that encircled the plate in front of her, trying to avoid catching Lord Gray or Mr. Sloane's eyes. No doubt her father had deliberately trapped her between these two relics.

Aunt Eugenia sat next to Lord Drayton while Miss Fairfax was relegated to the far end of the table, sausaged between two men Cassandra did not recognize. Neither of them was speaking to her. *Poor Miss Fairfax*, Cassandra thought. She and her father knew that Miss Fairfax was smart and sharp and beautiful, but everyone else turned down their noses at a governess at the dinner table. Cassandra imagined that most guests were silently wondering what on earth Lord Drayton was thinking by having her there. If only they had directed their talk toward Miss Fairfax, they would have been drawn in by her unaffected charm and impressed by her subtle, and at times, slicing wit.

Aunt Eugenia was particularly disdainful of Miss Fairfax, always questioning why she was invited to dine at her brother's table and taking every opportunity to dismiss her from the room. Before the dinner gong, Cassandra had caught snippets of a tense exchange between her aunt and father.

"James, really, why? Miss Fairfax coming to dinner. Again . . ."

"She is . . . sorry if you can't appreciate . . . Besides there are too few ladies at my little hunting party."

"James, there will be talk."

"It's a party, of course there will be talk."

"That is not what I mean. You're a wealthy widower . . . she's a governess."

"Then let them talk, Eugenia. I don't give a damn about it."

"If only Anne . . ."

"Anne! How dare you . . . That really is below the belt, even for you."

Cassandra heard the clipped beat of her father's footsteps and shared his anger. As always, Aunt Eugenia was ready to pounce on Miss Fairfax.

There was talk but most of it trended toward the War in the States, and particularly the success of recent shared investments in ironworks and munitions factories. It all seemed terribly dull to Cassandra. She stifled a yawn as Sloane cheerily announced, "Dividends are coming in stronger than ever, and they will do as long as the war goes on," and clinked glasses with father. At the mention of war, Mrs. Saunders, with her single strand of pearls, shuddered, which Aunt Eugenia took as a sign.

"Well ladies, I think it's time we retire to the Drawing Room and leave the gentlemen to their discussion," announced Aunt Eugenia. The whole party stood as the ladies made their way to the door.

Lord Drayton seized the chance to commence with his unfinished business. "Saunders, come sit with me. Forsythe, you too, you must hear this. I've had a letter from Mr. Fulton, the same Fulton that set us up with Iroquois Ironworks . . ."

Before leaving the room, Cassandra turned to see her father put his arm around Mr. Saunders, while Anthony Forsythe sidled up next to them. Like a conductor leading his orchestra, Lord Drayton gathered his friends with smooth gestures, drawing them in, feeding the fire of their self-interest in gain.

"It seems that Fulton recently met with a Mr. Jay Cooke, whose banking business is taking off. He sent me the Circular for Union War Bonds. Five-two-ohs they are called because they yield 5% in gold per annum, gold mind you. And there's no risk. The bonds are backed by the Union government, and we all know the Union is going to win the war. It's a sure bet, gentlemen."

This version of Lord Drayton—maneuvering, cajoling, deal-making— was so different than the overprotective man who kept her hedged in luxury. This James Drayton loved the chase and the art of persuasion. She knew her father, as a bachelor and a Lord, was the subject of much talk. He was occasionally the subject of rather unflattering articles in *The Illustrated London News* or the *Times*. Their authors hinted, without subtlety, that he was a hard, scheming man known for business dealings and clever manipulation. More sympathetic reporters noted shrewd risk-taking and unwavering persistence. Less sympathetic ones insinuated he would go to great and even questionable lengths to finalize an advantageous deal. Her aunt tried, unsuccessfully, to hide these papers from Cassandra, but it didn't matter—Cassandra did not believe them anyway. She adored her father.

Yet she could not deny or ignore that her father was filled with ambition. Long before it was acknowledged in fashionable circles, he was acutely aware that the world was changing—it was steely, mechanical, and relentless. She recalled him saying when he thought she was out of earshot, "I don't intend to look on like my forefathers, stuffing their soft mouths with tea and cake, as their fortunes crumbled." Lord Drayton was filled with a hunger to conquer the world and reclaim what his ancestors had let slip through their well-manicured fingers.

"Listen," Lord Drayton leaned conspiratorially toward Mr. Saunders. Cassandra slowed her step, hoping to hear what seemed so important and interesting, but her aunt was eager that they arrive in the drawing room before the other ladies. She hooked her arm in Cassandra's and sashayed forward as fast as her large frame would take her. Lord Drayton's voice faded away.

The ladies played whist and chatted for what seemed like hours, until finally, Aunt Eugenia yawned loudly, signaling it was time to retire.

"Miss Fairfax, would you please escort Cassandra to her rooms?" Aunt Eugenia asked with just enough condescension as to remind the room of Miss Fairfax's place. Cassandra feigned reluctance but rose to her feet and made her rounds. "It was so lovely to see you, Mrs. Saunders, Mrs. Sloane." She curtseyed slightly and then met each woman's eye. Stopping to say good night to Lady Winthrop, she heard the gentlemen coming in from the dining room. Forsythe emerged first. Oh, she would have a thousand times rather Lord Bedford had been the first to arrive in the room.

Forsythe honed in on her like a pigeon. "Is your auntie ushering you to bed so soon? What a pity, I wanted to be your partner at the whist table. I will have to wait for another night." So facetious and smug.

"Perhaps, but I suppose I might not see you again, Mr. Forsythe."

"Oh no, dear Cassandra—may I call you that? I am sure I will see you soon. Your father and I have much business to attend to."

Cassandra's tight smile hid her inward cringe at his tactless presumption. Vulgarity hovered in the air around him and instinctively it turned her stomach.

A s she got ready for bed, Cassandra thought about the one highlight of the evening.

For a fleeting moment, she'd escaped Aunt Eugenia, who had to walk into dinner with Lord Drayton. Cassandra should have walked with Lord Winthrop, but she deliberately held back in the shadows of the drawing room, just long enough that Winthrop went ahead without her.

Just as Winthrop was out of view, Lord Bedford offered Cassandra his arm. "Will you let me escort you?"

She did not refuse him. The expanse of years that had previously divided them melted away.

"I was sorry to miss the hunt today, I heard that you came to lunch."

Nerves getting the better of her, Cassandra blurted out a response that was far bolder than she had intended.

"Yes, I wish you had been there." To which, Lord Bedford responded with a broad smile and a wink.

"You'll be riding out with us next time, I hope?"

His question both ballooned and deflated Cassandra. She blushed that Lord Bedford desired her company, and then winced at the injustice of watching her father and his friends, especially Lord Bedford, head off to the hunt on horseback while she had been forbidden riding lessons.

Slipping on her nightdress, Cassandra dreamily replayed that moment in her head, mindful that Lord Bedford, Henry, was but a few rooms away. Her thoughts were interrupted by some shuffling in the hallway. Cassandra suspected it was Miss Fairfax coming to say goodnight, so she opened her door a sliver to peek out. But it wasn't Miss Fairfax at all; instead, Cassandra was almost certain she saw Mr. Forsythe walking down the hall in his dressing gown. He was going in the exact opposite direction of his room, toward the servants' stairway. Cassandra closed the door silently, not surprised—Forsythe was just that sort too, one to go courting upstairs in the day and downstairs at night.

CHAPTER 4

November 1863

Crispin saw Cassandra coming long before she saw him. Her figure, outlined by the sun, got larger and larger as she walked with a determined stride toward the stable. She wore a blue riding jacket, gloves, and a bright blue cap, under which her yellow curls flowed.

At first, Crispin thought to retreat, to disappear into a stall and pretend to rake straw or fill buckets with oats. But as she approached, rather than shrink away, he stepped forward and stood at attention. Out of some corner of his mind echoed his father's words. "Remember you are a gentleman's son." Would a gentleman scurry into a corner like a mouse? No, a gentleman would look a lady in the eye. And so he did. Taking two steps forward while dusting his hands off on his thighs, Crispin boldly welcomed the visitor to the stable.

"Good day, Miss Cassandra."

"You were looking at me during my father's hunting luncheon," Cassandra returned, raising an eyebrow. Boldness checked, Crispin was disarmed by her candid accusation, and his confidence faltered. Searching for words to explain himself, he wondered if he should pretend to not understand. Or should he admit his indiscretion and apologize? But he did neither. Instead, the lanky adolescent stood dumbly with his eyes fixed upon her.

"Well, never mind. That's not why I am here. I want to learn how to ride, and you can teach me." She looked about the barn with a possessive air.

"I'm not sure I should. I'm no trainer. I merely take care of the horses."

"But you know how to ride, don't you?"

"Yes, of course."

"Well, then you can show me."

There was a determined fire in her eyes, and Crispin sensed the danger he was in. Her father had not asked him to teach her. In fact, in the five months he had been at Drayton Manor, Cassandra had never stepped foot in the stables. The closest she had been was the day Crispin caught her crying behind the barn. Given the regularity of Lord Drayton's own riding habits, Crispin could only assume Cassandra's absence was deliberate; that Lord Drayton wished to keep her from the horses.

"My father doesn't want me to learn. He thinks I'll hurt myself. My mother died in a riding accident, so I need to be taught in secret," she said as if reading his mind.

She was direct and unabashed, and she confirmed the worst. If Crispin agreed to her request, he was opposing her father's wishes. If he valued his position and wages, he would never agree to such a thing.

"Miss Cassandra, I think you should listen to your father. He has not asked me to teach you."

"Has he told you not to?"

"No." It was the truth.

"Well then, I don't see any harm in it for you. If he's angry, I'm to blame. Besides, I am not asking you, I am ordering you." She said this with some hesitance as if she were trying on the words.

"Miss Cassandra, it wouldn't be right."

"It's 'Miss Drayton,'" she instructed and then teased, "Mr. Crispin, would it be right for you to ignore my request?"

He dodged the question by responding with one of his own. "Does Miss Fairfax know you are here?"

"No. Why does it matter? Neither one of us is going to tell her."

Cassandra was quick with her tongue and strong-willed. Crispin half expected a more demure, mild girl. For weeks now, he had observed her from a distance, catching glimpses of her gliding nymphlike through the garden walkways and noting coy gestures as she entertained Fairfax and her father. In his daydreams, he imagined her to be gentle and sweet. Yet here she was in the flesh, and he found her feisty, persuasive, and even insolent. He knew he should refuse her request. There were so many risks, and the reward was elusive at best. He wanted to play it safe, but a strange and wicked fluttering in his chest was creeping into his head—a desire to do the very the thing he knew he should not do.

"What are you thinking?" Her tone had changed. This time, she spoke as if they had been friends for a long time.

"I was thinking about my life on the street once your father sacks me." But Crispin was already leading her toward the tack room.

"He wouldn't do that." Cassandra smiled, keeping pace. "Besides, it will be our secret, I promise. In any case, the only one breaking the Lord of the Manor's rules is me."

Crispin rolled his eyes as he reached to take a bridle off the wall.

"That will be poor comfort when I need to pawn this silver bit on Drury Lane just so I can get a pot of porridge." Crispin offered Cassandra the reins and a bit he had recently polished.

"You're sorely out of luck there. You can't sell that one, it's not yours!"

"So, you'll make me a thief too?"

She laughed with mischievous delight. She could not have known that he had indeed seen the inside of such pawn shops, guarded by their toothless, grasping owners. Men with big red eyes and ladies who held pipes between their teeth. Nor could she know that he had met bona fide thieves, many of them. By and large, they were decent, desperate men, who headed to prison for trying to feed their families. To her, these people and places only appeared in the serialized stories that she read with her father as they sat by a blazing fire nestled in the safety of their leather chesterfield.

"Artemis of Avalon is a good little mare to start on. We'll walk her past the chapel to the edge of Blandford Heath. I don't think we can be seen there."

Cassandra squeezed Crispin's hand as she took the bridle from him. "Thank you. And you may call me Miss Cassandra if you'd like."

Smiling up at him, Cassandra's green eyes shone with specks of gold like the wild buttercups that dotted the low hills of Dorset. And for a second, Crispin was sure it was worth the risk.

CHAPTER 5

March 1864

"Come on Crispin." Cassandra tossed her head back, "Let's go to the hilltop." Finally, the days were lengthening, and Cassandra could escape to the barn after her tea. Over the months, she had become quite confident on Artemis, the mare they had secretly named hers, and now she rode ahead of Crispin. Prodded by a gentle heel to the side, Artemis began to canter up the path that wound up Bryanston Hill. The sky was cornflower blue, and the tall grass bent and bobbed in the breeze like a green ocean. The air was as fresh as a clear glass of water.

Cassandra had taught Crispin about the horse's namesake, the Greek goddess who strode with the moon and shot arrows with the precision of a man. She told Crispin that they were like Artemis and Apollo, the twin gods, moving sun and moon without anyone taking notice. He had no sister, so he did not know the intimacy of siblings, but he liked the image she painted of Artemis and Apollo riding through the woods carefree and independent. Yet did Apollo ever want to kiss Artemis's hand? Did he ever want to touch her soft cheek as Crispin had imagined doing so many times?

Some nights, Crispin slept on his hands just so he wouldn't run the risk of inadvertently reaching toward the snoring stable hand, who since the grouse hunt had become his full-time bunkmate. Heaven forbid he caress that face the way he had envisioned caressing Cassandra's.

At times he feared he'd gone mad. In his dreams, it was as if he could actually feel the tingle of her refined fingers drawing circles on his rough palms. He spent hours imagining that he was gazing into her green eyes as he mucked stalls and polished brass.

Dear God—he was insane. Crispin St. John was nothing but a humble, awkward stable boy who cleaned horse manure and whose mouth watered over the kitchen staff's leftovers, the food that barely kept his belly full. In his dreams, however, he was upright and self-assured. He called his new friend—a wealthy girl of breeding and the daughter of a Viscount no less— "Cassie" and imagined he courted her, flirting openly the way Lord Bedford did. When he woke, the cold reality remained unchanged. Even if his father had not been disgraced and Crispin had grown up comfortably as a gentleman's son, "Cassie" would still be far above him.

But the young are hopeful by nature, and Crispin felt buoyant as they climbed a verdant incline in companionable silence. The wind pushed the clouds like the white sails across the sky. *Someday,* he thought to himself, *I will rise from this station.* He had plans to lead a very different life. He just wished those plans were more definitive.

At the crest of the hill, Cassandra pulled back on the reins and came to a stop. Artemis stepped gingerly to the side, while Crispin pulled his horse, Cabal, next to hers. A chalky white line became visible off in the distance.

"What's that?" Cassandra asked Crispin.

"It's the old Roman Road."

"Really? I've never seen it."

"Never? Haven't you lived here your whole life, Miss Cassandra? Do they never let you out?"

His words seemed to hit home with her and ignited a sudden rebellious urge.

"I'll race you!" Cassandra challenged.

"You wouldn't."

"Would so!" She gave Artemis a swift kick, and they were off, galloping down the backside of the hill, across the green carpet of earth, nothing but a smattering of trees here and there cluttering their path to the Roman Road.

Crispin called to Cassandra, "You're crazy! You know that? This was not part of our arrangement." But she could barely hear his voice over the hollow clop of hooves and the rush of wind in their ears like a hurricane. If she had, she might have sensed the brightness in his tone that gave away his feelings. They were free, Artemis and Apollo, charting their own course and paying no heed to authority. And, they had not noticed the storm clouds roll in. The air was now damp, and mist clung to their cheeks and hair. Cassandra shuddered with the thrill of the chase and the cooling chill of the afternoon. Rain. It was coming.

The two riders reached the Roman Road just as the sky broke and fat droplets poured around them.

"There!" Crispin pointed to a large Hawthorn tree with branches that looked like a girl's long hair blowing in the wind. They charged toward the tree, and within minutes, dismounted and took shelter under her ancient limbs. The soothing music of the rain—the muffled plunk on the mossy ground and the staccato patter as it hit the leaves above—encircled them. Below, Drayton Manor seemed like a miniature doll's house, a red square in the distance. A patchwork of pastures and farmland, hedges and gardens, rolled on before them.

Trapped beneath the tree, Cassandra and Crispin did not pay attention to time. The rain did not let up, and they got lost in conversation, drifting away from their usual topics, which were grounded on the basics of horses and riding.

"I wish my father could see this," Crispin said, almost to himself.

"Was he a groomsman too?"

"No, but he was a horseman," Crispin chuckled dismissively. How pained his father would be to hear her question. "He bred racehorses and trained both The Barron and War Eagle."

"What are they?"

"Horses."

"Crispin." She groaned and giggled. "I'm not daft. What kind of horses? What should I know about them?"

He spent the next few moments regaling her with stories that his father had shared with him. It felt good to talk about his father and their happier days together sitting in the courtyard of Queen's prison. Crispin could almost see his father's rare smile and the twinkle in his eyes as he recounted steeple chases and horses racing with lightning power.

"And your mother, did she ride?"

"I don't think so. She died when I was just a baby."

"Oh. I'm sorry. How many brothers and sisters do you have?" Cassandra asked.

"None. There is only my father and me." Crispin neglected to tell her of his extended family—his aunt, who not a mile away, was secretly playing mistress of the house.

"So, you and I are both half-orphans. Motherless, only children. We have that in common." Her tone was light, but he knew she was familiar with the certain sadness that comes with missing and loving someone you don't even know. "Peas in a pod." Crispin liked the idea. Very much.

"Not too similar, I fear. You see, my father resides at The Queen's Bench."

"Queens?" She seemed taken aback. "The debtors' prison?"

"Yes."

He anticipated a repulsed response, a voice laced with disgust, but was happily surprised to hear soft sympathetic notes. "How sad. You must miss him."

"I do. We write to each other."

Crispin imagined his father's gray figure, hunched over as he stared absently out the window of his small room, waiting for his son's letters to arrive. In them, Crispin would tuck a few shillings wrapped carefully so as not to jingle and alert the postman.

Crispin told Cassandra about his childhood. He supposed that for her, his stories were better than a Dickens' installment: the motherly Mrs. Mayhew, his raggedy childhood companion Amy, and the bribable young prison guard Mr. Chickory. Recounting the stories, he felt a strange nostalgia for the prison courtyard, the dark halls, and musty smells. He missed the constant chatter and the feel of the cold bricks against his back in the quiet cubby hole he had found in Mr. Chickory's rooms. The jailor had let Crispin read his great stacks of *All the Year Rounds* and in between their pages, he told Cassandra, he met Oliver Twist and Nicholas Nickleby and Pip—stories that made him feel not so terribly alone.

Crispin realized things had taken a turn for the worse when his father stopped sending him to the pawn shops on Drury Lane. They had nothing left to pawn. Crispin was determined to help his father.

"I mean to free him," Crispin said, as much to himself as to Cassandra.

"Free him? How?"

"I will pay his debts."

"Are they terrible?"

"Many thousands." He shook his head.

"Perhaps I could ask my father."

"No," Crispin said more sternly than he meant to. "I can't trade one debt for another. I will work for pay and then we will be free, both father and I." In contrast to his tone, doubt gnawed at Crispin. *How long will it take?* he wondered. And would he ever be able to do anything more than simply free his father from prison? Could he actually earn the right to be among the list of Cassandra's suitors one day? The goals seemed beyond absurd. A more sensible person, world-wise and weary, might have accepted his circumstances, but Crispin had visions of becoming the master of his own manor. He recalled his first day at Drayton Manor when he had been summoned to the library by his new master, Cassandra's father.

Cowed by the scale and splendor of all that surrounded him, Crispin hunched his shoulders and stepped into the largest room he had ever seen. Lord James Drayton stood by a roaring fire, engrossed in reading a thick letter. Above him hung a painting of a red-coated rider on a chestnut mare, bounding toward a high hedge, hounds scampering around them. The rider glanced with confidence over his shoulder, dark curls blown helter-skelter by the speed of the hunt. Crispin had stood in open-mouthed awe for more than a few seconds before Lord Drayton chuckled at the boy's gobsmacked expression. In those brief moments in Drayton's library, something inside Crispin had changed, crystalized. A dream that had been foggy and distant took shape, the outlines becoming more definitive and crisper. *This* was what he wanted, *this* life. The leather couch, the gold-framed paintings, the easy confidence, the sense of being master of a room, a house, a world.

Cassandra looked at him with heavy eyes that seemed to have gotten greener with the afternoon. *I will deserve her one day,* he promised himself.

"Enough about me, I've gone on and on. You must be bored to tears with my sad stories. What about you?"

"Me? What's to tell? I've no interesting stories. My life has always been as it is now—with the exception of you, of course." She paused and gave him a smile.

He fixed on her admiringly, and for a moment he saw the feeling was mutual. Crispin resumed his lighthearted questioning. "So, we've established that you have been sheltered. But what's next for the Honourable Miss Cassandra Drayton?" He gave a jaunty bow.

Cassandra rolled her eyes at him

"Well, first I'd like to see some of the world. Even London would be a treat at this point. But more than that, I'd like to meet people who are different, with a different perspective. I'd like to learn from them. And, more than anything, I'd like to be taken seriously. Not treated like some sort of precious doll, dressed up and presented for admiration at various, permitted occasions."

Crispin looked to the wet ground beneath them as if trying to hide his reaction, but the corners of his mouth turned up in a smile.

"Are you mocking me?"

He shook his head. Cassandra was much more to him than the precious doll he'd first seen in the garden all those months ago.

"Then stop smiling. I know I sound ridiculous and spoiled, but I'm tired of it. Aunt Eugenia says I will marry someone with significant standing, that all of Father's ungentlemanly business dealings should surely result in something beyond restoring the family fortune. She's hoping for an Earl or a Duke—Lord Bedford would do just fine." She stopped for a moment as if considering the idea, turning it over in her mind. "Regardless of whom I marry, I want to be seen as a woman of substance."

A rogue raindrop snuck behind the lace of Cassandra's collar, and Crispin saw her shiver as it trickled down her spine.

"You must be freezing. Here, take this." Crispin took off his jacket and slipped the tattered green wool over her shoulders before she had a chance to refuse him. He worried the wool would itch her delicate skin, but she pulled it tightly around her as if she didn't notice. It smelled of hay and horsehair and dry dirt—a little acrid, but not unpleasant—she didn't seem bothered by it. Cassandra reached her arms into the sleeves, which hung over her hands, and buttoned the jacket up. The top button was missing.

"Sorry." Crispin grimaced. "Button fell off. I meant to fix that." He shrugged. "It is a good look for you. You look very . . . substantial." He laughed.

"Ugh, you!" Cassandra swatted him playfully on the shoulder, then twirled around for effect. "I hear it's all the rage in Paris. I'll have to order one from Worth's."

"From whom?"

"Charles Worth."

"Who's that?"

"Never mind. Just a ladies thing." Conversation lagged for a moment as they both shifted awkwardly from foot to foot. There was an expectant stillness in the air. Crispin kicked gently at a root that peeked up from the ground before he remarked, "I think the rain has stopped."

"Has it?"

A wave of disappointment flooded Crispin's body, and he let out a deep sigh. "We should go back."

For a while Cassandra said nothing. The leaves of the tree shed a few lingering drops, and the two of them looked back at the big house. Then, finally, she broke the silence.

"It is so pretty. I wish this day would go on forever and ever." Crispin too wanted to stop time. These were his most happy moments, but he could not find the words to tell her. "But you are right. I suppose we must. Miss Fairfax will probably be wondering where I've gone off to. And Father's coming home from London." Her voice quickened. "I'm terribly excited to see him. *And* he's bringing the Duke of Westmoor and his son Henry."

Crispin cringed. The mention of Bedford sent hot pins and needles up his spine. He had seen Lord Bedford at a distance and had to admit he seemed the natural object for Cassandra's affection: a Duke's son, well-born and well-bred with a good-looking face to boot. It filled Crispin with envy.

"Why are the Duke and his son coming?" Crispin clenched his jaw and tried, but failed, at seeming disinterested.

"I'm not sure. Westie's an old friend of Father's. But I hope Henry is coming to see me," she said wistfully. Cassandra teased, "Are you jealous?"

"Of course not. But we must return home, Miss Drayton." Miss Fairfax would be looking for Cassandra soon, and he was loath for her to check the stables.

"Crispin, you *are* mad. I know it."

He did not respond.

"Crispin." She played for his attention and batted her eyes conspicuously. He remained outwardly unmoved, until she asked in earnest, "Crispin, you won't ever leave here, will you?" Crispin's heart quickened in his chest. "You are . . . well, you are my best friend. I used to think it was Miss Fairfax, but now I'm sure it is you." Defenseless against her flattery, Crispin let down his internal armor and smiled at Cassandra. A wide unguarded smile.

"I'll stay for as long as I can."

The sweet scent of lavender filled the air as the late afternoon shadows closed in around them.

M iss Fairfax wasn't just wondering; she was in a full-out panic. Even from a distance, Cassandra spotted her pacing to and fro in front of the stable. And though they were not close enough yet, Cassandra could hear the swish of her gray silk bustle, as she pivoted back and forth, back and forth.

Trotting down the muddy path toward the house, Cassandra didn't want to mention what she saw to Crispin for they were about to get a wicked tongue-lashing. She hoped to spare him some of the anxiety she felt, but the quick sound of him sucking air through his teeth revealed that he saw what she did. The guilty pair said nothing but slowed their pace as if in mutual agreement. The air was charged, like the moment before the inevitable clap of thunder that initiates the storm.

"Where have you been?" Miss Fairfax's voice was high and shrill, so unlike the calm, unflappable governess who guided Cassandra through Latin and French lessons and coaxed her to bed when she pleaded to stay up late.

"I have been looking for you for hours! Hours! What were you thinking, gallivanting off on a day like this? And on a horse!" She looked up at Artemis, whose nostrils gently quivered, with visible disgust. "What would your father say? What would he do if anything had happened to you? The very thought of it!"

Her voice cracked and she shuddered. Cassandra didn't think she had ever seen her governess on the verge of tears before, and yet, here she was, glassy-eyed, the dams of her tear-ducts threatening to overflow. For a moment, the spoiled girl felt a terrible wave of shame.

Miss Fairfax held out her hand to help Cassandra dismount, the gesture giving her a chance to regain her composure.

"And you,"—she turned to Crispin, ice in her voice—"how could you?" Now, it was Crispin who shuddered. His eyes widened and his shoulders sank. Cassandra could see his spirit withdraw, like a turtle pulling into its shell.

"I'm . . . I'm . . ."

"It was my fault, Miss Fairfax. Absolutely and completely. I begged Crispin. I forced him to teach me to ride. I made him do it." Cassandra's pleas did nothing to melt the tundra of Miss Fairfax's mood.

"This will never happen again. Do you understand?" It was a statement, not a question.

Head bowed, Crispin muttered, "Of course, Miss Fairfax. I . . . I never meant any harm by it. I'm—"

"But Miss Fairfax," Cassandra whined, "I love riding! I've never had so much fun. And I'm rather good at it. Aren't I Crispin?"

He was silent behind the disheveled sandy locks that covered his forehead and eyes.

"We will not discuss it. Not unless you want to take it up with your father." Miss Fairfax knew that would put a conclusive stop to it.

"And Miss Cassandra," she said in a voice loaded with scorn and disappointment, "what are you wearing?" Cassandra had completely forgotten that she was still wearing Crispin's wool jacket. The frayed edges had ceased to irritate her wrists and neck.

"Take that off at once." Miss Fairfax sounded just like Aunt Eugenia at that moment, and Cassandra wanted very badly to say as much, but bit her tongue for Crispin's sake. She took the jacket off, one sleeve at a time. Without it, the early spring air was biting.

Miss Fairfax snatched it from her and, with an abrupt flick of the wrist, tossed it toward Crispin who let the jacket fall to the muddy earth. Miss Fairfax did not see. She was already marching, cadet-like, toward the house.

"Come, you need to bathe and change. Your father and his guests will be home any minute."

CHAPTER 6

May 1864

The letter was written in a schooled script with exaggerated capitals and unnecessary seraphs on the C and P. It was a girl's hand, a young one, that was still amateurish and danced around the page.

> *Dear Crispin,*
>
> *I am so terribly SORRY! I hope you were not in too much trouble. I'll never forgive myself. Please don't worry about Miss F. Her bark is worse than her bite. I know we gave her quite a shock. She likes things just so and sees herself as my protector, especially when Father's gone. It's horribly stifling, being treated like a china doll all the time, as if I'll get smashed to pieces, but I don't expect you'd understand. Never mind. Needless to say, again, I am sorry.*
>
> *Please, if you can, respond. There is a little nook between two of the stones along the garden wall, just opposite the statue of that fat little fiddler. It's always bothered me until now. Finally, I see it has a purpose. It's the perfect place for hiding secret notes! No one will find it if you leave a letter there.*
>
> *Apologetically yours,*
> *Cassie*

Thus began their correspondence. Not right away though. Crispin waited several days to respond. He was too nervous. The memory of his aunt's anger clung to him like a shadow. He wondered how much she regretted helping him with the position and half expected her to appear in the stables in the middle of the night, telling him to pack his bags. Or, worse yet, for Lord Drayton to appear demanding his departure. But Miss Fairfax did not. Nor did Lord Drayton.

In fact, absolutely nothing happened, which was even more disconcerting. Jones acted as if he'd never heard of the incident. He was as jolly and kind as ever, quick to smile or clip Crispin on the back. "There you go, lad. You're an 'ard worker, you are." Crispin had become a favorite of Jones, and the big-hearted man wasn't afraid to show it. He often brought the growing boy extra slices of mincemeat pies and cakes, as well as bits of cheese and half-eaten loaves of bread from the kitchen. "From Mrs. Jones. You're a growing boy and them folks in the big 'ouse ain't going to eat 'em."

Miss Fairfax, on the other hand, certainly did not seek Crispin out. When their paths crossed, she gave him a nod and a tight-lipped smile, the same as she had since his first days at Drayton Manor. It was as if the incident had never occurred. But here was Cassie's letter confirming, in black and white, that it had, and that she had neither forgotten about their time together nor wanted to.

A few days later, after the work of the day was done, Crispin sat down at the dusty table in the back recess of the stable and lit a lamp. The table was cluttered with papers and logs that kept records of the horses' care: farrier and veterinary visits, schedules for oiling saddles and polishing brass bits, the list of foals' birthdates and calendars for their breaking in, purchase and sales agreements, and a short but sad list of horses put down for one reason or another, a broken leg or respiratory infection. He pulled a thin sheet from the paper box. It was slightly yellowed at the edges, a fine contrast to Cassandra's thick ivory notepaper. Had she really signed her letter "Cassie"? Crispin read it again. He dipped the nip of his pen into the bottle of thick, oily ink.

Dear Cassie,

Could he? No. He crossed it out and crumpled the sheet, replacing it with a blank one.

Dear Miss Cassandra,
Thank you for your concern. All is well. In fact, I don't believe, Miss F . . ..

Crispin nearly wrote "Aunt Emma," but stopped himself just in time.

. . . told Jones. He's been as kind as ever, perhaps more so. I hope you too
did not endure any sort of punishment beyond the first "barrage."
Sincerely,
Crispin

For many weeks they passed notes through the garden nook, while the stone fiddler looked on. Crispin would find his way through the manicured hedgerows after his chores were done, when the afternoon gave way to twilight, and he was sure no one would be wandering the paths.

It was nice to have a friend and something to look forward to beyond the drudgery of mucking stalls and oiling and polishing endless leather straps and saddles. And he enjoyed stretching his mind, looking for big words his father had taught him like clemency (Miss Fairfax's) and somnambulance (his bunkmate, the stable hand's annoying habit), that he would never have used with Jones or the other stable hands and servants.

Cassandra wrote long letters that included accounts of dinner parties and her father's strange—or so it seemed to him—acquaintances. She wrote, *you can call me Cassie,* which was double underlined to assure him and started to sign *your friend, Cassie.* At the end of a shorter, more hastily penned missive,

Busy day. Must run.
Yours,
Cassie.

And then in mid-May,

Dear Crispin,

Father has gone to London for a fortnight. Please, let's resume our riding lessons. We'll go early, very early in the morning. Miss F will never know. She and I rarely have breakfast together. We won't go far, and I promise no more racing. But I do long to learn how to jump. Just low, perfectly safe, jumps. Please say "yes."

Yours,

Cassie

Dear Miss Drayton,

No.

Dear Crispin,

You are mean. Cruel. What a curt response. You didn't even sign your name. You've hurt my feelings, and my spirits are already so low with no friends and nothing to do all day but conjugate French verbs and practice my music and drawing with Miss F. It is so dull; I cannot tell you.

Sincerely,

Miss Drayton

Was it the switch from "yours" to "sincerely?" The "Miss Drayton," not "Cassie?" The hurt feelings? The low spirits? Crispin couldn't be sure. Perhaps it had nothing to do with her letter at all but his sense of drifting aimlessly through each day. Time seemed to stretch on like a gray fog that never lifted. Crispin was lost in it.

He missed his father and wanted to help him, but the few shillings he sent each month made little impact on his father's debts. His father's letters were filled with guilty sentiments and pleas for Crispin to keep his earnings so he could make his way in the world. His more cheerful letters made no mention of money, but said he was tolerably well, and that Mrs. Mayhew was looking after him. They were filled with prison gossip—Little Amy was now quite beautiful, and Mr. Chickory had gotten married and had a baby on the way—and best wishes for his sister-in-law, who was so kind to his son.

Crispin knew this was as good a position as he was likely to get. He was well-treated, well-fed, and well-paid for his station, but he was restless and wanted change and action. He wanted to be of use and be noticed, not to be some peon. He liked the idea of teaching something to Cassandra, who in so many ways was his superior. He enjoyed her admiring smiles, the way her eyes widened and brightened when he showed her a new skill or trick. She seemed to think highly of him and desired his company and even his friendship. Inadvertently, she had given him hope that one day he could—he *would*—be more.

So, Crispin pulled his rough wool jacket around his waist and fastened its two sad remaining buttons with resolution.

> *Dear Miss Cassandra,*
> *All right. If I must, I am at your service. Meet me at the stables, Wednesday morning at first light.*
> *Sincerely,*
> *Crispin*
>
> *PS: This is a terrible idea.*

Crispin's spirits lifted almost immediately. He went through the rest of the day feeling the sun—a warm, comforting hand on his back. He talked conspiratorially with the horses as he led them to pasture and brought them in and brushed them. When Jones commented on Crispin's noticeably good mood, heat flushed his cheeks as if he had been caught in some reckless act.

> *Dear Crispin,*
> *Brilliant! I'll be there! I am so excited, I can hardly keep still. Miss F thinks I've gone absolutely mad. Thank you ever so much.*
> *Yours,*
> *Cassie*

It was a cool morning. The mist hung so heavily in the air that Crispin could not see the big house from the stables. He saddled up Artemis and Cabal as quietly as he could for fear of waking the other stable hands and animals. Then he waited by the door. Through the trees, the dark sky gave way to the dusty pink dawn, and birds chirped their early morning songs. Those—along with the low, lazy clomping of horses as they shifted in their stalls—were the only sounds.

He waited. Nothing.

She decided not to come. Sense has gotten the better of her. He kicked himself for being so foolish, but his heart sank, and his insides felt like cold porridge. "You should be thankful she's not here," he said to himself, as he lifted the saddle flap, readying to undo the girth.

Just then, Crispin heard the crunch of gravel under footsteps, light, small feet running down the drive. They got louder and closer.

"Crispin," Cassandra called in a stage whisper. "Crispin." He stepped out through the stable door. "I'm sorry I'm late. Dressing without a maid is more difficult than you would think." She giggled, clapping a hand over her mouth to stifle it. "You're so lucky you're not a girl."

Cassandra's skirts rose and fell in a steady rhythm as she galloped in a wide circle around Crispin, who had dismounted and now stood in the middle of a meadow. The open space with a few low-lying shrubs was hidden from the big house by a vast stretch of tall elms.

Her form was quite good, her back straight without being too rigid. She leaned comfortably toward Artemis' neck, and Crispin could see her lips moving as if she were whispering something to the mare.

Cassie had begged him to teach her to jump, and he had agreed on one condition: that he could call a halt to the lesson if he had any reason to fear her abilities. He had none. She was a natural. She squared Artemis to the row of shrubs they were using as a jump. They were half a meter high. Horse and rider moved as one with graceful celerity as if on the wings of the wind, but there was no wind. Not even a hint of breeze. It was a still morning and the mist lingered, even as the sun rose.

Crispin could feel the beat of Artemis's hooves pounding the ground. Horse and rider dove through the air with gazelle-like nimbleness and landed. Cassandra's face filled with delight as she let the horse build speed, tearing for the edge of the meadow. Crispin whistled and called her back, fearful that she was too far away.

"Crispin! This is incredible. It's magic!"

"Your form is pretty good, but slow down for God's sake." He grabbed for her reins, but before his hand got to them, she swatted it away playfully.

"Stop being such an old man."

"And stop being such a foolish baby. You want to run before you can walk. Besides, your stirrup is too long." He put his hand on her ankle and pulled it away from the stirrup, which she allowed without any fuss. As he wrestled with the strap, he was painfully aware of how close she was. Heat billowed around his arm and face, and he could not tell if it emanated from the belly of the horse or the rider or both. Perhaps it was his own embarrassment at being close enough to Cassie to know the shape of her calf.

Meanwhile, Cassie sat cool and unabashed, looking down at him silently.

"There you go."

"Thank you."

Their hands touched, and for a moment they were frozen together.

Then she was off to try to jump again. Crispin climbed back on Cabal and trotted toward the south side of the meadow, while Cassandra cantered to the northern edge. She turned Artemis around and stopped, her back straight, her chin high. Framed by the pink morning light, she once again leaned toward the horse, whispering and stroking her mane. With a slight kick, Artemis started to move, accelerating quickly.

What happened next, Crispin couldn't be sure. He heard a noise like the rustling of an animal within the elms, but nothing of note. Artemis halted and rose on her hind legs, kicking madly at the air. She shook her mane, and with a terrifying cry, Cassandra fell.

Crispin vaulted off his horse and ran toward her, but it was too late. She had tumbled to the ground and now lay motionless. Her face, just moments before flushed and full of life, was gray and clammy. Crispin's heart was in his mouth, a salty mass of fear. He wrapped his arms around her slender body and awkwardly lifted her onto Artemis's back. Without thinking, he mounted the horse and, clinging to his unconscious friend, dashed for the manor.

"Please," he whispered to the wind, "please let her be . . ."

Upon receiving Emma Fairfax's note, Lord Drayton left his carriage in London, opting to ride solo, as fast as his horse's legs would carry him.

Jones, who now knew all that had occurred and the thunderous ramifications that were sure to follow, told Crispin to stay out of sight in the stables when the master arrived. But Crispin was certain it would not be long before Drayton summoned him to his study where, under the enormous painting of the hunter, he would send him packing with a snarl.

As it turned out, Crispin was not summoned. Lord Drayton came to the barn, red with rage.

"Is this him?" he demanded of Jones as his eyes bored holes into the wide-eyed adolescent. Jones barely said a word when Lord Drayton came at Crispin with the full force of his body, pinning him to the stable wall.

"How dare you?" He gripped the boy's shoulders, pulling him forward, and again slamming him into the boards, which shook with the combined force of their weight. "You could have killed her! You useless bastard. Who do you think you are? Guttersnipe!" The insults and curses cascaded from his lips like hot lava. Spit gathered in the corners of his mouth as he yelled. Petrified and consumed with guilt, Crispin did not think to run or protect himself until it was too late. Lord Drayton grabbed Crispin's neck and started to squeeze. His thumb dug into Crispin's breathing passage, and his palm pressed his Adam's apple so hard it seemed as though it would burst. Crispin's face grew hot and red, and his arms flailed.

Miss Fairfax appeared at the door, breathless.

"James!" She screamed. "Stop! You're hurting him!"

"I intend to!" he barked back.

"Stop! You are going to kill him!" She clung to his free left arm and pulled with all her might. Crispin saw tears streaming down her face before he tasted the saline drops on his own lips.

By now, Jones had interceded for Crispin, holding Lord Drayton back by the shoulders. Unlike Miss Fairfax, whose petite frame barely moved Lord Drayton an inch, Jones was a big man, far bigger than the Lord himself. But Lord Drayton's rage had given him strength, and it took several attempts to pull Drayton off. Crispin scurried and cowered in a corner, arms above his head.

"'E's a good lad, 'e is," Jones said feebly, doubled and panting with exertion, his hands on his knees.

Lord Drayton ignored him, and instead, stepped toward Emma. For a moment Crispin feared he would attack her next. He squared his face to hers and got so close the tips of their noses nearly touched.

"I never want to see him again," he growled and without looking back, stormed out of the barn.

CHAPTER 7

August 1864

The damp air crept into Crispin's thin coat, and though it was summer, he shivered as he approached the edge of the Western Docks at the Port of London. As a child, he had once ventured from The Queen's Bench prison to see the great ships along the Thames. It had been a sunny day with a good breeze then, and a line of ships with fat white sails paraded in and out of port. He had stared at the ships and dreamt of climbing into a cargo hold to be whisked away to an exotic port, where he would live a life rich in adventure.

Now, walking toward the quay where the *Edwin Fox* was docked, the scene was eerily calm. Out of the fog that hung midway between the water and the sky, emerged a lattice work of tall masts like smokestacks—dozens of them, layered upon each other, receding into the distance. The boats rocked with the undulations of the water, and the clinking of chains and knocking of rigging lines filled the air with a distant, creepy music. Tall ships with sails dripping half-furled off their yardarms, emerged ghost-like and awesome, towering over each quay and obscuring the large warehouses that lined the shore.

At just fifteen, he would be traveling to Calcutta as a passenger, albeit in steerage. His one-way passage had been paid for by Miss Fairfax. She had written to Crispin that she had good reason to believe he could find work in the East. The British papers had been filled with postings for positions on railroads, in cotton textiles, and at army outposts. They needed able-bodied young men who were willing to work for little pay.

As Crispin boarded the *Edwin Fox*, he was filled with regret. He had gone to Drayton Manor intending to act with honor and rise up the ranks in the stables, become a trainer, and ultimately a prominent horse breeder like his father, thereby resurrecting the family name. Looking back, Crispin saw the folly of the romantic notion that he would be taken under Lord Drayton's wing and apprenticed to some larger calling. In that, he had more than failed.

Though it had not been a tearful parting when Crispin left Drayton Manor, he had walked the long, tree-lined drive toward the town with a heavy heart. Within the space of a year, the Manor had become more than a refuge from London, from Queen's Bench, from his shameful past. It was a steppingstone. And he had been a success, at least at first. Jones had given him responsibility, had praised him. Crispin had seen his future take shape, but now it slipped away like a dream, one that he clung to in the early moments of consciousness.

His aunt's sad grey eyes spoke volumes when she came into the stable for the last time to wish him goodbye. "I am sorry, Crispin." And she'd meant it. But she had also warned him against his foolishness, and Crispin had not listened. She did not have to tell him that he had compromised her position as well. Her coarse guttersnipe of a nephew was caught interfering with the Lady of the house. Even if Crispin had not acted an outright scoundrel, he was to some degree guilty of the offense. His heart sunk to his gut. How could his aunt ever forgive him?

Before the house was out of sight, Crispin had turned back for one last look. He counted the windows, three over and two stories up. That was Cassandra's room. He stood for a long time, trying to pierce the glass with his eyes, hoping that she would come to the window, her blond hair loose about her face. Logically, he knew he would not be able to see her, yet he was sure he would feel her presence. But the window was dark. So, he headed for the London Mail and made his way back to The Queen's Bench and his father.

More than a fortnight passed before he heard from his aunt. Her letter to him was curt, but not reproachful. It contained fare for his trip and a strong recommendation that he keep to himself and work hard.

"Passage?" A gruff seaman barked at Crispin, bringing him back to the present. He smelled of sweat, tobacco, and stale fish. Crispin's stomach turned.

"I'm in steerage."

He took in Crispin's shabby appearance and the canvas sack slung across his back. "Down that way, boy." The seaman gestured toward the lower deck and turned to the next set of passengers, puffing up his chest at their fine attire.

Crispin walked down a few steps, surveying the sights and smells and the passengers just beginning to assemble. There were only six so far standing on the deck. Seated on a trunk was a young mother, her hands over her eyes as her three screaming children ran about. Two boys and a girl, all under six by the looks of them. She looked up at him with smudges under her eyes, both apologetically and imploringly.

Standing near the center of the deck were three middle-aged men, engaged in a deep conversation. At the railing looking out onto the docks, two tall, fair-haired soldiers in their gleaming regimentals smiled and waved at ladies who called tearfully to them from afar. Lastly, was an earnest-looking, attractive young couple observing the hustle and bustle of the port, smiling pleasantly at each other. He walked toward them, stopping at a fair distance to ensure he didn't appear too forward, and leaned over to look down at the black water beneath them. The husband, for Crispin was sure they were married, whispered something in his wife's ear, before patting her hand and walking away toward the gangplank. Moments later, a female voice with a slightly northern twang interrupted his thoughts.

"It's a long way down, isn't it?"

Crispin nodded quietly, not knowing what to say to this pretty woman. She looked out of place on a ship bound for India in her muslin summer dress. Her thin wrists and delicate heart-shaped lips suggested a sedentary and secluded life, yet her voice was strong and conveyed a soft confidence. Unlike him, she did not seem afraid of the journey that lay before them.

"Is this your first trip to India?" She did not wait for an answer. "I remember my first. I was terrified. But my husband—he's just gone over there to greet a friend." She nodded in the direction of the gangplank. "He was offered a wonderful post outside Calcutta, in a place called Serampore." She puckered her mouth as she enunciated the last syllable. "It sounded like an ugly insect or a disease then. We were newlyweds, and I couldn't bear to be separated from Colin. I felt I had to go. It was so long ago but feels like yesterday."

It was hard to imagine this spritely thing was old enough to be married, let alone a veteran of this long journey. Her fine, strawberry blond hair whipped in the breeze and blew into her eyes, and she tucked it behind her ear. Something about this simple act put Crispin at ease.

"I've never been." He exhaled.

"Well, it can't be described, but let me try," she continued cheerfully. "It is a place of contrasts—crowded and tightly packed bazaars a stone's throw from open avenues and marble palaces—stifling heat followed cooling monsoon rains. At first, the heat and the clatter will accost your senses. The ports are teeming with all manner of people, Indian and British. Some half-dressed and others in finery to rival any aristocrat and everything in between." She blabbed on as if to fill the silence and soothe Crispin's too-obvious fear, though her attempts did more to raise than soothe them. "And, the Indian caste system, it's a mystery to me. I only know that you must be sure to avoid the Untouchables. They are the lowliest of the castes, poor things, allowed only the dirtiest of jobs. Many have none and are forced to beg in the street. Once you have figured out whom to trust and whom to avoid, you'll be fine. Do you have someone meeting you?"

Crispin had no answer. He had not even thought about where he would sleep his first night. Had he been so foolish as to imagine that he would get off the boat and there would be work waiting for him? Room? Board? A hot shepherd's pie? Would Crispin become one of the Untouchables? Homeless, unwanted, a pariah?

She must have seen the fear in his eyes, which darkened with each terrifying unanswered question.

"Oh my. Listen to me. I must check myself before I run at the mouth so. Colin's constantly reminding me to hold my tongue."

"I, I am going to Calcutta to find a job," Crispin stammered.

"And I am sure you will find one right off. Colin will have plenty of ideas for you. Colin!" She called to the well-dressed, handsome man Crispin had seen earlier who was now making his way back to his wife. He looked to be in his mid-thirties.

"Colin, I have met a friend."

"How do you do?" He eyed the adolescent with a hint of suspicion, but held out a hand, "Colin Forester." Crispin wiped off his hand and reached to shake Forester's.

"Fine, sir. Thank you, sir."

"And you are?"

"Crispin, my name is Crispin St. John."

"This young man is headed to Calcutta,"—his wife paused—"to find employment."

"Well, that is a long way to go for a job, especially for someone as young as you. You must be, let me guess, fifteen?" He leaned back as if to assess the value of an object he was about to purchase.

"Exactly, sir."

"A fine age to start work. Why India, may I ask?" Mr. Forester's tone softened, and he patted the youth on his arm. Crispin realized Colin Forester was no sterner than his wife was taciturn, and he shifted from foot to foot as he framed an answer.

"My father cannot work, and my aunt purchased this ticket for me, thinking there were many good opportunities in India." He told a half-truth, rather than relay the whole shameful story. The ship's horn blasted into the air. Below them, the crew scurried from piling to piling, releasing lines thicker than Crispin's legs.

"Your aunt is a smart woman. India's a great place for a new start. We'll help you get settled."

The tension Crispin had carried with him since Cassandra's fall eased somewhat. With Mr. and Mrs. Forester, he felt strangely safe. The ship creaked out of its bay, slowly making for open water, while the Foresters told Crispin about their life in the railway villages of Serampore and Howrah, where Mr. Forester was an engineer who worked on the Banaras-Howrah line. They were good middle-class people who had no pretensions and few prejudices. That evening, he sat down next to Mrs. Forester for the first of many meals together, and he began to feel hopeful again, just as he had during his first journey to Drayton Manor.

Twenty-three days later, the *Edwin Fox* pulled into the port of Calcutta. Mr. Forester put his hand on Crispin's back. "You'll do just fine here, son."

They disembarked into a whirlwind of motion and cacophonous sound—the clank and growl of steam-cranes, the constant hammering of nails, the thud of masses of dirt and stone, the slap and shlup of mortar on brick. New, pungent smells filled his nostrils—the snap of cardamom and tamarind; the acrid swirl of sweat, oxen, and horses baking in the dust, even the dead making their final trip to the sea; and underneath the stench, the sweet, green draught of water lilies, palms, and palmettos.

Mrs. Forester squeezed Crispin's arm.

"It's a wonderful place," she said, "really. Though a bit overwhelming at first."

She had read his mind. The chaos that rose before them made him woozy. He had never seen so many people, teeming like a colony of ants, crawling over and under each other. Their costumes were curious; some looked as though they had stepped out of a cab in Belgravia Square, others wore no more than sheets. And the colors . . . everywhere was a dizzying kaleidoscope of colors.

A few times Crispin got separated from the Foresters and was swept into the crowd. Just as panic welled within, Mrs. Forester seemed to magically reappear at his elbow.

"Come, Caroline! Crispin!" Mr. Forester called to them. "We'll take this *tonga* to the village. Pradesh will get the luggage." Mr. Forester, a man of his word, was going to take Crispin to the railway village and make introductions at the train barracks at Howrah to get him a position at the East India Railway Company.

The next several hours seemed to blur together in a sea of activity. Mr. Forester was a take-charge sort of man and watching him was both energizing and exhausting. As the *tonga* rolled along he gave Crispin a detailed account of the settlement of the English in Calcutta and the industries that thrived in the bustling city.

"Cotton, tea, and the railway—that's what drives this city, Crispin. Calcutta is simply teeming with industry. I know we are all partial to London, but just look." He gestured his hand outside the carriage sweepingly. "Look at all the new structures and buildings. This is a place alive with opportunity.

See that?" he exclaimed excitedly. "That's Dalhousie Square. It's constantly under construction as they make it grander and grander. With more and more English settling here, the homes have become more luxurious. Some of the finest society is here as well. And you'll recognize the names of the streets when I show them to you—Park Street, Church Street, and the Esplanade. The British Raj has recreated London in the East."

"My dear," Mrs. Forester said sweetly. "While there is quite an elegant society here, I'm afraid we aren't a part of it."

"Well, not exactly, that's true. But you see, Crispin," he turned to his young friend, face beaming with excitement and sweat. "In London, Caroline and I are relegated to our little sphere. In Calcutta, we can meet officers and Lords—wealthy industrialists and intellectuals. It's a melting pot!"

"Speaking of melting, it's beastly hot dear." Mrs. Forester's delicate skin had flushed to a deep rosy hue. "It always takes me a few weeks to acclimate to the heat," she said apologetically as she fanned herself vigorously.

A short while later they boarded a small passenger vessel, which crossed the Hooghly River. The air was thick with the dank smell of the river, but the breeze provided some relief from the oppressive heat. From there, they took a short drive in an open carriage and approached what, at a distance, appeared to be a cross between a remote country village and an Indian outpost. One-story structures with thatched roofs lined the dusty road, which ultimately led to a large square with a park-like center and clusters of industrial buildings on all sides. On the opposite side of the park, small English-style houses in white stucco were nestled together. This coterie of Englishness was in sharp contrast to the buildings that lined the square. The sun beat down relentlessly, and having meandered far from the river, the breeze completely subsided.

"This is our little village of Howrah." Forester announced to Crispin and called for the driver to stop. "I'll get out here at the offices and ask about a spot for you. We are always looking for more help. And we'll need to get you set up at the barracks."

"Colin, there is no rush. He can stay with us for a little. Wouldn't that be nice?" She reached over and touched Crispin's arm, a motherly gesture.

"Please, you are both too kind. Mr. Forester, I'm sure you'd like to settle in. I can wait here for a while."

"Nonsense! There is no time like the present. And of course, he could stay with us Caroline, but I'm sure he'd rather stay with young men his own age at the barracks. They can get into a lot of trouble." Forester winked at Crispin mischievously, and Mrs. Forester flushed even more deeply. Crispin let out a laugh, knowing that he would miss their company.

After a few nights at the Forester's quaint home, Crispin began to explore his surroundings. True to his word, Mr. Forester had quickly found him a role as a clerk in the engineering offices with a bunk at the railway barracks. Though Crispin would be working in the offices, he would be living with the unattached men of the railway village. Mr. Forester explained, "Not everyone has a lovely lady like Caroline to take care of them, so you'll be staying with the lads. Some work on the trains, some supervise the construction, and some work in the offices. It will be great fun!"

The barracks was a rectangular structure with a low roof and two wide double doors opening onto a courtyard. It was an odd-looking building, the inside of which resembled a mead hall. The overpowering smell of sweat and dirty laundry mixed with spices stopped Crispin in his tracks as he walked inside. Mr. Forester clapped Crispin's back. "Come on then son, it's not too bad."

Standing in the entrance, Crispin observed the interior of the barracks with a mixture of wonder and apprehension. Three low cots lined each wall, separated by tables with white ceramic pitchers and basins for washing. In the center of the room was a crude round table, where a slight, native man had just set down a large bowl, an action that created chaos. .

A short, squat boy with straight dark hair dove at the bowl to grab a loaf of bread. Before he could put it to his mouth, he was shoved aside by a giant of a man, who Crispin later came to learn was only a year his senior. The bread flew onto the ground near Crispin's feet. Without thinking, he stooped to pick it up and, as he rose, he saw the short boy attempt to tackle the giant.

The boy jumped up, grabbing his shirt. They tussled good-naturedly until the giant spotted the stranger and stopped.

"And who's this? Come to join the chaos, eh?" His accent reminded Crispin of the shopkeepers around Queens, thick and cockneyed. He approached the newcomer congenially and stuck out his hand in greeting. His grip was crushing. Crispin handed him the loaf of bread in return.

"Cassidy's me name, from the streets of London." His broad chest puffed up with pride at the mention of his hometown. "You'll have to forgive Johnston here," he tossed the bread to his companion, who caught the loaf with one hand and chomped into its crust. "Didn't get a whole lot of food when he was a young 'un, thinks it's all gonna run out but I keep tellin' him, they need to keep us strong to help run these railways!"

Johnston grunted and continued eating.

"I'm Crispin. I've just arrived from London as well."

"Hmm." Cassidy took a few steps back, giving Crispin a thorough once over. "Sound right fancy, you do. Sure you haven't been sent by the bosses to keep tabs on the likes of us?" Crispin's accent had always placed him in a sort of no-man's land between the working and gentle classes. Like Jones at Drayton Manor, Cassidy didn't know what to make of him.

Crispin defensively stammered, "Well, no, of course not . . . I'm here to work like you . . ."

"You may sound fancy, but you don't look it, mate. Come on then, welcome home!"

"Go, go, go!" Cassidy jumped up and down with surprising agility despite his large frame. His sandy blond hair was matted to his forehead, and his face dripped with sweat as he cheered Johnston on. "He's pretty fast for a little guy." Cassidy was the consummate sportsman. Crispin imagined that if Cassidy had been born to different parents, he would have spent his days purchasing fine horseflesh and watching them race.

Cassidy had organized a weekly cricket match amongst the men of Howrah village. Each week, men young and old of all shapes and sizes, paired off in teams to play for the honor of winning the weekly game. The village had really taken to the idea of a standing event, and there was quite a bit of money that changed hands in advance of the game. There were five barracks in the village, each with its own team. But in the interest of opening the sport up to all, Cassidy had arranged for the married men to participate as well, so there was an engineering team and a train guards' team. He even had the serving women in the village prepare refreshments for each game.

"There he is! Good man Johnston!! And the match goes to us!!" He clapped Johnston on the back, who didn't stop to be congratulated for his efforts but ran straight to the refreshments table for some lemonade. Crispin, Cassidy, and Johnston's barracks had won for the last three weeks, a clear source of pride for Cassidy who proceeded to congratulate one and all for a great match.

Though it had been just six weeks since Crispin had joined this close-knit railway community, it already felt familiar. As a clerk in the engineering office, his days were busy, and he was exposed to every aspect of the business—from land surveys to equipment orders to budgeting. He was learning everything Mr. Forester had to teach. He hoped that with the right training, he would eventually become a guard for the railway line. Crispin had finally found the mentor he had craved, albeit not in the horse world. He especially enjoyed budgeting and bookkeeping. His education at Queen's prison had certainly not given him the opportunity to explore his interest in figures and problem-solving, and so he reveled in the pursuits his clerkship afforded him with shameful abandon. Each night he would sit huddled in a corner of the barracks, a gas lamp casting a dull glow on the entries from the day as he poured over them, balancing the figures in his head.

"Shut off that damned lamp Crispin! We have a big match tomorrow, and you need to rest up." Cassidy barked at him the prior night.

"Cover your eyes. This is important!"

"Cover my eyes? With what? It's hotter'n hell in here . . ." Cassidy had been in India for two years and still complained of the heat incessantly.

Now, under the raging sun, he threw his sweaty arm around his new friend in delight, directing them both toward the makeshift tavern that was part of the railway camp. "Let's us go for something stronger than lemonade, my friend."

"Not today. I have a few things to do back at the barracks."

"More numbers then?" He rolled his eyes, and Johnston chuckled.

"Nope. I have a letter to write. This one may take a while."

Crispin waved them off and headed back to the barracks. Without the others, it was unusually quiet and peaceful. The air seemed cooler, and the pungent odor no longer fazed Crispin. He took a deep breath and let the stillness wash over him.

Sitting down at the center table, he pulled out a sheet of the elegant linen paper Mrs. Forester had given him and began to write. "Dearest Cassie . . ." No, that was too familiar. "Dearest Miss Drayton . . ." Crispin wrote the salutations quickly, scratching them out and crumpling up the paper in a tight ball before beginning again. "Dearest" sounded somewhat absurd given the dramatic events at Drayton Manor. It seemed hard to find a way to address her. He had drafted and redrafted this letter dozens of times. Shortly after arriving at Howrah, Crispin had written his father to tell him of his plans and the path that he had set for himself. It would have been natural to have written to Cassandra and his aunt then, but something held him back. He wanted to wait until he felt established and secure.

> *Dear Miss Drayton,*
>
> *Words can barely describe the regret I feel about how I left Drayton Manor. I replay those wretched moments when you fell from Artemis's back in my head most nights. I can still hear the horse's cry and feel my heart stop when I saw you lying on the ground. Of course, by now you know the circumstance of my departure, but it devastates me beyond anything that I could not see you before I left, and that I didn't dare to write to you for fear of it being discovered. I . . ..*

Crispin stopped abruptly and looked down at his hand, which was shaking so hard the ink was blurry on the paper. He dropped the pen in disgust. The letter was dramatic to the point of hyperbole, the words of a tortured boy who was pouring out his emotions. *Do her feelings even remotely match mine?* he wondered. And how would this letter find its way to her without going through Miss Fairfax or worse still, Lord Drayton? They would surely tear it up on sight. Crispin tore it up himself and laid a fresh piece of paper on the table. He would write to his aunt. That would have to be enough.

> *Aunt Emma,*
>
> *In the past months, I have thought of you often and have hoped to be able to write the letter I begin now and share with you the news of my life in India. I arrived here over six weeks ago, and in that time, much has changed, dramatically so. Drayton Manor seems a world away, and, while I sometimes dream of the green hills of Dorset, I believe I have found my place in the world and a path to future success thanks to your kindness.*

He told her of his journey to India and his good fortune in meeting the Foresters.

> *My life in India is a full one so far. Calcutta and Howrah are indescribable. They are dirty and crowded yet filled with a certain vitality and beauty that does not exist in England. At first, I was overwhelmed by the noise, the color, the smells, but now I find comfort in them. My work keeps me very busy, and I've already learned much about the business of the railways. Here at the barracks, I have companions of my own age who have become good friends, but I shall not bore you with tales of my coarse life. Suffice it to say I am well and comfortable in my new situation and believe that my prospects are much improved.*
>
> *I have not forgotten the kindness you showed me even in the face of my shameful behavior at Drayton Manor. While I cannot excuse my defiance of Lord Drayton's wishes in teaching Miss Drayton to ride, I can only share that I think every day of the terrible position I put you in with your employer. I imagine you must have cursed me many times and even cursed yourself for your soft heart. My folly led you to nothing but embarrassment. I hope that you can forgive me and that you know I am eternally grateful for your generosity in paying for my passage to India.*

I hope you will not mind if I write to you of my progress, and, though I have no right to ask, I wonder if you would write to me of your life at Drayton Manor and of the family's wellbeing.

Your devoted nephew,

Crispin St. John

As Crispin reread his letter, he debated removing the last paragraph. He knew that it was asking a great deal for Miss Fairfax to continue to write to him and share news of Cassandra when his actions had no doubt caused her great harm. He steeled himself for a curt response . . . or none at all. Crispin dipped the nib of his pen in ink, addressed the envelope, and hurried for the post before nerves got the better of him. A weight was lifted. With a spring in his step, he set out to find Cassidy and Johnston.

PART II

CHAPTER 8

July 1869

The two-day journey from Banaras to Howrah seemed longer than usual to Crispin as the July rains had slowed the train's progress. It had been five years since his arrival in India, and in that time, his prospects had much improved. Though he still lived in the railway barracks with Cassidy and Johnston, Crispin had risen to the post of a railway guard, a point of constant pride for Mr. and Mrs. Forester, ever his friends in the railway village.

The train was held for four hours at Arrah, while workmen piled sandbags along the banks of the Ganga tributary, which was overflowing, turning the roads between Narhi and Koilwar into treacherous mud pits. Crispin could see nothing but the sideways rain from his guard's window as the train careened through the Alluvial plain. It was crowded and growing ever more so with each stop.

At Hooghly, the second to last stop, Crispin stepped out from the breakvan to call the "all aboard." The platform was thick with bodies—a motley, rain-soaked crowd. British men obscured by their umbrellas, pushed their way past the throngs of people native to India, who stood unmoved by the rain. They seemed to take all weather in stride, barely fanning themselves in the sun and lackadaisically guarding themselves with banana leaves against the summer torrents, resigned to the deluge. It made little difference, their thin cotton tunics and wide, white pants dried quickly. Unlike the Europeans, who were weighed down by garments built for other climates, laden with thick coats and dresses. British ladies were worse off than the men, their hems perpetually soiled as they swept along the curry-colored mud.

The waiting passengers surged anxiously forward, crowding the doors like cattle in the boxcars. Once inside they began to settle—British gentlemen, ladies, and children ushered into private, first-class cars along with commissioned officers; non-commissioned officers and a smattering of *Vaishyas* into second class; and rows of Indians, a sea of people—occasionally broken by a cinnamon-skinned Bengali or a redheaded Scot who had made his way to India to seek his fortune—pressed shoulder to shoulder in the third-class trucks. Everywhere the air was heavy with sweat and acrid breath and rain-soaked clothes. With a great groan, the train lurched forward.

Before Crispin could close the door to his compartment in the second-class car, he heard raised voices from the opposite end of the car. A lanky gentleman in a top hat stood stiffly in the middle of the aisle, while a swaying soldier drunkenly barked at him.

"If you want to move to your car, you'll have to pay," slurred the drunk.

"Do you mind, sir? I would like to pass."

The drunkard lunged toward him. "Like to pass, eh? Pay the toll and then pass."

"Excuse me, sir, there is no toll. I have already paid for my seat which, my friend, is in the next car." He stabbed the air with his umbrella motioning toward the door.

"No toll? This man says there's no toll, eh?" The drunkard glanced at his audience, his fellow second-class passengers, hoping to gain their support. "Well, I'll tell you what, you can pay the toll, or I'll beat you with that whale bone umbrella of yours."

"I think not, my friend."

The man in the top hat's unflappability merely served to further offend the officer, who spat, "Listen here. I am not your friend. I work for my country. Sent into God-forsaken, malaria-infested hellholes, while men like you get your boots polished by naked coolies. You pay the goddamned toll or—"

Passengers started to shift in their seats. A few stood and approached, trying to persuade the soldier to see reason. No one called for a guard, though the noise in the car was growing. Sensing the scene was quickly disintegrating, Crispin made his way toward the exchange.

"Is everything alright?" Upon closer inspection, Crispin noticed the tall gentleman was elegant and finely dressed, though his expression revealed a rising irritation. His vivid blue eyes, framed by the soft wrinkles of age, flashed brightly against his tanned face.

"I believe all is fine. I would just like to get to my seat."

"Just fine, he says! But he won't pay the toll."

"There is no toll to be paid, sir."

"Really!" The officer roared, reaching into his pocket. Crispin caught the glimmer of a blade.

Before another word was said, the officer flung his arm out and lunged at the gentleman, thrusting the knife forward inches from the man's waistcoat. The gentleman flinched, stepping backward and absurdly raising his umbrella in defense.

Crispin caught the officer's arm mid-swing and twisted it behind his back, gripping his wrist and applying considerable pressure until he dropped the blade. Nearly twenty, Crispin stood over six feet and was a strong figure of a man.

The loss of his weapon seemed to return some strength and coordination to the soldier's body. He pushed back onto Crispin, forcing them both to ricochet like billiard balls between the seats before tumbling to the floor, where the two wrestled until the officer's mass momentarily got the better of Crispin. Pinned as he was, Crispin saw the soldier's arm raise as if in slow motion and readied himself for a blow to the gut. He rained a storm of punches upon Crispin's chest before Crispin found enough leverage with his legs to push the beast to one side.

A number of concerned men had left their seats, trying to tear the drunk man off of Crispin. It took several attempts, but finally, the man was carted off to a third-class car, where he would be fettered to a seat until the train arrived at Howrah.

In the fray, Crispin had lost sight of the tall gentleman, who seemed to have slipped away to safety. The dust had settled, but the man's top hat rolled around at Crispin's feet. He picked it up, intending to find the man when the train reached its destination.

The train crossed the Hooghly Bridge without further incident, and the rain finally started to ease. Heavy clouds became less dense, as if an unseen hand pulled back the curtain revealing the rich green of the Ganges Valley and the roiling river that made its way to the Bay of Bengal. Crispin breathed more easily as the masts of Calcutta emerged above the city of palaces, the city he had come to call home.

Crispin studied Mr. Middleton's invitation as the passenger ship from Howrah pulled in to one of the long docks that lined Calcutta harbor. Several days after the incident on the train, he'd found the envelope waiting for him at the barracks. Middleton had inquired after Crispin with the railway company and, upon learning his identity, had extended an invitation to dine with him and his daughter as a thank you for Crispin's kindness and to discuss "a potential business proposition". Middleton did not elaborate. While vague, Crispin found the note intriguing. He'd learned from Mr. Forester that Middleton had amassed a sizable fortune in the cotton business and the draw of a meal at the home of a wealthy businessman was certainly a strong one.

Crispin disembarked from the ship and quickly hailed a hack for the ride to Hastings Street. Around him, the city was alive with carriages rolling in all directions, peddlers calling out, customers haggling, and *bhisti* rushing through the streets laden with their sacks of water. The rich smell of spiced lamb and goat wafted around his nose, and his stomach growled in anticipation of dinner.

The ride was short and, as the hack pulled up to No. 7 Hastings Street, Crispin caught his breath at the beauty and enormity of the house, a grand, glistening white limestone, which reflected the late day sun. Thick columns framed an impressive staircase to the entrance. Crispin imagined that this fashionable home and its equally imposing neighbors were not so dissimilar from the finer parts of London. In all his childish adventures at Queens Prison, he'd never really seen the elegant parts of the city in which he was born. Soon, when he had enough money to return and free his father from Queen's, Crispin hoped to see that part of London, to go to Grosvenor Square and Hyde Park and see how they compared with Dalhousie Square.

He descended from the hack and dusted off Mr. Middleton's hat, which he had brought to give back to him, though Crispin was sure the wealthy man had many more. He surveyed his own attire. He wore his one good suit—a navy blue cotton. This was as presentable as he was likely to get.

Before he could reach the door, it opened as if by magic to reveal a turbaned *durwan*, a butler dressed in the white pants and *kurti* of his station.

"*Sahib*," his voice boomed as he bowed and gestured for Crispin to enter the house.

In contrast to the traditional English exterior, the inside foyer opened to an Eastern-style central courtyard with a manicured garden and fountain. Long-armed fans circulated the air, providing a welcome relief from the breathless heat of the Calcutta streets and carrying currents of sweet-smelling hyacinths. Ornate, elegant staircases lined opposite sides of the piazza, ascending to the balconies and chambers of the many floors stacked above. The design married England and India.

Crispin entered the drawing room to find Mr. Middleton's lanky frame stretched across the sofa with a drink in one hand and a pipe in the other. In one fluid movement, the host rose and crossed the room to greet his guest.

"Crispin, my boy." He extended his hand in a grand gesture.

"Mr. Middleton," Crispin started.

"You must call me Joe." Middleton's words came out in a rush. "We can't stand on ceremony, seeing as you have saved my life!" He had a pleasant voice with just a hint of Cheapside in it. His warm blue eyes twinkled as he spoke.

"Of course, Mr. Mid—ah . . . Joe. What a fine house you have here. Thank you for inviting me. I, er, here's your hat." Crispin awkwardly thrust the hat out as if he were handing a bouquet of flowers to a young sweetheart. He was nervous and felt out of place and cringed at the stiffness in his voice.

Middleton sensed it immediately. He took the hat and tossed it on a nearby chair. "Unusual, isn't it?" He gestured around. "I bought the house from a Baron who couldn't wait to leave this 'godforsaken place,' as he called it. I'm so glad you were able to join us tonight." He put his arm around Crispin, leading him to the sofa.

"I am eager for you to meet my daughter Rosalind. You'll be a welcome relief from my usual dinner guests." Middleton had an easy way about him; his manners and tone conveyed a familiarity, as if they were old friends. Crispin felt his anxiety lift and break apart like a thinning cloud bank.

"Rosalind and I . . ." Middleton paused and rubbed his chin between his fingers as he sat down and gestured for Crispin to do the same. "Dear girl, she's spent nearly all her life here in Calcutta. We lost her mother shortly after she was born." Middleton winced as if he felt the fresh prick of loss. "I'm afraid I'm a sad substitute, and my business associates are even worse."

He shook his head, clearing his heavy thoughts. "Oh, how I go on! I want to hear more about you Crispin. You are more than just a railway guard, aren't you?" Middleton leaned toward Crispin, putting his elbows on his knees. "The way you handled yourself with that soldier, and the way you spoke impressed me. Tell me your story. We're all full of stories here—why else would we find ourselves in India? But first, a drink. Chetan," he called to a servant, who stood statue-like in the corner of the room—a waifish boy of no more than fifteen— his crisp white *Kurta* hanging down to his shins. "Fetch Mr. St. John a whisky." Within moments a glass was placed before Crispin.

Crispin hesitated, not at all sure he wanted Middleton to hear his history. He'd told the fellows in the barracks about his father's disgrace and his less-than-humble upbringing, but they were all like him, working men, and didn't care. Crispin debated altering the story to fit into these grand surroundings but thought better of it. Middleton's open and unpretentious manner invited honesty, so he told him the truth about his family and his father.

Crispin paused to take stock of his host's expression and gauge if he had misjudged Joe Middleton, but the man did not seem turned off. In fact, Middleton leaned toward Crispin as if to catch every word, so he continued.

"When I was thirteen, I took a position as a groom on a Viscount's estate in Dorset. I was happy there in the country, with the horses. Unfortunately, I displeased the master of the estate and was sent away."

"Displeased the Lord, how'd you do that?" Middleton playfully raised an eyebrow.

"It's rather a long story and involves my teaching the viscount's daughter how to ride . . ."

"It's always about the ladies, isn't it?" Middleton chuckled. "And then?"

"Well, my aunt, a generous woman, gave me passage to India," Crispin went on, relaying the most recent chapters in his life story, including his intentions to pay his father's debts. "Every month I send money back to London, but it barely makes a dent in his obligations. The longer father stays at Queens the more he is charged for 'necessities.'"

Mr. Middleton was just a stranger he had met on a train, and yet Crispin felt comforted sharing his burdens with someone.

"Crispin." Middleton sighed, leaning back into the deep linen couch cushions. He rested his chin thoughtfully in his hand and said with deliberative authority, "You need to get back to England so you can pay the debts in person," punctuating the statement by taking a swig of his whisky.

Crispin pursed his lips and swirled the ice around in his own glass. "You are right, of course, but a passage to England is long and expensive. And I can't run the risk of losing my position."

"Positions like that come and go. I suspect you are capable of more. What would you like to do?" Crispin knew Joe Middleton was not speaking of the railway or even of his father, but of his future. He hesitated. He barely knew this man, who was now asking Crispin to share his life's ambitions. But Middleton appeared earnest and not one to take a young man's dreams lightly. He waited patiently, while Crispin sipped his whisky and rubbed his lips together as he weighed his words.

"I'd like to have real success, to have something of my own to be proud of. Not just a wage, but more than that."

"Ah, success." The older man drew in the word and blew it out again like a puff of smoke. "How would you define success?"

Crispin looked around at the grandeur of the room. The architecture and décor were very different from Drayton Manor, but they shared an atmosphere of import. The spirit and exertion of the inhabitant were projected upon the space, the private reflection of the public self.

Middleton took that as his answer. "You want this then? This life?"

Crispin nodded, admitting that his ambition ran beyond freeing his father. He knew that once he had done that, he would not be content to linger in self-satisfaction. Cassie's words echoed in his brain—"a woman of substance." Yes, he wanted to be a man of substance. An elusive, borderless goal. How did one achieve that?

Middleton, as if clairvoyant, launched into his own rise through the ranks. "My father worked his whole life to build a men's clothing shop in London, making enough money to send me to university so that my fortunes would reach beyond his shop. When I got to University, I was surrounded by fellows who wouldn't have to work a day in their lives, who would never truly use their University education for anything more than drawing room banter and entrance to clubs." Middleton shook his head in disgust. "But I also learned of the opportunities abroad in China and India, where men who had come from relatively humble beginnings made fortunes and broke through the ivy-covered gates of *society* as they call it."

He rose and began to pace, his long legs covering half the room in three or four strides before turning and traversing the room again. Staring at the floor as he walked, Middleton continued, "In the summers, I would work in my father's shop, ordering, stocking, and folding bolts of fabric. That's when it struck me." He returned to the sofa with a soft thud and looked Crispin in the eye. "I would achieve more by being one of the few to participate in the cotton trade from its source, than one of the many selling the finished product in England. Coming to India was a risk, but it allowed me to start Middleton Cotton Exports." He settled back into the soft folds of the sofa and took another long draught of his drink.

"We struggled at first to find our way and there were a few unsuccessful crops. I wrote to anyone and everyone I could think of in the industry." As he launched into the tale of his success, Middleton's expression became more animated, and Crispin was glad to see his candor so tremendously reciprocated.

"Well, ultimately, the quality of our cotton far exceeded our competitors in other parts of India and sold well in England, directly competing with cotton from the American South. And then, as luck would have it . . ." He reached over and nudged Crispin's arm good-naturedly with his fist. "With the Union blockades of Southern cities during the hostilities in America, demand for Indian cotton exploded. London and Liverpool were practically begging us to grow and send more bales. So, in '62, I bought additional land and doubled the size of my business." Crispin's brown eyes widened in surprise.

"And since then?" He'd been hanging onto Middleton's every word. The man's story warmed the waters of his own ambition.

"Since then, our countrymen have realized that Indian cotton is as good as American cotton, at least the way my company grows it. Better still, two of my competitors made poor investments in the last several years and have closed up shop altogether." Middleton chuckled. "Middleton Cotton Exports and Rice & Cavanaugh are all that is left in Calcutta. The bulk of cotton exports are shifting to Bombay, but we have done well." Middleton paused, rather pleased with himself, and raised an eyebrow at Crispin prompting him to comment on the story.

While Crispin's wage as a railway guard was certainly higher than it had been when he was a clerk with Forester, the position wanted for any advancement in education or experience. Lately, Crispin had found himself missing the great debates in the engineering office about the merits and design of the proposed bridge across the Hooghly River. He missed his ledgers and the satisfaction he'd derived from solving the maze of numbers they created in his head.

"It seems to be a fine trade, sir, particularly when you consider the lack of resources in England. I've never spent time contemplating my clothing, beyond embarrassment at too-short pants and ragged cuffs. There's a story to everything isn't there? The suit I am wearing today is from Smith's Shop in London. When in fact I know that this cotton likely came from India, perhaps very near Calcutta, maybe even from your fields. And still, it needs to be shipped back to London, then to Manchester for milling, and then back to London for design and sale. That's a long journey for a single pair of trousers and a jacket."

"Quite right!" Middleton interjected, afire with excitement for his trade. "Now you are hinting at expansion and diversification! My mind often runs in the same direction."

Middleton went on to describe the mills he was exploring near Calcutta. He had an entrepreneurial spirit that clamored for an audience.

"It will take some time to change the perception of Indian finished goods, but we may pursue it one day," he said enthusiastically. "Crispin, if you truly want to save your father, you are going to have to take a risk." He stood, took a turn around the room, and drank the remainder of his whisky.

"I have a proposition for you: leave the Company and come work for me. My work causes me to travel a great deal to Tamluk and Benaras, and to England. And at my age and with this heat, it becomes more and more difficult."

Middleton seemed fit and relatively young, so Crispin, inadvertently, raised a curious eyebrow.

"As a clerk or secretary?" The prospect was not unappealing to Crispin.

"No, as my associate. I would like to have a young associate learn my business and take on some of my travel burdens. You have a sense of ambition and have overcome a great deal to get where you are. I can see that you want to go further, beyond even where your imagination can take you."

Crispin was overwhelmed. It was now his turn to pace the room. He took a few moments to compose himself. "Sir, you barely know me. How can you trust me with assisting you in a business you have spent your entire life building?"

"You saved my life, and I don't need to have known you for years to see that you have courage and a commanding presence. In fact, you remind me of myself. Besides, personal tragedies have a way of fueling the young and ambitious."

Crispin thought of his life in the barracks, of Cassidy and Johnston, of the endless trips from Howrah to Benaras. What further advancement could he possibly have at the East India Railway Company? He could become a driver and then perhaps a superintendent, but that would take years and would never allow him to build a fortune as Middleton's offer might. Unlike many his age, Crispin was acutely aware that his current life choices would form the cement upon which his future would rest. This risk just might pave the way to those dreams that had always seemed so unattainable. Then again, it could thwart his perfectly stable life at the railway. Things that sounded too good to be true usually were.

"Sir, your offer is incredibly generous. Might I think it over?"

"Of course. Whatever your wage at the Company, I'll double it. You will need to find yourself a suitable establishment in Calcutta, nearby to our offices on Church Street. Perhaps an apartment."

"That is too generous, really . . ." Crispin was nearly speechless, and Middleton must have known it was an offer he couldn't refuse.

"I'm sure I'll learn soon enough that you deserve more. I've long been delaying a trip to London to meet with some of my clients and bankers. I hate to leave Rosalind for too long because she is desolate without proper company. Why don't you take the trip in my stead?"

"Me? In your stead? But I am wholly unqualified. I really ought to think about it, and you should too."

Middleton barreled ahead as if Crispin had accepted the job offer. Pouring more whisky for the both of them from a heavy crystal decanter, he animatedly tipped his glass toward Crispin's, clinking the two together in salute.

"Posh, we won't arrange the passage for several months at least! Enough time for me to teach you what's needed. In that time, you will immerse yourself in every aspect of my business; visit the cotton plantations, understand the science of planting and picking, the figures, everything! By then you'll have made your decision. If the answer is yes, you'll go with the next cargo ship. There are some decent compartments on it for passengers."

Crispin's expression gave him away. He felt his eyes bulging out of his head.

"Don't be daunted, I know that you will learn quickly. Think on it, you will have free passage back to London and will be able to ascertain your father's final debts. How much do you estimate they are at this time?"

"Near 2,000 pounds, I should think." *Many years' salary*, Crispin thought glumly. No matter how much money he made, it was never enough.

"Now see here, I will advance you whatever money you don't have to pay your father's debts and establish him in London. I'll write to my bankers as soon as you decide."

"Mr. Middleton . . . Joe, I cannot possibly accept this charity!" Crispin protested, both knowing that he could not refuse the offer and reluctant to be so much in debt to a near-stranger.

"It is not charity; it's an advance. You will pay me back, through a portion of your salary and profits from any new clients you are able to procure."

It all seemed too perfect.

"Alright. Alright, I accept. How could I not?" Crispin knew he should be more prudent and make inquiries into Middleton's character. Mr. Forester knew him by name but not reputation. Still, he could not risk losing this opportunity.

"Wonderful!" Middleton was jubilant. "Tomorrow, I will write to my people in London and Liverpool. You will travel with the shipment to Liverpool, and Jennings, my man there, will give you a tour of the mill in which we have invested. Then onto our offices in London to meet Clarkson, the bankers, and the solicitors. I hope you are ready for an adventure!"

"Adventure Papa? Are we to take an adventure?" A lilting female voice drifted into the room. Rosalind Middleton was dressed in the latest fashions from London, her light-yellow gown stiffly hugging her slim figure. The young lady seemed crisp and fresh, despite the oppressive heat, and her coloring was extraordinary. Her hair was the brightest red and her porcelain skin was fair in the extreme, like a white English rose, not at all conducive to the Calcutta sun. She had her father's twinkling blue eyes and as she held Crispin's gaze, he found himself thinking about a pair of beautiful green eyes. Green eyes and blond curls.

It had been nearly five years since Crispin had seen Cassandra, but it had now become an inadvertent habit to compare any woman he met to her. And new female acquaintances always suffered in comparison. Even Miss Middleton, whose face could be called beautiful, did not compare to Cassandra—at least as Crispin remembered her.

Rosalind curtseyed elegantly to Crispin, and he managed a stiff bow. *Still,* he thought, *it has been some time since I've been this close to an attractive English woman, so near my own age.* His senses aroused; his eyes lingered on her for longer than they should.

Miss Middleton continued coquettishly, "Is your friend joining us on an adventure?" She smiled sweetly at Crispin.

"I'm afraid not my dear. The adventure is his. Allow me to present my new associate, Mr. Crispin St. John."

Miss Middleton held out her hand and batted her eyes. "Rosalind Middleton."

"Charmed." He grinned.

"He will be traveling to England without us." Middleton's voice cut through the flirtatious introduction.

"Oh Papa, why can't we go? I long to see London again!" She looked at him imploringly, suggesting she often got her way.

"No, I'm afraid we can't go this time my dear," Middleton said, ending the discussion. "Next time, I promise. Ah, here is Jayanta. Let us go into dinner." And with that, his daughter took his arm, and they strode out of the drawing room. Crispin followed them and the imposing *durwan* in a mild daze. In the space of an hour, his life had changed so dramatically it seemed impossible. Since his arrival in India, Crispin had been thankful every day for the series of events that had led to his steady wage and comfortable, if simple, life as a railway guard. But now, for the first time, he saw in front of him the beginnings of a future that would alter his and his father's prospects forever.

CHAPTER 9

February 1870

"So I said, are you crazy man? We can't fit seven of us in this little carriage—it's a thousand degrees outside," Thomas Henderson guffawed. He was a small man, but his voice carried throughout the room. Crispin was standing, as he often had in the last few months, in Mr. Middleton's drawing room. But this evening, he was not debating the progress of the latest crop or questioning orders from England. Crispin, always uncomfortable at these soirees, was wearing his newest and best dark suit.

Self-consciously clutching his whisky, Crispin hoped he did not look as out of place as he felt. He wished he were back at the railway barracks with Cassidy and Johnston.

"Can you believe that St. John? Trying to cram us into the carriage!"

Crispin nodded and smiled his agreement. Middleton had often spoken of Henderson. "Thomas is a great fellow. He can't do figures to save his life and doesn't know a wit about anything useful, but he really took me in when we got to Calcutta and we've been great friends ever since."

Henderson's family had come to Calcutta in the early '20s with a lofty name and very light pockets, but thanks to his grandfather's crafty dealings with the natives and the East India Company, Henderson himself had never known a long day's work. He enjoyed late mornings and leisurely afternoons at the club and lingered over tea before drifting to evening festivities. This Crispin knew vaguely from Middleton and now more directly, from Henderson himself, who managed to tell Crispin all about his family, his life, and the story of the over-filled carriage while taking down three whiskies and a port.

"My boy," he paused to put his arm on Crispin's shoulder as he drained the last drop from his glass. "Let's continue this later. I have to go see what my wife's up to over there. That's her third sherry and I want to be sure she lasts until after cards."

A moment later, Rosalind Middleton floated to his side on the sumptuous billows of her pale blue gown.

"Crispin," she whispered excitedly. "Don't we have the most marvelous guests? I'm so thrilled to see who has accepted our invitation. In addition to the usual drab crowd, we have three viscounts and two earls!"

Before he could respond, she familiarly grabbed Crispin's arm and directed his gaze to the group of soldiers in uniform on the other side of the room. "That,"—she paused for dramatic effect—"is Colonel Geary, and his father is an Earl. I think he's the third son, but does that really matter? I mean an Earl!"

Crispin didn't want to dampen her excitement by telling her that, no matter how much money a family had, it was highly unlikely a third son would inherit anything, let alone the title. Colonel Geary, though clearly dashing and welcome in society, would have to make his own way in the world.

"And here is Lord Douglas." She lowered her voice even further as a tall sinewy man with a boyish mop of ginger hair approached carrying two glasses of whisky. Her hasty whisper—"He is an Earl too,"—was not hasty enough to be out of his hearing.

"Ah, the lovely Miss Middleton." The ginger noble executed a flawless bow without spilling a drop.

"My Lord." Rosalind curtsied more deeply than was necessary if Crispin recalled correctly from his father's etiquette lessons—given more out of wishful thinking than practical need. Rosalind was amid an effusive introduction when Colonel Geary appeared at her elbow.

"Miss Middleton, forgive me for interrupting, but we are in desperate need of you. My fellow officers and I are engaged in a fierce competition over whose regimentals are the most handsome. I thought our beautiful hostess would be the perfect judge to help us settle this matter. Will you come with me?"

Buoyed by flattery, Rosalind left in a flurry toward the crowd of officers. Lord Douglas's deep and slightly cynical voice replaced her excited whispers. "These affairs are deadly, aren't they? They're even worse than dinners in Mayfair." He handed Crispin one of the tumblers of whisky and simultaneously threw back his own. After which, he stretched out his hand in a belated greeting. "I'm Archie. As our hostess said, the fourth Earl of something-or-other."

"Nice to meet you. Crispin St. John."

"As part of my penance, these old dust bags keep foisting their daughters upon me. My late father—the third Earl of Airlie—would have been so pleased. Before he died, he had been urging me to marry." His jovial expression momentarily turned, and his brows creased in remembrance before he continued. "I've just come to Calcutta to manage things here and have been greeted by a fresh crop of colonial daughters." He groaned as if there were nothing worse. Crispin imagined his new friend was universally admired by the fairer sex.

"So, Mr. St. John, what took you to India?"

"Work." Crispin was oddly tongue-tied despite several drinks. Whatever social rules bound the British on their isle, those rules seemed to constrict when imported to Calcutta's upper crust. Money opened doors, as it had for Middleton, but Crispin was still viewed skeptically as a stranger and an upstart.

"What kind of work?"

"I used to be a guard on the rail lines, but now I work for Mr. Middleton." That statement had stopped many a conversation that evening, but Archie was not offended by Crispin's humble beginnings.

"Ah, then you are fortunate enough to spend time with the lovely Miss Rosalind," he drawled, his gaze turning to Rosalind who was now surrounded by a circle of young men, all laughing rather too loudly to be believed. "She's not bad on the eyes, but she is rather forward don't you think?" Her enormous silk bustle accentuated her small frame as she animatedly turned from one gentleman to the next. Feeling it was not his place to comment on his employer's daughter's behavior, Crispin remained diplomatically silent.

Archie changed the subject. "So, how is the cotton business? As exciting as it seems?"

"Indeed. Mr. Middleton is tireless but a brilliant and considerate mentor. And the position has given me a chance to travel even more than I did with the railway." Crispin became increasingly animated as he spoke. "I've been inspecting the crops throughout the regions and monitoring the transportation, which has been critical. I'll even have the chance to get back to London shortly to see that side of the business. It certainly keeps me busy!" He stopped himself, realizing he must sound ridiculous to a peer who was politely asking about his employment and likely not expecting a response.

"Sounds wonderful," Archie said soberly. "I'd love to have a purpose beyond simply 'managing' things that already exist. It must be exhilarating to watch a business grow." Before Crispin could respond, Archie continued. "London, is it? I'll be heading back there shortly. When are you going? I haven't made arrangements yet."

"I need to be there by mid-March."

"Capital. I told my mother I'd accompany her and my sister to a multitude of tedious dinners and a debutant ball or two. Let's book passage together. Incidentally, I think we can cut out in about fifteen minutes without seeming rude. How about a night cap?"

By the end of the evening, they were as familiar as old friends. Archie told Crispin about his patrician upbringing and stern father and his subsequent wild impulses and reckless habits. Crispin too shared stories of his youth, all of which stood in sharp contrast to Archie's. Archie listened wide-eyed and jealous of his independence. At first, Crispin thought Archie might have befriended him because he needed a new acquaintance in a strange land or as a way to thumb his nose at his late father's stodgy ways, but his behavior never altered and within a few short weeks their lives became intertwined.

CHAPTER 10

March 1870

A single letter lay on the silver receiving tray in the foyer. *Miss Emma Fairfax.* The name was scrawled across the envelope in a masculine hand. *No. 37 Grosvenor Square. London. England.*

Cassandra stared at the letter, intrigued. She'd just made her way downstairs to join her aunt and Miss Fairfax for tea. It was one of many rituals she had become accustomed to since coming to London for the Season. At nineteen, she was a bit past the customary age of coming out, a fact that her aunt seldom neglected to mention in the constant stream of conversations about her marriage prospects. Still, Aunt Eugenia would always balance her worried titterings with the fact that Cassandra was "uncommonly beautiful" and had a "substantial dowry," making prospects for the would-be spinster as good as anyone else's.

Cassandra held the letter up to the light, but the envelope was thick, perhaps lined. It was the paper of a man of property and breeding. Was it a letter from a secret admirer? A love letter? As far as she knew, Miss Fairfax had no gentleman friends nor any male relatives. And this was not her father's neat and upright cursive, though it was vaguely familiar to her. What was in that envelope—a matter of business? Had she inquired about another position in an attempt to escape the peering eyes and disdainful jabs of Aunt Eugenia? The possibilities swirled through Cassandra's mind. Her curiosity begged for an answer.

There was no one in the foyer or the drawing room, and, though she could hear the faint clinking of activity downstairs, there were no sounds on the landing. She ran her finger across the address. Even that small gesture felt illicit. Cassandra put the letter back and turned to ascend the stairs. She had no right to read what it contained. If Miss Fairfax had a secret life, why should that matter?

As she placed her foot on the first step, Cassandra heard loud voices from a room above. It was Miss Fairfax and her father, engaged in a tense tete-a-tete. She could only catch the occasional word or phrase, Miss Fairfax's heated, "Lady Gray" and her father's dismissive, "don't be silly." Then there was silence followed by a deliberately loud, "Tell Eugenia that I won't be down for tea."

"Certainly, My Lord." Miss Fairfax said with a civility that in no way masked her contempt. In town, Aunt Eugenia's presence was nearly constant. It seemed that it wore on Miss Fairfax, just as it did Cassandra.

Overhead, Cassandra heard Miss Fairfax close the door with deliberate force and the clipped tap-tap of her slippered feet as she neared the top of the staircase.

There was no time to dally. It was now or never. Cassandra turned back to the tray and slipped the letter into her pocket where it burned like a hot coal. And there it remained throughout the long afternoon.

Outside the rain poured down, and the three ladies—Aunt Eugenia, Miss Fairfax, and Cassandra—sat down to a dismal tea. In the absence of having her own daughter as she and Lord Gray had never been blessed with children, Aunt Eugenia poured all her maternal energy into Cassandra's debut, and in that effort, she read aloud from *Morning Post.*

The Annual Ball in aid of the funds of the Yorkshire Society took place on Friday night at Willis's Rooms, King Street. In attendance were Her Grace, the Duchess of Rutland, the Earl, and Countess of Euston . . ..

She looked at Cassandra with a raised eyebrow that seemed to ask "aren't you intrigued?" It was her greatest joy to prepare Cassandra for the delights of the Season and all the "eligible and appropriate husbands" that it may present. Whereas Miss Fairfax clearly felt uncomfortable under the prying eyes of society and Aunt Eugenia.

Cassandra's father certainly enjoyed being in London as he could frequent his clubs and monitor his investments in America more closely. In the aftermath of the Union's victory in America, he had done extremely well, drawing the attention of his friends and the praise of Aunt Eugenia who reveled in how impressive Cassandra's inheritance had become.

Cassandra would have to wait until after her presentation in April to attend any large parties. A few years earlier she could think of nothing else—visions of waltzes and polka's had danced feverishly through her childish dreams—but now that the moment was upon her, she approached it with a tamed enthusiasm. While she did enjoy the idea of expanding her acquaintances and seeing more of the world, the purpose of these parties had been clearly set out by her aunt and, to a lesser extent, her father. Cassandra was to find a suitable match—period. It didn't need to happen this season, their wealth gave her that flexibility, but it needed to happen eventually.

For her part, Cassandra hoped that these forthcoming balls might give her the occasion to meet Lord Bedford again. They'd seen each other infrequently over the last several years, and she'd hoped that the passage of time, coupled with her newfound maturity and presentation to society, might make her more interesting to the Duke's son. She listened for his name as her aunt continued to punctuate the dreary morning with snippets of reports on fashionable social gatherings. By the time Aunt Eugenia got to the end of the first column, even she seemed to have lost interest. Looking out the window, Eugenia covered a yawn with her hand.

"It really is hard to get excited about anything today, isn't it?"

At last, Cassandra felt she could excuse herself. Fingering the edges of the letter through the fabric of her gown, Cassandra rose.

"Aunt, I think I will go read for a bit. Will you forgive me if I sequester myself in my room for an hour or so?"

"Do as you will my dear."

Cassandra kissed both her aunt and Miss Fairfax upon the forehead and left them staring out opposite windows.

When she got to her bedroom, Cassandra shut the door and pulled the envelope out of her pocket, slipping the silver blade of her letter opener beneath the seal.

Dearest Aunt,

I beg your forgiveness for the long delay in responding to your last letter. These recent months have passed in a blur, a blur of cotton—farms and bales and mills and markets. My work with Mr. Middleton moves at lightning speed. I am constantly occupied. Middleton has flattered me with praise of my progress, and I flatter myself that I have done right by his patronage. Aunt, you could never have imagined when you gave me passage to this faraway land that I would find my prospects so improved. I can now write to you of orders and contracts, the development and expansion of business, not train schedules and barracks for unmarried men. I too could never have imagined my fortunes would change so greatly. I, who was but a few short years ago, a luckless boy with no prospects in the world, have now taken a suite of furnished rooms near the company's offices. The rooms are in a very fine building and with a library, dining room, and parlor. Mr. Middleton's daughter, Rosalind, insisted on procuring some staff for me and I now employ a durwan (a man of all work) and a cook, who also acts as housekeeper. I think you would be pleased to see my small household, Aunt. I've even entertained a bit with some of my new acquaintances, though I scarcely have time for social engagements.

As for society, I live vicariously through your delightful descriptions of the goings-on in London. Your account of the soiree at the Summerton's was so vivid, I felt that I was standing there next to you sipping sherry. It seems your time has been full preparing for Miss Drayton's presentation to the Queen. Please give her my very best congratulations on the momentous event.

This brings me to some news I am bursting to share with you. In a few short weeks, I will be back on English soil, in Liverpool, where I will be managing some affairs for the company. But it is my visit to London that fills every waking thought. My chief purpose, at long last, is to resolve my father's debts. I've had the good fortune, with the help of Mr. Middleton, to amass the capital to do so. As Father has been ill, I've also arranged for my dear friends, the Foresters (the same couple I wrote of in earlier letters) to assist Father in settling down in a new establishment in Richmond, just outside of London. I have never been, but I hear from Mrs. Forester, who grew up there and still has family in the village, that it is enormously pretty with lots of green parks. I hope that Father will finally find some peace and comfortable living at last. A heavy burden has been lifted from my heart and mind, but I will not be completely at ease until I see it all come to fruition.

Once it does, I would dearly like to see you and share my happiness in person. Would you let a poor nephew take you to tea? I will be staying at Claridge's Hotel in Mayfair until the middle of April when I set out for Liverpool.

As always, your devoted nephew,

Crispin St. John

Crispin. Cassandra had not seen or heard his name in six years. Though certainly, she had thought about him. His ill-fitting clothes, his square face, his odd way of talking, hints of cockney peppering his otherwise wellborn speech—it was all etched in her mind. On summer days when lavender filled the hills behind Drayton Manor, Cassandra often reminisced about their secret riding lessons. She hadn't had many companions, especially friends her own age. Dolls and books were good company, but they paled in comparison to a real live friend. Before Crispin had arrived, Cassandra had not known how lonely she was, but she certainly did after his short stay at Drayton Manor came to an end.

The guilt of his dismissal had weighed on her, and while it had faded over the course of time, it still gnawed at her. She'd had no idea what had become of him—it was as if he had disappeared into thin air.

Yet this letter was filled with happy tidings and warmth. It was clear that he and Miss Fairfax had exchanged letters and that she had even written to him about Cassandra. Restless and wondering how much Crispin knew about her and her life since they'd parted, Cassandra paced the room. She moved back and forth between her enormous canopy bed and ornate vanity. It seemed unfair that she was entirely in the dark about him, save today's snooping. Her first thought was anger at Miss Fairfax for keeping this secret. Crispin was her nephew, but he had been Cassandra's friend and companion. She had a right to know about his welfare as much Miss Fairfax did.

Cassandra stopped pacing and collapsed in front of her vanity mirror, absentmindedly running her fingers over Crispin's bold script—a confident, educated hand. He must have grown up quite a bit since she last saw him. Cassandra stared at herself in the mirror, bright blond curls and deep green eyes stared back calmly, checking her frustration. She really couldn't justify being cross with Miss Fairfax who was in an impossible position.

Would she meet with her nephew now that he was in London? Cassandra was certain Miss Fairfax would not; she had enough conflict in her life. It was one thing to maintain a correspondence from afar, but to meet him just a short carriage ride from the Drayton home in secret? That would be too much. Her arrangement with Cassandra's father was infinitely more complicated when they were in town, with Aunt Eugenia hanging about, watching Fairfax's every move to catch flaws and inserting jabs and judgments whenever she could. Miss Fairfax would not want to give her further ammunition by sneaking out to meet her stable boy nephew, whose name would only dredge up old and painful memories for Lord Drayton. No, she likely would politely decline or perhaps defer a meeting to his next trip to England should he be fortunate enough to visit again.

An idea started to form in Cassandra's mind, one justified by her certainty that Crispin's news should be shared in person. And she could be that person. While he might be disappointed to see her instead of his aunt, this was her chance to see him and discover how the years had treated him. Besides, she wanted very badly to ask for his forgiveness.

So, Cassandra decided to write in Miss Fairfax's stead. As a young girl learning cursive, she had traced her governess's hand many times. She was sure she could still do a fair imitation; not perfect, but good enough to make Crispin believe it.

She placed a piece of paper on her vanity and began to write.

"Aunt Eugenia?" Cassandra poked her head into her aunt's dressing room. Lord and Lady Gray kept no home in town, and though Lord Gray frequently visited London, he stayed at his club. Alternatively, Aunt Eugenia had maintained her childhood rooms at what was now her brother's London home.

"Yes, dear?"

"I had a note from Charles Worth's Salon a few days ago. The fabric for two of my gowns has arrived. With all of the arrangements that you have been making I didn't want to bother you, so I wrote for an appointment on my own. It's this afternoon. I hope you don't mind."

Aunt Eugenia turned toward Cassandra with a swift and somewhat flustered gesture. Her long dark hair, which was usually bound up in a large bun, fell upon her shoulders. She looked surprisingly pretty in a matronly way. She carried her full body well and her features were soft, her complexion rosy and unwrinkled. She was close to Lord Drayton's age but generally appeared older than he did. This morning, she was more youthful.

"But Cassie, my dear, don't you need me to be there? Worth is the latest in fashion, and there is risk in that. You don't want to be too fashion-forward."

"Don't worry, I won't be easily persuaded to embrace the latest from Paris. I'll be very conservative. Anyway, I'll take Jane, so I won't be alone."

Jane was Cassandra's lady's maid, a new addition to their household since the Draytons had arrived in London for the Season. Aunt Eugenia had insisted that it was time Cassandra had a proper Lady's maid, not just Ruby, who had taken care of Cassandra's breakfasts and baths throughout her childhood—she was, as Eugenia pronounced, "just a housemaid" with a multitude of other duties. Though Aunt Eugenia had handpicked Jane, personally checking her references and instructing her in how to lay out Cassandra's clothing for approval and comb her hair into the latest fashions, she now looked a little crestfallen, momentarily feeling supplanted by the maid. Eugenia sighed, but did not protest any further.

"I do have rather a lot to do." With that, she turned back to her morning rituals.

In the carriage, Cassandra reviewed her plan to dismiss Jane, who was as observant as she was loyal and protective. She would not be easily convinced to leave Cassandra on her own. As they approached Claridge's, Cassandra turned to Jane with feigned agitation.

"Oh dear. Jane, I forgot my purse at home. Could you take the carriage and go back to fetch it? I will wait here in Claridge's lobby. It shouldn't take you long."

"Are you sure, Miss Cassandra?" Her tone teetered on incredulous.

"Yes, I'll be fine. I'm unaccountably tired. It will give me a chance to catch my breath."

Jane looked at Cassandra with skepticism followed by resignation. Smart as she was, she had no reason to suspect that her lady was being anything but spoiled.

"Yes, Miss. I'll be as fast as I can."

It would take Jane the better part of an hour to find the purse, which Cassandra had hidden deep in her wardrobe.

Cassandra waited for the carriage to roll out of sight before she entered the lobby, feeling small and awkward under the large romantic archways. Huge ferns and palms dotted the corners of the room and formed garden-like nooks for the tea tables. Guests glided across the shiny floor in pairs, and a few elderly businessmen pranced confidently from the front desk to the entrance where carriages awaited them. She passed several minutes looking around for people, who, like herself, were anxiously alone. She saw no one who looked like Crispin.

"Miss Drayton?" A tall, athletic gentleman approached. He was well-dressed, wearing a fitted frock coat that accentuated his broad chest. His face was framed by gentle waves of dark, honey-colored hair, and his golden skin was several shades darker than the other occupants in the room. Could this be Crispin? He was ruddy and handsome but looked like he'd spent his life circulating through places like Claridges. This was not the young stable boy from Drayton Manor. He walked toward her with an easy, upright gait, and suddenly Cassandra was overcome with nerves.

"Miss Drayton." He repeated with evident surprise. "What are you doing here?" His voice was deeper and more gravely, but Cassandra recognized it instantly. "Is Miss Fairfax with you?"

Oh, she had been terribly foolish. He was not happy to see her. She was the cause of his humiliation and degradation. He was expecting Miss Fairfax, his aunt. And Cassandra had tricked him. Tricked him and deceived him.

Though he was clearly confused, he smiled at her a bit sheepishly. "Forgive me. Miss Drayton, you may not remember me. I am Crispin. Crispin St. John. I was once the stable—"

Cassandra's face flushed with embarrassment, pink to the roots of her elegant coiffure. Here she was manufacturing a meeting to satisfy her curiosity and he didn't even think she recognized him.

"Oh. No. You mistake my silence. I do recognize you. Of course, I do. In fact . . . I'm not sure how to tell you this . . . the fact is *I'm* here to meet with you."

"Has something happened to Emma? Miss Fairfax that is. Is she alright?" Crispin tensed immediately, drawing his brows together and leaning into Cassandra to hear more closely.

"Oh yes, she is perfectly fine." *And, perfectly unaware that we are together,* Cassandra thought to herself.

At this, Crispin looked at her quizzically.

Cassandra felt ashamed. She had convinced herself that she was meeting him to apologize, when in fact she was merely satisfying her own curiosity. And, in doing so, depriving Miss Fairfax of seeing her nephew and keeping him from telling her his good news.

Cassandra twisted the smooth fabric of her green silk gown into knots as she clenched her hands. She stepped away from him as if quietly trying to retreat.

"I'm so embarrassed. I have made such a mess of this. I know you are here to meet Miss Fairfax, but I answered your letter in her stead. I wanted to see you, and, if I could, apologize for getting you sacked from Drayton Manor." She looked over Crispin's shoulder toward the hotel entrance, seeking an exit strategy.

"Miss Drayton. Please, there is no reason to apologize. Shall we sit down?" He offered his arm and led Cassandra to a small table in the corner, tucked behind two large potted palms.

"I'm afraid I have a great deal to apologize for. As always, I go plowing forward, going after whatever it is I want without thinking and, in the course of it, bungling everything."

Crispin leaned across the table and raised his hand to stop her from continuing, but she blathered on. She told him about her long illness after their last riding lesson, the hazy periods of fever, punctuated by brief moments of lucidity. Cassandra told him that she had never said anything in his defense, and how she knew that Miss Fairfax had pled for him, extracting a promise from her father to pay for Crispin's passage to India, but only if he left England for good. Then she told him about the letter, how she had seen it lying on the desk and read it without ever telling Miss Fairfax.

The only thing Cassandra left out of the narrative was the kiss she had witnessed between his aunt and her father. Somehow that seemed both sacred and taboo.

"Please, Miss Drayton." Crispin listened attentively, albeit uncomfortably, to her speech. He drew his hand through his thick, wavy hair, his crisp blue eyes engaging her in an intense and earnest gaze. "Please. You must stop all of this. It is all in the past, and it has all turned out well. For the best, in fact. If I had not been dismissed, I would never have gone to India. I might never have found the means to save my father. To Aunt Emma, my debt is unending."

"Crispin . . . Mr. St. John . . . I'm so delighted to find that you are well and have found happiness in India. You can't know how distressed I was when you left." The stiff words seemed absurd, even to Cassandra. She shoved her chair out a bit, preparing to go, her cheeks a deepening pink hue.

"Pardon the intrusion, will you be taking tea with us this afternoon?" A crisply dressed waiter appeared beside them. Cassandra jumped, slightly startled.

"Yes. That would be lovely." Crispin said with confidence.

At the same time, she said, "No, that won't be necessary," intending to dismiss the waiter as quickly and politely as possible so that she could make a hasty exit from this bumbling, awkward encounter. Confused, the young man looked at Crispin, then at Cassandra, and back again, like a sparrow searching for the wind. They stared at each other, eyebrows raised in surprise for an expectant moment, before bursting into laughter.

"I suppose tea would be fine." Cassandra acquiesced, even though she hadn't much time before Jane returned. She had a thousand questions but didn't know how to ask a single one. What had his life been like in India? How had he courted the patronage of this man Middleton? Did he ever think of Drayton Manor? Of her? Why must he insist on calling her Miss Drayton? He was so different from the boy she remembered, and yet so familiar. Youthful freckles still danced across his cheeks, and he still had the habit of gazing too intensely into her eyes, making her feel as though she really was the only person in the room.

Crispin and Cassandra stared at each other for another incredulous second, before blurting out simultaneously, "You must tell me everything." They laughed, and it was as if six years fell off their shoulders like a cloak dropping to the floor.

"You first," Cassandra said. "You've much more to tell." Without thinking she leaned forward to grasp his hands excitedly. It was Crispin's turn to blush. Cassandra withdrew her hands quickly with as much grace as she could muster and put them neatly in her lap.

"So, tell!" She cocked her head slightly to the side. This ruddy-cheeked Crispin reminded her of their youthful outings and a shared feeling of stolen freedoms.

"Alright. Well, since you read my letter . . ." Crispin paused for effect, leaning toward her and raising an eyebrow.

"Stop it! I'm shameless, I know. But seriously. How did it all come to be? How did your fortune change so much in five years?"

Crispin pushed back in his chair and tucked his thumbs into the pockets of his coat. "It's really remarkable, isn't it? Or rather, I'm remarkable, aren't I?" His broad smile winked at her.

"Oh you!" Cassandra flirtatiously tossed her napkin at him. It fell short and landed in the steaming cup of tea the waiter had placed in front of him.

"Lovely," he said trying to fish it out without burning his hand.

"Serves you right Mr. St. John." Cassandra leaned over the table, her lips upturned in a most winning smile.

Crispin caught his breath before he began in earnest. "It really was a lot of luck, I guess. On my journey out to India, I had the good fortune of meeting a wonderful couple, the Foresters, who took me under their wing. Without them, I would have been utterly lost."

And so, Crispin began his story and asked Cassandra to fill in the blanks of her own years since they had parted. Despite the years and vast differences in their lives, they began to rekindle the closeness of their youth until the unfortunate reappearance of Jane.

Cassandra's stomach sank as she watched Jane spin through the grand hotel entrance looking a little red-faced and frustrated. Her heart raced and cheeks flushed with feverish warmth. She felt like a child caught in the act of sneaking into her father's library after she had been told to go to bed. "Oh dear! I have to go."

"What's the matter?"

"It's just . . . I have to go. I am sorry. This has been . . ." She couldn't find the words for all she had to say. Cassandra wasn't even sure what she wanted to say. It was too much for the mere seconds they had before they would be discovered. She wanted to tell him about the guilty delight she took in seeing him again. She wanted to tell him she had never forgotten him and never would. She wanted to ask when and if they would ever see each other again. All the while, her eyes darted between Crispin and the lobby doors, which gave her away.

"Caught, are we?"

"It's Jane, my lady's maid. I told her I left my purse at home."

He smiled conspiratorially, and then as if he had read all the thoughts that raced frantically through Cassandra's skull, he asked, "May I to write you?"

She nodded eagerly. Too eagerly. They both knew such a correspondence would raise many questions; it would have to be conducted in secret.

"My employer, Mr. Middleton, has an office in Fleet Street. Here." He quickly scribbled the address on a calling card he had in the pocket of his coat. "I'll send my letters there. Perhaps Jane,"—he lifted his eyes in the direction of the lobby—"can pick up my letters and leave yours there."

"That's perfect." Cassandra's voice was clipped, and the words sounded strange in her mouth, but his plan *was* perfect, and her heart already raced with anticipation at reading Crispin's missives. As she stood to leave, he clasped her hand for a fraction of a second, and a feeling like a jolt of lightning shot through her veins.

"Please remember me to my Aunt—you can say we bumped into each other in the street—and tell her that I will be leaving tomorrow for Liverpool but will continue to write often and wish her all the best."

"Of course, of course. Goodbye Crispin." Cassandra tried to look dignified and nonchalant as she hurried away. Behind her, his voice, light and breezy, brought back the warmth of childhood memories, "Goodbye, Cassie."

Even as she climbed back into the carriage with Jane, Cassandra could feel the pressure of his hand on hers.

CHAPTER 11

April 1870

Preparations for Cassandra's presentation at St. James Palace and the party that would follow had taken over the household.

There had been countless trips to Madame Ferrier's Salon in the West End where Cassandra, Aunt Eugenia, and Miss Fairfax observed the latest styles of Charles Worth and Redfern's that were displayed elegantly in the salon's showroom. Although a part of her felt that the pomp and circumstance of coming out into society were undeniably excessive, Cassandra did love the chance to see and be seen and dove headlong into the sartorial delights of the Season.

While stuck in Dorset, despite her father's insistence on her having expensive gowns, she had few occasions to dress for anything. The countless hours Cassandra spent pouring over novels had set her head to inventing elegant ball gowns and dreaming up items for her future trousseau. So, she had sent away for some fashion journals and paid special attention to the details given to the gowns worn by the ladies of London society. Finally, Cassandra and her aunt had a shared interest. Lord Drayton told his daughter that her aunt was quite striking in her day and, while that seemed hard to imagine now, no one would deny that she was impeccably dressed. When Cassandra was a young girl, Aunt Eugenia had fussed over her niece's outfits much to her childish annoyance. But as she grew older, her aunt won her over, and Cassandra appreciated all she had learned.

Still, she knew that she was a constant source of worry to Aunt Eugenia, who had fixated on everything from Cassandra's hair to her wardrobe to making the right acquaintances in London, and of course to the fact that, on the cusp of twenty, she was two years older than most of the other debutantes this Season. Her father had insisted that they wait, claiming her to be too young. His fears that she might be swept up by opportunistic nobles who needed his money to buoy their falling fortunes galled him. He said as much to Aunt Eugenia behind closed doors as Cassandra eavesdropped. Cassandra was wise enough to appreciate her father's love but young enough to feel cheated of the exhilaration of London Society.

Aunt Eugenia fretted constantly that Cassandra's age would impede her prospects of finding a man with a substantial title and position. It seemed ludicrous. Any man who would have her at eighteen would surely have her at twenty. And while Cassandra was not quite as excited for all the balls and to-do as Aunt Eugenia was, she did look forward to the opportunity to meet new people, especially some her own age. Crispin was the only person her own age she had ever really associated with.

Cassandra's head was racing with such thoughts as she approached the drawing room. She stopped to pick up the newspaper from a side table. The smell of tobacco and freesia drifted toward her, revealing who was inside before she heard the conversation.

"Are we all ready for the Queen's reception, Eugenia?" Lord Drayton had happily distanced himself from the details of the preparations. The ritual of coming out was strictly in the female sphere, and he deferred to his sister accordingly. He'd spent many a late night at his clubs, enjoying talk of business, billiards, and the company of his friends and associates.

"Yes, Cassandra will look divine in her presentation gown. The brocade on that gown is gorgeous," Aunt Eugenia's voice nearly sang with delight. From where she was standing, concealed by a large armoire in the hallway, Cassandra could see the mirror above the fireplace. Aunt Eugenia was admiring her reflection and smoothing the silk bodice of her gown. It was exceedingly elegant, a pistachio green with small pearls sewn into the intricate folds that covered the back of the gown, the fashionable bustle only enhancing the appearance of her already ample frame.

"But James, I do want to discuss something with you before we begin the festivities of Cassandra's coming out." Cassandra was about to enter the room, but held back, curious. "We must talk about what's been going on in this house . . ."

"I'm not sure what you are referring to Eugenia." Lord Drayton had a hard edge to his voice. He knew exactly what she was alluding to.

"You know very well what I'm talking about James." Their eyes locked in the mirror. "Your completely inappropriate relationship with Cassandra's governess."

"She's not a governess. She's Cassandra's companion."

"I don't care what Miss Fairfax's position is." She said the name with withering disdain. "For years now she has been raising your daughter, running your household, and I assume doing other things that I dare not mention!" Cassandra's cheeks colored. Of course, everyone knew of their affair, but it was never spoken of openly.

"Eugenia, please. Lower your voice."

"James, it's not as though everyone doesn't know. She goes everywhere with you, and the way you look at her, it's completely unsuitable."

"Cassie doesn't know," James said defensively.

"Please, your daughter is many things—beautiful, intelligent, sometimes willful, but most definitely not stupid. She sees what we all see. It's too obvious." Aunt Eugenia paused and breathed deeply. "James, when you were at Drayton Manor, away from the prying eyes of Town, I didn't say anything. But now, Cassandra will be out in society and you will *all* be prey to gossip. This situation would not reflect well on Cassandra and might hinder her chances for a suitable match."

"No one will be concerned with our private business." Lord Drayton deflected.

"*Everyone* will be concerned with your private business. It will be spoken of in drawing rooms, clubs, gossip columns, and who knows where else! It's time that you grew up James. Cassie no longer needs a governess or a paid companion or any other name you choose to give her." The "her" was heavy with contempt.

"I will not give her up, I will not send her away!" Lord Drayton's voice boomed, and Cassandra was struck then by the force of his feelings for Miss

Fairfax. From the moment she had learned about their relationship, Cassandra had imagined them as characters in an Austen novel, formal and cautiously romantic. But her father sounded incredibly passionate in his defense of Miss Fairfax, as though they were Bronte-esque star-crossed lovers engaged in an all-consuming love affair. Suddenly, her anger rose. Aunt Eugenia was using her coming out as an excuse to put pressure on her father. Eugenia had never liked Miss Fairfax, and Cassandra was now sure she just been biding her time until she could get rid of her.

While Cassandra understood in theory why her aunt was so averse to a public connection between her brother, a Lord, and his child's former governess, in practice, Miss Fairfax had become family, as close to Cassandra as her father. She couldn't be compartmentalized, boxed in by her station. Wherever Cassandra was, there was Miss Fairfax, mother and mentor. She had a mild, calming presence that made their lives easier. She could blend with any company—Lord Drayton's schoolmates, his hunting partners, his business associates, their wives, and daughters—with chameleon-like ease, and her mind and manner were as elegant as that of a duchess. Aunt Eugenia was just being spiteful, and her fixation with society's rules rankled. With her aunt, those rules constricted like a too-tight corset. But surely others had a broader, looser view. Hadn't Jane Eyre and Rochester fallen in love and made a life together in the end?

"James, lower your voice. My God, there is no need to shout." Aunt Eugenia nearly hissed as she spoke. "I don't want to meddle in your personal affairs, but for Cassandra's sake, you need to be seen with ladies other than Miss Fairfax. Even if it's just for appearance. There are many nice ladies I can introduce you to."

Aunt Eugenia's strategy was clever. She knew that Lord Drayton would do anything to secure his daughter's happiness in an excellent match. She also knew that he would never be pressured to give up Miss Fairfax. But by inducing him to create a public flirtation with another lady, she could accomplish her goal of separating them, perhaps for good.

Lord Drayton balked, "I'm not going to carry on a flirtation with some young girl Cassandra's age."

"Of course not! I have many lovely acquaintances, widows in their late thirties, intelligent ladies with whom you can converse. Just allow me to introduce you to a few and whomever you find most interesting you can escort around town, go to a few affairs, and take a turn or two around Hyde Park. That will defray any suspicion."

He guffawed. "Well, I suppose that would be fine. Though hardly fair to a poor widow."

"I'm not thinking about the poor widow, I'm thinking about your daughter."

Cassandra felt a pang of guilt. Her aunt was doing what she thought was in her niece's best interests, but Cassandra knew this would drive a wedge between her father and Miss Fairfax even if it was just for appearances.

Even six years ago, when she first became cognizant of their affair, Cassandra had not been terribly surprised. Some part of her had always sensed a thread tying them together. The way her father looked at Miss Fairfax when she crossed a room, the blush that rose in Miss Fairfax's cheeks when he entered a room or left it, the looks over the dinner table that lasted two seconds too long, the shuffling of feet beneath it, Aunt Eugenia's scowl as her father helped Miss Fairfax into a carriage or took her arm in his on a walk. Perhaps that was the reason why Cassandra couldn't imagine life without Miss Fairfax, even when the time for her to have a governess had long passed. "Companions" were not really the thing anymore, and her aunt would have been more than happy to take up the mantle of Cassandra's progress herself.

But Cassandra had wanted Miss Fairfax to stay on because she loved her dearly, nearly as a mother. She'd known no other female influence, save Aunt Eugenia and the servants.

Then it dawned on her—would her father's social conscience overpower his feelings for Miss Fairfax and drive her away? She prayed it would not.

Having found a fraction of common ground, the bite in Aunt Eugenia and Lord Drayton's conversation softened, and they moved on to discuss the day's outing. Now, was her moment to enter. Cassandra pasted a smile on her lips.

"I'm ready Aunt."

Aunt Eugenia beamed with joy. "Wonderful, I'm thrilled for you to meet these new acquaintances. The Douglases are one of the best families in all of England! And Margaret Douglas is being presented with you to the Queen," she exclaimed with gusto.

Lord Drayton gave Cassandra's arm a quick squeeze as if steeling her for battle as he rolled his eyes and made his way to the library.

"You look lovely Cassandra," Aunt Eugenia said as she examined her niece from across the carriage. "Perfection. Well, almost."

She spent the entire length of the short carriage ride to the Douglases' home fluffing the ruffles on the front of Cassandra's rose-colored gown.

"They have wilted. It's despicable. I don't know what your maid is doing. I must speak to your father about employing better staff."

"Aunt! That isn't necessary." Cassandra attempted to push her hand away. "Jane is beyond attentive."

Undeterred, Aunt Eugenia joined Cassandra on her side of the coach and began primping the fabric between her fingers into neat folds. Cassandra sighed deeply and resigned herself to the humiliation. With Aunt Eugenia, it was best to pick one's battles.

"Cassandra, this is an excellent family, and you want to look absolutely perfect, don't you?" She hated her aunt's habit of making statements in the form of questions. "We may even see the young Earl today. Lord Douglas died rather recently, and his son has taken on his responsibilities quite early. He's extremely handsome by all accounts, or so I've been told." She gave Cassandra a knowing look, and Cassandra in turn bristled at her aunt's callousness. The debutante was all too aware that her aunt was on a mission for which she would be paraded around London to find a husband. Not that Cassandra objected to being married—she had developed a romantic sensibility over the years—but she looked forward to the adventures of the Season and to forming new friendships more than to attaching herself to any particular young man.

The day was overcast and the air damp and thick, though not unpleasant. Cassandra closed her eyes briefly and enjoyed the soothing smell of grass as they rolled along the edge of Green Park. For a brief moment, she was reminded of Drayton Manor until they came to a crashing halt. She had to catch Aunt Eugenia who pitched forward like a drunkard who had lost his balance. Cassandra's arms strained with the weight.

"Good gracious! What is this now?" Aunt Eugenia huffed and banged her umbrella on the roof to signal the driver's attention once she regained her composure.

"Overturned cart in front of us m' lady. Looks to be a mess of garbage." As soon as he said the word, the smell of grass was replaced by the raw stench of London city streets. Aunt Eugenia grabbed her handkerchief and used it as a guard against the odor, muttering about Lord Drayton's servants.

"We'll be out of this in no time."

Some five minutes later they drew up to No. 5 Mayfair Place. It was a magnificent home spanning nearly twice the width of the Draytons' London home with elegant, white-washed columns and a crisp limestone façade. Four footmen in green and gold livery, buttons polished within an inch of their life, appeared at the entrance, partially obscuring the wrought iron Douglas crest. The two women were ushered up the stairs, through the front doors, and into the marbled foyer.

"It's glorious, isn't it?" Aunt Eugenia hissed her excitement behind her hand fearing the footman would hear. "I've only been to the Douglases' once before." Her elation at the invitation was uncontainable. She twittered on recounting in excruciating detail the talk she attended for a charitable organization of which Lady Douglas was a patroness. Cassandra paid no attention, letting her aunt's voice fade to background noise as she took in the beauty of the house. The foyer was an imposing room with vaulted ceilings and an impressive white and black marbled floor. Elegant statues clearly collected over many generations' travels sat in alcoves, and comfortable settees dotted the space along the walls. The smell of fresh-cut lilies filled the air, emanating from a spectacular arrangement at the round table in the center of the room. The butler, who must have noticed their rapt expressions, moved slowly so that Aunt Eugenia and Cassandra might appreciate the details before escorting them to a charming day room, likely one of many that served the same purpose: entertaining. Green and pink wallpaper complemented the cherry-colored furnishings, and as large as the room was, it felt lived-in and warm.

"Lady Eugenia Gray and The Honourable Miss Cassandra Drayton." The butler announced their names with regal intonation as though they were the Queen and Princess of Wales. Cassandra could see Aunt Eugenia's smooth round cheeks flush with pride. The two ladies seated before them were pictures of elegance, both of similar fair coloring and bright blue eyes. The Countess's silver hair was swept up in a chignon pierced with a decorative feather. Lady Margaret, who couldn't have been more than eighteen, had raven-colored hair, which highlighted, by contrast, her vibrant peachy complexion. Combined with her sapphire eyes, she was an uncommon beauty. For a moment, everything in the room was silent and still as if holding its breath, until the Douglas ladies rose to greet their guests. Convention would not require either to stand and greet guests whom they clearly outranked, but the Douglases rarely stood on ceremony. It was one of the reasons they were universally well-liked.

"Lady Gray. How lovely to see you again!" The Countess clasped Aunt Eugenia's hand warmly. "Let me introduce my daughter, Lady Margaret Douglas." At her name, Margaret executed a flawless curtsy.

"It is a delight to be invited to your home Lady Douglas," Aunt Eugenia addressed the elder. "Please give me the honor of introducing my dearest niece, my brother's daughter, Miss Cassandra Drayton." With a nearly royal wave, she gestured to Cassandra, who curtsied to the Countess dutifully, feeling Margaret's smile upon her.

"Come and sit with me, Miss Drayton." Margaret grabbed Cassandra's hands and pulled her into a far corner of the room. Aunt Eugenia, usually so concerned with manners, was not bothered by their hostess's unchecked familiarity. She settled, as decorously as her large frame allowed, next to Lady Douglas, as the tea service began.

Out of earshot, Margaret began, "You are just as beautiful as people described. Suitors will swarm." She had a lyrical voice and her eyes sparkled nearly as brightly as her smile. Though Cassandra was new to Town and inexperienced in society, Margaret did not make her feel a stranger. Her manner was unaffected and genuine.

"Thank you, Lady Margaret, that's very kind, and I'm quite sure you will have many admirers this season."

"Please call me May, I can't stand formality. Mama gets upset with me sometimes. Especially when I get too chatty with the servants. I just don't care about it all—the balls, the soirees, the turns about Hyde Park. Of course, I think the parties will be fun and I certainly hope to have a romantic interlude in a secluded ballroom corner—wouldn't that be fabulous?"

Cassandra couldn't help but laugh. May hadn't taken a single breath and yet, she continued.

"But all this pomp and these ridiculous feathers that the Queen is making us put in our hair for the presentation, it's absurd," she had begun to whisper and looked over at her mother cautiously to ensure she had not heard. "Don't you agree?" May looked at her new friend hopefully.

Cassandra threw caution to the wind, leaning in so her aunt wouldn't hear. "I completely agree. I have been dying to get out of Dorset, and I'm excited to make new friends, but I'm so weary and bored with all the planning and the need for everything to be flawless, not a hair or ribbon out of place. My aunt says that all eyes will be on me and that I had better focus on the *goal*. She makes finding a husband sound like having your prize stag win at the Doncaster Cup! Though I have little experience with men, I think it's safe to say they aren't horses."

May chuckled and grabbed her hand in a conspiratorial manner. "From the talk I hear, the two beasts may be more similar than you would think. We are going to be great friends, Cassandra. That's a musical name but a mouthful, isn't it?!"

"You can call me Cassie if it's easier. My father does."

"Cassie. That's perfect. Anyway, back to the subject, men aren't horses, but you can certainly tame them."

"I would have no idea how to do that. Rest assured the women in my life are not focused on 'taming' their men." Her heart tightened as she thought about Miss Fairfax.

"I don't know Cassie, your Aunt looks like she could conquer King Tut himself." They both looked at Aunt Eugenia who was nodding vehemently at the Countess, the soft skin around her chin jiggling oddly as she did. Her girth seemed to overwhelm the delicate chair on which she perched. May and Cassandra looked at each other and giggled like schoolgirls.

"I'm serious." May continued. Though they had both grown up in relative seclusion—May in Scotland and Cassandra in Dorset—May had a head start on refining her social savvy. Cassandra had been told that May had spent the last few years in London. And she had an older brother.

"Men, all you have to do is charm them. I know the perfect way to do so and I'm going to teach you. We'll practice at our first ball." She pushed her chair back and angled her body slightly to the side, tucking her chin down and looking up at Cassandra.

"First, you bat your eyes just so, but not too much, and then you have to smile, but smile sweetly and don't show too many teeth."

"That looks rather like a sneer, not a smile."

"Don't interrupt me, I'm serious!" She grinned wickedly. "If the conversation lags, ask questions that flatter a man's interest in himself. And last of all, say something slightly shocking, just before you are whisked off to another part of the room."

Cassandra had a feeling that May didn't have to study to be charming, it came naturally to her.

"That's perfectly devious! How did you put that all together?"

"Easy, dear Cassie. I have a brother, and he taught me well. He has quite an ego and quite an interest in ladies."

"Sounds dashing," Cassandra said half-seriously.

"Not at all. He's more Wickham than Darcy." May laughed deliciously at her brother's expense.

"Do you like Jane Austen?" Cassandra said hopefully. If May loved romantic novels as much as she did, they'd be kindred spirits surely.

"Of course! I've read all of her books, *Emma, Sense and Sensibility, Persuasion, Mansfield Park,* even *Northanger Abby*. But *Pride and Prejudice* is my favorite. Really, we are living in the wrong time. Can you imagine what it would have been like to wear those frocks? My mother showed me one of my grandmother's gowns— she died before I was born. It was terribly low cut and positively see-through. What I would give to wear that to the Queen's reception!"

"May!" Cassandra exclaimed, imagining her in what amounted to a nightdress.

May winked in response. "I do love her books and I love the Bronte sisters too—not just because of the romance but how they truly transport you." May's look turned more serious and contemplative, and Cassandra had a sense that for all her shocking comments and animated speeches, May at her core had genuine substance.

"Girls," Lady Douglas called. "What is all that giggling about? Come join us. Let's discuss your gowns for the presentation."

"Yes, Mama." May jumped up dutifully, rolling her eyes at Cassandra before she moved to join the older ladies. Cassandra followed her and sat down next to her aunt. As May listened attentively to Lady Douglas, a wave of warm satisfaction washed over Cassandra. How excited she was to have the beginnings of what might be a true friendship.

A few short weeks later, as they approached St. James, Cassandra was filled with nerves and anticipation. It seemed every moment in the last year had been leading up to this one—her presentation to the Queen.

A long line of carriages formed on the Pall Mall and snaked around the palace entrance waiting to deposit their jeweled, beaded, and embroidered cargo. Anxious mothers and maiden aunts circled nervously around their charges making last-minute adjustments to curls and lace cuffs. The bustle of activity, as Aunt Eugenia and Cassandra descended from their carriage, caused Cassandra's heart to pound. Her father had insisted on coming with them to St. James, but he would remain in the carriage. Her aunt thought his presence superfluous, of course. As Cassandra's sponsor, Aunt Eugenia would accompany her into the anteroom and wait as she was ushered into the Presence Chamber. Though some men were present, most fathers chose to shy away from this distinctly feminine milestone. But Cassandra's father was stubborn as usual, and she loved him for it. His smile gave Cassandra encouragement as she set out for the palace.

"You look beautiful, my darling. You'll outshine everyone." He had said, beaming.

Still, Cassandra's courage faded as she struggled to put the long train over her left arm, ensuring the folds were elegantly draped. She'd had nightmares about today, envisioning herself tripping as she entered Her Majesty's chamber or falling flat on her face as she curtsied. Her mind raced wildly to these visions now.

"Come, my dear." Aunt Eugenia bustled. "This only happens once, and you look quite the part."

She referred to Cassandra's gown, which they had carefully picked out at Madame Ferrier's. A Worth gown in a pink so pale it appeared nearly white, but still managed to draw out the blush in her cheeks, which grew redder by the minute. The heavy silk folds fell gracefully to the ground.

The anteroom was abuzz with female chatter and the air was thick with perfume. The room had high ceilings, but the decor was rather more muted than Cassandra had expected. Aunt Eugenia sought out the Lord-in-Waiting and presented Cassandra's name card to him, while she shuffled nervously toward a cluster of other debutantes. She felt particularly awkward and friendless until she spotted May. Cassandra marveled at how much she had missed in not having friends so much of her life. After all the years being sheltered at Drayton Manor with no companions, except Crispin, she and May had become thick as thieves in a matter of weeks, and their friendship was a tonic that made every moment brighter.

"Cassie, thank God you've arrived." May rushed toward her. "I've been dying of boredom, but I am about to head out for my big moment, and now, I'm dying of nerves."

"You'll be the picture of grace. You look lovely, as exquisite as a pearl."

"Wish me luck!"

May's gown was rich ivory, which set off her striking looks. Her black hair was severe against the whites and creams that filled the room like a carpet of meringue, her complexion flawless, and her Adriatic eyes sparkling.

"Lady Margaret Douglas, daughter of the late Lord Archibald Douglas, the Earl of Airlie." Cassandra crossed her fingers for her friend and watched May glide gracefully toward the Presence Chamber.

Moments later, she too was ushered through the door.

"The Honourable Miss Cassandra Drayton, daughter of Lord James Drayton, Viscount Drayton." the Lord-in-Waiting's voice boomed, and Cassandra nearly jumped.

The presentation room was imposing. An oversized portrait of William III stared down from above a roaring fire. All eyes in the room were centered on Cassandra, and she silently prayed that she wouldn't trip. Her heart was beating so fast, she thought she might faint. Cassandra walked toward the Queen, who was perched on her chair surrounded by yards of deep crimson velvet. She longed to look up and observe Her Majesty, and it took all her willpower to keep her head bowed, but she managed to do so for the entirety of her slow march to the Queen's dais. Once she was before the Queen, she performed the deep, well-practiced curtsey, lowering her forehead until it nearly swept the floor. As she came up, Cassandra glimpsed Queen Victoria, who was small, short-waisted, and very round. She caught a whiff of Fleur de Bulgarie, her singularly powerful perfume. The monarch seemed so utterly human. Cassandra even wondered if her feet could touch the floor, and the thought made her lips curl upward. For a moment she feared she would be deemed insolent, but the Queen looked approvingly at her, kissing her forehead.

Cassandra lifted her head and regained her posture before backing out of the room as gracefully as possible. By the time she reached the entrance, an attendant was at her elbow, ushering her to the anteroom, where her aunt waited with a beaming smile. She had orchestrated Cassandra's presentation to the Queen, and now that she was "out" Aunt Eugenia could parade her niece around to as many balls as she liked. As for Cassandra, she couldn't have been happier. Finally, life was beginning. Everything before this moment seemed nothing more than a dress rehearsal for opening night, and at last, the curtain rose.

CHAPTER 12

April 1870

Crispin fingered the chain of his watch as he waited for Archie. Ten minutes had passed and the cramped entrance to the Liverpool Arms Inn was bustling with activity. He found himself jostled to and fro as patrons navigated the entrance. The thick smell of smoke, sweat, and ale signaled that another group of maritime men had just arrived, crowding into the dining room. They were a motley band of sea captains, some dressed quite nicely; others in shabbier coats with the smell of dead fish hanging on the threads. Crispin debated walking outside for air but was concerned that Archie would miss him as he came down.

"There you are!" Archie descended the stairs, valise in hand. "Everything took rather longer than expected. The Liverpool Arms doesn't quite have all the niceties of home."

"You didn't have to stay here." Crispin stood, smiling.

"Neither did you, you can afford better now!"

Crispin chuckled. "That may be true, but we were only in town for one evening and this seemed most convenient to our offices and the docks."

"A man of industry, that's what you are my friend!" Archie clapped Crispin loudly on the back.

With a good-natured shove, Crispin threw back, "And what does that make you? A man of leisure, I suppose." He ran his fingers through his thick, wavy hair and pushed past the raucous patrons to exit the inn.

"Certainly not. I'm a man of purpose, and my purpose is to show you the good life!" Archie puffed up proudly behind him. "So, we are off then, back to old Calcutta! Much more adventure to be had! Onward man!"

They left the Inn and walked along the water toward the dock where their ship awaited. With the cotton shipment safely delivered during their trip to England, the return journey would prove more relaxing. The low hanging clouds and thick, foggy mist obscured the masts of the many ships that dotted the dock. Liverpool was a rather grim place, offering little beauty to entice visitors, but it was a city bustling with industry. The docks teemed with an energy all their own.

"By the way, how did you find your aunt? Weren't you to have tea with her in London?"

Crispin was about to answer when two blushing shop girls passed them whispering. Archie, distracted from his line of inquiry, offered them a jaunty bow, and they giggled in return.

"Well?" He came back to his point.

"Rather different than I would have expected. It seemed my letter was misdirected."

"Please tell me it fell into the hands of a gorgeous singer with whom you shared some intimate moments . . ."

Crispin put his hand up in protest. "Actually, I did meet a lady, though not in the way you think. Cassandra Drayton. We were friends as children when I was living at Drayton Manor, even though I was just a stable hand. My aunt was her governess and now is her companion."

"Aha! And how did she look? Has she grown into a beauty with a slim waist and an eye-catching décolletage?" Archie pantomimed a woman's curves with his well-manicured hands.

"You're incorrigible!" But of course, Crispin was thinking about her, and her waist, and her décolletage. She had looked much the same as she did as a child. Even at fourteen, she had been beautiful, but her youthful prettiness had transformed into elegance. Her wild blond curls had been tamed into silky golden waves, tucked neatly beneath a stylish hat, and her flawless, milky complexion punctuated by bright green eyes. She did indeed have more curves, soft feminine ones. More than once at Claridge's, Crispin had found his eyes gazing over her figure. The memory of her hand in his brought a smile to his face.

"Wow, that pretty, eh?"

"Yes, she was looking very well. She's always been rather impetuous, so she intercepted my letter and responded in my aunt's stead. She had gotten it into her head to apologize to me for what happened ages ago. Still, it was nice to see her, even just once."

"Impetuous. Sounds delightful. And why would you see her 'just once?' You must stop being so conventional and rule-abiding. Why not see her again?"

Crispin mumbled, "You couldn't understand," but luckily Archie—ever distracted—didn't hear him or didn't listen as was more likely the case. Crispin wondered when he would see Cassandra again, if ever, but smiled. He had reason to hope. He had been astounded when not two days after their encounter at Claridge's, his clerk at Fleet Street presented him with a crisp white envelope addressed to him with an elegant flourish.

"Here you go, sir." The paper was thick and expensive, not that of a letter of business. "A pretty young lady dropped this by just now. Said her name was Jane and that you'd know all about it." He gestured casually to the envelope and left the room, having no idea the significance of the letter to Crispin. And just like that, their correspondence began.

"Ah, here we are!" Archie proclaimed as they approached the ship. "Our home, at least for the next few weeks." As they boarded, they noticed dozens of sailors scurrying about, set to the infinite number of tasks required before casting off. They were a motley crew of men, grizzled and bearded, not unlike those at the inn. Crispin nodded to the captain and shook his hand as he walked up the gangway. Archie trailed behind him.

"Well, enough about Miss Drayton, Crispin. She's ancient history and many miles away. Let's talk about Miss Rosalind Middleton. Now, she is a very pretty girl!"

Rosalind was pretty. Very pretty in fact, and she had the added benefit of being a practical, everyday reality. Thrown together as they were so often by Middleton's unsubtle matchmaking, Crispin and Rosalind were beginning to be seen by their friends as a pair. And while his acquaintance with Rosalind had been relatively short, Crispin could imagine a life with her. It would be so convenient, so comfortable. She was fun and had pluck, though perhaps too much. She coveted excitement and society, and she became the center of attention at any gathering.

But her porcelain skin and fiery hair paled in comparison to Cassandra's soft and inviting countenance. For years, Crispin had imagined what Cassandra would look like as a grown woman, and the reality was far more appealing than any imagining. Since their meeting at Claridge's, he couldn't help but see her face flicker before him every time he closed his eyes. She would always be the ethereal golden girl of his dreams.

Archie woke Crispin from his daydream with another violent pat to the back. "And she is quite an accomplished flirt."

Crispin turned to him. "You would know! Last time I saw Rosalind, you monopolized her for the entire dinner! Watch out *My Lord,* she may have her eye on you!" They headed toward their quarters below.

"I know!" Archie threw his head back dismissively. "My friend, I am not ready to settle down. Far too much fun to be had! But you and Rosalind . . ."

"Stop foisting her on me. You would have me married off in a fortnight, wouldn't you?" Crispin laughed.

"I've been told the state of marriage is very blissful for some, Crispin. Especially when one's father-in-law is one's employer!" He chuckled and pushed past Crispin to descend the portside stairs.

CHAPTER 13

April 1871

Cassandra waved the paper in front of her mouth, blowing gently on the last page of her letter to Crispin. It had been a year since their correspondence began, and Cassie found herself eagerly awaiting the arrival of Crispin's dry and witty missives. He had regaled her with stories of his life on the railroads and rivers of India, his various friends from a rough and tumble assortment of lads to the refined company of his mentor and business associates. Through his descriptions, Cassandra walked the streets of Calcutta and gained entry into an exotic world of color and chaos, so different from the orderly gray and green world of London and Dorset.

In return for his stories, she had tried to share her own. Her English life might be less colorful, but the circuitous nuances of aristocratic society and her new circle of friends made for engaging satirical chronicles. However, even Cassandra had to admit that today's letter was a bit more cynical than most.

Crispin,

You may snicker to hear it, but the excitement of my first season certainly did not last long. I confess these receptions and balls have blurred into one increasingly boring routine—the fittings for gowns, the hours spent getting ready, hair curling, ribbons and lace tuckers primped and plumped, pearl buttons and pins placed and replaced just so. My aunt's fussing never ends, nor does the reciting of the family lineage of every member of the royal family, and the peerage, and the gentry. All around me are people—mothers, aunts, grandmothers, debutantes, and their various masculine counterparts—poised with the focus of an archer on that singular target: marriage.

So here I find myself, at the beginning of a new season and I can barely recall the nerves that coursed through my veins when I tentatively curtseyed to the Queen just a year ago. After three weeks of balls, the familiar scene is becoming stifling: the crowded cloak rooms, the lemonades, and ices, the smell of cologne mingling with the scent of lilies and lavender, all covering the less pleasant smell of perspiration.

The rooms are always filled with little clusters of four or five ladies, flocking about a fashionable Miss So and So who has just come out. On the surface, they all—I mean "we all" for I too put on my widest smile—seem to be having the gayest of times, yet underneath the happy façade, panic boils over finding a husband, especially for those in their third or (heaven forbid) fourth season. While the ladies admired Miss So and So's dress—pale blush, heavily beaded at the décolletage and along the edges of delicate capped sleeves—they burn with jealousy, knowing her buoyant ringlets and carefree good spirit are far more likely to capture the attention of Lord Up and Coming, than their methodical social strategy.

Clusters of ladies gossip about the soldiers in their dignified red coats and the dashing young parliamentarians, such as Lords Silverbridge and Cartwright, who have precociously won seats only a year after leaving University. By my estimation, these cocky young bucks are far more interested in filling hopeful debutantes' dance cards and sneaking out to Regent Street for late nights than in the business of running the country.

Crispin, why am I bored with these festivities already? Aunt Eugenia seems to think I am naturally thrilled to the brim, and I don't want to disabuse her of this notion. She has gone to great lengths to introduce me to all the right people and to throw me in the path of some of the most eligible men in London. Even my father, who in the past has declared loudly that he has no interest in balls other than as a place for shoring up business with his cronies, seems glad to partake in the pomp and circumstance of it all. Yet here I am dreading the Winstons' ball for which I must leave post-haste. I'd really rather sit here and go

*on and on to you, honestly. Oh well, such as it is. I await your next letter. How
I prefer hearing of your adventures than living my own.*

> *Yours always,*
> *Cassandra*

After dispatching the letter to Jane, who planned on going to Fleet Street
the following morning as was her custom at the beginning of each month,
Cassandra had rushed to finish getting ready for the Winston's. Less than half
an hour later, her father led her quickly up the stairs into the grand drawing
room of Lord and Lady Winston's home at 29 Hyde Park Lane. It was an
immense and majestic room. Fires glowed from four hearths, and the
chandeliers were so highly polished they shone almost as brightly as the fires.
Enormous vases of flowers turned the interior of the house into a veritable
garden. Each room had its own bounty of delicacies: silver urns of tea, golden
bowls of crystallized fruit, and towers of petit fours—not that anyone would
eat a morsel, at least none of the ladies. The bones of their tight corsets left
room for nothing more than breath and little sips of sherry or champagne.

For the past three weeks Cassandra had harbored a secret hope that she
did not want her father or her aunt, or even Miss Fairfax, to know that she
desperately wanted to see Lord Bedford. But eight balls into the season, she
had seen neither hide nor hair of him. Cassandra caught sight of him once
last year across a vast court ballroom, but the room buzzed with bodies, and
they had never managed to be in the same place at the same time. If he had
spotted her, he had not sought her out, and debutantes did not do the
seeking, at least not overtly. Bedford had been in the London scene for nearly
five years. Perhaps he was engaged, but she dared not ask for fear of being
teased for wasting time on a childhood fancy.

"Oh Cassie, I'm so glad you've arrived," a cheerful voice exclaimed. "I've
been desperate without you. Mama is home with a headache, and Archie's
left for India, so I've come with my cousin, Thomas. He was directed to look
after me, but of course, all he wants to do is find his lads and talk about
cricket. I have to say, I don't give two hoots whether Bedford got a wicket
or not."

Her heart skipped a beat at the sound of Bedford's name. Luckily, May didn't seem to notice. By now the two young women were inseparable. May never ceased to impress Cassandra with her easy manner and quick wit. Her observations of people were as keen as any seasoned socialite, but she lacked their hardened edges. She turned everyone into a friend, giving out silly nicknames that disarmed people and set them at ease. May and Cassandra shared a mutual contempt for the rigidity of society.

Yet, within minutes of entering the ballroom, the two were in the center of a gaggle of debutantes, who admired their hair and gowns. "Miss Drayton that is the most gorgeous gown, wherever did you get it? No, let me guess—Redfern's."

"Yes, Miss Devon."

"Well, it is just beautiful. You have the most impeccable taste."

"And the most generous father. If he had any other children to spoil, I am sure he would never let me purchase this gown."

While Miss Devon and others showered Cassandra with compliments, Miss Anne Lancaster made a move for May.

"Now, Lady Douglas, where is your dear brother?"

"Miss Lancaster, he's not dear, not a bit, don't let him fool you. I swear he's the devil himself."

"Oh, I can't believe it. I won't. Did you watch him in the cricket last summer at Lords? He bowls brilliantly. The Gentleman never would have won without him."

"I successfully avoid nearly all of his matches, but alas not that one. Yes, I was there," May said with an especially jaded sounding sigh. Then leaning conspiratorially toward Cassandra, she snickered, "I can't get enough of cricket, can I?"

"Is that Lord Bedford?" rang out one of the company, followed by a chorus of, "Where?" "Do you see him?" "Could it be?"

All eyes leaped toward the drawing room door. It was indeed Lord Bedford, the one-day Duke of Westmoor. He was still handsome and broad-shouldered and thin in the way of athletic youths who have left childhood gangliness behind, but not yet filled out into middle-age. His square jaw was framed by rather long golden curls that peeked insolently out from behind his ears, and he had a wide, pouty mouth that gave the impression of having just done something mischievous and not giving a damn. A smile touched Cassandra's lips, her breath quickening as she realized her childhood crush had not faded a bit.

He was clearly aware of the gaggling girls, who chattered away, glancing indiscreetly in his direction. Excited as she was to see him, Cassandra did not want to appear overly enthusiastic. Embarrassed to be part of such a silly coterie of debutantes, she tried to plot a getaway for May and herself.

Then, Cassandra felt Bedford's eyes on her. The high-pitched whir of female voices faded as she watched him approach the group. He moved with the easy grace and inner assurance of one who knows he has nothing to lose. The color rose in her cheeks as he looked at her with obvious approval. The thirteen-year-old girl in Cassandra wanted to avert his intense gaze and stare timidly at the polished floors but she met his eyes with convincing confidence.

"Well at long last we meet each other, Miss Drayton! I have waited too many Seasons for this moment. But now, here you stand before me the picture of elegance. And quite grown up I see." He stepped back, grinning. Cassandra hoped he didn't notice her flushed cheeks. Bedford clasped her gloved hand, bringing it to his lips. She could feel his breath through the lambskin. His eyes were trained on hers, and they stood that way for many seconds. "May I have this waltz?"

Cassandra's dance card was not yet full, so she had no excuse to check his boldness. He led her to the dance floor and walked a wide arc around her before bowing deeply in the old fashion style. Determined not to let him unnerve her, Cassandra returned a Regency curtsy.

They stood without speaking in a flirtatious standoff, waiting for the music to begin. As soon as it did, he moved with jaunty grace, leading her around the floor, smiling teasingly each time he caught Cassandra's eye.

"I wanted to dance with you because I hear you have become quite saucy." Lord Bedford raised his eyebrows.

"From whom?"

"Oh, I don't know. Archie, I suppose."

"Impossible. His sister and I are very good friends. I am always on my best behavior when he's around."

"Really?" he replied incredulously. They made two or three turns in amiable silence. "Well, actually, I made that up to see your reaction."

"You like to test people, then?"

"And you?" He answered the question with one of his own.

"Me? Never." Cassandra blinked a few too many times to be believed, and Bedford threw back his head and laughed.

"You've changed a great deal since you were a little girl. Being out in society agrees with you."

"Once upon a time, you paid me no attention."

"Oh, it has been a few years now that I have had my eye on you . . ."

Cassandra could scarcely believe him and struggled to contain her excitement.

The music began to slow, but she felt no desire to stop dancing. His palm was solid and warm on the small of her back, as they sashayed between the column of gentleman and ladies on either side of them. From across the room Bedford smiled at Cassandra, one corner of his mouth a little higher than the other, an idiosyncratic feature that only made him more attractive.

The music stopped, and May rushed toward Cassandra, asking what she thought of Lord Bedford, who likewise was encircled by his own group of friends the moment the dance ended.

"Archie says he's a bit of a cad," she cautioned. "Careless with money and the reputations of others. And from Archie, that is saying something."

"I wouldn't doubt it," Cassandra confirmed. "But he is more fun than some of the bores here. His father and mine are old school chums. I've known him since I was young."

"It's true that he's from a very old family, but as I'm sure you know the Bedford fortune is dwindling fast. At least that is what I've heard, so be cautious Cassie. You smiled a bit too much."

Cassandra felt her cheeks flush. May was right of course. It was widely known that the dashing Duke of Westmoor's pockets were very light. Generations of his predecessor's reckless gambling and wanton spending had resulted in the near depletion of the once-grand Bedford fortune. The Duke, or his son, needed an heiress—and fast. Still, the warm crush of girlish infatuation was starting to creep through Cassandra's blood. She wanted to stop it, control it, but after a few more dances with the puffy young sons of her Aunt Eugenia's friends, Lord Bedford appeared at her side again.

"May I have a second dance?"

"I should refuse."

"Yes, probably."

"But I've been warned about you, so I am safe."

Laughing, he led her to the center of the room.

"Shall we get some refreshment?"

"Yes, please." Cassandra could feel the unladylike perspiration at the base of her neck and along her hairline. She withdrew the fan from her reticule and snapped it to attention, casting a sideways glance at Bedford, hoping he wouldn't notice her appearance. He, too, was ruddy and his hair a bit unkempt. Bedford offered his arm, but when they got to the door, he took a sharp turn to the left rather than to the right to the stairs that lead to the drawing room.

"Lord Bedford, we're going in the wrong direction."

"I know." He made no excuses. "There is something I want to show you."

It seemed innocent enough and intriguing. Though Cassandra knew she should be cautious, and that Aunt Eugenia would not approve, she followed where he led. Shortly, they found themselves in a quiet, private library.

"This is rather intimate," Cassandra said. Shocked at her own boldness, she immediately wanted to take back the words and made a move for the door, suggesting that they should return to the party.

"I think not, Miss Drayton." His tone was firm, but he held his hand out gently in an almost childlike gesture, irresistible and sweet. "I want to show you something." He drew back heavy organza curtains, revealing a balcony that looked out over the darkness of the street and the park beyond.

He seemed to know the Winstons' house quite well, and, when she asked how it was so, he told her that he'd spent many days at Hyde Park Lane with the youngest Winston, Lord Graham Winston.

"We used to spend hours playing hide-and-seek in this very room. And then, we'd perch on this balcony, concocting fantastical battles in which we had claimed the hilltop and the pedestrians below were bloody opponents. We ravished them all with our swords and bayonets." He made a definitive swooping gesture with a make-believe long sword.

"That's absolutely charming, Lord Bedford. I wish I could have played such games. But girls are not given license to entertain themselves with battles. In any case, I had too few childhood playmates to engage in such elaborate fancies." Distractedly, Cassandra drew her fingers across the length of the dark mahogany table that stood next to the balcony doors. She had slowly moved away from him but, just as slowly, he closed the distance between them.

"You? No friends? I don't believe it." He reached the other end of the table.

"You should know, I had a very sheltered youth. And, when we were together you didn't give me the time of day."

"Well, it's never too late. I could teach you to play battle now." He made a playful lunge that brought him face to face with Cassandra.

"Lord Bedford, you're ridiculous."

"I don't think I am ridiculous. I would like to teach you,"—he paused for a moment becoming exaggeratedly serious—"a lot of things." Now he was barely a foot in front of her. Goosebumps rose on the back of Cassandra's neck.

Bedford looked her steadily in the eye for what seemed like a long time and then put his arms around Cassandra's waist and deftly drew her in for a long, forceful kiss. His lips parted, compelling hers to do the same and his tongue, sensuously and slowly, circled her mouth. It was terrifying. And thrilling.

Cassandra pulled away in heated horror. "Lord Bedford!" Fuming, she couldn't decide if she was madder at him or herself. She could only imagine what Aunt Eugenia or, God forbid, her father would say if they heard about this compromising situation. This was the sort of episode that could lead to her complete ruin if they were discovered. Even a large marriage portion could not remedy the salacious rumors that might arise about her "loose morals," deterring other possible suitors for her hand. Cassandra knew this but she had still followed him there. She heard the voice in the back of her mind telling her not to, but had been delighted with his silly story, and she pushed back on his lips, half-enjoying their pressure and, worse yet, the warmth of his tongue.

"Why don't you call me Henry?" he asked, totally unruffled.

"Goodbye, Henry." Cassandra turned on her heel and rushed from the room, her cheeks on fire. Silently cursing him and herself, she was sure she heard him chuckling calmly, having a good laugh at her expense.

Feeling violated and humiliated by this overly assured young duke and betrayed by her willingness to follow him, Cassandra rushed down the stairs and in doing so, ran straight into Miss Fairfax.

"Cassandra, I am afraid we have to gather our cloaks." Miss Fairfax said calmly.

"Leaving?" Lord Bedford appeared behind her. He must have been fast on her heels. "But the night is young. Miss Fairfax, a delight to see you." He bowed with the manners and smooth swagger of a fashionable man about town.

"I am afraid we must be going; Cassandra's aunt is not feeling well."

"That's too bad." He picked up Cassandra's gloved hand and kissed the air above it. "We'll see each other again soon. I am sure."

Cassandra sat in the window seat in her bedroom staring out over the shared garden of Grosvenor Square and chewing the tip of her thumbnail. It was a terrible habit she'd had since childhood. Aunt Eugenia would often chide her for it—"Ladies do not bite their nails, Cassandra"—so it gave her a devious double pleasure knowing that in the seclusion of her own room she could do as she pleased and defy her aunt. Now, even after a season and a half of her supposed maturity, Cassandra fell back on her clandestine habit, especially when she was lost in thought, which she was.

Cassandra was anticipating a walk with Lord Bedford in Hyde Park. To her surprise, the day after the Winstons' ball, he had stopped by 37 Grosvenor Square and left his calling card with Braxton, the Draytons' butler. Hours later a brief note was delivered.

> *Dear Miss Drayton,*
>
> *Please forgive my appalling behavior. Of course, it's an insufficient excuse to say I was living out a childhood fantasy, but there you have it. I can be a gentleman, I assure you.*
>
> *I would be honoured if you would join me for an afternoon stroll in Hyde Park tomorrow. You will of course be obliged to bring a chaperone, so I will be on my best behaviour. I hope that you will be satisfied by the seasonal splendor of the Park, and my mundane topics of conversation. Meet me at the fountain circle some ways west of the Park gate.*
>
> *Yrs.*
>
> *Bedford*

The notion that she had somehow factored into his romantic "childhood fantasies" tickled Cassandra's ego more than it should have. She could feel the blood rush to her cheeks as she read the words again. Cassie had always assumed that her crush was one-sided. To discover that he had been watching her out of the corner of his eye was like finding a gold coin in the pocket of a dress she had not worn for quite some time—an unexpected treasure.

Cassandra wrote back in the affirmative: *Hyde Park. Twelve noon. It just so happens I am free tomorrow afternoon.* Aunt Eugenia was thrilled. Miss Fairfax much less so.

C assandra insisted they leave the carriage at the Park Gate and walk west toward the appointed spot.

"I still think it would have been more appropriate to have this first meeting at Grosvenor Street, not a turn about Hyde Park." Miss Fairfax fussed, as she smoothed a wrinkled pleat out of Cassandra's gown. It was pale blue organza with delicate lace ribbons. Cassandra could see that her companion was uncomfortable, even slightly nervous about the propriety of the situation, about her appearance, and about Cassandra's as well. It should be Cassandra who was nervous. She was going to be "taking a turn" about Hyde Park with *Lord Bedford*. But strangely, she was not.

An outing with an eligible Duke, even one known for his family's dwindling fortune, would send Cassandra's friends as well as this season's crop of fresh debutantes gossiping. Yet, May's warning turned in her mind as she considered Lord Bedford. He had a dangerous edge to be sure, but despite his behavior at the ball, Cassandra had been reassured by his invitation, which seemed to be inspired by more genuine attraction than improper motives.

For all her bluster about adventure and her general disdain for the confines of society, May had a mostly traditional, if romantic, notion of marriage. Cassandra imagined May secretly hoped that someone largely suitable would sweep her off her feet. Having witnessed her parents—happily married for thirty-five years before the Earl's passing—she had a rather high point of comparison. While the idea of a romance for the ages was certainly appealing, Cassandra's view of the estate was probably closer to Bedford's than May's. She wanted to find a suitable partner in life. And he was a good deal more than suitable.

"Well, whatever my perspective is on this rendezvous, it couldn't be a more picturesque day." Miss Fairfax lowered herself gracefully to one of the benches that surrounded the picturesque pond and shaded her eyes as she looked across it. She was right. It was a perfect spring day with only a few stray wispy clouds dotting the glorious sky above them. The rains brought a lushness to the manicured greenery of the park, and the pond reflected both the sun and the sky, shimmering white and blue, like crystals. It seemed all of London society had come to the Park, and the ladies' colorful gowns were in bright contrast to their green surroundings.

"How about a dip in the pond, Miss Drayton? It's rather warm for April."

Bedford's gravelly voice carried as he walked toward them. His gray coat and black trousers were the picture of fashion, and the sun made his golden curls something of a halo around his handsome face.

"Lord Bedford, I don't think I'm dressed for sea bathing." Cassie could imagine her governess flushing. Though Cassandra loved her dearly, she hoped Miss Fairfax wouldn't play the part of the elderly duenna today. She quickly changed the subject.

"You are acquainted with my dear friend Miss Emma Fairfax?" Cassandra gestured to her companion who had risen and curtsied to the Duke. He bowed with a flourish.

"Of course. Miss Fairfax, I'm delighted you could join us today. Should we walk toward Kensington Gardens?" He offered his arm to Cassandra, and Miss Fairfax fell behind them at a discreet distance.

"I'm afraid Miss Fairfax was a bit unsettled to be chaperoning today," Cassandra said in a hushed voice.

"Why's that? Does she find me unsuitable?" He smiled slightly, clearly pleased at the notion, but continued to look straight ahead as he walked with deliberate, confident strides. Cassandra was close enough to smell his fragrance, a pleasant musk.

"Not at all. I think she is just out of sorts, chaperoning the son of a Duke."

He finally turned his gaze to Cassandra. "So, she's in awe of me, eh?" Bedford's chest puffed up as he leaned in close.

Cassandra laughed. The smug look on his face was priceless. "I can see you have a healthy ego, Lord Bedford."

"Well, I need something to recommend me, other than my title." His brown eyes twinkled, and Cassandra smiled both outwardly and inwardly. His cheerful banter was such a welcome change from the colorless gentleman she had met in her last season.

"For most women, I imagine that your title is enough." This time, she looked straight ahead and warmed with the feel of his gaze on her.

"I can tell already Miss Drayton that you are not most women."

Cassandra bit the inside of her cheeks to contain her smile. A few more strides down the path and she had all but forgot Miss Fairfax's presence. "You are incorrigible, Lord Bedford. But you know that don't you? Don't you ever have a serious conversation?" Cassandra had stopped to face him and though her words were severe her tone was not.

"As a general rule, I avoid serious topics, Miss Drayton. There will be time for them, plenty of time for them soon enough." The corners of his lips turned down for a fraction of a second, and his eyes, typically sparkly and gay, became somber. It was strange to see his natural buoyancy, like a tethered hot air balloon, reach the end of its ropes. "My father is not in good health, you see." He looked to his feet, which for a few strides he kicked out in an exaggerated march.

"Oh, Lord Bedford. I am sorry to hear that. Is it very bad?" Cassandra raised her gloved hand to rest on his arm, feeling him tense in surprise and then relax. If Miss Fairfax had seen the gesture, Cassandra knew she would object.

"Yes, I'm afraid so. Has your father not mentioned it?"

"No." She withdrew her hand and cringed to admit it. Was it an oversight? Had her father meant to protect Cassandra from upsetting news? Or, as she suspected was more likely, was he so consumed with his latest American investment that he had let his old friendships fade into the background, assuming he could pick up where he had left off at any time?

"As the eldest and only son," Bedford continued, "I'll have to take on the burdens of our household estates. Rather a daunting prospect. Ah, but enough about that." His eyebrows raised roguishly, and his mood ballooned again.

"What did you think of Mrs. G's dress?" He was referring to the newly widowed Mrs. Gresham who wore the latest from Paris rather too soon. The Parisian necklines plunged dangerously low for English tastes. "Rather much, eh. Though, I suppose it depends on the model."

"I don't know what you mean."

"For example,"—he lowered his voice and raised his left eyebrow—"if you wore that gown, I'm quite sure I would appreciate it." Cassandra slapped her reticule upon his forearm.

Bedford and Cassandra spent another hour touring the park, speaking about their families, her impressions of London as a relative newcomer, and Bedford's plans for a European tour.

When they returned to Grosvenor Square, her father asked, "Well how did it go with Bedford?" He couldn't hide his enthusiasm, for the premature possibility of a match with a soon-to-be duke.

"About what you'd expect, I guess."

Chapter 14

May 1871

Cassandra sighed as she entered her room and tossed her reticule on the bed. She was winded from the short climb up the stairs. After three long nights—two balls and a soiree—she was exhausted, and tonight her father was hosting a dinner. She wanted to rest before getting ready for another evening on show, but just as she sank down on her bed, she spotted the envelope on her vanity, perched on the edge, the address obscured. Jane always left Crispin's letters that way, in case anyone should come into the room. Cassandra snatched it up, eager to hear Crispin's news.

> *Dear Cassandra,*
>
> *I hope that this letter has braved the long journey to London to find you well. As always, I was delighted to read your last letter. It has been so many years since I lived in London—and my experience there shared little with yours of course— but your letters transport me to an entirely different world from this one.*
>
> *You cannot possibly imagine what has transpired since my last letter—I'll impart it now—if only to warn you away from the hazards of the cotton trade! As I've written previously, I'm often engaged in ensuring that the harvests are transported without incident from the fields in Tamluk to Calcutta and from there to Liverpool by boat.*
>
> *But I've learned that nothing in India goes quite to plan. Sadly, the train derailed but a few miles from the Tamluk station, and I had to revert to a more rudimentary method of transport—large carriages driven by horse through the hot*

plains—and decided to lead the transport to Calcutta myself on horseback. You would have laughed a great deal at my expense, Cassandra. There I was on a majestic white horse under the terrifyingly strong sun at the head of a great caravan. I'm sure you have seen such a scene depicted in your novels, but hopefully, the heroes of those vivid stories do not meet the ending that I did.

The rains began almost immediately after we left Tamluk. My clothes were drenched through and caked with mud. Though this was no great trauma, what followed was—we were just a few miles from Calcutta when not one, but two carriages slipped their wheels and literally toppled over. Nearly as large as boats, they listed to and fro in a sea of mud until they finally gave up their fight and creaked over with a thunderous crash. The cotton threatened to spill out and be taken by the elements, but the men and I worked feverishly to save every last bit.

It was nearly 8 o'clock in the evening when I arrived at Mr. Middleton's home to inform him of our near disaster. Disheveled as I was and exhausted beyond belief, I hoped for a bath, some dry clothes, and a strong whiskey. So, imagine my surprise and their shock when I knocked at the door to find it was, in fact, the night of a soiree planned to celebrate Miss Middleton's twentieth birthday. I had completely forgotten and was greeted by Mr. Middleton, Miss Middleton, and many of my new acquaintances and friends—including Archie Douglas, of whom I have written previously—who were shocked at my bedraggled state. Suffice it to say, I was the butt of many jokes that evening.

Miss Middleton was so overwhelmed by my appearance, she asked if they should send for the physician, but Archie took one look at me and doubled over in laughter. Then, he foisted a glass of champagne in my hand and dragged me to the party. We stayed up until the wee hours laughing about my misfortunes— Archie, Miss Middleton, and I.

The Middletons—that is Rosalind and her father—have been so incredibly welcoming—as has been their circle of friends. I've felt quite at home here in my new surroundings. Though, occasionally, I still miss the hubbub of the barracks and my old pals Cassidy and Johnston.

Cassandra giggled at the prospect of Crispin's harrowing cotton journey. She always enjoyed his letters—in addition to conveying her to a world that she would likely never see, they brought Crispin to life as vividly as if he were sitting right there beside her in her room. But as Cassandra laid back and reread the last paragraph, she wondered, *who is this Miss Middleton? What is she like?* In the corner of her mind, a sprout of jealousy took root.

The gong sounded. Cassandra looked about the room at present company, her father holding court with Misters Saunders and Forsythe, and Miss Fairfax engaged in a genial conversation with Mrs. Saunders. Miss Fairfax's rich auburn hair glowed in the firelight. Her nerves had been frayed lately, and it was no wonder with the icy looks she continually received from Aunt Eugenia. A second season in London, and Lord Drayton and Miss Fairfax could no longer hide in plain sight as they had done in the past. Cassandra could see the toll it took on her.

The overwhelming smell of roast wafted into the drawing room. Miss Fairfax's face turned slightly green as she took in the aroma. Cook had been ordered to make her famed crown roast of lamb, even though Lord Drayton knew how much Miss Fairfax detested it. It was Mr. Forsythe's favorite. That unctuous man was preening over his latest thoroughbred purchase.

"I tell you, Drayton, I have an eye for horseflesh," he practically bellowed, while stealing glances at Cassandra, who knew she needed to rejoin the conversation.

"Dinner is served," Braxton's deep voice bellowed. Offering Cassandra his arm, her father led them into the dining room. Saunders followed near behind, and, unfortunately, Miss Fairfax was forced to walk with Forsythe, who smiled smarmily at her.

As the evening chugged along, Cassandra tried to force herself to engage in polite conversation, while Forsythe gobbled each dish greedily. When the roast arrived, he beamed and, greasy with delight, grabbed four ribs of lamb from the silver tray the footman carried and began chomping. *With his mouth otherwise engaged, at least his conversation stopped*, Cassandra thought to herself. A momentary reprieve, thank heavens, but incredibly, he had managed to consume all four ribs in the space of a few seconds. He wiped his lips indelicately and called across the table, "So Drayton, tell us about this new venture of yours in America. You haven't steered me wrong yet my friend. I'm anxious to hear about all the money to come."

"Now that you mention it, I do want to talk to you gentleman about a new investment." He cleared his throat and went on pridefully about the "excellent Union War bonds" he put his friends into years prior. He stirred the waters of ambition, projecting confidence in investments and drawing his companions in with the prospects of larger and larger fortunes.

"Of course," Saunders interrupted. "That interest in gold allowed my dear wife to renovate our townhouse."

"My dear, please." Mrs. Saunders reddened.

"Anyway, the very same company that helped us invest in the bonds— Jay Cooke & Company, you remember—now has an office here in London, and my old friend Fulton brought me over there the other day. Seems that Cooke and his group are allowing for an exchange of those Union bonds to an even higher interest bond. I think it's a great deal."

"What's *this* bond for?" Forsythe clearly liked the idea of more gold.

"It's to fund a new railroad across America. Similar to the one they just completed but further north. It's called the Northern Pacific, and it goes all the way to the northwest corner of the continent. It's a great venture. The news of this offering is spreading like wildfire. We must get in sooner than later, I'm sure of it. I'm going to go over to America this winter to see it for myself."

This was news to Cassandra. A trip to America and her father hadn't mentioned it?

"America! Papa, how exciting, when are we going?!"

"My dear girl, I'll be going there by myself. Remember you have to plan for the next season. You don't want to miss all the fun in London with your friends."

"Papa, I'm sure you couldn't possibly describe the railroad to Mr. Forsythe as well as I could. Isn't that right Mr. Forsythe?"

Forsythe grinned and bobbed his head at Cassandra as he sucked at the remaining bits of meat clinging to the lamb ribs piled on his plate.

Aunt Eugenia clucked in disapproval. Her position on Cassandra accompanying her father to America was obvious. Mrs. Saunders' too.

"But Miss Drayton," said Mrs. Saunders. "Wouldn't you rather spend your time touring the London social circuit, looking for love and seeing your friends, than shivering at some railroad site amid the American wilderness?"

Cassandra's encounters with Lord Bedford had changed the tenor of her socializing. They had been spotted in the Park and with that came chatter and a general understanding amongst society that he'd taken an interest in her. Aunt Eugenia had not been able to hide her enthusiasm and, less than twenty-four hours after Lord Bedford and Cassandra's first rendezvous, began to discuss the "tactics" necessary to ensure their next *chance* encounter. Lord Drayton laughed outwardly at his sister's "overly fastidious stratagems" as he called them, but inwardly he—and now it appeared several of his friends—felt he was judicious.

Cassandra shrugged them off. In the tug of war between solidifying her connection with Bedford or an American adventure, America won.

"I think I've had my fill of parties for now." She declared to the table. "I'd like to see the New World. Besides, my closest friends will all still be in London when I return. They are in no rush to marry." She smiled and leaned forward, hoping to cover up the half-truth of her statement with enthusiasm for her father's travels. "Papa, it would be a wonderful adventure."

He shook his head in a mixture of mild amusement and uncertain refusal, but Cassandra's mind was made up.

She couldn't contain her excitement as she raced up the stairs two at a time. She was sure she could convince her father to take her with him. Cassandra couldn't wait to tell May, who would be green with envy. To have an adventure in a faraway land was a dream come true for both of them.

"Cassandra, do stop for a second please dear." Though the evening had ended, Aunt Eugenia was determined to catch Cassandra privately before they all turned in for the night.

"Yes, Aunt?"

"All this talk of a trip . . . I just wanted to be sure we discussed this more fully."

"What's to discuss? Papa has basically agreed." Cassandra's tone was bordering on the edge of rude.

"My dear, I know you crave adventure. And what young girl wouldn't? To be honest, your dear papa has sheltered you a bit too much." Her expression was nearly sympathetic, and Cassandra was pleased that her aunt had noticed her confinement over the years. "I don't blame you, truly I don't. In my day, before I met dear Lord Gray, I had a few adventures myself." She tittered, and Cassandra found herself struggling to imagine her aunt in intrepid circumstances.

"But dearest, this is your second season. I know everything looks so easy to you at this stage. You've caught Lord Bedford's eye, which is wonderful, really, but this is not an easy process. What if Lord Bedford is not interested when you return? He might not be. Even worse, he might be attached to someone else. You are as charming as anyone my love, but someone else might catch his eye."

Cassandra was not going to be deterred. "Dear Aunt, we'll be back before you know it, and it's only one season, not even the whole season. Besides, Lord Bedford is going for a European tour himself, so I doubt I'll come home to find him otherwise engaged. It might make us more . . . oh, I don't know, connected." *Besides*, she thought to herself—the echo of May's remarks in her head—*he will still need the Drayton fortune.* She was not so naïve as to be unaware that he was attracted to more than her golden ringlets and sparkling humor.

"Cassandra you are still so young and idealistic where men and marriage are concerned. I don't blame you for it but take it from someone who has lived a bit. The first season or two always seems inconsequential to pretty young ladies; it seems you have all the time in the world before you, but you don't realize how hard it can become as time marches on. Too often I have seen young girls left waiting with apprehension for the right match. And sometimes it never comes. You don't know it now, but the world is awfully cruel to women who have no partner. It's not just for you, you know; it's for your family as well."

"Aunt Eugenia, please don't be so melodramatic. It's just a few months, several maybe. Not a lifetime." Cassandra tried her best to soothe her aunt's worries, but the older woman sighed the placation away, dismissively shaking her head.

"I just don't think a lengthy voyage before you've established yourself is wise." Having said her piece, she smiled confidently, fully expecting her niece to back down.

"Aunt, I appreciate all you have done for me; the trips to the dressmakers, my presentation, introducing me to dear May. I know this is important to you and I do take that very seriously. But I will be miserable if Father goes without me. Plus, I'll write to my friends and hear all the news and be excited and ready to go next year. I promise." Cassandra clasped her aunt's hands and planted a warm kiss on her soft, jowled cheek.

Seeing that cajoling was having no effect, Aunt Eugenia changed course. "If you won't see reason, I'll have to speak to your Papa about this. It is too important. And just too foolish for you to leave London at this point."

Cassandra stiffened, resolved. "I'm afraid you won't be able to convince Papa otherwise. He prefers to have me around and would miss me too much. And my mind's made up. I really will insist." She matched her best steely gaze with a tight smile. Aunt Eugenia inhaled deeply in frustration but did not press her further. Cassandra could almost see the gears of Aunt Eugenia's brain turn, already scripting her petition to her brother. She quickly said her good-nights and exited for her room.

Cassandra smiled to herself as she passed Miss Fairfax's room. She debated asking for her help in extracting a promise from her father to let her accompany him on the trip to America. At the end of the day, he valued Miss Fairfax's advice above anyone's when it came to raising his daughter. She could tell him that seeing the world would do Cassandra good—it would be edifying and enriching.

As she raised her hand to knock on the door, Cassandra heard the sound of her father's voice. She stopped to listen. At Drayton Manor, Miss Fairfax's room was in another wing. But here, in the townhouse on Grosvenor Square, it was close to her own. The door was cracked slightly.

"James, I received a letter this morning."

"You look so serious. What's this about? A letter from whom?"

"From my relations in Aberdeen. I've mentioned them to you." They moved further away from the door, and Cassandra strained to hear. She didn't know that Miss Fairfax had relations in Scotland.

"I suppose so. Well-to-do as I recall."

"Yes, they have done quite well in fact. He is in shipping I believe. At any rate, understanding that Cassandra is grown, they've offered me a position as governess to their daughters, Fiona and Clarissa. They've proposed a very fine salary and have arranged a suite of rooms that are quite spacious for my accommodation.'

"You seem to know all the particulars then." His tone was cold.

"The letter was very specific."

"And I suppose you have been in correspondence with them for some time?"

Miss Fairfax was silent, and the tension was palpable. The thought of Miss Fairfax leaving sent a shock through her spine. Cassandra couldn't remember a time when Fairfax hadn't been in her life, a constant warm and loving presence. She fought the urge to rush into the room and tell her not to go.

"We've kept in touch over the years, and they have always offered their support. But I never accepted."

"So, are you resolved? Is that it? Is this how it is to be? You announce this to me without any question or discussion? You talk to me about salary and accommodations? What nonsense is this? You are not leaving!" Cassandra heard a shuffle in the room. One of them was coming toward the door. She stepped back a few feet, torn between rushing away to avoid discovery and staying to hear the rest of their conversation.

"James, you must have known this would happen eventually. Cassandra is grown. She is a lady now. I have done all I can do for her education. Very soon she will find a husband of her own. This situation cannot continue as it has."

"That's nonsense. Of course, Cassandra needs you, you are her companion. She needs that and she needs to learn the ways of society from you."

"She has your sister for that, and God knows she has already learned the ways of society. She was a perfect hostess tonight. My work is done; it is time for me to move on." The two of them were making this about Cassandra, but she knew she was a decoy. This was about their relationship.

"No!" Lord Drayton bellowed so loudly, Cassandra jumped and looked about, concerned the servants would come. "You are not leaving and that is it. That is final. I am not releasing you from your position."

"I do not need you to release me from my position," Miss Fairfax's anger rose with each word. "I am not some sort of indentured servant. I have the means to go to Scotland and no need for your good reference. I shall do as I please since I have no reason to stay."

Cassandra gasped sharply, then clasped her hand over her mouth to muffle the sound. She'd never heard Miss Fairfax speak to her father so forcefully. Though she winced at the idea of Fairfax leaving, she also felt a certain pride at her determination.

"No reason to stay?" he exclaimed. She had unwittingly struck a blow. "What the hell do you want from me? I don't understand this. I have done everything to ensure your comfort and happiness. I have included you in all aspects of my life. We have a shared affection. What more can I give or say to you to make you stay?"

Cassandra cringed at her father's lack of romantic sensibility. How little he understood Miss Fairfax. Her heart was racing, and she knew she shouldn't stay to hear more, but instead leaned closer to the door. Cassandra had to know the outcome of their quarrel, one way or the other.

Lord Drayton spoke again, more softly this time. "Emma, please don't leave me. I need you." He sounded vulnerable, the fury drained from his tone. "Please stay. Please. Give me more time. Once Cassandra is wed, things will be different. We'll be free to do as we choose. I will be free to do as I choose, and I choose you." There was a long pause and, though she could not see them, Cassandra expected her father's plea continued in more silent forms.

After several minutes, Cassandra heard a deep sigh from Miss Fairfax. She still had said nothing.

"Besides, we'll all go to America, together. Without Eugenia. I promise things will be different."

Finally, in a breathy, wistful voice Miss Fairfax said, "Fine. I'll stay. For now, until we are home from America."

CHAPTER 15

January 1872

Crispin smiled at the familiar, feminine script in the letter's address. Cassie's p's and s's had a distinctive and elegant swirl to them. He had collected his correspondence from his study and was now lounging in the coolest place in his eight-room flat—the parlor. It faced full West and did not take any early morning sunlight. There were a few other letters, but he tossed them aside as he flopped down unceremoniously on the sofa. He was half-dressed in preparation for his outing with Archie that day and could think of nothing better to do than read one of Cassandra's colorful letters. They always made him smile as he imagined her life in London.

Dearest Crispin,

She began as she always did. It never ceased to delight Crispin that the vast difference in their stations had been bridged first by a youthful friendship and now, by an unlikely correspondence from many thousands of miles away. "Dearest" he read again.

I know my notes are usually lengthy and probably bore you to death with the latest ridiculous gossip from London. You flatter me to care and be polite when I tell you about all these goings-on! But this one finally has some exciting news! What a relief my letter won't sound like the Society Column in the Post. I've hesitated to write even a word about this until it was fully confirmed because it's taken a great deal of convincing on my part (a great, great deal!) I hope you will be excited to hear that I'm finally getting the adventure I've always wanted. I won't keep the suspense for much longer—Father and I are going to America! And Miss Fairfax is coming too.

I cannot describe how excited I am to take this voyage, which will be (if you can believe it) my first sea voyage. My dear Papa has kept me cooped up for too long, but now I'll be seeing America replete with all her teeming splendor. We are planning—though our itinerary is not entirely etched in stone—to land in New York in January, and after staying there and taking in the sights while Papa has meetings for his business, we will journey to Boston, Chicago, and finally to Thompson's Junction, Minnesota. Though the last location is not much of a destination per se, it's where the Northern Pacific Railway is beginning construction and where Papa will have some more of his meetings and survey the substance of his investments.

I'm so thrilled! It will be so exciting to witness a different culture and people and to see new things . . . though I'm sure it won't compare to the exotic climes of India. I imagine some will be strange and some not very much so, but either way, it will be different. Aunt Eugenia is apoplectic of course. She thinks my prospects for a match will dim after a few exotic months abroad, but of course, I'm not deterred by that at all. Oh Crispin, can you believe my good fortune? I hate to dash but there is much to do before our journey. Your dear aunt is a bit apprehensive about all the particulars, but rest assured, I'm taking care of it. I'm not sure how often I'll be able to write from America but expect my next letter to be filled with tales of the Wild West.

Yours as always,
Cassie

"I still can't understand why you insist upon coming to the market yourself. You have a man for that now, Crispin." Archie gestured to Anuk, a small and wiry man, who moved as quickly and efficiently as the wind. He held a large basket that was nearly filled with fruits, meats, and fish, the wares of Dalhousie Square.

Since his early days in India, Crispin had come into the city to wander the markets, losing himself in the kaleidoscope of sights and sounds as men and women hawked their goods under the warm January sun. The rich smell of spices seeped out of tandoor ovens. Crispin reached for a plump mango, at its peak of ripeness, its tangy smell setting his mouth to water.

"We look perfectly absurd in our suits. We must be the only Englishmen here. Plus, all these smells. I'm famished. Can we please go to the club now?" Archie ran his hands through his thick auburn hair in frustration. His tan suit coat, normally an image of starched perfection had wilted in the heat and sun.

"Stop going on like a little girl! I'm finished now." Crispin plopped the mango down into the basket.

"Anuk, please take these home and tell Cook that I will be dining out this evening." The man nodded and briskly walked away seemingly unburdened by the large basket.

"At last! We can be at our leisure. This hard work has been exhausting," Archie sighed in exasperation. Crispin raised an eyebrow, but Archie, usually a master of irony, was slow on the uptake today.

"You do look fatigued my friend. Did you sleep in that jacket? How can you possibly show up at The Bengal Club dressed like that?" Crispin laughed at the way Archie attempted to beat the wrinkles out.

"Alright, I admit it, I was rather hard at it last night. Do I look absurd?"

"Only a little." They walked the rest of the short distance to the club in silence. Its limestone façade was awash in the late afternoon sun. The door of the club opened, and a cool breeze swept over them, lifting Archie's spirits.

"On top of a raging headache, I've had another letter from my sister, Margaret. She's such a prolific correspondent, I feel terrible that I write one letter to her three." Archie nodded at a smart-looking officer as he walked into the club lobby, handing his hat to a waiting footman.

"What's her news then? Has she found a husband yet?" Crispin enjoyed hearing Margaret's stories of London society. While his Aunt's letters had vivid descriptions of the balls and dinners and news items that she thought might not reach Crispin in India, they were more formal. Cassie's were peppered with sarcasm and conversational nuggets, whereas Margaret's letters were rich with commentary about all the people she met. She painted her characters as richly as those in a Trollope novel.

"Enough. She won't be finding a husband until I approve. He'll have to ask *my* permission. Poor bastard, whoever he is." Archie threw his head back in laughter.

"Archie! Your sister can't be that bad."

"She's a handful, that one. I pity the man who scoops her up. There was her usual blasting of the old biddies and their antics—I'll read that to you later. But you'll be most interested to hear, she wrote that your old friend Cassandra Drayton has headed to America."

Archie watched Crispin closely to gauge his reaction.

"Really? What brings her there?"

Crispin had kept his correspondence with Cassandra to himself, so he let Archie jabber on. He knew that if he told Archie, he would have to endure a brotherly teasing. Crispin wasn't afraid of Archie's jovial mocking or his judgment. He might gossip about others, but they shared a sort of easy confidence with one another. It just seemed best that this alone was his secret. Somehow it made the anticipation of the arrival of Cassandra's letters more exciting.

Archie paused as they reached the entrance to the dining room.

"Lord Drayton's business matters apparently. Margaret is of course envious. I think she dreams of a great American romance or something like that."

"Romance with an American?" Crispin sucked in his cheeks. Would Cassandra Drayton fall for an American? No, everything he knew of her told him she'd have to marry an aristocrat, with a title greater than her own. And why did the thought of her finding a husband, American or otherwise, gall him so?

Crispin was himself in many ways attached to Rosalind Middleton. They had been spending a lot of time together, and their names were often paired in conversation around the British ballrooms and society halls of Calcutta. They made entrances at parties with one another and were seated together at dinners. Usually, it was circumstantial—Crispin traveled to and from events with the Middletons quite often. James would invite him for tea after work or for an early drink, which would drift into dinner or the start of a regimental ball. But Crispin knew that James approved of him and their connection. It wasn't something that Crispin objected to in principle—Rosalind was lovely to be sure and much admired. She was in many ways a wonderful match for him. Crispin's mind drifted back to one hot evening earlier that week.

"Crispin," Middleton said swirling scotch lazily in his glass. "Thank you for entertaining my little Rose. I was afraid when I brought her here that she would be homesick and find the society as stifling as the heat. And she was indeed growing restless, but your companionship has been a great joy for her." He raised an eyebrow, signaling he had something more to say, something he thought Crispin already knew, as if the two of them were in cahoots. Instead, he said, "You two fit rather naturally together don't you think?" Was his question rhetorical or was it supposed to be answered? The answer was, Of course, you and I both know you could do worse than align yourself with my daughter and her fortune, *but neither man said it aloud. Crispin smiled like a guilty schoolboy and took a slow sip of the scotch, letting its cool bitterness work across his tongue, followed by the burning warmth in his throat.*

Archie collapsed dramatically into a chair, signaling to Crispin to sit down by patting the table, thus recalling the daydreamer to the dining room and the slow whirring of the fans overhead. "I know it's farfetched. Only reason to marry an American is if you are tight on cash, and old Drayton's made bags of money so there is no need for that. Surprising, though, that she'd take up all this time with a big trip to the States when parties and possible suitors await her in London. My dear Mama would never allow Margaret that leniency."

"It is surprising, but her father's devoted to her. I'm sure she convinced him." Crispin felt oddly relieved. If Cassandra was engaged in an American tour, she was less likely to become attached to some suitor, a would-be husband. Crispin shook his head, trying to shake the image of Cassandra from his mind. He wondered if she spent half as much time thinking about him as he did thinking about her.

Rosalind pressed her hand insistently into Crispin as she clung to his arm, gaping at the reliefs. Despite his protests that her father would not approve, Rosalind had convinced Crispin to take her to Kharagpur to see the erotic paintings in the 11th-century Hindu temple. As always, she got her way, but he was relieved that she at least wore a colorful scarf over her red hair, in case one of the officers making a pilgrimage to the temple recognized her.

Though the firelight was dim, they could easily see the reddish-gray figures that lined the edge of the wall. They demonstrated a myriad of illicit positions, suggestively pressed to each other.

Innocently she reached out to touch one of the reliefs, which depicted a man mounting a woman from behind as she threw her head back in pleasure. The tip of Rosalind's finger ran slowly over the outline of the male figure. *Does she understand what she's looking at?* he wondered. She was barely into her twenties and had led a sheltered life. But the pale skin of her cheeks, only slightly obscured by her scarf, flushed in evidence of her cognizance.

Crispin's mouth had gone dry, and he struggled to speak, distracted by the look on her face. "Rosalind, I don't think you should be touching that. They are very, um, ancient. You wouldn't want to damage them." Her eyes widened innocently, but Crispin could not mistake the kittenish streak of curiosity in them. Rosalind had a surprisingly sensual nature, which snuck up on him now and again. At times the backs of their hands would brush against each other as they entered a room or sat in a carriage, and Crispin knew that she had intended the touch, planned it. Though he was sure she was a virgin, the general culture of passion in Calcutta had clearly piqued her interest. Unlike her British-based counterparts, she had seen more of the human body while living in India, midriffs and shoulders, ankles, and elbows. Both she and Crispin had seen *Nautch* girls spin and sway as they performed at evenings hosted by even some of her father's most conservative-minded friends and associates.

"I'm sorry Crispin, you are right. I shouldn't be touching them." She rested her hand lightly on his chest, communicating the opposite of remorse, and Crispin felt his body tingle as he was drawn into her powerful gaze.

"Look at this one, old man. My, my, these Indians certainly know how to get an old heart pumping." Two aging soldiers, clearly in their cups, leered at the relief. Crispin immediately positioned himself to block Rosalind from their view and ushered her out of the temple.

As his eyes adjusted to the bright light, the peach of her dress glowed, and shadows danced before his eyes. Rosalind had taken an active role in establishing him into both his lodgings and society. Though reluctant at times, Crispin didn't argue with many of the changes she had brought about. She took pride in smoothing some of his rougher edges, and, in many ways, he appreciated her for it. It was clear that she had taken to him and was molding him into the type of man that she wanted. While Crispin may have thought this was at Middleton's direction, he knew she was far too headstrong to obey her father in everything. Crispin was aware he was marching toward an inevitable match with her and, though he felt no great passion for Rosalind, he was quietly and gradually accepting his fate. Practically speaking, it was for the best, and he was sure that those things they did have in common would far outweigh the differences in their natures.

Rosalind had walked some distance from the temple, removing her scarf after discretely peering around to ensure no one was nearby. She looked at him with excitement. "Thank you for taking me here Crispin. It was exactly what I had expected! I know you think I'm mad for asking you to do it, but I was so curious. I've heard about this temple my whole life. Please don't tell Papa. He is scandalized enough."

Crispin laughed and rolled his eyes. "Well, we had better head back. I'm entertaining the Foresters and the lads this evening. I have to ensure everything is in order at home." While he was somewhat relieved to have an excuse to leave the temple, Rosalind's glowing face dimmed a bit.

"My darling Crispin, you know I understand how you like those rough men from the barracks; they are quite funny, and you need your male companions. But really, Mr. and Mrs. Forester, they are rather provincial, aren't they? And those strange costumes she wears, it's as though she is trying to blend in with the native women."

Crispin stiffened. He was devoted to the Foresters and completely in their debt. He had tried so often to convince Rosalind of this, but her views remained, so he simply changed the subject. "I thought you had a fine appreciation for the culture in Calcutta." He gestured to the temple, which was now some ways in the distance.

"Please, Crispin. One can appreciate from afar without forgetting where one came from."

"Rosalind, the Foresters took me in when I was a child, and Colin gave me my first employment here. And even more, they have helped my father immensely. I owe them a debt I can never repay. They are far above me in every way that is important." He softened his strong words by laying a hand on her shoulder.

She let out a sigh and tapped the side of his face lightly with her fingers. "Crispin, you have changed. You are now wealthy and successful. You have reinvented yourself here in the colonies. Do you really want to associate with such people?"

Her question made his ears throb with anger.

"That's enough, Rosalind," he snapped.

They walked in silence for a few minutes, making their way to the shade of a Banyan tree. Rosalind looked up at him with bright eyes and batted her eyelashes a few times.

"Alright then, do as you will," she said. She put a hand on his arm, a peace offering, and let her fingers brush over his with a feather-like lightness that gave Crispin goosebumps despite the heat. They moved closer to each other, and then to his surprise, Rosalind leaned in to kiss him gently on the lips, making him forget her mean-spirited condescension.

Chapter 16

January 1872

"You don't think it's a little strange, that we are staying with the Howards?" Miss Fairfax asked, her face drawn from the long sea voyage. After disembarking from *The Cutty Sark* at New York Harbor, Lord Drayton had arranged for a carriage to take them uptown, as it was called, to Gramercy Park. The harbor was not unlike London Harbor with an endless series of tall masts receding into the skyline and the heady smell of fish and coal fires hanging heavily in the frigid air. Lord Drayton had warned them that New York was colder than home, but it was a brisk cold, less damp than London. Walking across the gangway, Cassandra caught a glimpse of the expansive city. It seemed to go on for miles, and her heart raced with exhilaration at the promise of something new.

"I mean you are barely acquainted with them, James." He raised an eyebrow at her subtle disapproval but was not taken aback. Tossed about on the open ocean, Lord Drayton and Emma Fairfax had dispensed with certain formalities and subterfuges. For one thing, they had started to call each other by first name in front of Cassandra. Another difference was that Miss Fairfax openly questioned some of Lord Drayton's decisions and actions. Not many, but enough to establish that she had a mind and spirit of her own. Cassandra wondered if this had been part of the deal they had struck before they left London: Miss Fairfax would, for now, put thoughts of Aberdeen aside and stay with them as Cassandra's "companion" as long as she would be free from Aunt Eugenia's scowls and from the tightrope walk required of those who tottered between household staff and friend.

Lord Drayton sat across from Miss Fairfax and Cassandra as he often did when they traveled by coach. He'd once said that was the best view—the two loveliest ladies in the world.

"Emma, don't worry. They are a lovely couple. I did indeed meet them just once on my last trip to New York, but we've corresponded for several years now and they insisted that we stay. This is America, it's much less formal. I promise you'll enjoy it."

The carriage moved briskly up Park Avenue. They'd been traveling for over an hour and had yet to reach the Howards' home in Gramercy Park. Cassandra marveled at the continuously changing scenes of New York. Some parts were like Mayfair with elegantly dressed men and women walking briskly to avoid the bitter cold, while others were teeming with tradesmen hawking their wares in front of rough-hewn storefronts. As they passed the Bowery, they were overwhelmed with smells and shrill, high-pitched sounds of children's voices as they banged on the carriage asking for coins. There was a palpable energy to the city, a nearly constant hum, not unlike that of a steam engine. Cassandra could hear the distant buzz swirl around her as she snuggled more deeply under the fur blanket. Struggling to fend off sleep, she closed her eyes as Miss Fairfax, quietly whispered,

"Alright James, alright. We'll see."

The carriage stopped, and Cassandra awoke with a start. Had it been a few seconds or several minutes? Outside the window was a quaint, tree-lined street coated with a dusting of snow.

"Ah, here we are! Isn't this charming?" Lord Drayton flung the carriage door open without waiting for the driver.

Cassandra descended from the carriage at No. 2 Gramercy Park, a handsome house, with a crisp, red brick façade and elegant wrought iron gates. Each window on its five stories was festooned with evergreen garlands and the house was tucked in by heaps of white snow, a picture postcard of the Christmas season. As Miss Fairfax directed the coachman with their baggage, Cassandra wandered around the carriage, curious about the small park the house looked out upon. Surrounded by a low gate, the park housed several magnificent trees, which Cassandra imagined in the summer months were lush with greenery. She took a deep breath, and the cold, clear air pricked her nose.

"Come, Cassie," her father said. "There will be plenty of time to explore the area once we have met our hosts."

"Lord Drayton, there you are!" A striking woman stood at the door to the house waving a gloved hand in greeting.

"See Emma. This is America." Lord Drayton waved back as he strode toward the house. He of course referred to the fact that their hostess was braving the January cold to welcome them herself. A tall, equally handsome man hovered behind her. Miss Fairfax linked arms with Cassandra, eager to get inside.

Unlike many London townhomes, the entrance was not at street level, nor above it. They walked several steps down to a small landing that marked the entrance to the house.

"Come inside my friends, you must be chilled to the bone. I think it's not quite as cold in London." Mrs. Howard appeared to be Miss Fairfax's age, somewhere in her mid-thirties. Her hair was deep chestnut brown and her eyes, emerald-blue, shone large and bright. Despite her intimidating beauty, her smile was warm and reassuring. She smelled of hyacinth and wore a smart gown with an intricate black and red pattern that hugged her slender, graceful curves. Certainly not the picture of American ruffians and upstarts Aunt Eugenia described in her futile attempts to persuade Cassandra and Lord Drayton that his daughter would be better served spending the Season in London than "gambling with her future thanks to a shortsighted obsession with adventure" as she put it.

Charles Howard stood behind his wife. At well over six feet, with broad shoulders that seemed to burst out of his topcoat. Though he may have been dressed as a gentleman, he did not look the part. His untamed hair, rugged face, tanned skin, and wide sensual mouth set him apart. He may have been closer to the sort of ruffian Aunt Eugenia envisioned they would meet in America but, when he smiled at Cassandra, he radiated charm.

Her father had told them that upon first meeting the Howards, he thought them an unlikely match. Mrs. Howard, he had learned, was, in fact, Lily Mayhew Howard, of the Philadelphia Mayhews. Apparently, they were an excellent family—a Mayflower family—with a great deal of money and the best breeding. Yet, she had managed to find Charles Howard, once a poor boy who had moved west as a young man to become a very wealthy cattle rancher in Minnesota. Cassandra could see how Mr. Howard might have enchanted Lily Mayhew and enticed her to leave her fine family and join him in the wilderness of Minnesota.

Mrs. Howard reached out her arm and clasped Drayton's hand in greeting, "You are most welcome Lord Drayton. And this must be your lovely daughter Miss Cassandra. Charles, we'll be bombarded with questions about Miss Cassandra when we bring her about town." The hostess hugged her young guest as though they were old friends.

"And here must be her equally lovely friend, Miss Fairfax." She moved onto Miss Fairfax who colored at such a familiar welcome.

"You are so kind Mrs. Howard. We are delighted to be here and look forward to becoming better acquainted and exploring New York." Miss Fairfax, though stiff by comparison, seemed genuinely content. Her anxieties diffused as she looked about the small hall.

"Oh now, I know it doesn't look like much compared to London, but we have some lovely rooms upstairs. Our man will take up your trunks." She guided Miss Fairfax up the stairs. "You must be exhausted from your trip and ready for a nice rest. We've made no social engagements this evening and we'll have a quiet family dinner at home." They followed the Howards and listened while Mr. Howard explained that Gramercy Park was a relatively new development established in the 30s. At the time the area had been seen as rather avant-garde, though not nearly as risky an investment as uptown. By the 1860s many new houses had been built, yet the area had remained peaceful. It was just far enough away from the center of the city. "Me, I'd rather be at the ranch all year long, but my Lily wanted to keep a place in New York, and this is the only spot I'd buy. Plus, they've just opened up a nifty pub nearby called Pete's Tavern. I know some residents are turning their noses up at it, but I think it's a great addition!" He winked at Mrs. Howard.

"Oh, Charles! I think he rather wishes it was like one of those rugged saloons out West, but it's a great deal nicer than that." She gave him a good-natured shove as she continued the tour.

"Here is where we entertain." She ushered her guests into the rooms on the second floor, each tastefully decorated. The ceiling of the parlor stretched high, and a great deal of natural light streamed in from the tall windows. Cassandra was struck by the mixture of comfort, function, and formality, so unlike their homes at Grosvenor Square and Drayton Manor, which were filled with ancient dark paneling and heavy brocades.

"Now ladies," Mrs. Howard addressed them with conviction. "I know you have not brought any maids on your journey, so I've engaged two trustworthy girls, both nieces of our housekeeper, to care for you during your stay."

"Mrs. Howard, that is too much," Miss Fairfax objected. She glanced at Cassandra, eyes wide with surprise. "We do not need two new maids in addition to your own staff. We are happy to make do with one of your housemaids."

"Please, let us." She spread her arms out in a warm gesture. "It's not often that we have ladies as houseguests. Frankly, we don't do too much entertaining. As you've heard, Charles prefers the ranch, but I've been looking forward to your visit and introducing you to New York society. It won't compare to St. James and Mayfair, but I'd like to ensure your coiffures are the best in town. Please indulge me." She gazed imploringly at them.

"You are too generous Mrs. Howard, but we won't refuse your hospitality." At that moment, Miss Fairfax's whole demeanor changed, strengthened by their hostess's kindness and acknowledgment of her position. She spoke for both of them in a way that Cassandra had not seen since she was much younger and under her charge. Cassandra congratulated herself for convincing Lord Drayton to take them along on this journey. It would be good for everyone.

Within a few short days, it felt as though they had known the Howards for eons. Though Lily Howard was easygoing in her manners and had a spontaneous, jovial spirit, the corners of her eyes curled, communicating constant vigilance. She was alert to all that went on around her. If a room was cold, she called for someone to light a fire before the chill was felt. If a glass was near empty, she would make sure it was filled before the drinker got the last drop. If a guest entered the hallway, she stood upright to greet him before he was announced. Cassandra had to wonder if Mrs. Howard had been deliberate in placing her father in the room beside Miss Fairfax's.

"Tonight will be an interesting evening my dear, Miss Drayton," Mrs. Howard said with more than a hint of sarcasm. "Cousin Lina has invited us to one of her grand soirees. We'll be going up to her house on Fifth Avenue and we'll see what fun we can have." She raised a mischievous eyebrow.

They were seated in the parlor. The roaring fire and smell of evergreen made Cassandra want to curl up on the sofa like a little girl despite the stiff boning of her taffeta gown.

"By cousin Lina, she means her distant cousin Mrs. Caroline Schermerhorn Astor, who among many other things, had the good fortune to marry Mr. William Astor Jr. She holds court uptown at that monstrosity of hers." Mr. Howard clearly did not approve of his wife's cousin. He moved behind her chair, resting his broad hands on her shoulders as his index finger wandered in delicate circles over her exposed skin.

"It's large but it isn't a monstrosity. It's actually quite elegant, if a little overly opulent." Mrs. Howard awkwardly craned her neck to look up at her husband. "Charles, I know you aren't jumping with excitement, but this evening will be a wonderful opportunity to introduce our guests to society."

"It sounds lovely, Mrs. Howard. You've been so kind, showing us all the sights and shops in the city. I'm sure tonight will not disappoint. Thank you for including Papa, Miss Fairfax, and myself. I do hope we will be pleasant additions to the evening."

"Of course, you will be. Cousin Lina will love meeting you and who knows, maybe you'll find a handsome young American man and decide to move to New York!" She laughed, delighted by that idea.

"American men are much different from English men," Mr. Howard followed his wife in her matchmaking intentions. "I'm sure you've already noticed that we are more forthright. And for the most part, we are industrious. We don't just wait around for the next horse race or event. All but those in the highest circles."

"Quite true," Cassandra's father chimed in. "Except, they all live very far from England!" Though he might have admired the American sense of purpose and drive, she was sure he would rather die than see her living in New York or Boston married to a merchant or industrialist, however rich he might be.

The chief subject of Lord Drayton's admiration was Jay Cooke, to whom he had been formally introduced the day before. He'd come back from the meeting raving with praise and even a little bit of envy. The meeting had given him confidence that exchanging the War Bonds for Railway Bonds was indeed one of the soundest investments he could make.

"Today was simply ripping, Howard," Lord Drayton began excitedly, repeating what he'd told Cassandra earlier. "Jay Cooke is a brilliant man, brilliant!" Mr. Howard smiled politely. Just as Cassandra was taken aback by their American friends' refinement, she suspected Mr. Howard was surprised by her father's overt enthusiasm. At times, even Cassandra wondered how he could have emerged from the taciturn ranks of the British aristocracy. "He's been using the newly laid transcontinental telegraph to communicate with his office in England and take bond orders," Lord Drayton said with childish glee. "He's invited us to visit the railroad site in Thompson's Junction. They'll be breaking ground next month."

"Well, I'll be dammed!" Mr. Howard exclaimed. "You know that's very near my ranch."

"Our ranch, dear." Mrs. Howard chided, blinking her lashes at him.

"That's right, *our* ranch." He tucked a delicate curl behind her ear adoringly. "Where are you staying Lord Drayton?"

"I was told there would be some temporary accommodations constructed near the ground-breaking site. It will only be for a couple of weeks."

"Nonsense," Mr. Howard continued. "You'll stay with us. There's plenty of room. Wouldn't that be wonderful Lily?"

"We couldn't possibly . . . you are too generous."

Mrs. Howard stood up with finality. "Absolutely. It's settled then. I'm excited to have company at the ranch. It can get a bit lonely out there."

Mr. Howard put his arm possessively around his wife. "That's right, and I won't have it any other way. I get what I want. Ask Lily. The moment I saw her, I told her I'd marry her, and she barely put up a fight!"

"Charles, please!" Mr. Howard beamed at his wife and then turned his attention to Miss Fairfax, who had just entered the room.

"Are you looking forward to this evening Miss Fairfax?" He asked. Lord Drayton's eyes widened. Her gown was a deep lavender that hugged her waist intimately. Its intricate folds and flounces gave it texture and richness. Most catching was the rather daring and low square neck and the diaphanous sleeves that outlined her delicate arms. She wore her hair in loose curls that framed her face. The style was not the height of fashion, but it served to enhance her unwittingly seductive look. Between Miss Fairfax and Mrs. Howard, whose deep charcoal gray evening gown was in the finest silk and adorned with miniature white and pink rosettes, Cassandra felt positively girlish and nun-like in her modest pink gown. Her father continued to stare at Miss Fairfax in a way that made Cassandra blush.

They approached from the south, coming up Fifth Avenue. Carriages gathered in a long line down the street so Cassandra couldn't get a good view of the house until a footman opened the door of their brougham. It was an impressive red brick building, which took nearly the entire block. Grand Corinthian columns framed the entrance and a light burned at each window so that the interior of the house seemed aglow. Mrs. Astor's home was every bit as grand as the finest in London.

Guests rushed to escape the biting winter air, and they joined the stream hurrying up the stairs into the foyer. Passing quickly through entrance rooms, they gave their cloaks to the attending footmen and went onward to meet their hosts who received them at the entrance to the ballroom. Mrs. Astor, rail-thin with deep brown hair and piercing eyes, commanded the room with iron-like grace. Her gown was gorgeous, if severe, a rich black velvet, overlaid with an elaborate gold pattern, vaguely reminiscent of the East. The heavy texture was a stark contrast to her fair skin. Cassandra imagined that the many hopeful debutantes in the room found her terrifying.

"There she is. Cousin Lina," Mrs. Howard declared as they reached the entrance to the room. "She looks very elegant this evening." Charles Howard grumbled something inaudible, but clearly unflattering.

"Charlie, you must not antagonize her, she's our hostess *and* my cousin," Mrs. Howard put her hand on her husband's arm.

"I'll try to behave."

"Her home is quite impressive," Cassandra said politely. Though, having experienced the London season, she was less awestruck than some others in attendance.

"Cousin Lina, you are looking lovely this evening. Thank you so much for including us." Mrs. Howard's tone was as warm as her smile. Mrs. Astor showed the beginnings of a smile, which flattened quickly as she took in Mr. Howard's hulking frame. Clearly, there was no love lost between Lina and Charles.

"My dear Cousin Lily, you are looking so well. Time never seems to trouble you. And . . . hello Mr. Howard." Her tone was so saccharine it bordered on nasty, but she gave him little time, quickly turning her attention back to Mrs. Howard, "I'm glad to see you back in town, my dear. How have you enjoyed rusticating on your ranch?"

"Well, as you know, I'm a country girl at heart, in love with my horses and cattle. They might even be preferable to the opera."

"Amen to that!" Mr. Howard boomed. "Cousin Lina." He executed an overly grand bow. Mrs. Astor cringed.

"And who are your friends?" Mrs. Astor was happy for the distraction.

"May I present Lord James Drayton, Viscount Drayton, and his daughter the Honorable Miss Cassandra Drayton. And this is Miss Emma Fairfax. Our dear friends from London."

Mrs. Astor was clearly impressed by two words, "Lord" and "Viscount." It seemed that even American "royalty" coveted a more official noble position.

"Welcome. How delighted we are to have you in our home, Lord Drayton, and your lovely daughter and her friend." She beamed. "How are you finding your stay in New York?"

Drayton responded with American-style enthusiasm, "Very pleasant, Mrs. Astor. Our gracious hosts have introduced us to your fine city. We are enjoying ourselves immensely."

"Wonderful. And you, Miss Drayton? You must think us very shabby."

"Not at all! Everyone has been so kind, and the town is full of such energy. Thank you for including us in your lovely party, Mrs. Astor. My friends at home will be terribly jealous."

"Tell me Miss Drayton are you engaged?"

Cassandra stiffened and then smiled, reminding herself how very direct Americans were.

"I am not, Mrs. Astor. I have been out for two seasons, but after much pleading, I convinced my dear father to allow me to join him on his tour of America."

Lord Drayton smiled and interjected, "My daughter is an adventurer, it appears. She would not let me leave England without her."

"Indeed? Well, we shall have to find some young people to entertain Miss Drayton. With any luck, perhaps one of our young, unattached American gentlemen will strike your fancy. I will think on it . . ." Mrs. Astor trailed off, gazing over Cassandra's shoulder. She was distracted by the appearance of new arrivals, decked in velvet and pears, and as a result, did not catch Lord Drayton's frown at the notion of an American son-in-law. With Mrs. Astor's tacit dismissal, the group was released to enter the ballroom.

Lord Drayton turned to Miss Fairfax with a raised brow and held out his arm, which she took. He clasped his hand over hers, a possessive gesture that did not go unnoticed. As the couples walked toward the ballroom,

Cassandra caught Mrs. Howard regarding them curiously. She was a sharp one. The moment the Draytons had arrived, she seemed to glean the nature of their relationship. Then again, Cassandra's father *had* changed in New York. Outside of the confines of London society and Aunt Eugenia, he seemed freer to show his emotions. Each night at the Howard's, he'd taken Miss Fairfax's arm and escorted her to dinner, and later in the parlor, he would linger by her side. At Drayton Manor, they had always deliberately excused themselves separately at the end of an evening. In New York, her father and Miss Fairfax would say goodnight to the group together. They'd even explored the city on their own.

Cassandra noticed her father stiffen when Mr. Howard asked Miss Fairfax for the next dance. As Mr. Howard swept her away in his long arms, Lord Drayton's lips tightened and did not ease until the set ended and Mr. Howard swept Cassandra off for the quadrille. For such a large man, he was surprisingly graceful in his movements.

"Miss Fairfax is quite lovely tonight. That color becomes her." Mr. Howard's gaze drifted toward Miss Fairfax, who was now dancing with a tall red-haired gentleman.

Cassandra arched her neck to look into Mr. Howard's handsome face.

"Yes." She smiled, and he spun them neatly through a cluster of other dancing couples. "You're quite a good dancer, Mr. Howard."

"Not nearly as good as my partner." As they circled the floor, he changed the subject. "I've been wondering, Miss Drayton, how long has Miss Fairfax been connected with your family?" He was clearly intrigued.

"Oh, since I can remember—nearly ten years, I think. She came to us as my governess, and now she's my companion. Really, she's part of our family."

"She doesn't look like any governess I've ever seen. I associate that word with gray-haired spinsters."

"Her father was a gentleman, but I gather he managed to squander his property away, forcing Miss Fairfax to find work." Entranced by his warm smile, Cassandra found herself saying more than she should.

"Lily and I have really enjoyed spending time with your father. He is an easy-going fellow. Not at all what one would expect from an English Lord."

The Draytons had been staying with the Howards for over a week and this was the only private conversation Cassandra had had with Mr. Howard.

"Papa is a rare breed. A warm Englishman and a devoted father, but I'm biased of course."

"Well, he seems up for adventure, and I'm sure you'll enjoy Minnesota. You'd be surprised how the plains of the West can change your perspective."

"Excuse me, Mr. Howard." A tall, handsome dark-haired man with a pleasant smile approached them as the music came to an end. "I was wondering if you might introduce me to your friend and if she might do me the honor of accepting my hand for the next dance." Mr. Howard made the introductions, and the cotillion began.

CHAPTER 17

February 1872

A blade of sunlight cut through the slit in the heavy curtains. It was early at Thomson's Junction in Duluth, Minnesota. Cassandra thought about ringing for tea but decided against it. She liked this peace and solitude. She liked watching the particles of dust slowly float through the air and listening to the low calls of the ranch hands and the atonal clank of the cowbells as the herds moved from one pasture to the next.

She got up from the bed and drew open the curtains to the Howards' ranch, which spread out below her. A small wave of homesickness rippled through her and she wondered what May was doing at that moment. Cassandra had stayed up late into the night the day before writing letters to May and Crispin. She glanced over at her letter to Crispin which she had laid out to dry.

> *Dearest Crispin,*
>
> *It has been so long since my last letter and I doubt this will find you for several months as I won't be able to post it until we return to New York, but I must write now before I forget any of what I've seen in this part of our American Tour.*
>
> *I'll begin with our train ride which was unlike anything I've experienced.*

She described how the train snaked its way from Chicago, Illinois, to St. Paul, Minnesota, to the tip of Lake Superior, and how it charged through dark tunnels that seemed to be cut from the bowels of the earth and sped by towns so small they disappeared behind them before she had even registered that they were towns at all. They passed forests of silver birches and poplars, occasionally broken by a farm-clearing and a cluster of bark-roofed log cabins.

> *With each turn of the wheels, the landscape seemed rougher, the trees taller, and the climbs steeper. The last miles were the most dramatic as the train wound around the broken bluffs of Lake Superior, the icy water below us darker and deeper than the ocean.*
>
> *Just when I thought I would go crazy with the restlessness of being confined to a train car for days on end, we lurched to a stop in Duluth. My legs felt wobbly beneath me as we stepped onto the platform and the ribs of the unfinished depot roof opened above us. Standing on the nearly deserted platform, the place could not have felt more foreign than if we had arrived on the surface of the moon.*
>
> *Of course, father insisted we go directly to the Northern Pacific Railway offices. He wanted to meet with his associates and take a tour of the Thompson's Junction site.*
>
> *At the site, I felt I had stepped into another world. I had never experienced the sting of such cold.*

She wrote of the wind that cut across the desolate, snow-covered plains, and how she had to bury her face in her father's chest to guard against its blow. Once she became accustomed to the harsh conditions, she was able to look out upon the expanse before them: a white world with endless frozen fields and a pale, frosty sky. It was a lonely place. But also, free.

> *I took a deep breath—the smell of snow and pine filled my lungs. It reminded me of galloping through the Dorset hills on Artemis' back. Those days seem so long ago.*
>
> *Crispin, I have led a life of privilege, have beautiful gowns, know people of fortune and breeding. I recognize the creature comforts of my world, one filled with delicate teacups, grand staircases, and balls. But in the barren wasteland of*

Duluth, stripped of all that was familiar and assaulted by the biting cold, I felt that I had broken away from my perfect life.

After our frigid tour of the site—we were unprepared for the cold—we hurried to the Howards' ranch. I had no idea what a Western ranch would be like, but it is certainly a great deal dowdier than their home in New York. I can only imagine what May would think of ranch living. She might not be impressed with the inside of the house, but I am sure she would marvel at the splendor of the land, just as I do. The house is situated in a broad clearing with glorious, majestic oaks framing it. In every direction, the acres sprawl out farther than the eye can see. The West is untamed, expansive, and desolate. Description can't do it justice.

But I must leave you as it's very late. Mr. Howard has promised to take me riding tomorrow. Don't be shocked, Crispin. Papa doesn't know and I didn't exactly tell Mr. Howard about my riding experiences. But I couldn't resist. Being here reminds me so much of you and our long rides together. I'm going to keep it a secret from Mr. Howard as long as I can. Hopefully, Papa won't find out!

Thinking of you and the hot Calcutta sun as I freeze in America.

Yours always,

Cassandra

It was an impossibly long letter and Cassandra hoped Crispin would enjoy it. She folded it gently and rang for breakfast.

"Off to the construction site my dear?" Mrs. Howard caught Cassandra by surprise as she was fastening her heavy cloak in the front hall. Cassandra had slept a bit late and was rushing to join her father and Miss Fairfax in the coach.

"It's a warm day for February, so you should be comfortable in that coat." As always Mrs. Howard was aware of the movements of everyone in her household, but somehow no one felt put out by it. She looked lovely as usual, in a Western-style blue plaid dress with a very straight skirt. Aunt Eugenia would have been shocked by the lack of petticoats. Cassandra wasn't even sure if she was wearing a corset.

"Yes, I'm looking forward to it, Mrs. Howard. Papa is so excited to show us the progress and to meet with those in charge of the project." She was nearly at the door when Mrs. Howard spoke again.

"He does seem to be *very* enamored with the railway project and heavily invested in Jay Cooke." Her tone was wary, suggesting something in Lord Drayton's involvement was inappropriate. Cassandra met her gaze.

"What do you mean?" Her response was more brittle than she'd intended. Mrs. Howard's subtle disapproval of her father sparked Cassandra's indignation.

"Only that based on the amount of time he spends talking about the project, it sounds as though he has focused all of his efforts in one direction." She looked unwaveringly at Cassandra, convinced of her point.

Cassandra squared her shoulders to face Mrs. Howard, her anger rising. She knew it would be best to bite her tongue but couldn't help herself.

"Mrs. Howard, the success of railroad investments is well documented. It's a very sound investment. My father has been involved in schemes in this country for years, and frequently engages his friends as well. It is his way, and he is always successful. I should think Americans would respect his industry and work ethic." Mrs. Howard had no right to pass judgment on her father's affairs. Propriety dictated that Cassandra remain polite, but she could not. Yet, even as she defended her father, Cassandra wondered why Mrs. Howard's words had stung her so sharply. And she regretted not being able to temper her reaction.

"Miss Drayton, I didn't mean to speak out of turn. I'm sure Lord Drayton knows what's best." She spread her hands out in apology, but her posture remained assured. She moved to open the door for Cassandra.

"Indeed, he does. Thank you, Mrs. Howard." Cassandra turned quickly toward the carriage, her host's words following her like a shadow.

As they walked around the bustling construction site, Lord Drayton turned this way and that with frenetic energy. "This is brilliant," he said under his breath, repeating the phrase more loudly as they marched closer to the action. "Look at that, Emma!" He grabbed Miss Fairfax's arm and pointed toward two lines of steel tracks, the sun glinting off of them. They sliced through the empty land for several hundred meters and then stopped abruptly.

"Soon they will stretch to the edge of the westward horizon and beyond. Just a few months ago people might have considered this a wasteland. Now, it will connect the continent and open more markets than the Union Pacific. It's a gold mine."

Cassandra had become distracted by a group of men, an array of races, features, and skin tones, but all covered in grime and half-dressed despite the cold. They were hard, stony-faced, numb to their sublime surroundings. Their massive arms yielded axes almost as large as the men themselves, which they swung up and down in steady rhythm. In these men, Cassandra caught a glimpse of an icy truth that their hosts, who sang the praises of this railway venture, wanted to brush aside. Their breezy confidence did not match the cruel work required to bring the project to fruition.

"There's Fulton!" Lord Drayton pulled Cassandra around to face the naked scaffold of the train depot, where Mr. Fulton stood, deep in conversation with two mustachioed men, who looked as though they were part of the rugged landscape.

Catching Lord Drayton's eye, Mr. Fulton extracted himself and strode toward them.

"Drayton! Miss Drayton and Miss Fairfax." He bowed. "So, what do you think?"

"Magnificent. It's the only word that comes to mind. When do you imagine you'll finish?"

"We hope to reach Montana by June and Puget Sound by November of '72. Our timeline is ambitious, but without the government to bog us down, we should be able to work more quickly than the Union Pacific folk. As long as we get the appropriate funding. To be quite frank,"—Fulton paused—"we need to raise twenty million dollars to guarantee we meet our deadline." As the last word left his mouth, he glanced sideways at Lord Drayton, gauging the impact the number would have on him. "So, I *am* glad you've come. I understand you have serious interest?"

"I do. I have a number of investors, who will certainly commit sums to me on the condition that I report back and recommend the project."

Cassandra felt uneasy at his claim. Saunders was always a skeptical investor, requiring cajoling and assurances. Forsythe, though eager and opportunistic, had promised nothing more than his interest in sitting down for dinner at her father's expense. Cassandra's uncle, Lord Gray, definitively denied his support of past schemes, until he was absolutely sure his money was safe. He took small risks and enjoyed relative gains. Cassandra feared her father was speaking out of turn, and she imagined it could entangle him in an embarrassing ordeal. Mrs. Howard's warning rang in her head and a nagging worry took root in the pit of her stomach.

"I speak on behalf of Mr. Cooke, with whom I've discussed this issue at length. We will be happy to reach a rather liberal agreement with any investor who can supply us with 10 million."

Lord Drayton's eyes narrowed, and Fulton took a hopeful breath before uttering, "He has spoken of a *finder's* fee in the range of 10% of the total investment."

Lord Drayton stopped mid-stride and turned toward Mr. Fulton. Taking off his hat, he leaned toward the man. "Mr. Fulton, I think you have found 'yer man,' as they say in Ireland. I am confident that my colleagues and I will meet your needs,"—he paused—"if you can offer assurance that there is proper oversight and regular reporting of progress. Speed is of the essence. We are looking for relatively fast returns and don't want to find our assets tied up in a project that gets bogged down in politics or tripped up by unexpected obstacles."

"Of course. Mr. Cooke is sensitive to the needs of investors. He delegates operational authority to reputable businessmen who have a proven record. Here is one of our best men now. You must meet him."

A tall, barrel-chested man with a round face and a full beard, strode toward them purposefully.

"Ira!" Fulton called to him. "Come meet Lord Drayton."

After introductions were made, Ira Spaulding asked the obvious question. "What brings you to these desolate Minnesota climes?" He gestured toward the frozen land. "I don't imagine you've brought your wife and daughter here on a sightseeing holiday." He winked at Cassandra and Miss Fairfax in kindly good humor.

Cassandra wondered if her father would correct him, but before he had a chance to say anything, Fulton chimed in, "These good folks are here to assess an investment."

"Ah." Spaulding stopped to cough loudly. "Excuse me. This cold gets in the lungs." He coughed again before regaining his composure. "You can't go wrong with the Northern Pacific. It must be built and fast. At present, the land is untamed and under-populated, but it won't be that way for long." He smiled and coughed again.

"Ira has been with us since '68. He's instrumental in surveying the land. If anyone knows about the promise of this project, it's him." Fulton turned to his shivering guests. "Shall we escape this wind and have a cup of something warm? I am sure we can brew some fresh coffee."

"Yes, let's go in Mr. Spaulding." They trudged toward a small log cabin. Cassandra tried to catch her father's eye in hope that she could silently warn him to temper his enthusiasm, but he had fallen into step with Fulton who was ahead of them.

Lord Drayton rubbed his hands together quickly. "Fulton, if all goes well, I can cable the money to you as soon as I get back to New York."

Mr. Fulton grabbed Lord Drayton's hand with something akin to glee, shaking it vigorously. "I will wire Cooke directly. It will take a few days for the bank to draft a note. In the meantime, you can contact your man in London."

After they climbed back into the carriage, Fulton shut the door and bowed an obsequious goodbye. Lord Drayton released a great sigh, falling back into the seat. Cassandra did not know if it was a sigh of relief or panic. For several minutes they rode along in weighty silence. Miss Fairfax's eyes were downcast, and Cassandra sensed they both felt the same way.

"What if you have to go back on your word?" Cassandra said slowly.

"Do you really believe I will have to do that?"

"How can you be so sure?"

"Cassie," he took his daughter's hand, which she squeezed tightly as if to try to convince him of the danger in his overconfidence. "I see why you may be skeptical, but trust me, I have a plan." Cassandra bit her lip and looked skeptically out the window at the piles of newly cut timber and the uneven pyramids of rail ties. Doubt had taken hold, and the clunk-clunk of hammers and axes became a steady drumbeat to her unease.

The train came to a slow halt and the guard jumped to the platform calling out, "Buffalo! Exchange Street. Buffalo." A trickle of well-dressed first-class travelers merged with a larger stream of shabbier second and third-class riders. Porters swarmed the doorways to help unburden passengers of their trunks and valises. Hellos and goodbyes were hastily exchanged and soon they were off again, jostling through the hills and rocks of New York.

Miss Fairfax had been drifting in and out of sleep until the guard opened the car door letting in a stiff breeze. She blinked her wide eyes several times and shifted position, straightening her back. She and Cassandra both looked out the window, watching the silent world go by.

Cassandra turned her attention back to her letter. She was trying to complete what would be her last letter to Crispin, which she planned to post before they set sail from New York, but she sensed that Miss Fairfax was staring at her, so she paused mid-sentence and tucked the papers under a blank sheet.

"London will seem strange, won't it?" Miss Fairfax broke the silence.

"Very."

"But we'd best get used to the idea." Her words were something of a warning to herself.

"I suppose."

"It's unlikely we'll find ourselves in America again." Miss Fairfax was right. Cassandra might exchange letters with the Howards but doubted they would ever cross paths with them or Mr. Fulton and Ira Spaulding again.

What would they all do when they returned to their familiar hemmed-in world? Her father and Miss Fairfax would have to go back to the way they were. For that Cassandra was sorry. And it would be some time, if ever, before Cassandra would be able to see exotic places or have any of the experiences she'd had in America and, though Cassandra hated to admit it, she was also aware of the passage of time and knew it would be best for all if she settled down. Aunt Eugenia's words about missed opportunities and wasted time echoed in her mind. There was some wisdom in her warnings. The truth was, if Cassandra wanted even a fraction of the excitement she had tasted in America, she could not stay a girl at her father's home. And she certainly couldn't travel the earth on her own. The idea of doing such a thing was as unreal to her as traveling to the moon.

Cassandra's only hope was to marry someone who, like her, craved travel and new experiences.

Chapter 18

April 1872

Archie thought this was a good idea, but as Crispin followed him through the dark alleys at the far end of Dalhousie Street, he regretted coming. During his stays in Calcutta, Archie spent his time managing his family properties, drinking as much whisky as possible, and visiting every notable brothel in town.

"Come, Crispin," he slurred the words together. "That pretty Rosalind of yours will never know, and besides, I'm sure she expects to share you with some native girls, at least for a little while."

Crispin wished he hadn't mentioned Rosalind. An image of her pale skin and fiery hair flashed in his whisky-muddled brain. He recalled the feel of Rosalind's soft, petal-like lips as she whispered in his ear earlier that evening, "Crispin, don't go out with Archie. Stay with me. We can sit in the garden after Papa goes to sleep."

"C'mon mate, let's go inside. I promise you'll thank me later. Madame Fillette's is the best in town."

Despite the building's shoddy exterior, they were ushered into a grand parlor and offered claret and a hookah pipe. Within moments they were lounging listlessly on the low silk settees piled with ornate pillows. Crispin, languid with alcohol, felt as though his limbs were floating.

"*Messieurs, bon soiree.*" An older, dark-haired woman with alabaster skin, dressed entirely in black, entered the parlor. She carried her age well, and Crispin could see that in her day she had been very attractive.

"Crispin, let me present Madame Fillette." Archie had pulled himself away from the hookah pipe and jumped up unsteadily to kiss the lady's hand.

"Madame is the most unconventional patroness in Calcutta. She employs both Indian and European *kasbis* and educates them in the pleasures of both societies. Imagine that. But of course, she is the most beautiful woman in the house."

"Lord Douglas, you flatter me." She chuckled, unconvinced. "Because of the late hour, I'm afraid most of our girls are taken, but since My Lord is such a fine gentleman,"—she paused and gestured to Crispin—"as I'm sure is his friend, I have found two ladies to entertain you this evening."

Two young women dressed in brilliant silk saris entered the parlor. Each had long dark hair intertwined with pearls that caught the light and glistened like diamonds. One was tall, fair, and clearly of mixed race, and the other was a petite Calcutta beauty. The taller girl strummed a *viol de gambe*, while the other's body moved sensually to the music's rhythm. As the song continued, she shed the layers of silk that hugged her. Within a few moments, she was naked and had moved toward Archie. He reached up to touch the smooth skin of her exposed breast, and her long hair fell forward as she enveloped him.

Crispin's mind was thick and dull from the pipe as he watched the woman remove Archie's jacket. Mesmerized by the gentle curves of her body, Crispin felt himself grow rigid. The fair musician lowered her instrument and moved toward him. Though the music ended, she danced as her companion had, removing her clothing as she approached. Her body lithe and delicate. She kneeled before him, and Crispin saw that her face was equally so. Her dark eyes shone, but even in his stupor, he sensed sadness in them. She brought her fingers to Crispin's face, tracing the outline of his features with both hands before resting them on his chest. Crispin lost his jacket and shirt in moments, and lowered her to the plush carpet, burying his head in her hair and inhaling the fragrant scent of clematis flowers.

He was lost in the sea of sensations. Her hand moved smoothly toward the hardness in his groin. She stroked up and down, up and down. Crispin's breath quickened as she deftly slipped open the buttons of his pants. He opened his eyes to find himself staring straight into hers, huge and deep brown and glassy. He wanted to push himself into her, to feel her warmth envelop him. That was why he and Archie were there. But those eyes—empty as if her real self was in another room—were windows through which Crispin could see all her wasted youth and sadness. He pulled away, fastening his buttons.

"I'm sorry, so sorry," he said as he fumbled for his jacket and stumbled toward the door.

"Archie. Come on. We've got to go."

"Drop the rates? Don't be daft Middleton!" Thomas Henderson thumped his fist on Joe Middleton's desk, rattling the tea service and rousing Crispin from his brutal hangover. Middleton, a maverick to many colonials, preferred to have business meetings over tea. He turned to his protégée.

"What do you think Crispin? Should we drop our rates to accommodate the Mattlon Mills order? I say we can give a little. I don't want to drag this out and it's quite an order."

"What's that?" Crispin shook his head. The rattling teacups echoed in his ears like the thunderous hammers of a railway chain gang. It was four in the afternoon, and he'd barely made the meeting. Crispin hoped his clammy pallor wouldn't give him away and that he could hold his nausea at bay.

"Whoa! Better lower your voice, looks like our boy Crispin is a bit delicate this afternoon. Were you entertaining late last night?" Henderson reached over and clapped Crispin's shoulder so sharply he jolted upright. Try as he might, Crispin couldn't help closing his eyes to block out the afternoon sunlight and calm his throbbing head.

"Crispin, you *are* looking rather low. Should I send for Chetan? He can set up a room for you if you need to rest." Middleton was so obliging and earnest, Crispin felt even more guilty for last evening's indulgence.

"No, no I'm fine, really. Just a bit tired. I was dining with Archie last night. He kept me out quite late."

"I'll bet he did." Henderson saw through Crispin's stony face. Henderson, always jovial, had known more than a few late nights himself.

"Lord Douglas has really taken you under his wing. Wonderful." Mr. Middleton beamed with pride over Crispin's rise in society. But then his broad smile wavered. "I do so worry for Rosalind. She hasn't found an appropriate female companion of her own age to share her experiences and confidences. And Lord knows I despair of her prospects for marriage." He looked to Henderson for validation. "I know Henderson is tired of me going on about this over the years, but I'm constantly worried about her future, especially when I'm gone."

Henderson cleared his throat and looked at Crispin. Mr. Middleton's implication couldn't have been clearer if he'd taken out an advertisement in *The India Gazette.*

"You're such a very good influence on her Crispin. I do hope you continue to spend time together." Over the course of the year, his hints had become more obvious and public. Crispin could sense Middleton's growing frustration over his inaction in proposing to Rosalind.

Crispin fidgeted in his seat and changed the subject. "The Mattlon Mills order. It's very big, nearly twice the size of the last one. They must be running over capacity to order that much. Are they behind?" As soon as he said the words, Crispin realized he knew the answer. He cursed his brain, which stumbled to keep up with the conversation.

Middleton cocked his head to the side as he often did when puzzled. "Are you quite alright, Crispin? Don't you recall they had a strike last month?"

"Yes, of course. It just slipped my mind," he said. Chetan silently entered the study to refresh the tea. "Chetan, might I trouble you for a coffee?" The servant bowed and slipped out of the room.

"That's the ticket Crispin, it will perk you right up! I can't imagine what you were up to with that derelict Douglas—no good, I'm sure." Henderson guffawed.

"Archibald Douglas comes from one of the best families in England," Middleton said indignantly. "He enjoys himself, but I would hardly call him a derelict."

"So, about the strike," Crispin once again changed the subject. "I can't recall, how long did it last?"

"Those workers in Liverpool held out for quite some time—three weeks if you can believe it. Mattlon held his orders before the strike and has doubled them after. I don't know how he will manage it all and hope he won't lose too much business because of it. And of course, the impact on the city was devastating. All those workers idle, without pay or occupation for weeks. Many families suffered, I'm sure."

"What was the outcome of the strike then?" Henderson asked, only somewhat interested in the response. Middleton launched into a long speech about how management had won but that the workers had made a good showing. His humble roots put him firmly in the liberal camp. Though he was now a wealthy industrialist, his sympathy for the common worker always came out.

Henderson, like many of his class, was adamantly non-political and now indicated so by distractedly wiping his spectacles. "How do they move all that cotton? That seems like a challenging business."

"By rail of course. The train system in England is second-to-none really. Not quite like the bits and pieces of lines we have here. Crispin can tell you all about the railway, that's how he got his start in Calcutta, years ago." Middleton once again beamed at Crispin with obvious pride. The young man blushed. If he only knew where Crispin had been just twelve hours earlier. The color quickly left his cheeks, and he took stock of the nearest exits should he need to vomit.

"You were a railway man?" Henderson chuckled.

"Yes, that's right." Crispin held onto his composure, tenuously. "You don't know the story? How I saved Middleton from certain death at the hands of a drunken, ghoulish officer?"

"Yes, I had heard something of that!" He chuckled. "You're quite the hero, though I can't imagine you miss that life."

"Well, not any more of course." Crispin stretched his legs out and took a deep gulp of the hot coffee Chetan had just brought in. He waited for it to work its magic. "I did at the start though. For maybe a year after I left the

Company, I would still dream of the ground shifting beneath me, the sway and shimmy of the railcar. It was like rocking a baby to sleep."

Henderson leaned forward in his chair to take a biscuit from a gleaming silver tray. "It seems to be good business too! Maybe better than cotton." Henderson mulled this over as crumbs of biscuit fell on his waistcoat. "There are all sorts of railway schemes here in India and America. People want to build them everywhere."

"There is a lot of expansion, but not all for the best, I think. You can't just build railways to build railways. You have to have demand, people who want to travel throughout the country. It's hard here in India, it's so vast and underdeveloped. And then there is the capital required, of course, it's a damned expensive business," Crispin said, perking up a bit.

"That's true. Maybe when you get back to England, you can start building some railways too, eh?" Henderson suggested to Middleton.

"I think I'll stick to cotton. I'm afraid I'm not accomplished enough to do two things at once. Another reason I need you, Crispin—to be my eyes and ears in London. Have you set the date for your voyage home?"

Middleton had asked him to run the London office, and Crispin was to split his time between Calcutta and London. In his efforts to bring Crispin and Rosalind together, Middleton wanted Crispin to establish himself among London society so that Rosalind would have a comfortable life, free from the heat and hazards of the colonies. Crispin understood that his acceptance of the new assignment was a tacit agreement to the match. Still, he could not quite bring himself to propose.

Middleton rose and pulled the bell, instructing Chetan to call for Rosalind. Crispin wished he hadn't. His stomach turned afresh, this time with guilt at last night's escapades. He cursed Archie's bad influence, but even more, Crispin cursed his own weakness.

Over the back of Crispin's chair, Middleton placed his hands on his shoulders. "Rosalind's a beautiful girl, but you will have your work cut out for you to keep her happy."

Crispin sucked in his breath at the notion of a lifetime of making Rosalind happy. Then, he cursed himself for his own dithering; Rosalind was everything he should want in a bride. He thought of her refined features and the way her smooth skin felt when their hands touched.

"She's far too good for me," he said as nonchalantly as he could, knowing the moment would soon come when he could no longer put off an engagement.

"Ah, here she is, the lady of the hour."

Rosalind swept into the room. Her gown was a deep blue to match the sapphires at her throat.

"Of course, I am! And I see you gentlemen were talking about me." She placed a small kiss on her father's cheek.

"Good afternoon Mr. Henderson, you are looking well." She reached a gloved hand out to him, which he took to his lips. Then, she swung about to look at Crispin, beaming with unexpected excitement.

"You didn't tell me you would be here today." She leaned in to touch her soft cheek to his, lingering so that Crispin could smell her jasmine perfume. As she pulled away, she gave him a look that was both possessive and seductive. The dark eyes of the young *kashi* filled Crispin's mind with a sharp pang.

"My dearest, we were just talking about Crispin's move to London."

"Oh, I long to join you there, Crispin!" Her voice filled the room, a deliberate blend of girlish innocence and womanly confidence. "You will let me visit." Her perfectly curved eyebrows, raised in anticipation.

"Of course, Rosalind. Of course."

CHAPTER 19

May 1872

Cassandra and Miss Fairfax entered Hyde Park on a sunny afternoon. They decided to leave their carriage near Queen's gate to enjoy the long walk to the luncheon—their first social event since returning to London. Cassandra paused to take in the English spring, which was bursting to life. The boughs of the cherry blossoms were weighed down with an abundance of pale pink flowers and tulips of every color lined the wide walkways.

"There she is! Returned from the American Wilderness." May flew toward Cassandra, her dark hair reflecting the afternoon sun. "You have been gone for a decade!"

"Margaret, dearest, there is no need to run." Lady Douglas called after her, her tone mild and restrained. "She's not going anywhere."

Ignoring her mother's soft reproach, May threw her arms around Cassandra and they spun like giddy schoolgirls. Cassandra had so much to tell her. When May's mother caught up to them, she clasped Cassandra's hands and pressed her soft aging cheek against the young woman's face.

"You do look well, my dear. You are positively glowing, I think," Lady Douglas began. "Isn't she, Archie?"

Archie sauntered to his mother's side and offered an exaggerated bow, so low that the corners of his grey topcoat brushed the ground. As he came up, his smile was bright and infectious.

"She is indeed."

Cassandra had met him only a few times during his infrequent visits to

London over the last few years, but May had spoken of him so often and Crispin had written so frequently about their escapades in Calcutta that she felt as though they were old friends. "Miss Drayton, America certainly seems to have suited you. You look even more stunning than usual. And you too Miss Fairfax." Archie offered them each an arm to escort them toward the party.

Cassandra felt her cheeks flush warmly under the spotlight of praise. "It really was wonderful. Wasn't it, Miss Fairfax?" She hooked her arm through May's and the four of them began to walk down the dappled path, sunlight shifting through the green canopy overhead.

"Yes, quite. We saw New York, Chicago, and even the Wild West."

"Oh, do tell us, Miss Fairfax, was it as wild as all that? I can't imagine. Archie, can you believe what Cassie has seen?"

"Will Lord Drayton be joining us today?" Archie asked.

"I'm afraid not. He is engaged with business affairs." *Even on this beautiful day,* Cassandra thought to herself, *he is consumed with the Northern Pacific Railway.* The moment they had returned to London, he called his solicitor and banker and shut the door to his study, barely emerging for meals.

They had come to the clearing before Round Pond where a pristine white tent stood in contrast to the green bloom of the Park. Chairs littered the clearing and guests mingled, sipping champagne in the midday sun.

A footman moved toward them with a silver tray filled with crystal flutes. Archie took two, handing them to Miss Fairfax and Cassandra, before serving his mother and sister. "Something to fortify you."

"To your return!" May raised her glass in the air.

"You must tell us all about your adventures across the Atlantic. You have been gone for far too long." Lady Douglas engaged Miss Fairfax, asking her to recount stories of their journey to New York and Thompson's Junction.

Cassandra took a moment to observe the party. Lord and Lady Harrington, their hosts, stood with Mr. Tovington, who had a reputation for being an outspoken Tory representative in the House of Commons. By his side was the amiable Lady Lawrence, recently widowed as May had recounted in one of her last letters. She caught Cassandra's eye and nodded her head slightly. The constancy and restraint of London society seemed both comforting and stale. In London, everyone moved and spoke and interacted in predictable circles, with perfectly choreographed timing. Cassandra was happy to be among old friends and slipped easily back into the social dance, yet she missed the excitement of the unfamiliar.

As Cassandra scanned the scene, her gaze fell on Lord Bedford, who was standing alone by the pond in a pool of sunlight. His blond hair was still a little unkempt, and he was staring at her with unnerving intensity. In short order, he approached their group.

"Ah, Bedford," Archie reached a hand out in welcome. "Join us and hear the stories of Miss Drayton's experiences in America."

"Miss Drayton." He acknowledged Cassandra with a short bow. "And Miss Fairfax, a pleasure." Bedford took his place to Cassandra's right, so close, his arm brushed her shoulder.

"It would seem that your time overseas was exhilarating." Bedford rather impolitely addressed Cassandra alone in his comment. She looked to the rest of the group to reengage them, but Archie had become distracted by another round of champagne, and Lady Douglas, Miss Fairfax, and May were chatting about the fashions in America.

"Yes, it was a very exciting trip. And how have you found the past year? Enjoyable, I hope."

"Passable. But this past season hasn't been the same without you." He raised an eyebrow. "I missed you and hope to make up for lost time." Bedford leaned in so close, Cassandra could smell sandalwood and cigars. "I mean to fill up your dance card and would take this opportunity to secure the first two dances at the Tovington's ball."

"My Lord! You are very forward." She pulled back, indignant, but amused.

"Did you expect anything less?"

"And what if I don't accept your offer? My dance card may already be full."

He burst into laughter, drawing Lady Douglas' attention. "My dear Miss Drayton. Saucy as ever, I'm glad to see. Perhaps a bit more so after your trip to America. Shall we take a turn about the garden?" He offered his arm, knowing it would not be refused, and they started down the path toward the rose garden, away from the others.

"And I find you the same, charming and devilish as ever."

"Well, I aim to capture your heart." He bowed with great flourish. It was all in jest, but inwardly Cassandra was flattered by his attention and hoped that some small part of his behavior was sincere.

She had learned, through Margaret's letters, that his father had passed away mid-winter, leaving Henry his title—the Duke of Westmoor—and a large estate to maintain. Cassandra half-expected that she would return to London and find him connected with an appropriate debutante.

"I suspect you say that to all the eligible ladies, your Grace." She lightly smacked his arm with her reticule. Bedford caught it quickly before she could snatch it back, and used it to pull her toward him, much too close. He released the purse, but Cassandra did not step back. His eyes met hers and held her gaze much longer than was appropriate.

"Not all the ladies, Cassandra. Just one," Bedford whispered before he turned and walked away.

Chapter 20

October 1872

Cassandra sat in the drawing room watching the rain as it hit the windows. The streams of water reflected the dim gaslights that dotted Grosvenor Square, making the windows appear nearly as green as the silk drapes that framed them. She'd chosen the fabric on a recent trip to Oxford Street. Miss Fairfax was impressed by her choice and pleased to see Cassandra take a larger role in managing the household, satisfied that she had trained Cassandra in the duties of a lady. Cassandra was now ready to take on the mantle of that responsibility.

These days Miss Fairfax spent less time doling out advice and more time listening. Even Aunt Eugenia treated Cassandra differently, particularly given the prospects of a marriage with Bedford, which pleased her beyond words. Society knew the benefits of a match between Bedford and Cassandra. Lord Drayton's wealth would protect Bedford's holdings, and his ancient name and title would elevate the Drayton family's position. Aunt Eugenia looked forward to the new connections Bedford would bring. Her constant stream of unsolicited advice to Cassandra had dwindled, replaced by knowing looks and a self-satisfied smile at the progress of her protégé.

Even May had warmed to the idea of an engagement between the two. Though she openly balked at the idea of "losing" Cassandra to that great pile of stone at Westmoor Hall, she knew the match was what everyone hoped for.

"But do you really love him? More than anything? Enough to leave your family, and me, behind?" May was forever the romantic and Cassandra loved her for it.

"May, he's handsome, charming, and has all the qualities I would want in a husband. I think that is enough. Besides, nothing is decided!" Cassandra smiled at May's worry over losing her and absentmindedly ran her fingers over the black embroidery on the cuff of the new gown she wore— royal blue silk, richly ornamented. The risks, she told her friend, were low. If she knew Bedford, he would want to spend most of the year in Town. He could not stand to be far from the action.

"Miss Drayton, when can we expect Lord Drayton's guests?" Cassandra turned from the window to face Marjorie, a recent addition to the household. They'd taken her on a few weeks after returning from America. She had reddish curls and a lilting Scottish brogue. Her lovely accent must have reminded Miss Fairfax of her relatives in Aberdeen, whose offer of employment Cassandra gathered Fairfax had definitively declined though no mention had been made of it.

"We will be expecting the guests at seven o'clock. Thank you, Marjorie."

"Very good, Miss Drayton." She dropped a small curtsey and left to inform the cook of the schedule. It was Marjorie's habit to curtsey to everyone in the household, even the housekeeper. She might have curtsied to the chimney sweep if he had been standing in the drawing room.

Normally, Cassandra would have looked forward to an evening of easy conversation with Mrs. Saunders and Mrs. Ogilthorpe, who were regular guests at the Draytons' table. Tonight, however, Miss Fairfax and Cassandra would be the only ladies present. Highly unorthodox, Lord Drayton had insisted that his friends not bring their wives, who were bound to get in the way of business. He felt that women often derailed the conversation, favoring the weather or the latest announcement in the *Morning Post*. For some reason, he excluded Miss Fairfax and Cassandra in this assessment. They belonged to a more masculine sphere in his eyes, perhaps because so often the two had been privy to his private speculations and would not interfere.

During and after their trip to America, Lord Drayton had spent a great deal of time at Jay Cooke's offices and had been commissioned as a "referring agent" for the offering of the Northern Pacific Railroad. While Cassandra wasn't sure if this was an official title, her father had taken it very seriously. He was to solicit one million pounds to further the offering of the bonds, which would raise funds and confidence in the continued construction of the railroad. He'd accepted and pursued the task with a feverish energy, spending hours every day in Jay Cooke's offices and in meetings, convincing his friends to pursue the investment. He'd even impressed upon Aunt Eugenia the amazing returns and absolute security of the scheme. She was supportive but had politely declined, claiming that she would only do so if her husband approved. That was unlikely. Lord Gray was risk-averse, more inclined to breed horses and improve his land than dabble in speculative investments.

Outwardly, Cassandra supported her father's ambitions; inwardly worries festered. When she questioned Lord Drayton, he would insist, time and again, his investments had always proved sound and reaped great returns, and that this time would be no different. So, Cassandra held her tongue and prayed this would be the same. Yet Mrs. Howard had planted the seeds of doubt, and the enormity of the sum and the voracious way he courted his friends left a knot in her stomach that was not easily untied.

What motivated her father? Cassandra could not help but wonder. Over the years Lord Drayton's quest for money had safeguarded her fate and fortune. It was widely known that Cassandra had one of the largest marriage portions in London. Drayton Manor and the house at 37 Grosvenor Square had been luxuriously refurbished. Lord Drayton had reestablished the family wealth and name, retrieving it from near ruin brought on by Cassandra's grandfather and great grandfather. There was nothing left to accomplish.

The thud of the knocker announced the first arrival. In came Mr. Saunders, followed shortly by Mr. Forsythe, and Misters Strong, Ogilthorpe, and Blanche. There were ten gentlemen in all. In the absence of female company, the men dispensed of the usual drawing room formalities in exchange for firm handshakes and chummy greetings. Cassandra's presence didn't prevent them from talking horse races and boxing matches, just as they would have had they been at Brooks. When all had assembled, she stood up, inviting the group to move to the dining room.

As Cassandra smoothed the blue skirt of her gown, removing a stray feather that had fallen from the elaborate comb in her hair, she noticed Forsythe's eyes lingering on her breasts and body. When his eyes finally reached Cassandra's, he showed no signs of remorse, only a steady gaze that set prickly goosebumps to her skin. Miss Fairfax let out an inadvertent harrumph revealing that she too had observed Forsythe's gesture.

At dinner, Cassandra was flanked by Forsythe and Saunders, and Miss Fairfax by Mr. Ogilthorpe and Mr. St. John-Brown.

"Cassandra," Forsythe leaned in close. "I must say you look beyond exquisite tonight. I'm not at all sure I will be able to focus on our business discussions with you seated next to me." His oily skin glistened in the candlelight.

She could see Miss Fairfax's feathers were ruffled at Forsythe's obvious advances, but she did not say anything. And, as was his custom, Lord Drayton remained willfully oblivious to Forsythe's advances toward his daughter. Cassandra and Miss Fairfax had never discussed the matter directly but rather relied on knowing glances to convey contempt for Lord Drayton's would-be confidant.

To his credit, Mr. Saunders seemed to intuit the awkward change in the atmosphere. He asked pointedly, "I have been hearing rumors, Miss Drayton, of a forthcoming attachment." Forsythe's eyes locked on Cassandra's. "Will you have some news for us soon? I'm sure your father would be very pleased if it is the lucky gentleman I think it is." Saunders was thinking of Bedford of course, though he was discreet enough not to say so. It seemed that everyone had noticed Bedford's advances. Since they had returned, Lord Bedford had been a constant presence at every party, rarely leaving Cassandra's side.

Forsythe drew back momentarily as a flicker of frustration crossed his face. Recovering himself, he called out to his host, "James, you haven't mentioned a forthcoming engagement."

"Why would he?" Cassandra interjected. "I'm not engaged. Not yet at any rate. I've been acquainted with Henry since my youth. Our fathers were friends. Are you not acquainted with him? If not, I'll have to introduce you.

He has just left for the countryside for some time, but we'll have to arrange an introduction when he returns."

The footman made his serving rounds, and the exchange was interrupted by a clinking of silver to china.

"Gentleman, I want to thank you all for joining me this evening." Lord Drayton stood up and stepped away from his chair, pacing the length of the room. "Each of you has expressed interest in the Northern Pacific railway. While many of you have taken my recommendation for investments in the past, some have not. Let me take this opportunity to assure you that I only invest in projects that have an absolute guarantee of performance. You can ask Saunders or Forsythe—" He gestured to both men, waving his hand in a broad sweep.

"Hear, hear!" Saunders boomed.

Lord Drayton continued, "And never in all of my years of investing in America have I been more certain than I am now. You've heard all of the particulars—7% in gold per annum—and I've shared the circular prepared by Jay Cooke's firm regarding the land values and the progress of the construction, but there is one point I cannot stress enough." He paused, turning his gaze to Cassandra as if willing her to fuel his impassioned plea. She smiled as brightly as she could in encouragement, but her enthusiasm was tempered.

"The United States government has allowed the war bonds issued during the recent war between the states to be converted to these railway bonds. That means that the government endorses this investment and believes it to be even more valuable than an investment in its own bonds."

Hanging on every word, the guests were riveted by the promise of additional riches. As Lord Drayton spoke, they contemplated the multitude of ways they would spend their growing wealth. Before putting forward half a crown, they had far outspent their prospective returns in their minds.

"I believe in the Northern Pacific Railway. As proof, I myself am putting up a great deal of money, well over 100,000 pounds. Change is afoot in America, tremendous expansion and growth. My daughter, Miss Fairfax, and I spent several months there, and you cannot imagine the promise this land has to offer. What we beheld in Chicago and Minnesota is indescribable and, for an Englishman, nearly unfathomable. There is more land and more opportunity than any of us can imagine." Ogilthorpe, normally reserved, had managed to throw back an entire glass of wine during Lord Drayton's speech and plunked it down on the table with a resounding thud. Lord Drayton nodded to the footman to refill his guests' glasses.

"This is why I have asked you here this evening. We all have an opportunity. I have committed to raise one million pounds for the railroad."

Cassandra noted a few audible gasps at the staggering sum. Her father must have registered the surprise as well for he added, "Which, considering the potential, is a modest sum." The men lowered their glasses and tried to catch each other's eyes.

"Now, don't plan my farewell party just yet. I'm not saying I intend to move to the American West and raise cattle." The group laughed heartily. "And I assure you, I did my best to keep those American lads away from my Cassandra."

Cassandra cleared her throat politely, signaling he was getting off track.

". . . But the country, and this investment in particular, is truly inspiring. I urge you to consider this proposition, and I hope to have discussions with each of you as we continue dinner and afterward." Lord Drayton made his way back to the head of the table. Before he had taken his seat, Saunders was talking numbers. "Perhaps 100,000 or 200,000 pounds, do you think that's suitable? My wife has some interest with her marriage share as well."

The table was aflutter with conversation. Mr. Ogilthorpe and Mr. Blanche spoke across Cassandra animatedly. They considered how much they would invest, perhaps 50,000 or even 100,000. Her father had energized the group, and Cassandra's heart lifted to see him so satisfied.

"And you, Mr. Forsythe," she asked quietly among the din of voices. "How much will you put in the railway?"

"Oh 10,000 pounds, I think. Sounds like a good number to me." He murmured between bites of lamb.

"Only? A man of your means?" Cassandra knew the part her father wanted her to play, particularly with a man like Forsythe.

"Much of my money is tied up in some real estate investments I made last year. I've told your father I'd give him 10,000 and he should be happy with that."

A fter the last of the guests left, Lord Drayton leaned back contentedly in his plush chair by the fire. He stared at the dying embers intently. His handsome face, starting to show the signs of age, relaxed in relief.

"A roaring success, my dear, don't you think?" He caught his daughter's hand and squeezed it, but his eyes did not drift from the fire. "I anticipated interest, but this exceeded my expectation. All this work, the meetings, and the lunches, the dinners, the prospecting . . ." He rambled on, exhaustion and wine slurring his words.

"Have you reached your goal?" Cassandra asked. She and Miss Fairfax had excused themselves after dinner while the men talked on.

"Nearly. We have 600,000 pounds. But no matter, I will put in an additional 100,000. I can mortgage Drayton Manor for the remainder; I have already consulted with my bankers at C. Hoare & Co."

Cassandra's heart stopped for a moment and then began beating so rapidly she felt lightheaded. *Mortgage Drayton Manor?* Surely, he would not. The idea of borrowing against their home, the home her father had finally restored after decades of disrepair seemed beyond her comprehension.

"Papa, are you sure?"

He drew his eyes from the fire and faced her with a steely, determined gaze.

"Of course, I'm sure. I told the group I would be putting more of my own money in. They have to know that I am committed." He was behaving so coolly, as if 400,000 pounds wasn't that much money.

"Yes, I understand that, but it is so much. I know you said you can't lose, but Drayton Manor? You've dedicated so much effort to restore it to its former glory. If something were to happen . . ."

"My dear girl, I know you've seen a little of the world now, but don't instruct me on my investments."

Cassandra kneeled next to him, their eyes locked. "I understand the gamble you are taking Papa. I hope you are right." She pushed herself up from the floor, feeling much older than her twenty-two years. "Goodnight." Cassandra kissed him brusquely on the cheek and left him staring at the fire, swirling the ice cubes in his glass of whisky.

CHAPTER 21

December 1872

C rispin couldn't quite put his finger on it. Even the greeting seemed more formal.

Dear Crispin,

Was it a shift in the turn of her script? Less scrawling and hasty. A careful comma, definite and defined.

This may be the last letter I write for quite some time. Lord Bedford and I—I'm sure you remember him from our youth—

Yes, Crispin did, and not very fondly either. He was a careless, cocky lad, who knew all the genteel gestures and clever quips that would charm both the ladies and the men in a room.

We have an arrangement. We are soon to be engaged to be married. It has not been announced in the papers yet, but perhaps will be this season. Henry—

Cassandra deliberately dropped in his first name as if to confirm that they were indeed on intimate terms, whispering sweet nothings into each other's ears in dark corners, seated comfortably side by side on too-small settees, hips brushing. *Henry.* And that *we. We!* As if they were a foregone conclusion.

They were, of course, and Crispin had known it years ago when he and Cassandra trotted up and down the hills of her father's estate. His mouth filled with a bilious sour taste.

Crispin read the lines again. Why the delay? Did he sense hesitation? The bile receded. Between the elegant arches of her script, Crispin suspected aloofness on Cassandra's part. She didn't, wouldn't, couldn't, intend to follow through with a marriage she was not whole-heartedly committed to, not Cassandra whose impetuous nature had guided so many of her actions.

Then, why write him? Why tell him at all? The burning in Crispin's esophagus returned.

> *Henry has some affairs to attend to, and father is too consumed with certain business matters to plan a proper wedding. Of course, Aunt Eugenia would be happy to step in as the family matriarch, but I've insisted that Papa must be involved.*
>
> *Henry's much more serious now. You would barely recognize him as that carefree lad you met in Dorset all those years ago. Although, he still has a mischievous twinkle in his eye and a charming, lopsided grin.*

There it was: affection. She did care for him.

> *But now he has more purpose. You see, his father passed away a year ago this January.*

Her letter went on to describe the Duke's demise and the responsibilities left to the formerly-roguish Bedford.

> *We will be quite happy together, but I do hope that you and I can one day share an acquaintance. Perhaps you too will be settled, and we'll have a brood of children between us.*

The word *acquaintance* stuck in Crispin's throat like a fishbone. That, and *settled*. It seemed so final. It was final. He filed the letter way back in the bottom drawer of his desk, hoping that in the mahogany darkness it would disappear, evaporate.

Outside the window of his office, Indian men in their long white *dhoti's* and turbans rushed past, and carriages with well-dressed cargo rolled languidly by. *This is my world*, Crispin thought, and his murky sadness turned to anger and defiance. Crispin was not a child. Maybe he had never been one. For years he had confronted harsh realities and made his way out of necessity. He had achieved his goal, paying off his father's debts and restoring his dignity, and was now on the path to resurrecting the family name—*erasing the stain of debtor's prison—the St. John's would be people of status once again. He would secure their future.* Doing so required putting childish romantic notions to bed and facing reality. Life soldiered on and so would he.

Rosalind. It was time. Crispin grabbed his top hat and walking stick, as he rushed out the door, rehearsing the speech in his head. He would talk to Middleton first. This had to be done right. *It took some time*, Crispin would say, *but I wanted to be sure I could take care of her in the fashion she was accustomed to living.* He had to be sure he would not disappoint Rosalind and her father. They had been so good to him. They had built *his* world—he would emphasize that point. Now, Rosalind and he could share a life together, and, once he was set up in London, they could move between their homes in Calcutta and London. It might take some time, a little more time, but they would be perfectly happy once . . . once they were married.

Yes, Crispin could say all of that. He rehearsed the words, modifying sentences here and there as he made his way through the familiar maze of streets to the Middletons'.

Crispin's jacket clung to his back in the oppressive heat, but he marched on, swiftly, picking up his pace as if this were a race, one he must win.

PART III

CHAPTER 22

September 1873

"" $\mathbf{L}$ ord Drayton took a fall, I hear."

"I've heard he's ruined. Completely ruined."

"What? Drayton?" scoffed a gray-haired gentleman in disbelief as he stroked the velvet lapels of his jacket. "Never. The man has the Midas touch."

"Not anymore," returned a younger man with buck teeth and a soft chin.

The men of Brooks, previously scattered around the wood-paneled library, were pulled as if by centrifugal force into the conversation.

"Worse yet, his investors have gone down with him." More heads turned, and the conversation drew in a wider circle. "Saunders, Ogilthorpe, Blanche . . . All done for."

"Impossible," snorted the velvet jacket.

"Sad to say, but it's true," was the retort of a heretofore invisible man, who popped his head up from behind a newspaper. "I read it in yesterday's post. Jay Cooke and Co. has gone belly up. They could not meet the demands of their depositors. And all the investors are out of pocket entirely."

"That doesn't mean he was so foolish as to put all his money in."

"But he *was*, my friend. He *did*. He talked to me about it in this very room," said a slick man with a thin moustache.

"He said it was the safest investment he'd ever made; he'd stake his life on it. And by God, he did." There was a chorus of muffled groans punctuated by a few guffaws. The latter came from men who clearly thought James Drayton was a conceited aggrandizer. With a dismissive grunt, the man once again disappeared behind the pages of the *Telegraph*. Only a white wisp of smoke signaled he had any interest in the conversation and conjecture that continued to fill the room.

"A drink, Mr. St. John?" asked a waiter, who had silently appeared at Crispin's elbow. He ordered scotch and water and found an empty chair along the edge of the room where he could watch and listen unobserved.

A footman placed another log in the fire, which crackled and spat angrily, seeming to remind everyone that the conversation had become too public. The expected hushed tones of the library resumed as men broke off into smaller, quieter groups, their exchanges muffled by the heavy curtains and the even heavier clouds of cigar smoke. Crispin could only catch the tiniest fragments of sentences.

"I knew from the start . . . very unwise."

"His father would never have conducted himself in such a manner."

"Do you think he'll still marry her?"

Crispin's ears perked at this last line. He pulled a book from the shelf and feigned concentration on an arbitrary page while straining to hear more.

"Doubtful. He's a cad. Besides, Westmoor didn't leave him a cent . . ."

"The property's worth a fortune, but it costs a fortune to keep it up . . ."

"That's the curse of the peerage, all the expense but none of the means to support it . . ."

". . . perhaps Drayton wasn't so foolish after all. Just unlucky."

"She's the unlucky one really. Beautiful girl." The two men walked toward the double doors leading to the gaming room, and their conversation was swallowed by the din within.

Was it true? Had Lord Drayton lost his fortune? Who had he taken down with him? Crispin recognized some of the names. Blanche—it was familiar. Saunders? Yes, he remembered Saunders. A sort of gentleman farmer. Crispin remembered feeling bad for his wife, who had looked so out of place at Drayton Manor. Even now he could hear Cassandra chattering on animatedly about her father and his friends as they had trotted up Coad Hill and traversed the white hills of Blandford.

Was all that gone? The stables, the horses, the endless hills, would they be sold off?

What about his Aunt? Would she stay on? Could she? And Cassandra? Had Bedford really deserted her?

The image of Cassandra's bright, fresh face devastated by the loss of her family fortune and of Bedford flashed before his eyes. It was followed quickly by one of Rosalind's coy smiles and soft touches. A tight knot began to form in Crispin's stomach.

He resolved to call on the Draytons and find out for himself but squashed the thought. It was too vulgar. He had been in England for the better part of a year and had not called. To do so now would be out of the question. Crispin didn't want to join the other vultures hovering over their misfortune.

CHAPTER 23

Cassandra hadn't seen her father in hours. Nobody had. She had checked with Marjorie and Ruby and Cook, and they had not seen him since the morning papers had been delivered. After pacing uselessly around the drawing room, she decided to call for a tray of cold dinner to bring to his room as an excuse to check on him.

Cassandra tapped at the door. There was no answer. So, she turned the knob and let herself in.

The room was oddly quiet, and the fresh smell of cigarette smoke hung in the air. She looked around for its source but saw no feather-like tail curling up in the dim glow of the lamps. The atmosphere was stifling and still and the only sound was the low ticking of the clock on the mantle. Then she noticed a cool breeze. The door to the balcony was open and there, barely perceptible in the London gloom, was the outline of Lord Drayton's figure.

He seemed to be staring out across the city skyline. It was lonely, black, and unforgiving. The ruddy light from the streetlamps and figures silhouetted in other houses merely punctuated the loneliness. Across the street a solitary man sat in his library turning the pages of titleless book, a butler turned out a light, a silent lamplighter worked his way through the quiet street. Untouched by the ruin of Lord James Drayton, they went about their business, each wrapped in their own lives and troubles.

Then Cassandra saw it, at first just a sliver of reflected light, the glint of metal in the gloom. But as her eyes adjusted to the dark, shapes emerged like paper cutouts from the black canvas of the night. A revolver. Held snug to his temple. His arm, bent upon itself, trembling. His body shivered and shook.

Cassandra wanted to cry out, to run toward him. She saw herself leaping across the carpet, flying through the French doors, knocking the gun from his hand and down to the street below. Instead, she did nothing. Like a stone fixed in the ground, she could not move.

He clicked back the hammer, which in the silence, echoed across the room. She gasped and dropped the tray. The sound of china shattering exploded like shrapnel. The spell was broken. He turned with a jerk and in so doing let his hand fall to his side. The gun dropped with a thud. Her feet became unstuck, and Cassandra lunged toward him.

"Papa, Papa!" She clutched his shoulders.

"Shhh, shhh." How was it that he was comforting her? "Shhh, my dear, shhh."

"You can't do it! You can't do such a terrible thing!"

"I won't. I am an utter wretch and a ruin and," he sighed heavily, "a coward."

"Promise me you won't do this. You can't do this to me, or to Emma."

"I won't. I promise," he whispered. Together, they walked back into the room, and he dropped into his leather chesterfield. Cassandra poured him a whisky and sat down. He took the glass, absently turning the amber liquid around and around before downing it in one gulp.

"I have been such a fool. Such a colossal fool." His words communicated something final and irrevocable. In all her life, Cassandra had never seen her father like this.

"It's all gone, my dear. I'm ruined beyond imagination. You must be thinking of your words of caution last December. About mortgaging Drayton Manor. You were right. It's lost to us now. The bank will repossess it. All because I bet our fortune on a losing horse."

"But Papa, surely there is a way to recover some of your investment?" Cassandra had moved to kneel beside her father and clasp his clammy hand. She couldn't believe rational words came to her, given what she had just witnessed.

"Jay Cooke & Company is gone. All of our money is lost. Now, we have to salvage what we can." He shook his head and closed his eyes. Dejected and shrunken, the ebullience and energy that had characterized his every move were gone. The fire of his ambition, his love for life, his zest extinguished. The future, which had once seemed to open expansively at his touch, closed fast. Cassandra's heart was breaking. Her father had spent his life rebuilding the Drayton family, and he had done it for her.

What could she do to help? Though she was young, she felt she would do anything.

CHAPTER 24

The day was fresh and cold, and a crisp wind seemed to have swept yesterday's thick smog away. Old ladies were turning out, cloaked in fur, sitting haughtily in their landaus, and running myriad useless errands. Crispin closed his front door behind him and stepped out into the busy masses. Though he was unsure of his purpose, he knew his direction: 37 Grosvenor Square. He had written the address countless times in letters to his aunt, but this was the first time he would be calling on the Drayton home.

Crispin's pace slowed as he neared his destination. After hearing the news at Brooks, he'd confirmed the particulars of the situation with Archie. It was indeed dire and, though May and even Lady Douglas, had tried to be helpful, it was clear that Cassandra was devastated. During his time in London, Crispin had tactfully avoided meeting her. He'd confined himself to the male sphere of his office and club and had chosen not to enjoy the season despite May's countless attempts to entice him. It had seemed easier that way, and there would be time enough to embrace society when Rosalind arrived. But now, his relatively reclusive world would fall open.

How would his Aunt Emma receive him? Crispin justified his visit by telling himself that he would be a friendly face when others had turned their backs. Yet since arriving in London months prior, he had not called on Emma as it would have resulted in an encounter with Cassandra. He had not even notified Emma that he was in town. And now here he was rushing over, unannounced. Crispin didn't have the slightest idea of what he would say or what he would find or how he would offer comfort. The news of Lord

Drayton's misfortunes was relatively new, so he suspected that the family would still be there, hunkering down for the social storm that was sure to ensue. But perhaps they had already fled, leaving Crispin to find traces of their hasty exit—empty, echoing rooms that still smelled vaguely of perfume and fresh ashes in the fireplaces.

He crossed Avery Row and turned the corner. Lost as he was in his thoughts, Crispin nearly knocked over a woman, who rushed along, head bowed. His hat tumbled off his head and, bending to pick it up, Crispin sputtered apologies. The woman was oddly quiet in response. When he looked up, he knew why. It was his Aunt Emma. A strange expression danced across her face, a mixture of relief and excitement, fear and confusion.

"Crispin? Is it you?"

"Yes. It is." He bowed. "I was coming to call on you."

Emma Fairfax moved as if to embrace him, but her reserved nature got the better of her and she pulled her shawl tightly around her neck.

"Unfortunately, the timing couldn't be worse. I'm in no position to receive you. But I am glad to see you. Truly glad. You look so well. The years have been kind." It was half question and half statement. When Crispin thought of the boy in too-short pants and a borrowed shirt and coat, slinking in shame from Drayton Manor, he was tempted to blush. "I did not realize you were back in London." She reached forward as if to touch his arm, but quickly pulled back. "I only wish . . ." her voice started to trail off. Her complexion was wan and her cheeks drawn.

"I intended to write sooner and tell you of my arrival, but I've been so busy settling in and working. Mr. Middleton's business keeps me occupied, and then . . . well, I heard the news." It felt right to come out and say it. She clearly could not have brought it up, and it would have been awkward for both of them to let her manufacture reasons why she could not see Crispin. After all these years, he'd envisioned their meeting as a warm and lighthearted moment between relations separated by time and distance, but the reality of the Draytons' affairs made their reunion stilted and strained.

"Oh." She sighed. "Where did you hear it?"

"It's in the papers. And men at the club were talking." Crispin could see her face tighten. "I'm terribly sorry for the family. How is Lord Drayton?"

"Not well. Not well at all. We were to have gone back to Drayton Manor for the grouse, but there will be no season now. He needs to be here, in London, to monitor the situation. Not that he can do much. Now, I fear we'll stay here for the winter and perhaps longer. And every day will be a reminder of this nightmare." She shook her head sadly.

Crispin was shocked by how forthcoming Miss Fairfax was. This sad turn of events seemed to have unlocked the dam of her reserve. Normally, it would be inappropriate to pry, but emboldened by her candor, he asked, "Is there any hope of a recovery of his investment?"

"I couldn't say for sure. He seems hopeless enough. Banks have inquired into his mortgages, asking for financial statements and for monies he does not have. His friends do not call—even those who invested alongside him. So, he is left to wrestle with his own thoughts."

Crispin struggled for something comforting to say. He had to restrain himself from clasping her arm, knowing she would not appreciate the contact.

"We've let go of the staff at Drayton Manor, and here some will have to go as well." It was odd to hear her speak of "we" as if she were mistress of the house. Crispin wondered if she was to be kept on, or was she no longer considered staff. It was a question he could not ask.

"How is Miss Drayton?"

"As well as can be expected. She is quite the lady now. You would not recognize her. Well, perhaps you would." Her eyes brightened with the hint of teasing but dimmed again as if a cloud had swept in overhead. "She is more serious. She knows the world is not the steady and delightful place she was born into."

"I think she knew that even as a girl. She was less innocent than her father imagined." Crispin said. His boldness surprised them both. "I'm sorry. I spoke out of turn. I don't know what I'm saying."

"Perhaps you are right, Crispin. You saw a side of her that . . ." She drifted off again. "But those days are gone. Best not to dredge up the past."

"If I can be of any assistance—"

She seemed to recoil at the suggestion, reluctant to be the recipient of charity, especially from her nephew.

"You have shown great kindness to me, and I would like to return the favor." Crispin handed her his card, confident that she would not contact him.

"It *has* been nice to see you." She patted Crispin's hand and walked away, pulling her shawl around her shoulders, leaving him standing awkwardly on the street with no excuse to knock on the door and no opportunity to see Cassandra.

"Mr. Oliver! I distinctly remember telling my son's man of business that we would only be seeing homes that were five stories at least!" Lady Douglas shook her purple reticule imperiously at the beleaguered agent. "Is this even four stories?" She asked the question of Crispin in horror. As if renting a four-story house in a well-heeled neighborhood was a dreaded fate. Crispin first met Lady Douglas at Archie's house just after he'd decided that his last trip to London would be a permanent one.

Not one to mince words, Lady Douglas announced, within minutes of meeting him, "I hear you are renting rooms in Piccadilly, Mr. St. John. You must find a proper home. Now, I know you are a handsome rake and a dear friend of Archie's,"—she smiled warmly—"but appearances matter in London. When you two were running wild in India anything was permitted, but if we are to make you an established gentleman in society you must play the part!" Her manner was so charming, Crispin didn't mind her direct words. She was the mirror image of May, or rather May was of her. Lady Douglas must have been stunning in her youth.

"Not to worry. We'll find you the perfect place and one that's not too far from here, so you won't get lonely. You know," she continued, "it's too bad you are spoken for. I mean, you would be a tremendous catch to the right young lady. Archie tells me that you are not just Mr. Middleton's employee, but that you are his partner."

"Mama," Archie had chimed in. "There is no need to pry into Crispin's position."

"I'm not prying, Archibald. This is all widely known." She turned to Crispin. "A partner. Well, that's very respectable."

"Yes, Lady Douglas. I am grateful to Mr. Middleton, who has taken me under his wing. Thanks to him, I find myself able to set up an establishment for Miss Middleton."

"Yes, yes. Now let's discuss that. It takes some time to find the right place, so we mustn't rush you. While you are looking for something more permanent, you should let. Something in a fashionable area, but not more than you can manage as an affianced bachelor. You know there are some lovely houses on Green Street. I'm going to call over to Mr. Channing, who manages Archie's business affairs. He will know what's what, and we will find you the perfect way station until you are settled!" She had been true to her word and arranged today's house-hunting expedition.

"This is the third house we have seen and it's entirely unsuitable." She turned to the waifish agent, who was clearly intimidated by Lady Douglas. "Mr. St. John must have a fifth floor for the servants he will employ."

"Yes, your ladyship. Well, in that case, I think you'll be liking the last house. It's just down the lane from here. Perhaps you should call your carriage." He looked at Crispin imploringly. Archie had bowed out of the excursion, so it was just Lady Douglas and Crispin. What a pair they made.

"Excuse me, sir! Am I so much in my dotage that I can't walk down the lane? Crispin, tell the driver to follow us." She stomped out of the house with Mr. Oliver trailing in her wake. In the sunlight, Green Street was exceptionally picturesque. Over the last five hours, they had seen homes at Bryanston Street, Upper Brook Street, Portman Square, and Park Street. They all were merging into one in Crispin's mind, but Green Street, only a few blocks long and running perpendicular to Hyde Park, felt like a small village within the city. Few carriages passed and the odors of London did not linger, Crispin noted as he took in the crisp fall air. It was certainly more peaceful than his office at Fleet Street.

"Here we are, your ladyship." Oliver stopped not 200 feet down the road in front of a tidy brick house with freshly painted white windows. Its grand mahogany door was framed in limestone and the entrance was just two steps from the street level.

"The house is five stories in addition to the kitchen, so I think it will be an adequate amount of room for Mr. St. John and his bride." Mr. Oliver began, consulting his notebook. "The family has holdings in Jamaica and have been away for some time. The house can be let for one or two years depending on your preference."

"Two years, minimum." Lady Douglas declared with authority. "It may take time for you to find a home you wish to purchase, and this will give your bride a chance to become better acquainted with London. What do you think Mr. St. John?"

Five stories and a kitchen—Crispin couldn't imagine what he would do with so many rooms. It was not as grand as Rosalind was accustomed to, but she would appreciate that there was space to entertain, her favorite and primary occupation.

"I like the look of it. Let's go in."

Lady Douglas was thrilled, and Mr. Oliver was relieved.

"I'm sure this is the right one. Afterward, we'll go back to my home, and you and Mr. Oliver can discuss the particulars."

Mr. Oliver opened the door to a handsome, marble-lined foyer. "Ah some furnishings, that's good. But you'll undoubtedly need to supplement . . ."

As he followed them inside, Crispin admired the airy entryway and thought with an odd sense of pleasure that it was only a few blocks from 37 Grosvenor Square.

Just two weeks after settling the arrangements to let the house with Mr. Oliver, Green Street was now home. Crispin laid his hat on the entry table and checked for letters; a small ivory stack awaited him. The smell of a rich roast wafted up from the kitchen below. Though heady, it was a stark contrast to the pungent spices he had grown accustomed to in Calcutta.

"Good evening, Mr. St. John," Nora said as she opened the door to the study. "Did you have a good day, sir?"

"Yes, thank you."

Nora was part of Crispin's small household—two maids and a cook. Lady Douglas thought he should get a butler, but it had seemed excessive. Rosalind would sort that out when she arrived.

"Some letters arrived, sir. I put them in the library. Will you be going out again tonight? Cook is preparing a roast."

"No, I'll stay at home tonight, lots of work to do," Crispin said, absently rifling through a stack of papers that littered his desk.

"You're always working, sir," she said with motherly concern. "But I expect that will change when your bride arrives. No time for all this endless toiling then . . ." She chuckled, looking at the islands of papers that dotted his desk. Nora was a pleasant woman in her late 30s. Most would find her a little too familiar, though Crispin suspected that she was responding to his lack of formality. Crispin treated his staff more as equals than most employers, feeling rather like an imposter in the role of master of the house. Nevertheless, he thought Rosalind would like Nora. Lady Douglas agreed, particularly given her homely face.

"I'll take some claret when you have a moment, please."

"Right away sir." And she was off.

The study was a warm room, with rich mahogany panels and heavy red silk drapery. Crispin sat down at the large wooden desk and sorted through the day's letters. Most were business-related, though he spotted one from Rosalind, which he set aside. He put orders and invoices in separate piles and quickly skimmed a new contract. He would read it more carefully later, as was his habit.

Before Nora returned, he took a strong draft of whisky, then opened Rosalind's letter.

"*My dearest Crispin,*" it began.

Rosalind had a flair for flowery language and detailed description. It was unfortunate that her subject matter didn't often match her skill. She commenced with warm greetings and longings to see him and proceeded with frustrations about India, the heat, the servants, the fashion, the assorted company, as usual.

> *The weather as always is insufferably hot, I think more so since you left this last time. I have been forced to change gowns more than is my custom during the day (three times as you know). And since there is no one worth seeing me in these*

lovely gowns, it's all for nothing! Oh, how I long for the cool breezes of London
and the dinners and soirees with handsome people and beautiful frocks. I hope
you are not frightfully bored without me, working and taking tea with Archie.

Just think, in the new year, we'll be there together—as Mr. and Mrs. St.
John. It will be so exciting! When I arrive, we will dazzle London!

Crispin chuckled. True to form, Rosalind was overly confident in her
ability to charm anyone in any locale. He tried unsuccessfully to envision her
dazzling May and Lady Douglas at a ball. Despite her hopes, Crispin doubted
her limited social circle in India had prepared her for the intricacies of
London society. Her letter continued with descriptions of the latest
"disastrous" soiree at the Cummings' home in Calcutta.

Mrs. Cummings, who you recall is both dreary and plump, wore the most
horrible gown ever. It was made for London and was terribly heavy, so she sweated
through the silk like a greasy piggy. How awful!

Crispin hoped that Rosalind had maintained her composure at the event.
Mr. Cummings was a key business associate and his aid in transport had been
critical to their efforts to get their product to Manchester with efficiency and
speed.

The one saving grace of the party was that Colonel Geary of the 4th Light
Dragoon Regiment was there. Do you remember him? His commission in
Calcutta was extended just a few months ago and he has been touring the country
with his regiment. Did you know, he's a native of Gloucester and the third son
of the Earl of Cottingham? As you can imagine, we have much in common and
found a better conversation between ourselves than the rest of the group. I do hope
he will find himself invited to more gatherings as he is a welcome relief from this
dreary set.

The letter had ended as it had begun, and Crispin turned, with mild relief,
back to the contract for a second read-through, ready to engross himself in
more substantive matters.

CHAPTER 25

October 1873

The ladies looked resplendent in their evening gowns. Cassandra had never before appreciated the craftsmanship, the fireworks of beads that burst in symmetric patterns down the long silk skirts, the tumbling bouquets, and the kaleidoscope of colors. She'd never pondered the hours that went into each lady's costume, from the tips of her satin slippers to the crown of her head. Plaits and curls, pinned and wrapped, dotted with jeweled combs and exotic feathers. Lady India Worthington, the hostess, wore a beautiful indigo gown, punctuated with midnight gray sunbursts. Lady Lydia Hastings looked like a tropical bird, a bold green and royal blue peacock feather tucked between the locks of silver-gray hair.

Eugenia led her niece through the foyer and up the grand staircase. Their hellos were uncharacteristically hasty.

"Oh, Lady Worthington, my dear Lydia. Charmed to see you tonight. Cassie and I must rush. Cassandra told the Duke of Westmoor we would meet him, but I will be back to talk at length." Kiss. Kiss. And so they jumped from one *dear* friend to another, never stopping for conversation, never lingering long enough to make others feel uncomfortable in their presence. Cassandra wondered what people said as they passed. Did their conversation turn to her father? It must have. She was sure that whispered remarks traveled from one lady to the next. *Did you see Lady Eugenia Gray and Miss Cassandra Drayton? Pity. A great pity.* Perhaps they were less kind. *Why ever did they come? Don't they have the good sense to stay at home and ride out this storm in private?* Perhaps they were wise to Eugenia and Cassandra's true motive.

Normally, they would never have attended any Little Season ball or party, as they would be at Drayton Manor setting up for the autumn grouse. But there would be no hunts this year. And Aunt Eugenia was determined that Cassandra's position should and could be secured in society despite the collapse of her father's scheme.

Tonight, she insisted that they find the Duke as quickly as possible, and so she rushed with steady and inelegant purpose, glancing around the banquet table and the ballroom, looking every which way. Aunt Eugenia was certain that once he and Cassandra were together all would be happily resolved.

"You must stay by his side, my dear. It is about proximity. If you are near him, he'll stand by you," she whispered into Cassandra's ear. She did not go so far as to say, he cannot leave you once society is reminded of your attachment. To her, it was a matter of manners. Her aunt could not comprehend that even those of good breeding could be moved to breech the walls of politeness and propriety.

Though Cassandra was much younger than her aunt, she felt more cynical about the world. She saw with stark clarity that financial interests and embarrassment were powerful motivators. They had their claws in those born to the manor, just as deeply as they did in those from lower circles. Aunt Eugenia's upbringing, shivering through Drayton Manor's more ramshackle years, before her marriage to Lord Gray, and before her enterprising brother restored the family estate, should have taught her that, but she had revised the world, editing it to suit her vision, creating order out of chaos and comfort out of instability. Cassandra both pitied and envied her for her narrow-minded view. It limited her world but protected her from harsh realities.

Music drifted through the Worthingtons' elegant Mayfair home like smoke, getting thicker and louder as they approached the ballroom. Young couples spun across the dance floor, floating and turning. They bobbed up and down like snowflakes pushed by the breeze. A sea of white and pale pink, punctuated by the occasional rich red or deep violet gown of matrons and dowagers. Like many of the younger ladies, Cassandra wore white—it was her third season, but she was still unmarried (though, Aunt Eugenia declared, she would not be single for long). Cassandra's gown was from Paris, ordered two years earlier. She had never worn it.

Earlier that evening Cassandra had slipped it on with Miss Fairfax's help. Even the act of dressing had been laden with nostalgia. She was bowed down with the sobering knowledge that all of this—the new gowns, the balls, the social maneuverings—was frivolous. She would never again approach them with the same carefree spirit of the past two seasons. Cassandra ran her hand over the delicate rosettes that danced along the neckline and climbed up the edges of her capped sleeves before diving down the back and cascading along the train.

A young woman with bright red hair caught her eye. As she spun in graceful circles, she leaned back in her partner's arms with near illicit intimacy and let her hand run seductively along his lapel. It felt almost voyeuristic to watch her dance so unconcerned with the watchful eyes of the old gossips. Who was she? She threw her burning head back and laughed with glee. Then Cassandra noticed the girl's partner. It was Henry. He smiled eagerly at this young and reckless nymph in his arms.

Cassandra waited for the heat of embarrassment to climb up her face, sure she would feel the burning in her cheeks. But she didn't. Nor did she feel the icy chill of rejection. She felt nothing. An empty space where feeling should have been.

Luckily, Henry did not see her, nor did her Aunt Eugenia see him.

"Aunt, he's not here. Let's get some champagne," Cassandra urged her. "We'll do another circle of the party. I'm sure we'll run into him as we do." She led Aunt Eugenia out of the ballroom, nodding to those they called friends as they left.

For the rest of the evening, Cassandra worked to avoid Lord Bedford, and until the end of the evening, was successful in her efforts. When finally, Aunt Eugenia had gotten tired of their constant movement, Cassandra took her hand and led her to a seat.

"Here, you rest for a moment. I will see to our cloaks."

"Thank you, my dear. I am so sorry that he is not here." Her words were filled with genuine sadness for her niece. As Cassandra turned the corner, she spotted the Duke and his dance partner sitting cozily on a settee. They were close, their bodies touching beneath the barrier of their evening dress. At that moment, Henry gazed up and saw her. Their eyes locked. They were stone still. It was as if the rest of the party fell away—the music, the tinkling of glass, the laughter, the chatter, all of it faded into the air.

His blue-grey eyes were filled with pity, but not regret. He did not move toward Cassandra, nor did he separate himself in embarrassment or hurry away from his redheaded dance partner. Instead, Cassandra was the one who turned around. She left knowing that a great change had occurred and that he was free.

In the morning, Cassandra wandered into the parlor, feeling purposeless and restless. She was glad she had gone to the ball that prior evening, even if it was to be her last—even if it was an awkward catalyst to a final encounter with the Duke of Westmoor. She would think back on those nights with their free-flowing champagne and flickering candelabras as happy days and remember herself as another girl.

Still, that left today to face, and the day after, and the day after that. She fluffed a pillow and ran her hand along the piping on the chaise lounge and debated sitting down, but ultimately decided to return to her room. As she turned toward the stairs a flash of ivory caught her eye and she saw that the morning's letters had come in. There was a small stack of correspondence, mostly from solicitors and agents addressed to Lord Drayton. Cassandra put them aside, she would read them later. Owing to his current state, she was now managing all of her father's correspondence. One letter was addressed to her. She recognized the crisp script. Her heart sank as she opened it, knowing what it would say.

Dear Miss Drayton, it began.

Cassandra's eyes dropped to the bottom, only one page.

Your Servant, Henry.

She barely needed to read the words. *I'm sure you can understand . . . Circumstances have changed . . . disengage from our understanding . . . .*

After the ball last night, it was no surprise, but the sharp finality of his words stung, much more than their silent exchange had. A heavy weight fell on her shoulders. All that her father and Aunt Eugenia had hoped for her was dashed in just three weeks. May's warning to her when she had first seen Bedford in London had not fallen on deaf ears. He was a fortune-hunter, as so many from the *great families* were. He sought to bolster up his crumbling grand estate by marrying money, and Cassandra had accepted what she would bring to their arrangement. Now, he would find another heiress, whose money was secure so his fortune would rest on steady ground.

A noise interrupted her thoughts. Ruby was crying in the hallway. She let out a few quiet sobs, drew in a great breath of air, and was silent. Cassandra could imagine the maid wiping her tears with the back of her sleeve, dabbing the corners of her eyes, and then pinching her cheeks in the hope that no one would notice. But Cassandra did. For days now Ruby had been red-eyed. Cassandra knew she was to blame. She had let Jane, Ruby's best friend, go a fortnight prior.

Cassandra had discussed it with Emma at length—who would stay on and who would go? Neither of them wanted to send anyone away, but they couldn't continue to support a full household. Jane, who acted as Cassandra's lady's maid and chief courier for her secret correspondence with Crispin; Marjorie, the newest addition; and Paul, the second footman, were the first to go.

Cassandra didn't feel at all good about it. In fact, she felt awful and trapped. She could barely look Ruby in the eye. How could she ask Ruby to brush her hair and wash her frocks, when Cassandra couldn't even assure her that her place was safe. As much as she wanted it to be, Cassandra knew that without a sudden reversal of fortune, Ruby too would have to return home, wherever that was.

Ruby entered quietly.

"I have mended your dress, my Lady." She held up a rose-colored gown that Cassandra had ordered from Worth's last season. Along the hem were airy layers of decorative ruffles, which seemed to catch on the foot of every desk and corner. In the last year, Jane had had to replace at least half of them. Now the job fell to Ruby along with her other responsibilities.

"Thank you, Ruby."

She smiled sadly and looked out the window at the gray London skyline.

"Ruby, do you know where Jane lives?"

"She said she was going home to her mother's house on Stew Lane. She'll look for another position from there, I suppose."

"So, she's well taken care of?"

"I suppose you could say that. She's one of six children, My Lady. The oldest. I suspect she's a help to her mother." Ruby's expression tightened. It spoke words of its own. *With five brothers and sisters and no father, you can imagine money's tight, can't you? She would be more help if she had some wages to send home.*

"I see."

Ruby picked up a brush and started to run it through Cassandra's hair.

"I can do that myself. I'm sure you have much more important things to do."

The maid put the brush down, gave a little curtsey, and moved brusquely for the door.

"Ruby?"

"Yes, My Lady."

Cassandra was tempted to say something assuring. That had always been her way. Now, she had to learn to bite her tongue. "Never mind. It's nothing."

After Ruby left the room, Cassandra opened her jewelry box and rummaged through the drawers. Each bauble seemed significant. An emerald necklace from her sixteenth birthday; a black cameo of her mother's; pearls and more pearls; her grandmother's wedding ring; diamond chandelier earrings that she wore at her debut. From an early age, her father had showered her with these extravagances, gifts that should have gone to her mother. It bordered on inappropriate as Aunt Eugenia had often warned Lord Drayton. Even May, who had as rich a collection of finery as anyone, would ogle Cassandra's emeralds. Cassandra picked up each piece, holding it in her hands and running her thumb over the smooth stones, feeling the weight of gold chains. She wondered when she would have occasion to wear these dramatic jewels again.

The contrast in their circumstance hit her forcefully: Jane in a cramped flat on Stew Lane, while Cassandra, by all standards "ruined," sat surrounded by a fortune in gems at Grosvenor Square.

She must have something she could give Jane to help feed all those mouths. Cassandra picked up a pair of gold earrings. Little white cameos set in pale blue enamel nested in a circle of gold the size of a halfpenny. What did they cost? They couldn't have been cheap; her father never gave her cheap gifts, even her dolls were dressed in silks in the highest fashions from Paris. What would they bring at a pawnshop? Cassandra had never set foot in one. To her, they were fictional places concocted out of the minds of Charles Dickens and Anthony Trollop, but she knew, intellectually speaking, that they were real. Could she go to one? How would she find one? She could ask Ruby.

No. Ruby wouldn't know how to respond. And Cassandra could only imagine the reaction of the other servants: Braxton, Cook, the remaining maid, and footman. The shock of the question would reverberate throughout the house no less powerfully than a bolt of lightning. There would be panic, further questions about the stability of their jobs. God forbid her father or Aunt Eugenia found out. The embarrassment would be overwhelming. Perhaps she could go to Stew Lane, to Jane's home to give her the earrings. She would know what to do with them.

S tew Lane was a small, water-side street beyond Cheapside. It was a long walk from Grosvenor Square, so Cassandra asked the coachman to take her to the National Gallery, which was about halfway there. The rest of the distance, she would go on her own two feet. Cassandra couldn't tell Miss Fairfax as she would have scolded her and then insisted on accompanying her. So, she told Miss Fairfax and Aunt Eugenia that she was to meet May at the Gallery for the afternoon.

After Cassandra stepped into the hustle and bustle of Trafalgar Square, she waited a moment for the carriage to roll away and disappear around the corner. She counted to thirty, then walked toward Nelson's monument and crossed onto the Strand. In her hand, Cassandra held a small map she had scribbled quickly before leaving the house.

The streets were crowded and tight, and the further she traveled toward her destination, the more crowded and tighter they got. They were filled with dirty carts swerving and dodging each other, loose cargo tumbling into the gutter—a potato here and pebbles of coal there. The jostling wheels blended with the commercial calls of vendors—"onions, onions, get yer onions," "here's a pheasant, just caught," "lovely lady, don't you want a bolt of cloth, fine Indian cotton, just in from Calcutta?"—in a cacophonous, frantic drumbeat. At times Cassandra was rudely jostled and at times she drew curious glances. She stood out as a foreigner to these parts.

Finally, she reached the intersection of Newgate and Bread streets. She was close but doubts consumed her. How would Jane receive her former employer? What about Jane's mother? They wouldn't be happy to see the lady who had damaged their livelihood. They couldn't be.

Cassandra looked down at her clothes, her fur muff and her green velvet skirt shimmering like sunny water in contrast to the muck of the street. She reached up for her hat, which was perfectly cocked and decorated with ribbons and a fan of feathers. How stupid she was to think this was wise. She should have sent Ruby in her place, but Cassandra had wanted to do it herself. To be a savior with a little gift of expensive earrings. She felt pathetic as she faced the house, a ramshackle dwelling with a warped wooden façade that was covered in peeling white paint. There couldn't have been more than two or three rooms within. Just as she reached for the knocker, which was askew on the door front, Jane opened the door, clearly on her way out.

"My lady, whatever are you doing here?" Her high-pitched voice interrupted Cassandra's thoughts.

"I . . . I . . ." Cassandra stumbled indelicately. "I'm here to see you."

Her eyes lit up. Cassandra's heart sank. Jane thought she was going to ask her to come back to work. A little face peered out from behind her dirty calico skirts. "This is my brother. Joseph, say 'hello' to the lady."

"'ello." He appeared to be about five years old and had a sooty smear across his bony cheek, which Jane, suddenly embarrassed, tried to rub off with her thumb.

"I want to give you these. They're not much, but I thought they might help."

She looked inside the bag. "Thank you." Her expression was flat. It was clear Jane didn't know how these frivolous earrings would help.

"I'm sorry," Cassandra said dumbly and turned to walk away.

"Miss Cassandra, it's awfully nice of you to think of me. I am grateful." And she was, Cassandra could tell. "I know it's not your fault." Jane smiled a sympathetic half-smile. Her rosy skin tightened across high cheekbones communicating without words a combination of courage and a shared sense of humanity. Somehow it all made Cassandra feel worse. Tears welled up in her eyes as she scurried back toward the land of limestone mansions and broad, tree-lined streets.

CHAPTER 26

It was getting late, and Crispin still had work to do, so he politely excused himself from the Douglases' company. They had spent the better part of the afternoon chatting in Archie's library. Though the room was imposing with dark wood paneling and a massive mahogany desk, May's presence somehow made it feel light and cozy.

"You can't go yet, Crispin, not before telling May about the Kandrapoor disaster."

"You can't be serious, Archie. Do you want me to bore your sister to death?"

"I'm not bored at all. This is the most excitement I've had in weeks. And you're a brilliant storyteller. Do go on." May moved jauntily around the room and flounced down on the sofa fanning her skirts with a dramatic gesture.

"I wish I could Margaret, but I am afraid that I'm that most banal of all creatures, a working man, and thus I must wish you a good day. Besides, Archie does a much better job weaving that tale. And by weave, I mean expand and distort the truth."

"You're no fun. If you don't stay, I won't forgive you and I'll ignore you at the Gregorys' ball."

"I'm almost gullible enough to believe that. But, dear Margaret, I know you are too kind-hearted to snub me."

"Well, I might not snub you, but I won't introduce—or rather reintroduce you—to the most beautiful girl in the room."

"May, Crispin is an engaged man. You can't entice him with other ladies.

Besides, you ought to be saving your loveliest friends for me. Who is this beauty?"

"I'm not going to tell you. You are an inveterate flirt, and Crispin needs to have some fun. We can't expect him to be a wallflower at the ball. Crispin, you must stay. You'll regret it if you don't."

"I know I will."

Nonetheless, Crispin stood and took her hand, bowing slightly, while May pretended to be angry. Like her brother, May had an effortless charm. She was careless with her remarks and could tease and flirt without raising suspicions about her intentions or causing a stir amongst the older generation. She had extended a filial warmth toward Crispin, letting him into her circle as very few others had done. Only those most confident in their position could take such risks on a friend with no history and no social standing, and Crispin was thankful for her doing so. It was due to her and Archie's total acceptance of him that the doors of London society had begun to swing open.

"It has been a lovely visit, Margaret, and I promise on our next meeting I will regale you with stories of my heroics and your brother's misadventures. Consider this visit a prologue to a longer tale."

May and Archie finally capitulated to Crispin's leaving them and rose from their seats, walking with him to the foyer, where their butler, Tollingham, stood with his hat and coat. Tollingham was either a master of anticipation, or more likely a skilled eavesdropper, listening for his cue. That is the life of servants; unseen and unheard, yet all-seeing and all-hearing.

"Well, it has been diverting. I intend to keep you to your promise, so make sure you dream up all the dramatic details."

"Your wish is my command." Crispin popped his hat on as Tollingham opened the door. Then he stepped out, right into Cassandra Drayton. There she stood, hand raised. In the act of reaching for the knocker, which had been pulled abruptly away from her, she inadvertently hit his chin. It had been years since Crispin had last seen her and a year since they last wrote to each other. Yet, he had thought of her so often that in his mind's eye, he knew exactly what she looked like.

Flustered, she avoided making eye contact.

"Oh my goodness, I am so sorry. I haven't hurt you, have I?" For a moment, caught so off guard, she did not seem to recognize Crispin.

"No, not at all. I'm fine. Miss Drayton, what a surprise."

"Crispin?" Her eyes widened.

"Cassie? Oh, Cassie is that you? I'm so glad you are here. Crispin is such a beast. He wouldn't stay and entertain us, even when I tried to bribe him with a chance to dance with you at the Gregory's. But now that you are here, and he's seen what he's missing . . ."

Crispin sucked in his breath. Cassandra was as beautiful as ever, more so. Blond curls framed her face, and her eyes shone in afternoon sunlight. Crispin had wondered if his imaginings had built her up into an impossible beauty. But in the flesh, she was true to his vision.

From the corner of his eye, Crispin could see Archie's inadvertent perusal of Cassandra. Though she was his sister's dearest friend, he was a long-standing admirer of the fairer sex.

"Of course, you know each other already from another life." May said, "But you are both so much changed, like fine wine better with age." She laughed.

"Yes, Crispin is an old friend," Cassandra said earnestly as she embraced May. "We have not seen each other in a long, long time." With that, she eliminated any questions about where and how their friendship took shape and the Douglases were none the wiser about the intricacies of their connection and their extended correspondence.

"Damnation!" Archie bellowed. Startled, May and Cassandra both jumped. "I forgot I have your coat upstairs, the one you lent me the other day."

May cocked her head to the side wondering what on earth Archie had gotten up to that he needed to borrow Crispin's coat. Tollingham moved toward the stairs to retrieve the coat but Archie stopped him.

"I've got it Tollingham. I could use the exercise." He bounded up the stairs two at a time, passing Lady Douglas, who moved with as much slow elegance as her son moved with athletic haste.

"May," she called to her daughter, not fully conscious of the comings and goings of her children's guests. "I need you desperately to help me decide upon the menu for Saturday's dinner. Your uncle is coming and, after that last battle with gout, I can't remember what it is he can and cannot eat."

"Coming mother." Turning to Cassie apologetically, May assured her she would be right back. When Tollingham excused himself as well with Cassandra's cloak, Crispin and Cassandra stood awkwardly in the foyer alone.

Crispin seized the opportunity. "Miss Drayton, it really is wonderful to see you. I know it's been a difficult time for your family, and I want you to know that I called at Grosvenor Square."

"You did? When?" Her tone was distracted and slightly defensive. She didn't look him in the eye but rather busied herself by smoothing her gown, her brow slightly furrowed.

"Last week, but I ran into my aunt just as I arrived, and she said it wasn't a good time."

Cassandra had moved to the gilt-framed mirror at the entrance of the house to check her reflection. Her pale skin was taut. Crispin drew closer to her but resisted the urge to put his hand on her shoulder in comfort. He stood behind her and held her green eyes in the reflection. There was a profound sadness in them, and they clouded over with tears, which she quickly brushed away before spinning around to face him.

"She's quite right you know, it's never a good time to call these days. It's a gloomy house, Crispin. I can't imagine why you'd want to stop by, except perhaps to revel in our ruin," she said with a biting edge.

"Cassandra please," Crispin spread both arms out. "We're old friends. I just wanted to see if I could offer any help."

Cassandra held her hand up to refuse him. "Crispin. The situation is quite beyond help. I appreciate your concern but I'm sure there is nothing anyone can do, least of all you."

"But—" He was cut off by the return of May, followed by Tollingham.

"I knew you wouldn't be able to leave once you saw her," May called out in delight. "Now stay for tea!"

Crispin looked at Cassandra. Her expression had not changed, signaling their conversation was over. He made hasty excuses to May and took his leave. He would collect his coat another time.

"Mr. St. John, were you planning to accompany me to Liverpool to meet the latest shipment?" Thompson, Crispin's clerk, stood at the door wrapped in his greatcoat and hat.

"Yes, Thompson. I'm just finishing this letter and then I will join you. Has the coach arrived?"

"You know it really isn't necessary, sir. I'm sure I can manage it. I've done so before."

"Of course, you can manage it." Crispin knew Thompson was a very able clerk who had done an excellent job these past months. "I'm not concerned with handling the shipment, but I do need to speak to the captain on certain matters."

"Well, we should be leaving then. We don't want to miss the train."

"Alright. I'll meet you outside. At least I won't be delayed putting on my coat. It's so cold in here I can barely hold my pen!" Though it was late November, the fires had not yet been lit. Not wanting extraneous expenses, Crispin had held off on buying coal for as long as possible. He knew this was not something Middleton would have done, but it seemed unnecessary to heat the whole floor when there was just his and one clerk's comfort to think of.

Thompson chuckled. "I'll engage someone tomorrow to see to the heating. I'm thinking all those years in India made you vulnerable to the cold . . ." His voice trailed off as he left the room.

Crispin wasn't in the habit of writing to Rosalind while in the office, but he'd received another letter since the last and needed to ensure that this letter made it aboard *The Calcutta Rose* for speedy transport to India. His letter seemed sadly short compared to her flowing prose.

My dearest Rosalind,

Please forgive my delay in responding to your last letter. I have undertaken a great deal of work to set us up in London and hope you will be pleased by the progress I have made in finding us a proper home. You mentioned Belgravia in your last letter . . ..

Rosalind had gone to great lengths to explain that residences on Belgrave Square were the most fashionable these days. She had written: *I've had this from Colonel Geary, my dear, Belgrave Square is where we must live if we are to be considered fashionable at all. Dear Geary is so knowledgeable, having spent a great deal more time in London than we. We should take his counsel. He also said yesterday, as we took tea at Auckland's, that if we have the means, which of course we do, we should consider a box at the opera.* Her letter meandered on, filled with the assurance of the uninformed. Crispin knew he would need to educate her gently.

You mentioned Belgravia in your last letter. Let me assure you I have inquired after and viewed several houses there but did not think them as suitable as those in Mayfair. Lady Douglas recommended that we let a house first and as her advice has been indispensable, I have secured a suitable home on Green Street. It is a very fine house in the Georgian style with a large parlor and even a ballroom for entertaining. Once you are here, we can begin looking for a house to purchase.

I do not mean to discount the opinion of Colonel Geary, whom I hope I am fortunate enough to meet, as you have recommended him by your continued acquaintance, but I do believe that we must heed Lady Douglas's counsel in this. She and her family have shown us great kindness, and Archie has helped in securing my membership to Brooks.

I believe you will find the house on Green Street to your taste, and I have already engaged a cook and two maids, who can join us in our new home once we have found it, along with any other staff you think we require.

Now, I'm off to ensure this letter finds its way to you with all speed. I remain yours, affectionately,

Crispin

Crispin closed his eyes and breathed in the sea air. *The Calcutta Rose*, named for Rosalind, stood proudly against the gray landscape of Liverpool harbor. The cold smell of the sea mingled with the earthy scent of cotton, which drifted from the bales as the crewmen unloaded them, bringing back years of memories. This dock felt far away from Green Street and Brooks.

"Hello there, Mr. St. John. You are looking fit!" Captain Dean huffed breathlessly as he approached from the ship. On the water, Dean was as full of life as a man in his twenties, but as soon as he hit land, his fifty-seven years showed.

"Well now, let me look at you, sir. Very fashionable indeed. And less gangly too. I see all that fancy London food is finally sticking to your bones."

Crispin didn't mind Captain Dean's familiar jibes. Over the years, he had seen Crispin grow from a pupil to a master and he took pride in the transformation. They had spent many hours together during their long journeys from Calcutta to Liverpool and back. From the first, he had invited Crispin to take meals with him, in large part so that he could regale Crispin with stories of his maritime triumphs and adventures and dispense fatherly advice. Dean was a childless man, who, as he often said, had chosen the sea as his bride, yet Crispin sensed he craved a family, and so the captain had taken him under his wing.

"I am enjoying London, Captain Dean. It's far nicer than a cramped bunk aboard the Calcutta Rose. No offense of course!"

"None taken, my boy. But what brings you out to the ship? That clerk of yours is managing the shipments just fine these days."

"Yes, yes. Thompson's getting on very well. I came on a double errand, not merely to check on the shipment but also for a personal matter." He pulled the letter from his coat. "I'd be obliged if you would deliver this note to Miss Middleton. I'm afraid that I haven't been able to keep up with our correspondence as well as I should." Embarrassed, Crispin stared at the dock. Rosalind had sent four letters to his one, and Crispin felt that if this one made it to India in haste, she might not deduce his distraction. Dean chuckled good-naturedly. "I thought it would be faster if it went with you as you will start your next run tomorrow."

"Quite right, sir. I'll get this to your pretty young lady. She's quite busy and popular about town in Calcutta." He tucked the letter in his coat pocket for safekeeping.

"Did you have a chance to see her on your last trip?"

"Yes, I did. I had some business with Mr. Middleton, and he was kind enough to include me in a dinner party at the house. Miss Middleton looked very elegant, and she had so many admirers among the men that evening, even some of those officers the ladies are always getting weak in the knees for. Be on guard my boy!" He clapped a good-natured hand across Crispin's back and led him toward the harbormaster's office. Crispin hoped that Rosalind wasn't making a spectacle of herself. Even Archie had noted her forward ways more than once.

Crispin wasn't jealous by nature but still he asked, "Miss Middleton did mention a Colonel Geary, a recent acquaintance of hers. Do you know him?"

"Yes sir, he was there and another Major something or other. The lot of them, strutting about like peacocks in their uniforms. Not quite sure how Mr. Middleton knows all these young chaps. Big one, that Geary, tall as a giant in his red coat. But enough about that, tell me more about your fancy life in London."

Inexplicably, his thoughts drifted to his tense exchange with Cassandra. Strange. A few minutes in the whole of his London life and yet this is what came to mind. He shook his head and launched into a description of his new home on Green Street.

Chapter 27

November 1873

"Father?"

Lord Drayton's chambers were perpetually dark these days, the thick embroidered curtains always drawn to keep out the light. *Headaches plagued him,* he said.

"Father, are you awake?"

"Yes, my love."

"Shall I open the curtains a hair? It's a beautiful day. I think the sun would do you some good."

"If you must, but not too wide."

He squinted in the half-light, backing away as if Cassandra had thrust a lamp in his face. His beard, growing thick, made him look ages older, as did his sallow skin and unkempt hair. He had not been bathing regularly and a stale smell hovered thickly in the room. In the slim beam of light, dust gathered and swirled upward in tiny tornadoes.

Trinkets and keepsakes that documented her father's life were scattered about the room: silver hunting trophies, a pocket watch hanging on its stand, the Drayton family signet ring, a photograph of a young James Drayton on his favorite mare, Calliope. Not long ago these were little validations of a life well-lived, promises of exciting times to come, petty confirmations that the Draytons were people of importance, always had been and always would be.

Her father coughed dryly. Cassandra tried to muster up the courage to reveal the purpose of her unhappy visit but held on to the words as if saying them out loud would turn this dingy dream into reality.

"Father, there have been several communications from Soanes." For the last two months, Cassandra had been reading her father's mail. The usual correspondents, who wrote letters on clean linen leaves in rounded script, had ceased and were replaced by tighter, far less circuitous notes. "They have expressed concern that we cannot meet our obligations."

Her father nodded slowly, bringing his hands up to his face and rubbing his eyes deeply. His soft brown hair, streaked with silver, fell across his forehead. He did not attempt to push it away and took a long breath but said nothing.

"We have cut back on some of the staff, but that does not go terribly far toward reducing our monthly commitments. And I'm afraid the income from the estates takes us only so far."

His shoulders rose and fell. Cassandra thought she saw him shudder as if a chill ran through his body.

"I think that if we sell a few personal effects, and some of the investment pieces, we can hold them off for a time, just to show we won't fall behind. Right now, it is a question of confidence. It will give us time to come up with a more complete plan and perhaps in time—" She nearly said, "things will come round right," but held her tongue. False hope would only hurt them both.

Outside, carriages crunched along the boulevard, the turning of their wheels deafening. Cassandra waited. In time, her father took a cigarette from an elaborately decorated enamel case on his bedside table. He lit it with a tremble, drew in a breath, and, tired by the effort, exhaled a meek gray cloud of smoke. Finally, he gave his slow response as the afternoon sun carved a violent tear across the room.

And so they decided to sell the Degas of the chestnut mare, a Fattori that had been a wedding present to Cassandra's grandmother, a fine mahogany dining table, two Ming Dynasty urns that had been taken from China by her great uncle Charlie during the Opium Wars, the tigerwood dresser, a set of silver, a vanity set, a number of little-worn gold pieces, and her much-admired emerald necklace. Her father had objected at first, but Cassandra had insisted. She loathed to part with it but knew it would fetch a significant amount.

A life's fortune to some. To the Draytons—two month's reprieve—three if they were lucky.

CHAPTER 28

"And here we have a lovely Chippendale dresser in mint condition. The woodwork is exquisite; dialing on each drawer, brass nobs. The bidding will start at 100 pounds. I can't go under 100 pounds."

A paddle in the front row went up tentatively.

"100. Do I hear 110?" An interminable pause, and then a paddle rose in the back left corner.

"110. Do I hear 120? It is a steal for something of this fine a quality." The bidding went on for a few more minutes, ending at 150. It was a steal. A piece like that should have sold for over 200 pounds. More items sold to thrifty bidders, some the representatives of wealthy Lords and Ladies who did not deign to attend an estate auction, let alone one in which items from a member of their own social circle were being sold. Many were wealthy merchants, who could not resist a bargain even if they felt reluctant to furnish their homes with the cast-offs of the aristocracy.

Crispin's heart sank. The Draytons' furnishings were paraded around the dark room. Everything looked washed out, dreary. The rugs looked worn, the curtains faded, the paintings cracked. The prices smacked of a second-rate life. How were these people to know that when hung in the grand hallway, that portrait looked regal? He wanted to leave but was mesmerized by the travesty. The cartoonish auctioneer kept raising the hands of the marionettes in the crowd as if they were attached to strings.

Crispin had reluctantly agreed to attend the auction as a favor to his aunt. After settling at Green Street, he'd written to her that he was nearby and offered his services again, expecting Emma Fairfax to decline. Though for years an ocean and thousands of miles had kept Crispin and Emma apart, their correspondence seemed to solidify a bond between them, much stronger than the one when he was a boy at Drayton manner. But now, in the wake of Lord Drayton's meltdown, a handful of streets seemed a greater distance than the Arabian Sea. So, it was a great surprise to Crispin when Emma called on him unannounced. She'd sat in his library, a forced smile on her face.

"Crispin," she said. "I hate to impose on your good nature. You offered your services to me and I find that I would take you up on your offer. You see, we . . ." She shifted in her seat uncomfortably. "That is, the Drayton family is selling a great deal of valuables at auction. And I would very much appreciate your attending it for me."

"Attend? How can I be helpful? Would you like me to purchase some items?"

"Purchase! No! Crispin, I ask because I cannot bring myself to attend. I could not risk running into any one of my or the Draytons' acquaintance, and it would be totally inappropriate if Cassandra did, of course. The talk would be overwhelming." She'd shaken her head vigorously and continued. "I'd like an account of what happens and how it's managed, that is not provided by the auction house. I'd like the real story, so to speak." Crispin could not refuse her this small favor, no matter how uncomfortable it made him.

A vanity set was now on show. Was it Cassandra's mother's? Or her own? Was it his Aunt Emma's? Crispin strained to recreate his one trip to her rooms, to see the brush and comb that he had caught a glimpse of. Nothing came to mind.

"Thirty pounds. Do I hear . . ."

Crispin raised his hand. "The gentleman in the back without a paddle. Can someone get him a number?" The auctioneer called to a gray-haired lady, who sat scribbling notes near the entrance to the room. She nodded.

"Do I hear forty pounds? No? Going once. Going twice. Going three times."

What was Crispin going to do with a lady's vanity set? He hadn't the first idea, but for thirty pounds, he had saved something from the wreckage. Crispin sat, lost in thought, as several more items were presented and sold too cheaply. He had just finished convincing himself not to buy anything else when the Charles Towne painting came up. A chestnut brown mare trotted across the canvas, gleaming and sinewy with the effort of the hunt. Astride her sat a red-coated hunter, looking casually back, hat in hand, toward other hunters who lagged behind just out of the frame. The curls of the hunter's dark brown hair jutted about, and his broad back and well-cut jacket pointed to an easy, moneyed confidence. A pack of hounds sniffed the ground about the horse's heels and barked into the air, and another pack leaped over bushes making their way toward a fox who hid somewhere in the hills. Crispin would have known the painting anywhere. It had hung in Lord Drayton's study and had welcomed him to Drayton Manor all those years ago.

He purchased the Charles Towne painting and stayed until the auction's end so he could give his aunt a full report, but he wouldn't mention the 500 pounds worth of the Draytons' memories he had bought.

CHAPTER 29

"Uh, Miss Drayton, the mail's come in." Ruby hesitated as she poured Cassandra's tea, trying to make her voice as small and light as possible. "There are several letters for Lord Drayton, should I bring them to him?"

"No!" Cassandra said too harshly. She softened her tone. "No Ruby, as I've said Lord Drayton is resting. I will manage the correspondence."

Ruby came back quickly with a pile of ominous letters. Cassandra remembered her former excitement when the letters came in, when they had first arrived in London for her debut; they were all filled with invitations to parties and events. Now, she looked at the envelopes in front of her and knew there were no well-wishing invitations within. The solicitors, the bank, investors . . . . on and on they went as usual.

As she spread them before her, Cassandra spotted the flourished hand of Mr. Smythe of Christie, Manson & Woods, Auctioneers.

"My Dear Miss Drayton . . ." The letter began. Mr. Smythe was an efficient, kindly man, but given that his life's work was to sell people's most cherished belongings to the highest bidder, Cassandra took his accountings of the goings-on at the auction with a grain of salt.

> *My Dear Miss Drayton,*
>
> *I do hope this note finds you in good health and that Lord Drayton is tolerably well, given the circumstances. You will find enclosed an accounting of the items you solicited on behalf of Lord Drayton that were sold at the latest auction, held on 25 November at Christie, Manson & Woods. You will see*

that we were able to sell all 30 items presented. While some did not fetch the highest of bids, I'm sure you will be pleased to accept the attached bank draft for 2,476 pounds, deducting, of course, our commission for the sale.

You will be happy to hear that I did not chance to overhear any of the ugly talk regarding Lord Drayton that took place at the last auction we held on 28 October. In fact, all present appeared to be pleased with the quality of the goods and the efficiency of our auction process. One gentleman, in particular, did distinguish himself. You will forgive me for calling attention to him. He purchased seven of the thirty items, with a value totaling over 500 pounds. As he was late to the auction event, he had not obtained a paddle or number. Thus, I was forced to acquaint myself with him, and—although we at Christie's are known for our discretion—I still feel compelled to inform you of his identity, as he has a connection to your family. Mr. Crispin St. John indicated to me that as he is setting up a new establishment for himself, he had been told of the excellent quality of items at Christie's by a dear friend. During the course of the auction, he happened to recognize the lady's vanity set as having possibly belonged to an acquaintance of his or perhaps his aunt. Given that he mentioned Miss Fairfax's name, whom I know has a strong connection to your family, I thought it appropriate to inform you of his participation.

I look forward to our further association. If you have any future items you may wish to auction at Christie, Manson & Woods, do not hesitate to write.

I remain yours, respectfully.

Mr. Edwin Smythe

Christie, Manson & Woods, Auctioneers

King Street, St. James

Cassandra let the letter fall to the table. 500 pounds? Crispin had spent over 500 pounds purchasing things for his new home, her family's things. Since seeing him at the Douglases', May spoke about him often, relaying the story of his success, his engagement, and his close connection with her family. Could Crispin have known that word of his behavior at the auction would come back to the Draytons? Was he flaunting his wealth and capitalizing on their misfortune?

Breathing deeply, Cassandra checked herself.

That was not the Crispin she knew. While nearly ten years would certainly have changed him from the boy he was at Drayton Manor, the man she met at Claridge's and corresponded with over the years was kind and humble, not one to flaunt his position at the expense of others. She was allowing her newfound cynicism to get the better of her. Perhaps he had been trying to help the only way he could, from a distance. Or, he could have been repaying Emma's kindness from all those years ago. Still, Cassandra wondered, how had he heard about the auction? Who was this friend who had advised him to go? She would ask Emma.

CHAPTER 30

December 1873

Archie shook drops of rain from his uncontrollable hair as he entered the small drawing room at Brooks.

"Have you ever seen such a downpour?"

"Miserable." Crispin agreed from his melancholy post at the window where he had been watching sheets of rain cascade down the panes. It was the kind of day where the cold got into your bones. Crispin had been spoiled by his sunny years in India and wondered if he was now ruined for the damp British gloom.

"Let's have our drinks by the fire." Archie nodded toward one of the room's crackling fireplaces and a trio of empty leather chairs. The room was hushed as if the weather had dripped indoors. Three men played a silent game of cards. Occasionally, one of their mouths would move, but the sound was absorbed by the rich oriental carpet and barely a whisper's worth reached Archie and Crispin.

Archie picked up the poker and stabbed at a log, sending sparks flying. "You're awfully glum my friend. What's eating you?"

"Nothing."

"Really? You're a terrible liar, you know." Archie's brows rose but he continued pushing the glowing embers.

"I'd let you in on it, but I'm not quite sure myself. I just got a note from Middleton. He's all set to release the reigns of the Fleet Street office to me and suggested that Rosalind and I set our wedding date for early summer.

Everything seems perfect and I can hardly believe my good fortune. What could possibly be wrong?"

"I'll tell you what it is old chap." Archie looked over his shoulder and even though no one was within earshot he leaned in and spoke in a low voice, "I'm not sure you love her." He paused for a second. "She's a fine girl, but you don't love her. Do you?"

Crispin didn't answer. Not right away. Staring into the crackling fire, finally, he said, "Do you know, Archie, that last week I bought a lady's vanity set at Christie, Manson, and Woods? That and a mahogany wardrobe, and a painting of a chestnut mare, and a couple of other fine things. The thing is I didn't buy them for Rosalind. I'm not sure I'll ever put them in any house I own."

"Why'd you get them then?" Archie stood up and nodded to the footman who handed him a drink.

"They belonged to Lord Drayton. To Cassandra and their household." Crispin took a large mouthful of scotch. "I can't very well give Rosalind *that* Lady's vanity, now, can I?"

Archie was kind enough not to comment. Most of the time he was all laughs and the pains of the world never seemed to permeate his quest for a good time, but he knew when to be silent. Crispin appreciated his friendship, and, despite Archie's penchant for storytelling, he trusted him with his secret.

"I should be perfectly happy, shouldn't I?"

"Probably. But I wouldn't put too much stock in contriving to be 'perfectly happy.' That's when you'll find yourself most trapped. Isn't life most fun when it's not perfect?"

"That's easier for you to say; you haven't been where I have."

They were interrupted by a familiar, nasal voice: "I didn't expect to see the two of you here, not on such an ugly day."

"Hello Forsythe," Archie said as if biting into a lemon.

The little man stood in the door of the drawing room, slicking his glossy dark hair back from his forehead. He had the odd habit of pursing his lips and sucking on his cheeks like a man getting ready to eat a roast pig.

"Boys, come dine with me." The thought set Crispin's teeth on edge, yet the club was near empty so there was no way to politely decline. Though Forsythe had no memory of him as a child, Crispin recalled his first encounter with the man in vivid detail. It had been at the Draytons' grouse hunt, where Forsythe had taken every opportunity to make sure the stable boy knew his place. His former disdain was now replaced with condescending camaraderie, but no amount of backslapping and awkward jokes could expunge his demeaning remarks from Crispin's boyhood conscience. Because of his friendship with Lord Douglas, Forsythe assumed Crispin was a part of the old guard and sought to ingratiate himself. But Crispin had the advantage of knowing they were both outsiders. He saw, clearer than most, that Forsythe's glib ways were studied; he was a man with a barely veiled agenda, and it angered Crispin that other men, those of Brooks's old world and even the new one, would allow him to slither along in their midst.

At dinner, he sucked on his wine and picked his teeth with abandon, while regaling them with tales of the fluctuations of his fortune.

"It's a bad business, you know, this thing with Drayton. Of course, I count myself lucky. I invested a decent handful, mind you, but not so much that I've got to sell the shirt off my back. I hedged my bets going in. That's the problem with Drayton." He dove headlong into his critique without waiting for encouragement from Archie or Crispin.

"He got overexcited. Over sure. Never do that, my friends. If anyone says 'you can't lose' they are dead wrong. History does not lie. Of course, I invested enough to make him happy. I wanted him to know I was on his side. Or rather I wanted little Miss Cassie to know." He raised an eyebrow, and Crispin fought the urge to slap him. He couldn't bear the familiarity with which he spoke of Cassandra. "Now, I can be indispensable, a true friend to our damsel in distress."

He chuckled and smacked his lips, before devouring a large mouthful of pudding.

"By now, I'm sure you've heard that the Duke has done a runner. He's attached himself to an American."

Unable to listen to one more word out of Forsythe's mouth, Crispin threw back a glass of claret and motioned for another.

"We've had one too many, my friend. I'll be glad to see my bed tonight. Though I might not be glad to see the morning." They'd had too much scotch and not enough soda, that was for sure. Crispin chuckled and struggled gracelessly into his coat, while the attendant, stern and knowing, helped Archie find with some difficulty the sleeve of his Coburn greatcoat.

"Quite right. You know, about your bed. But I'm thinking we might find some more comfortable beds tonight." He winked.

"Archie!" Crispin glanced around, thankful that the attendant had returned to his post. Being a newly elected member of the club, he didn't want to give the wrong impression. "Keep your voice down."

"Oh, it's fine, don't worry about it. But, anyway, I was thinking, and I know you don't love to do this, but there is a little place on Church street that you might like. Very classy girls, nothing out of the ordinary." He stumbled on to St. James Street.

"Well, that's reassuring." Crispin followed Archie into the street. Though the rain had stopped, the night was damp and bone-chilling. "I don't know why you insist on trying to get me to go to these brothels with you. You know I'm not up for it."

"They're not brothels. I keep telling you, these are fine establishments with very clean and well-mannered ladies. Besides, who else am I going to ask, that creep Forsythe? I hear his tastes are unconventional."

"What do you mean? I hadn't heard." Crispin didn't need anything to convince him that Forsythe was repugnant, but he couldn't resist learning more.

"Yup, he loves this house on Norfolk Street. I've never been of course. It caters to pleasures of the exotic variety."

"How exotic?"

"Well let's just say that Forsythe prefers young ladies, very young . . ." Archie's voice trailed off as he stared glassy-eyed into the dark street. His tone was matter-of-fact despite the startling comment.

"What? Do you mean . . . ?" Crispin couldn't put words to the awful thought.

"I think you know what I mean."

"That's repulsive." The image of a lecherous Forsythe reaching to grope a young girl, her stockings showing beneath her skirt sprung into Crispin's mind. The face of the girl was Cassandra's, the way she looked when they had first met. Shutting his eyes tight, Crispin tried to erase the image.

"Yes. It's too dissolute"—he slurred the "s's" and dropped the "t"— "even for me. But, you know, my fre'nd, I think maybe we shoul' call it a night. I mi' actually be swaying right now. I'll embarrass myself in this condition."

Archie made for his coach. Crispin started after him shaking his head.

CHAPTER 31

December 1873

"I have a brilliant idea!" May exclaimed excitedly as she pushed past Braxton into the drawing room. Cassandra rose and kissed her on the cheek. May's cheeks bloomed to match the deep pink color of her gown.

"Thank you, Braxton." Cassandra smiled apologetically at him as she and May walked arm in arm to the sofa.

"Now don't say anything until I have finished. I promise this is a great idea." She plumped her skirt around her distractedly and looked at Cassandra with a determined glare.

"May, don't keep me waiting, what is it?"

"Scotland! We're going to Scotland!" She waved her hands in the air like an excited child.

"Scotland? I don't really think I should be leaving London right now . . ."

"Before you start in with excuses, hear me out," May squeezed Cassandra's shoulders and looked her squarely in the eye. "I'm not finished. You know my family's estate in Scotland, Airlie Manor," she began.

"Yes. 'A paradise in the Highlands' I think you've called it."

"No need to mock, my dearest friend. But yes, that's the one. Well, the paradise is quite old and needs a lot of work. Our staff there has been supervising one of the projects—a refurbishment of the stables—and Mama wants me to go check-in and see how it's progressing." Cassandra couldn't imagine why Lady Douglas would think that May was qualified to supervise a barn renovation. Clearly, her doubt showed.

"Don't raise your eyebrows like that." May was genuinely insulted. "I'm perfectly capable of checking in on the workers." She paused to take a teacup and saucer from Braxton. "Besides, I offered because it's so peaceful there in the winter, and I thought it would be the perfect getaway for you. It will be just you and me. We'll take walks around the grounds and then warm up by the fire with steaming chocolate and gothic novels."

It sounded heavenly. Cassandra thought it would be nice to put some distance between her and the horrible mess that was her life, but it wasn't possible.

"May, you are very dear but . . ."

May cut Cassandra off, "Cassie, you've been having a horrible time of it. As if it wasn't bad enough your being in this position but the fact that you are now managing everything for your father and that he's taken to his bed . . . it's too much. You are going to grow old before your time. In fact, I think I spot a gray hair sprouting up from your brow, just there." She pointed to an imaginary spot on the crown of Cassandra's head and playful pursed her lips, before resuming with resolve. "You need a break." An edge rose in her voice, and she put her cup down forcefully.

Cassandra looked at her friend sheepishly, wondering how she could refuse her kind invitation and knowing that she had to.

"I'm sorry, I don't mean to sound so stern." May reached over and put her hand on Cassandra's. "But you really do have too many burdens and too much time to think about them. A break will do you a world of good. And I'm only suggesting a fortnight. Nothing will change in so short a time." Oh, if only it could, Cassandra thought, wishing that she could go to Scotland and come back to find all her worries melted like snow in the spring.

"But here is Miss Fairfax. I know she will agree with me." May quickly rose to greet Miss Fairfax. "Miss Fairfax, don't you think it would be wonderful for Cassandra to join me on a trip to my family's home in Scotland just to get away for a while?"

Since receiving the news in September, Emma Fairfax's once radiant features seemed to be perpetually drawn, as though she had not slept in days. But May's question brought a great smile to her face.

"That is a marvelous idea, Lady Margaret." She turned to Cassandra with lightened spirits. "It's best to take your mind off of everything."

"Emma, I don't think this is a good idea. Father is still beside himself, in bed all day long . . ."

"Your father will be fine. I will be fine. It's time for you to lighten your burden for a little while. Please, think of yourself."

Cassandra's face colored, and she stared down at her tea, amber-colored and nearly cold. Margaret took her silence for resignation.

"Brilliant, I'll arrange it. And don't worry Miss Fairfax, we'll travel with at least two footmen and my maid in the coach and then there is the housekeeper at Airlie, Mrs. MacDonaugh, to act as a chaperone, though we won't need one." She kissed Cassandra's cheek quickly and hugged a startled Miss Fairfax, before rushing out of the room. "This will be wonderful, Cassie. I promise."

"I suppose you are both right," Cassandra told Miss Fairfax later that afternoon as they sat in the drawing room, discussing the prospect of a Scottish getaway. Cassandra was torn, but Miss Fairfax was urging her to go.

"She's right, you know. Nothing will change in a fortnight, and it will do you good."

Cassandra turned the idea over in her mind. A fortnight, it was not very long, and May seemed set on the idea.

"May does go on about Scotland," Cassandra said as much to herself as to Emma. "I'm embarrassed I've never been there. All these great lochs and hills she talks about, you'd think she was describing a world full of heavenly creatures instead of cold, grey Scotland!"

Miss Fairfax smiled with matronly affection.

"But are you sure you will be alright without me?" Cassandra flushed and closed her eyes, leaning her head back for a moment. Composing herself, she looked straight into Miss Fairfax's eyes. "You must truly love him."

The words hung in the air and neither woman made a sound. It was a thing they had never spoken of openly. Of course, Cassandra had known about Miss Fairfax and her father's long attachment; they had spent so many years under the same roofs and traveled as a unit. And Miss Fairfax knew that Cassandra knew. But everyone had always maintained careful silence—except the occasional biting quip from Eugenia behind closed doors. Miss Fairfax now looked at Cassandra with sad eyes and sighed.

"I suppose he has his shortcomings."

Cassandra thought of the years she had idolized her father. He'd seemed so clever and winning. Perhaps that was the worst of it, to see one's childhood idol, so dear to the heart, toppled. When she thought of her father now, she saw a myriad of flaws and foibles—the aggrandizing, the maneuvering, the ego—and yet she loved him so. Cassandra's heart seemed to break into a million pieces all over again.

Sensing the fall in her mood, Miss Fairfax cupped Cassandra's hand. "We will be fine, I told you. Besides, Margaret will find so many fun things for you to do, I hope you won't think about us too much."

"Miss Drayton, Miss Fairfax." Braxton's voice boomed like an alarm bell. "Mr. Forsythe has arrived."

"But we weren't expecting his call," Cassandra said taken aback by the afternoon's second unexpected visitor. Why would he choose to call when he knew Lord Drayton was not receiving visitors?

"No, we were not." Miss Fairfax looked up at Braxton. "Please tell Mr. Forsythe that Lord Drayton continues to be indisposed."

"Yes, Miss Fairfax. However, I already told him as much. He said he isn't calling on Lord Drayton, but rather he is here to call on Miss Drayton." The butler's expression of stymied disbelief reflected their own.

After a long pause, Cassandra stood up and smoothed her skirt. Miss Fairfax did the same.

"Well then, please show him in Braxton." Steeling herself, Cassandra's voice was edged with ice.

"I will stay here of course." Miss Fairfax assured Cassandra. Forsythe's presence always aggravated Miss Fairfax, but she would persevere for propriety's sake.

"Thank you, Emma. I'm not sure I have the energy to be witty and entertaining."

"Well, we will have to keep this brief then." Miss Fairfax smiled as Forsythe entered the drawing room.

"Mr. Forsythe, what a pleasant surprise. We weren't expecting you." Cassandra gestured for him to sit on the armchair. Instead, he moved so he could join them on the sofa. Realizing that there wasn't enough room to appropriately accommodate three, Miss Fairfax moved to the armchair. As they all took their seats Cassandra was struck by how short he was. She hadn't noticed it before, but he was barely her height.

"Yes, I imagine this is a surprise. I suspect you don't have many callers these days." His oily cheeks stretched into a smug, tight-lipped smile. Miss Fairfax drew back inadvertently, as though he had slapped her.

Cassandra tried to salvage the awkward moment. "Have you been well Mr. Forsythe?"

"Me? I've been fine. Very well. However, I'm sad to hear that your father has been indisposed since word spread about Jay Cooke's collapse." He waited for a response and when none came, bounded on. "I suppose I'd be indisposed too if I'd gotten my friends to sink their money into a disastrous investment."

Too shocked to speak, Cassandra turned to Miss Fairfax, whose stony expression barely veiled her fury and hurt.

"Mr. Forsythe, please." Cassandra's words were halted. She struggled between tears and rage. "These are difficult times for all of us."

"Oh now, there is no cause to be concerned on my behalf, Miss Drayton. I didn't invest very much, even after you batted your pretty eyes at me." He moved closer to Cassandra on the sofa and wagged a pudgy finger in her direction as if he were about to tap her nose.

"Only invested 10,000 pounds. That's not too much for me to lose, so don't you worry, I'm not put out." He paused, breathing heavily, his mouth just inches from Cassandra's cheek.

"Your father became overly excited by the prospect of his riches. He never should have invested that much. Mortgaging his family home, really was an absurd and irresponsible tactic. He's never had a head for business, has he?"

Miss Fairfax rose from her perch unable to take anymore. "Mr. Forsythe," she said with warning. That he would say all of this about Lord Drayton, his friend. It was despicable.

"Well, perhaps I've said too much. Or my visit may have been premature." He turned to Cassandra and took her hand. Her instinct was to draw it back, but she let it sit in his clammy palm. "Miss Drayton, I know that this will be a challenging time for you, as you adjust to your new reality." He was insufferable, but Cassandra was determined to be polite. "I would like to invite you to attend the opera with me, that is, to take your mind off of your circumstances. It would please me greatly to do so. There is a new production, *La Traviata*, and I have heard that it is wonderful." His greasy face glowed at the prospect of the opera with a pretty young lady in his box.

Cassandra's face brightened as well. *May,* she thought, *dear May.* How could she have known her invitation to Scotland would be so timely? Cassandra looked to the ceiling sending a silent "thank you" to May, or whatever higher power watched over her at that moment.

"Mr. Forsythe," she began with a great sigh of relief. "I regret that I cannot join you for the opera. I am going to Scotland for a fortnight with May Douglas. We will be traveling very soon, so you see it is quite impossible." Cassandra hoped he wouldn't press the matter and rose as if to signal permission or rather invitation for him to leave.

"Not impossible my dear, just impossible for a little while. I will call on you when you return, and we will have our evening together." His voice had a possessive ring to it.

Cassandra moved toward the door, and thankfully, Braxton approached from the hall, preparing to escort Forsythe out. "I'm afraid I have to go pack my things. Given our circumstances, I'm sure you'll understand, I have to see to these nuisances myself." Cassandra said. Her smile dripped with insincerity, but Forsythe took no notice.

"I will leave then and wish you well on your journey." He looked at Miss

Fairfax and nodded, then grasped Cassandra's hand again to kiss it. She smiled evenly as Braxton escorted him to the door.

"That man! He is so . . . vulgar, crass, uncouth. I can't think of a word that could possibly describe how vile he is!"

Cassandra had never seen Miss Fairfax so angry.

"I think you've come up with several good ones. But I would add 'opportunistic.' At least now I can be just as excited about this trip to Scotland as you are. It certainly couldn't have come at a better time!"

Chapter 32

At the crossroads, the Douglases' carriage turned left and started to climb a steep hill. The road was rocky and rough, and the horses navigated slowly and deliberately. Winter had carved deep ruts into the dirt. The grass was a shaved brown stubble, and the heath was frost-bitten and ashy.

Cassandra bit the inside of her cheeks and tried to look cheerful. It took all she had not to think about the daily letters she would be missing by going to Scotland. Letters that demanded payment for this or asked for documentation of that—mortgages, bonds, securities, contracts, all of which required study on her part. A few months prior, in what seemed a past life, Cassandra had known little of the Drayton family finances, but in the wake of the unexpected crash, she had been forced to dive headlong into the maze that her father had created. She had scoured complicated ledgers, noting income from various small investments and from tenants that lagged far behind the mounting debts that were being recalled. Other ledgers listed household expenses and inventories of valuables. Most pathetically, was a black leather-bound book labeled NPR, in which her father had made elaborate projections for future income, dividends, and sales of shares from the Northern Pacific Railway. Of course, the family's financial mess was not all James Drayton's doing. His father before him had dug himself into quite a quagmire, which James had sought to escape.

The carriage rolled on and patches of snow gave way to the odd mound of emerald green, a holdover from the wet fall or a precursor to a lush spring, nature's way of reminding the travelers of the season's muscle. Cassandra had to admit that even after just one day's drive, she felt a little better. Her worries had not disappeared, of course, but they were interrupted by thoughts of other things. For one thing, May, in all her excitement, was continually pointing out the delights of her childhood.

". . . And over there, Cassie, is where our friends, the Bothwells, live. Oh, the hunts they host! You have never seen such a fleet of horses and their picnic is immense. You'll have to come for it this season." May practically climbed over Cassandra to get to the window on the east side of the carriage. "Let's open the window, Cassie. There is nothing like the smell of Scotland." It was an earthy smell, frozen moss and snow.

The carriage turned the final corner and gravel crunched beneath the wheels. "Here we are. At last!" May announced proudly. The manor emerged from behind a thick line of barren-looking trees. It was handsome and grand. Four spires, one on each corner of the house, pierced the gray sky. A silver-gray lattice of ivy and wisteria vines covered the south wall. They were colorless now, but Cassandra imagined that in the spring and summer the imposing limestone mansion was dressed in a green mantel that turned it into a fantastical fairy castle. The door was set deep in a stone portico embellished with gothic rosettes and diminutive gargoyles. At its peak, was the Douglas family crest underlined with 1503. The Douglases were an old family, but Cassandra had not realized how deep their roots ran. She was about to ask her host for the history of Airlie Manor when May exclaimed, "Brilliant. They're here!"

"Who?"

"Archie and Crispin, of course. I was sure we would be settled in when they arrived, but they've beaten us to it."

"May you didn't tell me . . ." A mixture of shock and embarrassment flooded Cassandra's cheeks. She wanted to shake May's shoulders and reprimand her, but all she could muster was a feeble, "But I haven't packed any of my formal gowns. I'm woefully underprepared for a social visit."

May cut her short. "Never mind that, Cassie. You can borrow some of mine. I knew you wouldn't come if I told you. It would have been too dull, wouldn't it? Just the two of us roaming around alone. Now, we'll make a full party. Don't be mad. Please don't. I know that he used to work for your father, but times have changed a great deal, and Crispin really is a gentleman. If Archie can overlook his past, so can we."

How could Cassandra tell her that her reluctance had nothing to do with Crispin's humble beginnings? Cassandra was ashamed. How could she spend a fortnight with Crispin, knowing he knew all about the Draytons' miserable situation *and* had in his possession 500 pounds worth of their peddled furnishings? Not to mention their last encounter in the foyer of the Douglases' townhouse. Cassandra's cheeks reddened further with the memory. She had been so curt when all he had done was say he had intended to visit her. *What had I expected from him?* she wondered.

May leaped out of the cab as the footman opened the door.

"Hello Campbell. It's good to see you."

"You as well, my Lady. I hope you will find everything to your liking. We are anxious for you to see the progress of the stable. It's nearly complete and I think you will be pleased."

"Of course, I will. What a relief to finally be here." Pulling Cassandra along, May greeted Mrs. MacDonaugh, the housekeeper, with equal warmth.

"We have the Rose room made up for you, Miss Drayton. Denton will act as your lady's maid." She nodded toward a petite brunette, who stood a careful distance behind the heads of the household.

Thanking May and Mrs. MacDonaugh for their consideration, Cassandra was reminded that she would no longer bring her own maid when she went visiting. But this, she knew, would be the least of the barbs that would pierce her new life.

Denton filled the large enamel tub with piping hot water perfumed with lavender bath salts. Cassandra stepped in gingerly and let the warmth seep into her bones. She closed her eyes and breathed deeply, letting her cares wash away with the long day's travel. *I could—no, I will,* she told herself, *make amends for how rudely I greeted Crispin and for rushing so quickly to my room upon my arrival.* She had to gain control of herself, she reasoned, before dipping her head beneath the surface of the water.

Once dried and dressed—Cassandra found one of May's silk taffeta gowns hanging in the wardrobe—she sat at the dressing table while Denton curled and pinned her hair.

"No need to fuss over me, Denton." Cassandra felt guilty for taking the maid away from her regular duties.

"Not a worry, ma'am. We have been so quiet here, it's a real treat to have company and noise in the house, not just us servants rattlin' our bones about." She tucked a pin into a bun at the back of Cassandra's head. "That should do it. You look lovely. That young guest of Lord Douglas's won't be able to take his eyes off ya now. Not that he could before mind you." Denton winked at her as she exited the room, before Cassandra could ask her to clarify her remark.

Denton had laid out the few items of jewelry that Cassandra had packed, among them amethyst and gold earrings that mysteriously matched the braided detail on May's gown. As Cassandra attached them to her ears, she gazed at her reflection in the mirror as if she were looking at a stranger. She wondered who Crispin saw when he looked at her: the spoiled adolescent who teased him at Drayton Manor or the melancholy young woman Cassandra feared she had become. She pinched her cheeks a couple of times to draw the color back into them and made for the door.

When she was ready, Cassandra headed for the library in the hopes of finding a gothic romance she might sink her teeth into before dinner. She was sure May had many in her collection, but as she shut the door behind her, Cassandra heard the crackle of a page being turned. Crispin looked at home in a big leather armchair, a book spread across his lap.

"Oh dear, I didn't know anyone was in here. I'm sorry to disturb you."

"Not to worry. In fact, thank you for saving me from this deadly tome— *Holinshed's Histoire Scotland*. Everyone says I must read it to have a true appreciation for the country, but it's beastly. If one more thane lops off the head of his predecessor, I don't know what I'll do."

Cassandra laughed at his account of Scottish history.

"You've never been to Scotland then?"

"No. You?"

"No. We Draytons stick to the South. We have thin skins, I guess."

"You? You're more rugged and adventurous than you let on. I seem to remember you dragging me across the Dorset hills in a rainstorm, with no thought to your comfort—or mine for that matter."

Cassandra smiled at the recollection, but more than that, she was tickled that Crispin too had remembered that early spring morning when she compelled him to adventure with her to find the old Roman road that ran near the edge of the Drayton property. They had been quite far from home when the skies opened up on them.

"You have a long memory!"

"I was laid up with a devilish cold for days afterward."

"You were? I never knew! I'm terribly sorry. Is there a statute of limitations on apologizing for poor behavior?"

"Actually, yes, there is. You'll have to make it up to me some other way." At that moment, the dinner gong echoed in the hall and the Douglases' butler, jolly Campbell, poked his head around the door to let Crispin and Cassandra know their hosts would meet them in the dining room.

"Just in time." Crispin smirked. "Now, you'll have to wait to hear my plan."

Crispin took Cassandra's arm and tucked it into his, pulling her a tiny bit closer than necessary as they walked toward the drawing room. From this angle, she could see the chiseled line of his jaw framed by short, sandy curls. He was handsome, anyone could see it, though a little less rakish than Archie and a little more studied. Cassandra supposed he had to be, given his upbringing. He did not have the freedom to break the rules that someone like Archie had. Yet, Crispin was unaffected and spoke what he thought without hesitation. Cassandra was sure that many young ladies, and even older ones, were drawn to him. As soon as the idea entered her head, a warm wave of jealousy washed over her.

Dinner was a simple, jovial affair. Archie and May quickly dispensed with the formalities that Lady Douglas would have insisted upon. As the four friends swallowed creamy butternut squash soup, and sliced into crispy roast duck, and sipped bottomless glasses of red wine, the rest of the world fell away. May insisted that Crispin tell colorful tales from his days in the barracks at Howrah, and Archie added all the ribald details that Crispin tried to leave out.

When at last the final course, treacle pudding, emerged on silver platters, Archie claimed with delight, "Oh Cook! She never forgets my favorite!" May chimed in that Archie, who was forever getting in trouble with his parents and nannies, was nonetheless Cook's favorite and she tried to fatten him up at every opportunity. Cassandra had the feeling that time had stopped and that she, and May and Archie and Crispin had dined like this, in this room, with these stories and jokes, every night of their lives.

After every last sweet morsel was scraped from their plates, Archie took his wine to the French doors, which opened to a balcony overlooking the lawn and the Scottish highlands beyond.

"Come." He called with excitement. "Look at the sky. It's never like this in London, there's either too much light or too much fog." The foursome looked to the heavens. Stars peppered the sky and a white sliver of moon hung as if on a string, part of the mobile of the velvet night.

"It's enough to make me feel rather poetic," Archie joked.

May rolled her eyes. "Well, I'm feeling rather cold. Come, Cassandra, let's go back to the fire." Cassandra followed her friend, pulling her shawl around her shoulders, but beneath her skin, she felt warmer than she had in months.

Cassandra lingered in her room the next morning, enjoying the comfort of the large canopy bed and the distant sounds of the waking household. Outside, clouds hung low in the gray sky. All was still in a peaceful, happy way, and for a few moments, she closed her eyes, wishing time could stop.

Finally, she got dressed and went to join the others. The house was so oddly quiet as she descended the stairs that she started to wonder what time it was and feared she had missed the day. But as she came to the lower landing, she saw Crispin dressed in his riding coat, looking absentmindedly out a large picture window in the entrance hall. The rustle of her skirts must have disrupted his thoughts and he looked up at her.

"There you are! I thought you would never wake up."

"Where is everyone? It's ghostly quiet."

"Our hosts have gone visiting. Archie said something about a deaf uncle or cousin and such. They'll be back by tea, so we have the whole house and the whole day to ourselves. And I have an idea." His face lit up with boyish excitement.

"I'm all ears."

"Picking up on last night's unfinished business . . . your apology."

"Oh dear, now I'm quite nervous. Is this your retribution?"

"We're going out for a ride. We'll explore these Scottish Highlands, just like old times. I've already spoken to the stable master who's happy to furnish us with two fine and sturdy animals. I'm sure by now, given your malingering, they're ready."

"Well, you certainly have this all figured out and tied up neatly with a bow." Cassandra feigned haughtiness, but fearing he would take her at her word, quickly added, "How can I refuse?"

"You can't. Besides you're honor-bound." Crispin grinned.

"True, though I'm not dressed for riding. Will you let me get my cloak?"

"I suppose. I've already been waiting for nearly an hour, so what're a few more minutes?" He pantomimed disappointment and sunk into a chair at the base of the stairs. "I'll be right here when you return." Crispin turned his smiling eyes to Cassandra, who dashed up the stairs looking less demure than a lady should.

The old friends headed out into the bracing air. An early morning cloudburst made the land wet and what colors there were—the green ivy, the white gravel path, the crimson and gold quince—stood out more intensely against the gray backdrop and the mist.

A wave of nostalgia hit Cassandra as they strode toward the stable. Feeling like a young girl again, sneaking off for a secret ride with her erstwhile companion, she looked over her shoulder though it was obvious no one was watching. Crispin and Cassandra looked at each other and giggled, the same thought crossing their minds.

"I'll race you!" Crispin took off and Cassandra tried to catch him. By the time they reached the stable, they were breathless.

CHAPTER 33

After trotting up hills and meandering through low heaths for the better part of the morning, Crispin and Cassandra stopped on a gently sloping hill and dismounted. They looped the reins of their horses about the bare limbs of a windswept tree. Before them was an expanse of wheat-colored grass that stopped at the foot of an ominous craggy climb. Behind them was the Douglases' estate. It looked no bigger than a parson's cottage in the distance.

Cassandra's hair, which hung loosely about her shoulders, was in disarray and a few stray curls clung to her face, wet with the mist. But rather than disheveled and soggy, she seemed to have grown more striking, almost unearthly, as she gazed into the distance. Crispin silently watched her, not wanting to disturb her reverie. After a few moments, her face seemed to fall, and her shoulders sunk.

"What are you thinking?" Crispin asked.

"Sometimes I wish I could close my eyes and pluck the days of the past year away like the petals of a daisy." She sighed and her cheeks tightened as if wincing with pain. The last few months had softened her, taken away the sharp edges of privilege that had once intimidated Crispin. With a barely perceptible shudder, she continued, "It's not very romantic, you know, losing your fortune."

"I do know. Or at least I know how it is to fall on hard times."

"Of course, you do. I am sorry. I'm being daft."

"You don't have to apologize. You've done nothing wrong."

"But I have. I was so rude to you the other day, and it was the first time we had seen each other in so many years."

"It's my fault. I caught you by surprise. I should have written." Crispin tried to make her feel better. He wanted to tell her how much he cared but the words seemed simultaneously insufficient and inappropriate.

"I have missed your letters," Cassandra said with a frankness that caught Crispin by surprise.

"I've missed yours as well." Those letters had been highlights for him and, in the last year of chilly silence, he often wished for the thrill of the familiar script, the weight of multiple pages tucked into his pocket, the sound of Cassandra's voice in the ink.

"I'm sure you've heard, I've been jilted. Seems silly now that I called a halt to our correspondence," Cassandra said with a self-deprecating shake of the head.

"Bedford didn't deserve you," Crispin said with conviction. It wasn't a mere platitude. The adolescent jealously that plagued him at Drayton Manor had never lessened, he thought to himself. At least he now had the satisfaction of knowing Bedford was as much of a cad as he had always suspected.

"Didn't he though?" Cassandra returned, and as if she had read Crispin's thoughts. "He's not as bad as you think, *and* I was exactly the kind of bride he expected, spoiled and shallow. Crispin, until a few months ago, I led my life without a care, believing that everything would always be just so. The only decisions I had to make were what dresses to wear. I read novels, *Vanity Fair*, *Anna Karenina*, and such, and thought those women were so tragically romantic. I envied their pain and the purpose it gave their lives, and then I would close the book and call for Miss Fairfax and ask her to do this or that for me: play with my hair, get me a doll, play chess. I'd stomp my feet and pout when I did not get my way. I wandered listlessly through our manicured gardens, bemoaning my boring and protected life. I wanted something to *happen*. And now it has."

She sighed a weighted, sad sigh. Crispin reached his hand toward her shoulder, wanting to comfort her, but stopped himself. Her straight, graceful back was rigid in the wind.

"And now it has," she repeated.

"No one should expect you to understand a tougher world than the one you were born and raised in."

"I was so naïve. It's horrible, watching everything around you crumble. Letting servants go, selling furniture," she said.

At once, he knew she had heard about his purchases at the auction.

"When I heard of the outcome of the auction . . ." She continued, turning to face the horizon, her hair hiding her features. "I was humbled and touched by your generosity Crispin." He edged closer to her. When she looked at him, her eyes glistened with tears.

Crispin grazed her shoulder hesitantly with his fingertips. For some reason, he felt he owed her an explanation.

"My aunt told me of the auction. I recognized some of the pieces from a happy time in my life and couldn't help myself. Were you upset with me?"

"Only for a moment, at first. But then I was glad that you were thinking of us, of Emma and me. I can't imagine what Father would make of it. You see, he's become a shell of the man he was, like a painting that cracks and fades before your very eyes. And all I can do is stand still and look on. I feel so helpless."

"How is your father? I wish there was more I could do to help." Too late, Crispin realized his sentence was shamefully hollow and vaguely insulting. He hoped his words were carried away by the wind so that Cassandra didn't hear them.

"You've done all you can. The Draytons have dug themselves into an abyss." She did not seem angry, just resigned. They stood in silence, looking out over the Scottish hills, the harsh winter wind slicing through the air.

"You are a fine man, Crispin. I hope Rosalind Middleton knows that."

With an abrupt jerk, Cassandra turned away and started to walk toward her horse. Crispin could tell she was crying. For several minutes, he stood dumbly, watching her stroking the mare's mane, her frame silhouetted against the gray-green land.

Finally, he mustered up the courage to approach her. He put his hand on her shoulder.

"Cassie?" In the blink of an eye, she was in his arms, her head cradled in his chest. Burrowing into him, she cried quietly.

After a while, she pulled away and wiped her eyes with the back of her wrist and smiled weakly. Crispin brushed a hand across her pink cheek. She was soft and warm and delicate. But she was also sturdy, poised, sure. The tears on her cheeks fell over his fingers. He didn't want to let go of her, didn't want to let go of this moment, so he wrapped his arms around her slender waist and drew her tightly to his chest. The wind knotted their hair as they stood on the hill under a darkening sky, exposed for anyone to see. It didn't matter.

They were easy companions—Cassandra, May, Archie, and Crispin—and though the sun rarely shone, they made the most of each day, occupying themselves with chilly walks in the hills and long games of whist. Cassandra and Crispin were rarely alone, but when they were, they fell into a comfortable silence. They sat side-by-side on the velvet settee slowly turning pages of books they were barely reading or looking out the diamond panes of the big picture windows at the frosty, dormant gardens. Cassandra pointed to a vermillion spot darting here and there, a red-headed Chiffchaff that finally found a perch in the palm of a granite fountain, shut dry for winter.

"Look."

Crispin caught her hand in his, and Cassandra lay her cheek softly on his shoulder. Wishing to slow the passage of time, Crispin shut his eyes. *But like Christmas or Spring*, he thought, *just when you most want time to creep, it speeds up.* May and Archie broke in with their jovial, live-out-loud manner, and he separated slightly from Cassandra but held her in his gaze.

One snowy afternoon, the four friends were cooped up in the drawing room, content to be listless and bored. Archie and Crispin were playing a distracted game of chess, occupied more with suppositions about what horse would win The Oaks Stakes than with their moves. May played the piano, her fingers dancing lazily across the keys. It was a Brahms melody that matched their quiet, happy mood. Cassandra, nestled in a bay window and silhouetted by the steel sky, was reading a novel. Every once in a while, she would emerge from behind the pages to add a witty remark to the conversation, the only sign that she was not fully transported by her book.

"The post has come," Campbell said, walking toward Archie and Crispin. He extended a silver tray, which held two letters. "For you Mr. St. John."

"Two! You *are* popular Crispin! I don't think I've gotten two letters the whole while we've been in Scotland." Archie let out an exaggerated sigh.

"Who are they from?" May asked indelicately.

"Middleton and Miss Rosalind!" Archie broke out before Crispin had a chance to respond.

"They must miss you so," May added, a little too treacly to be believed.

Crispin read the letters quickly, hoping nothing was wrong.

Nothing was.

And everything was.

"What is it, mate? You look like you've swallowed a gnat."

"Sadly, I must depart sooner than intended. Tomorrow even."

"Tomorrow!" May balked in genuine distress. "But you can't!"

"I don't have much choice. Middleton writes that he is on his way to London and the letter was posted a little less than a month ago, so he'll be arriving any day. This is much sooner than I anticipated, and I must make sure our office is ready for him."

"And your Miss Rosalind, does she travel with him?" May asked, intrigued.

"No. Not this time. However, it appears that she too is planning an early arrival. The first of April. I am sorry. You are the consummate hosts, and I hate to leave in such haste. You can't imagine how disappointed I am."

"Hardly." Archie scoffed. "This is rather good news, isn't it?" His voice was laced with something that sounded like sarcasm. Crispin gave Archie a sideways glance but didn't answer. He got to his feet with a purpose and bowed to May, making a hurried exit.

As Crispin left the room, he tried to catch Cassandra's eyes, but they did not move from the pages of her book. Her expression was unreadable; her chin set with marble-like resolve and she stared intently at the pages as if she was held hostage by the plot.

CHAPTER 34

March 1874

Cassandra had seen the opera before. *La Traviata*. It was not one of her favorites. No opera was for that matter. The fat men and voluptuous women crooning in the intense spotlights and pretending to be youthful lovers never captured her imagination. The louder and more mournful they became, the more Cassandra saw them for what they were: players stuffed into voluminous costumes, their faces caked in grotesque paint.

Forsythe did not seem to share her skepticism. Cassandra had not been home from Scotland for two days when Forsythe had caught wind of her return. He renewed his invitation to the opera. She had put him off again, claiming a head cold from her travels, but at his third request, she could not muster a legitimate excuse. *Besides*, she told herself, *it was generous of him to stand by her family*. In his unappealing way, he was trying to be a good friend to her father. Or so she tried to convince herself. On the short carriage ride to the theater that night, Forsythe had situated himself too close for comfort. Cassandra could feel his hip pressed against hers.

"I hope, Miss Drayton," he had said, sliding toward her, "that this is the first of many such evenings together."

Now, as they sat in the rather confined opera box, shared with only two other spectators, Cassandra observed Forsythe's profile. Enraptured, his mouth fell slightly open as Alfredo fell to the feet of the ailing Violetta. Observing him watch the opera, it seemed Cassandra finally found his genuine interest. Most of the time Forsythe himself was the player, but his genre was not the melodramatic; it was more a pantomime in which he ironically played the part of a dashing young lord.

Caught up in her analysis, Cassandra had looked at him too long. He sensed her stare and turned away from the stage. Open-mouthed, he drew in a deep, meaningful breath. Cassandra smiled quickly and turned away, hoping to break the awkward tension. But she had triggered something that she could not stop. The dark, velvet box seemed to close in on her even before Forsythe moved his hand toward hers, his fingers sliding over her gloves. Cassandra could not speak or make sudden movements or shift her chair for fear of drawing the attention of their companions in the box, a Mrs. Jennings and her daughter Anne. And so his hand moved unchecked up Cassandra's arm toward her shoulder and neck. It inched down her back and crawled along her hip and stomach.

Cassandra was sure the Jennings must have been aware of some movement behind them. Why did they not turn around or clear their throats? Surely, that would break this moment. But in the stillness, Forsythe's hand pressed its way along the silk of Cassandra's skirt: her thigh, knee, calf, ankle. Her body froze. She could not move a muscle, not even to stay his hand. He must have taken her goosebumps as encouragement. His hand was at the base of her skirt, wandering along the hem of her crinoline. Wanting to scream, but knowing she could not create a scene, Cassandra bit the inside of her cheeks as his hand crept further, only stopping when she squeezed her ankles and knees together sharply. Cassandra's whole body was rigid and pinched tight. He could not ignore her reaction now. His lustful gaze froze, hardened, and then resumed a feigned ease, as he leaned close to Cassandra's ear.

"I have longed for a moment like this." His words were hot and moist on her neck. A wave of nausea came over her.

"To have you in the dark and by my side." He breathed. "I can save you, you know. You and your father." Lecherous, suffocating breath. "I'll wait until you are ready . . . and you *will* be ready. In the end, you'll need me."

Finally, the opera ended, the lights rose, and the audience spilled out into the gallery. What a relief to see the teeming crowd. Cassandra exhaled and unclenched her jaw at last. As they made their way through the crush of people, Cassandra tried to ignore the whisperings and murmurings that were surely directed at her and her companion: one the daughter of a disgraced lord, and the other so much older and so often the subject of gossip.

Cassandra saw him first. He was standing in the hall, pulling on his gloves and talking seriously with a gray-haired man. He spotted Forsythe and inadvertently cinched up his face. But then he saw Forsythe's hand touching her arm as they descended the stairs. Noticing Crispin's distraction, his friend looked in their direction, then turned away with a disdainful curl of his lip. Cassandra watched their silent exchange a few seconds longer. The gentleman must have said something snide, which Crispin dismissed politely. The interaction was followed by an awkward lull in their dialogue, but they parted as friends, shaking hands before heading to the street.

Cassandra had not seen Crispin since he made his premature departure from Arlie Manor in Scotland. She simultaneously was desperate to hear from him but also dreaded the inevitable news that Rosalind Middleton's early arrival would hasten Crispin's wedding day. A spring wedding. She and Aunt Eugenia had once—it seemed an age ago—talked of a spring wedding with Lord Bedford. No wedding hovered on Cassandra's horizon now, unless of course, she capitulated to Forsythe's attentions. The thought set her teeth on edge, mostly because the idea became more real with each passing day. Her father's depression and inertia did not lift, and the money from the auctioned items slipped away like sand. More could and would be sold; more furnishings and keepsakes and jewelry closer to the heart than the last lot. *And what then*, Cassandra's mind wondered feverishly as she waited for her cloak.

It took nearly twenty minutes for her to collect it, but once she did, she drifted through the doors, once again on Forsythe's arm. She was surprised to see Crispin there on the sidewalk, not waiting for a carriage or hailing a hack, but standing straight by one of the tall columns of the opera house. He was waiting for her, Cassandra was sure. He watched Forsythe put Cassandra into a carriage and kiss her hand, a long, lingering, possessive kiss.

"I will call on you tomorrow?" Forsythe blinked his eyes suggestively. Was it a question or a statement? Cassandra couldn't tell.

"I wish Father were well enough to see you."

"I don't come to Grosvenor Square to see your father."

"It was a charming evening. Thank you, Mr. Forsythe. Good night."

"Good night." He shut the door and tapped the window to signal to the driver. As they pulled away, Cassandra wanted very badly to look back and see if Crispin was still there. She was almost certain he was, but if she looked back, Forsythe would take it as encouragement, and she was all too aware that she had encouraged him enough for one night.

Forsythe did call the next evening. And the next. And the one after that. Cassandra tried as best she could to find his good qualities, ones that made his company bearable. He was generous and gracious and even chivalrous. Each day he arrived with an enormous bouquet of expensive flowers.

"Mr. Forsythe, you've practically turned the drawing room into a greenhouse!" Cassandra exclaimed as she accepted the fourth bouquet. "Peonies, my absolute favorite." She buried her nose into the pink cloud puffs of blossoms. They did smell delicious.

"I suspected as much. They are not in bloom yet in England, so they had to be shipped from southern Spain. They symbolize wealth, did you know?"

"I did not. You are full of interesting tidbits. Braxton, could you find me another vase?"

Braxton moved with haste to leave the room, thankful, Cassandra imagined, for a reason to exit. Miss Fairfax, on the other hand, stayed put, doing all she could not to roll her eyes. Later that night she warned Cassandra. "He's getting too friendly, you know. You shouldn't encourage him."

"What am I to do, Emma? He arrives invited or not. And they are beautiful flowers. I think he's trying to be nice."

"I'll give him that, but why? That man does nothing without a motive."

Cassandra couldn't have agreed more, but other thoughts clouded her mind. Bills piled up day by day, and every time she did an accounting, the negatives loomed, a craggy mountain of red against a tiny green divot of positives. Her father had still not emerged from his room, not for more than the odd and unpredictable hour.

When Cassandra told him about Forsythe's multiple visits, pleading with him to play host for a night or two, he dismissed her request.

"Cassie, he's here to see you."

"I know but I don't enjoy his company. Not the way you do. You and he have things in common." Cassandra racked her brain for what those things were. "Hunting, gaming, business interests." Oh dear, how had she let those words exit her mouth?

"Business. I've had enough of business for now, Cassie." He was so defeated, she shivered. Why could he not pluck himself up? Why couldn't he find some ember of his former fire for life? Why did he leave it to his daughter to put together the shattered pieces of their household affairs? Cassandra let out an exaggerated sigh, hoping he would hear her thoughts. But if he did, he made no show of it.

"Do you want a tray of supper, father?" Cassandra made her way to the door.

"No thank you." He did not lift his head to look at her. It was as if she was a ghost that floated, unseen, in and out of his room. But he knew she was still there, hand on the brass knob. Her father gave a sad cough and raised his darkened eyes to his daughter.

"He's a rich man, Cassie. You know that don't you?"

She closed the door. Yes, she knew that.

A few days later, Cassandra spotted Mr. Forsythe emerging from the master suite. Turning the corner, she reversed her step and stood stone still, back against the wall, hoping she had not been seen. Forsythe strode confidently down the hall and hopped, giddily, down the stairs.

Other than Emma, Cassandra, and Braxton no one had entered Lord Drayton's room in months. Not even Aunt Eugenia. It took a moment for

Cassandra to understand Forsythe's purpose, and then, as she stood at the top of the stairs, it washed over her like an icy wave. She heard Forsythe ask for her.

"Where might I find Miss Drayton?" His voice was light and pleasant, comfortable and proprietary. Her weeks of suspicions were confirmed.

Braxton stated in his most regal voice. "Please wait in the library Mr. Forsythe, I will inquire after Miss Drayton."

Feeling the weight of this moment, Cassandra descended the stairs. She heard Braxton through a distorted haze. "A guest . . . in the library . . . would you like me to say you are unwell? Miss Drayton?" Forsythe would ask for her hand, she knew this with the same certainty that she knew the sky was blue and the sun rose and fell to make day and night. "No, Braxton, I'll go. Tell him I'll be there in a minute." If she accepted, she would face a lifetime of his unsettling stares and unwelcome touches. She arrived at the library door.

"Miss Drayton, you are looking exceptionally lovely today." Forsythe's voice was uncharacteristically low, nearly husky. He approached her with a purposeful swagger. Cassandra stared at the gray flecks of dandruff on his ill-fitting but expensive suit. Visible beneath the folds of his jacket was the thick gold chain of his pocket watch.

"Thank you, Mr. Forsythe. It is nice to see you today. Were you visiting Papa?" She did her best to maintain a cool detached demeanor despite her clenched stomach and dewy brow.

"Yes, my dear, I was. We had a nice chat, and he suggested I come down and talk to you afterwards." He took her cold hand in his damp one. "You see, I've asked his permission for your hand."

And there it was. A proposal.

"Cassandra. You must have noticed that I have had a regard for you for some time." He cleared his throat. "I find myself in a position now to take a wife. Given your family's circumstance and our connection, I think this would be a suitable match for both of us."

Everything in her screamed to deny him. Reject the life he offered, one of monetary comfort but personal torment. And still, the only thing

Cassandra could think of was her father. Papa and Drayton Manor and all of the work he had done to build his legacy. In one moment, it had evaporated, and she could save him, save their fortune and perhaps even resurrect their good name. With just a few kind words.

"And my father gave his consent?"

"Yes, of course. Your father has long been a supporter of mine, and I'm honorable enough to forgive him for putting me into a losing investment. Mind you, as I've said I didn't lose that much. Your father sees the benefit of this union. I will be able to bolster his coffers and pay off the mortgage on Drayton Manor."

Cassandra must have winced inadvertently, and Forsythe must have noticed, for he continued with a softer approach. "I am sorry if I have offended your feminine sensibilities. He couldn't have kept it secret for long though. His banker is a great friend of mine and told me some of the particulars of your father's mortgage. It wasn't a wise move, but your father always was impetuous. So eager, I suppose, to make up for the lost fortunes of his ancestors that he put himself into risky situations. The road to hell is paved with good intentions and all that." Forsythe chuckled. The condescending edge in his voice had returned.

The words were vulgar but not without truth.

"Anyway, let's not talk about money matters." He ran his thumb and forefinger down the gold watch chain. "I don't want to bother you with that. When we are wed, there will be no more worries for you and your family. I will solve everything, you will see. Your father will take his position back in society again, gradually, and you all will be able to go out to parties and balls. We will entertain in grand style I promise you. Now, what do you think? Do you accept?"

Cassandra took in what he said, her mind doing somersaults over Forsythe's words. She tried to weigh her options, to think clearly and calmly, rationally. She wanted more time to think, but she could hear the ticking of his watch.

"Miss Drayton?" Forsythe's voice was a cocktail of condescension and impatience. "Cassandra? I may call you that, can't I?"

It was one or the other, she either accepted his offer or accepted losing Drayton Manor. Accepted the persistent humiliation and social exile of those she loved. Accepted being turned out of Grosvenor Square, as would eventually happen when the funds raised at auction were depleted. She would watch her father and Miss Fairfax be put into the position of having to rely on the charity of Aunt Eugenia and Lord Gray. Miss Fairfax would surely be sent away. Or she could save them all, right now, starting now.

She nodded wordlessly, and Forsythe pressed a ring onto her finger. Cassandra looked at the shimmering stone, a clear diamond, smooth and glassy, like a square of ice.

It was a practical arrangement, a decision many women in her position had made before and many would make after.

CHAPTER 35

April 1874

Having finished several glasses of wine, Crispin struggled to follow the contents of the rather involved contract he was reviewing. He read and re-read paragraphs, until finally, giving up, he tossed the papers to the rug and fell back into the leather chesterfield, rubbing his eyes and loosening his collar and top shirt button. There was a gentle knock on the door. It was Nora.

"Mr. St. John, Miss Drayton is here to see you." Crispin hurriedly tried to put himself together as Cassandra swept into the room, her cheeks flushed and her gold curls slightly in disarray, betraying that she had walked from Grosvenor Square. Crispin had not seen her since that night at the opera when that unctuous Forsythe clung to her like a bad cold. She had looked pale, almost ill, as if Forsythe really had given her a chill, but tonight she was rosy and alive.

"I hope I am not intruding." She said a little breathlessly.

"No, no. Of course not. It's beastly out. You must be frozen." Crispin cupped Cassandra's hands and led her to the fireplace.

"I'm fine." Her voice was low and even.

"I'm sorry for the state of the room. I've taken to eating my dinner here since I'm just a bachelor with no one to please but myself." He attempted excuses, but she dismissed them. "Would you like something to drink? A sherry?"

"Yes. Thank you." The room was silent except for the sound of the decanter clinking against the glass and the crackling of the fire. Crispin passed Cassandra a delicate crystal cup filled near the brim with caramel-colored sherry. She sipped it slowly, while he took indelicate draughts from his tumbler of whisky. He waited for an explanation. *Why had she come?* But none was forthcoming. Cassandra walked over to the bookshelf where Crispin kept various treasures from his travels: an elephant tusk, a photograph of Archie and himself with mates from the "Pig Sticking Club" in Howrah, an opalescent conch shell. She looked at the shelf, lingering on each item.

"Do you miss your life in India?"

"Not really. I suppose I miss the weather, though most in London find that hard to believe."

"I wish I had traveled more. There are so many magnificent places to go and beautiful things to see."

"You've been to America. Not everyone can say that."

"True."

"While I was in India, I missed the cool mornings and the lavender hills and even the fog. There is a certain harshness in the air in India."

"The same could be said of America. At least the West." She held up the conch shell. "Where is this from?"

"Goa."

"It's lovely." Her voice seemed remote. She put the shell down and ran a finger over its perfectly, imperfect ridges.

"If you put it to your ear, you can hear the ocean."

She followed his instructions.

"That's magical. I feel as though I'm there." And, for a moment it was as if the crash of waves filled the silence of the room. Cassandra clearly had come for a reason. Crispin took the shell from her hands and placed her palms in his.

"What is it?"

She raised her bright, sad eyes.

"I don't know. I just had to see you and tell you myself."

"Tell me what?" Crispin moved his hands to her shoulders and pulled her close. He wasn't sure he wanted an answer. His lips brushed her hair, which smelled faintly of gardenias. For a moment she was motionless, her cheek resting on his heart.

When she finally pulled away, he didn't want to let her go, and for a moment too long he held her upper arms firmly, pressing her close to his chest. He thought of her sad beautiful face looking up at his in Scotland. He wanted to kiss her and to keep kissing her. Whatever piece of himself was attached to Rosalind floated away and he made no attempt to catch it. Instead, he reached for Cassandra, again.

"I can't, Crispin. I came to tell you something. It won't change anything for either of us, but I needed to tell you anyway."

"It can wait, whatever it is." He said as much to himself as to Cassandra. His restraint evaporated, and he lowered his lips to hers, tasting salt and sherry. He kissed her searchingly once, twice, three times, each time lingering longer. The air between them was charged with electricity. He wrapped his arms around the small of her back and kissed harder, pushing heavily into her. She pushed back. They dove headlong into each other, their tongues meeting, barely coming up for air.

Crispin knew what it was to touch a woman, to feel her flesh on his, but this was Cassandra. He had longed to hold her for as long as he could remember. She shivered, and he could feel the soft hair on her arm. Desire rose from the pit of his stomach, shooting outward like lighting. His body stiffened. He wanted her. Impropriety be damned. She had come to him.

Crispin's tongue trailed along Cassandra's jaw and down her throat. He pushed her against the desk, clearing papers aside with one hand and pulling the neckline of her dress with the other. *Could this be happening?* he thought to himself. He crumpled the question up like a piece of discarded paper and threw it to the back of his mind. He kissed Cassandra's shoulder, before daring to go further, dipping beneath the lace to her perfect porcelain breasts.

"This isn't right. Crispin." Cassandra breathed in his ear, but as she did, she clasped his back and did not let go. He pulled her skirt toward her waist to shower kisses on her smooth calf, the delicate inside of her knee, her thigh. She exhaled faster and faster, yielding at his every touch.

"Good God, Cassandra. Stay with me." He kissed her again and again.

"Crispin," she whispered suppliantly, "we must stop."

"Shhh." He put his finger to her lips. "Please stay."

Then, Crispin picked her up and carried her to the couch, laying her down and pressing his whole body into hers. Through the layers of clothes, they melted into each other. He could feel her rise to meet him. Their muscles strained. Heat swelled up and exploded like fireworks through all their limbs.

Cassandra shifted under him and finally struggled to get up. "Crispin." She pressed the silk of her skirt down definitively.

"Cassie, I—"

"No, Crispin, don't." Her voice had a piercing edge.

"Why not? What is it?"

She said nothing, but her tears came fast. For a moment, they were still; side by side, before the tugging of the outside world broke them apart.

"Forsythe has asked me to marry him." All the air was sucked from the room. "And I have said yes."

"What? You cannot! You cannot do that!" Crispin leaped up from the couch, shouting, "Cassie, he's a snake! What could he possibly offer you?" He slammed his fist upon the desk.

"I have no choice. It is the only way I can help my father. He is a broken man. His life is in shambles. I have to make things right again."

"A life with Forsythe is too high a price to pay. What about your life?"

"I will survive. I will make this work. You of all people should understand. I have to save my father."

"No. You cannot do this. There must be another way. I will help you." He knew he sounded like a pleading schoolboy, his voice raw and high at the same time.

"But you can't. You can't," she cried. "No one can help, but me. I have chosen this fate."

"You don't love him. I know you don't love him." Crispin gnashed angrily. "If you are going to go ahead with this sham of a marriage, tell me you love him!"

She shook her head sadly. That she could not do.

He approached her again, cupping her face between his hands. They were both crying now.

"It's not right," Crispin nearly whimpered.

"You are one to talk," Cassandra said in a low accusatory voice. "What would Rosalind think of all this? I must go. I should not have come."

"Please don't do this." Crispin grabbed her hand, but she slipped away too fast, and he heard a sob as the door slammed.

CHAPTER 36

Out in the night air, Cassandra ran as fast as she could down Green Street, past Mayfair and Kensington, past the Grand Park Arch and the Queen's Mews. Panting, she kept running. *What would Aunt Eugenia say if she saw me now?* she thought to herself. The hem of her skirt was speckled with mud; her hair unkempt, her face smeared with hot tears, her upper lip beaded with sweat. She knew she must look like a street urchin, but she kept running as far as her feet could carry her.

As she ran, her chest felt tight as if her heart were a clenched fist beneath her corset, knocking against the walls of her rib cage. It battled, boxer-like, against the nightmare of the last few months. Cassandra cried out, a wordless sob, the sound swallowed up by the dark, starless night.

In the silence, she tried to think her way out of the knot of confusion that filled her head. Could she really go through with marrying Forsythe? Could she sleep next to that greasy little man? Could she kiss his hard, narrow lips? Let his reptilian tongue linger in intimate places? She shivered at the thought.

She could still feel Crispin's kiss, his wide, soft mouth on hers. He had held her so tightly that the heat of his skin radiated through his clothes, and his heart had thumped against her chest, which now rose and fell heavily with the effort of breathing. Cassandra could still feel his enveloping embrace, his broad shoulders, and strong arms. She had felt faint, faint but alive. She should never have gone to his house, Cassandra cursed herself for the folly of it. Because, of course, now she knew, and would always know, what it felt like to be held like that and to be kissed and to want to kiss back. Her cheeks were a mess of tears and her feet hurt.

Cassandra stopped at the corner of Upper Brook and Park Street and grasped the spikes of a cast-iron gate. Though they were cold and damp, she held them tight. It was as if she could feel Crispin's fingers laced in her own.

As she stood there, mind still racing with indecision, Aunt Eugenia's voice seemed to float in on a cool breeze, reminding her about the challenges that life presented, the importance of their social sphere, the sanctity of family, and the need to be pragmatic. *It's not just for you, you know; it's for your family as well.*

In the not-too-distant past, Cassandra had dismissed Aunt Eugenia's warnings as the dim, shallow musings of the middle-aged. When, at fifteen, Cassandra had declared that she would marry for love, Aunt Eugenia had gently mocked her niece, dismissing the thought. That kind of love is short-lived, she advised. Yet maybe that kind of love did exist. Cassandra had first sensed its possibility in Scotland, like a flickering candle set on the sill of an open window, and she had felt its heat again tonight. It was both real and unrealistic. In the darkened streets and looming houses, everywhere she looked she saw sadness. A light turned on in a window above her, and the silhouette of a woman looked down at the street curiously. At first, Cassandra thought the woman was watching her, but then the silhouette leaned her forehead upon the windowpane and lingered there as if to cool a fever. Her long hair fell over her shoulders. Cassandra saw loneliness and worry, and the memory of Crispin's touch grew cold, replaced by the pull of blood and a single sober need: money.

A wave of calm descended upon her. Cassandra would do what was needed. She would forget Crispin and even herself. She exhaled deeply, acknowledging that her momentary insanity had passed, and walked home, hugging her shawl around her shoulders.

CHAPTER 37

Crispin was not normally a restless pacer, but tonight he could not sit still. He walked back and forth across his study nearly a hundred times before sitting down at his desk. He picked up a pen, dipped the quill in the well, and put it down again. He got up. Did several more turns about the room. Poured himself a second glass of scotch. Sat down again. Same routine.

He knew he needed to write to Rosalind—Middleton too. It would change everything, but it was changed already. He could put up with a life of talking about chintz and Col. Geary and what they were wearing in Paris, but he could not spend his life thinking about Cassandra Drayton for hours on end. He couldn't enter into a marriage with that kind of false pretense. Every thought Crispin had of Rosalind was eclipsed by Cassandra's image. For the last three hours, he had tried to imagine a life with Rosalind, walking arm and arm in St. James, taking tea, sitting at the table, the bedside, the nursery, but the image refused to crystalize. Everything he tried to conjure up brought him back to Cassandra.

Dear Rosalind,

Crispin wondered how Middleton would respond and anticipated that his retribution would be painful. He would have to give up Fleet Street of course. Unless Middleton was willing to sell it to him. Crispin snorted at the idea, the absurdity. He was about to jilt the man's daughter. Surely, he would be in no mood to sell the boy a business, no matter how rational he was or how much he had appreciated Crispin prior to this moment. Crispin crumpled the paper in his hands and pushed it aside. Grabbing another sheet, he began again.

Dear Joe,

Better to write to Middleton and get the worst over with. The ink splattered as Crispin pressed down on the tip of the pen in determination and frustration. He explained as best he could.

I find myself compelled to end my engagement to Rosalind . . . great respect for you and your daughter, yet my feelings are those of brotherly affection . . . It is my sincerest hope that we maintain our business connection . . . of course, I will understand if . . ..

As he read the letter, the words blurred into a murky black jumble, and the knot that had been growing in his belly tightened. The second glass of scotch hadn't soothed it. Joe Middleton had been a mentor, a partner, and a better father to him than his own. Crispin felt sick to his stomach with regret at the pain and embarrassment he was about to inflict, but he sucked in his breath and sealed the letter quickly, before losing his nerve. This had to be done. He couldn't embark on a marriage to a woman he didn't love, no matter his affection for Joe. This he knew. Crispin rang the bell, and Nora appeared instantly.

"Nora, post this immediately." He practically threw the letter in her face.

"But sir, it's far too late. I'm not sure it will make it out tonight."

"Find a boy to run it over. This must go out with haste." Thankfully, Nora sensed his urgency.

"Alright, Mr. St. John. I'll get it out straight away." She ran from the room. Crispin grabbed the decanter and filled his glass to the brim. There would be no sleep tonight.

The bright morning sun sliced through the window pulling Crispin reluctantly from his slumber on his desk. His head pounded. Disoriented, he looked down to find he was still wearing yesterday's suit, wrinkled and stale-smelling. As Crispin attempted to reconstruct the evening, Archie's too-cheery voice boomed from the foyer.

"Nora, a pleasure. You look ravishing as always. I'll let myself in." Crispin did not even have a chance to rouse himself from the desk before Archie was in the middle of the room.

"Good God! You're a mess! Did you sleep here?"

"Please, your voice. It's like a trumpet."

"And you're drunk!"

"No. Just dreadfully hungover."

"Don't you remember? We were to check out the sales and take lunch at the club. Crispin, you *are* looking rather bleak this morning. And you smell terrible." Archie joked good-naturedly. "Nora asked that I give you these." Archie's ginger bangs fell across his forehead as he shoved a short stack of letters toward Crispin. "I think she was afraid to come in. And now I see why. By the way, I think Nora fancies me!"

"All the ladies fancy you, my friend, regardless of their age or station. In fact . . ." Crispin stopped dead as he noticed Joe Middleton's handwriting in the pile of post. His stomach dropped in dread of the letter's contents; the happy tidings and marital planning it was sure to convey. He slowly fumbled with his letter opener, unable to catch the crease.

"Who's that from? You look like you're going to swoon. Positively green."

Finally, Crispin ripped the letter open, careless of the paper. It was likely a routine letter of business matters, yet his heart was beating so hard he thought Archie might hear it across the room. Crispin scanned the first paragraphs.

"My God."

"What is it?" Archie rose and came to the desk.

"It's from Middleton. You read it." Archie grabbed the letter from Crispin's shaky hand and read aloud.

Dearest Crispin,

I do hope this letter finds you well and that our affairs continue to prosper in England as they do here in India. I am delighted and indeed proud of the excellent progress you have made in moving our business forward in these modern times. I have made no better decision than to take you under my wing those years ago and to make you an equal partner last year.

My boy, I have always looked upon you as the son I never had. And it is because of the affection I have for you that writing this letter and the news that it brings is so difficult for me.

I will not waste ink. My dear Crispin: she is gone. Rosalind has run off with an army colonel, Colonel Geary. I cannot begin to express my shame in relaying this news to you. I have long known of Rosalind's high spirits but could never have imagined her capable of bringing this sort of shame on our family and of hurting you so profoundly. I will not offer any excuses for her behavior, and I do hope that Geary has honorable intentions and will marry her. As the third son of an earl, I suspect he will be easily enticed by the hope of winning her fortune. He will be sorely disappointed, however, when he learns that I have adjusted my will to protect my property from his fortune-hunting. But I won't trouble you with my profound embarrassment.

I know you will be as shocked by this news as I have been and expect that upon reading it, you will consider your engagement with Rosalind broken. It is my sincerest hope that this news will not cause you to end our connection. I would like for us to continue in partnership and hope that you do as well. But of course, if you would prefer to release yourself, I will buy your share.

I had so dearly wanted you and Rosalind to find happiness together. I suspect I am as heartbroken as you are, perhaps more so. Crispin, I wish you all the best in finding that happiness elsewhere.

With warmest affection and hope for your speedy response,

Joe

Archie punctuated the close of the letter by raising both eyebrows as high as they would extend.

"Whoa. 'My God' indeed." He paced back and forth before the windows, his dark silhouette a contrast to the morning light. "This is really something. Shocking. Geary . . . I . . . uh, know the family. Not, of course, this scoundrel of a Colonel, but the rest of them. Not a bad lot, I guess."

Archie stopped pacing and walked toward Crispin, balling the letter in his left fist and clenching the right, before placing them both on the edge of the desk. A smile overtook his face.

"But look, Crispin." He lowered his voice as if to keep others from hearing, "I think you have really dodged a bullet here my friend."

"What?" Crispin dragged his fingers shakily through his unwashed hair. His head was pounding, and he couldn't concentrate, fragments from the night before came back to him like a flickerbook. Cassandra in his door frame, her hands in his, the taste of sherry and salt on her lips, his frantic letter writing, pressing Nora to send the missive without delay. What would Joe think when it reached him? Perhaps it wouldn't matter.

"I said I think you've dodged a bullet. I mean you said yourself that you don't love her."

"I never said that! You said that." Crispin stood challenging his friend, indignant and uncertain at the same time.

"Alright, maybe it was me, but you can't tell me you aren't somewhat relieved. I mean, since you've been in London, you haven't once told me that you missed her or were eager for her arrival. You'd be bored with her in a fortnight for God's sake! And I needn't remind you of the other ladies you have met. Cassandra Drayton for one. We saw you in Scotland, May and I. You look at her like a man enthralled."

Cassandra. Images of last night continued to dance across the stage of Crispin's brain. What would Archie say about *that*? No, doubt he would be impressed and think it the greatest stroke of luck in the world.

"Let's leave her out of this," Crispin grumbled.

Archie harrumphed.

"The truth is, the reason I look like hell is I stayed up all night agonizing over a letter I posted to Middleton yesterday."

"What did it say?"

"Oh, not much, only that I wanted to break it off with Rosalind and hoped that our business relationship would survive! And then I wake up this morning to this. Christ." Crispin dropped back into his seat and recounted to his friend the whole of the prior night's adventures. Well, not the whole. He left out the details that were perhaps the most crucial, such as the gentle pressure of Cassandra's lips and the feel of her body pressed against his.

"But that's terrific! Now, he doesn't have to feel guilty about his faithless floozy of a daughter."

"Please, is that necessary?"

"Damn right, it is! You have been toiling away, working dutifully, setting up a home, and she has been setting her sights on some no-good third son of an earl. It's clear from the letter that Middleton wants to maintain your business connection. It's an out, and at least *your* reputation is intact. I say, well done, you!" Archie reached around to clap Crispin firmly on the back.

It started to sink in. Crispin raised his eyes to the ceiling. For the first time that morning, his spirits lifted. Archie was right. He might get what he wanted—to break with Rosalind, to keep Fleet Street, and in a tiny corner of his mind, a spark lit in the hope that he might have the slightest chance, however minute, to thwart Forsythe. To win Cassandra's hand.

"Well Archie, I think you've covered it all. Let's go check out those horses. It will help me clear my head."

"I think you'd better change first. And wash. For the love of God."

CHAPTER 38

May 1874

"So, have you decided on where you will purchase your trousseau, my dear? I'm sure Forsythe will contribute and that no expense will be spared. You will be a stunning bride!" Aunt Eugenia's ample body bobbed up and down in her enthusiasm over her niece's engagement, while Cassandra stared at her soup with the same feeling of nausea and apprehension that had filled her stomach every meal since she'd decided to accept Forsythe, and particularly since she'd visited Crispin. Cassandra greeted well-wishers with her best smile and stopped trying to convince May that this was the right decision. May in turn had ceased her lengthy diatribes about romance, love, and passion, particularly when Lady Douglas was present.

Cassandra glanced up from her soup to see her father, clean-shaven and in relatively high spirits. He was looking much better these days. Color had come back to his cheeks, and he was starting to regain some of the weight he had lost. Seated at the head of the table, Lord Drayton had resumed eating dinner with his daughter and Miss Fairfax almost immediately after Forsythe and Cassandra had announced their engagement.

"Yes! She will look marvelous as always." James beamed at his daughter. She knew it must have been the same smile he bestowed on her as a younger girl, but now it seemed empty and insincere. "I knew this would all work out. After all this terrible business, we will have a happy ending." Her father was relieved to the point of elation that Forsythe had agreed to pay off the mortgage on Drayton Manor in exchange for the marriage. With the estate secure, the income from the rents would be enough to cover the expenses in the country and in town. "We will resume our position. It will be no time at all before we can entertain and go into society again."

His words gnawed at Cassandra. Was he really as self-centered and avaricious as he seemed? Previously, Cassandra had accepted her father's constant search for monetary gain as a minor idiosyncrasy that was overshadowed by a preponderance of other, finer attributes. But now, she sensed it was the hard pit at the core of his nature. His months of self-induced exile seemed to have vanished the instant Forsythe remedied his financial situation.

"Papa, let's not be overeager. We are not as popular as we once were. Many of our friends lost a great deal this past year. Mr. Forsythe is not universally admired."

"Cassie, dear, these things blow over in time." He patted his daughter's hand lovingly, his signet ring clipping against the diamond of her betrothal ring. "Times change. The classes mix. You see it more and more."

Cassandra's stomach turned sour with anger, but she noted that if *she* looked out of sorts, Miss Fairfax looked as if she had been slapped in the face. She visibly recoiled before violently shoving her chair back and rising cadet-like to her feet.

"James, you are a fool . . . you've sold your daughter to that odious man." Momentarily stunned by her outburst, Cassandra looked to Aunt Eugenia and her Uncle, who were both riveted. Miss Fairfax walked around the table and squared off against Lord Drayton. He too rose from his seat and reached his hand toward her as if to soothe her. She knocked it away. Aunt Eugenia's lips pursed in disapproval and amazement.

Miss Fairfax's face burned with rage and her hands trembled. She snapped. "When you collapsed with the news of your ruin, my heart stopped. I thought, no one knows his pain, how much he is suffering. No one but your daughter." Her voice grew more strident, stinging with its force. Aunt Eugenia gasped indignantly, looking at Miss Fairfax, then Lord Drayton, and then Cassandra in bewilderment. While Cassandra warmed with pride that Miss Fairfax had come to her defense, even she could see this heated outburst could come to no good. "But they were right, those who thought you got what you deserved. And the worst part is that you have learned nothing! You are consumed with selfish desire. The ambition that drove you into this mess is just that, ambition. Ambition and greed!" She paused, collecting her breath.

"For years you held yourself above Forsythe, thinking yourself a man of family and breeding. But you and he are cut from the same oily cloth. More outrageous yet, you are willing to let your daughter take the fall for you. Even Forsythe has not sunk that low. He at least knows the value of his prize." Miss Fairfax looked at her young companion, no longer the little girl in petticoats skipping up and down the stairs at Drayton Manor, with tears in her eyes.

She then scanned the room, her gaze stopping on Aunt Eugenia and Lord Gray, who still held their forks delicately in their hands, raised as if frozen. "And all of you." Miss Fairfax nearly growled, turning on the Grays. "You are just as bad, just as cowardly. Willing to let Cassandra be your pawn just so you can show your faces again at balls and banquets. In the hopes that those who have shut their doors to the Draytons, and their kin will open them again. Ha." Miss Fairfax laughed with derision. "What a dear price to pay for such tepid acceptance." She wrung her shaking hands and bit her lip so hard Cassandra was sure drops of blood were going spill.

After an extended, aching pause Miss Fairfax whispered harshly, "I won't stay to watch this fiasco," and hastened to the door. Cassandra grabbed her hands, trying to stop her.

"Emma, don't," Cassandra pleaded, squeezing their palms together as if in prayer.

"I am sorry, but I cannot stay." She rushed out of the room.

"Emma, please . . ." Lord Drayton called after her.

"See James, this is what you get for elevating her beyond her station. There's no need for these hys—" Aunt Eugenia's voice trailed off as the color drained from her cheeks. Despite Aunt Eugenia's huffing and puffing, Emma's words had not fallen on entirely deaf ears. Ideas were shifting, questions forming.

Cassandra followed Emma out of the room and toward the stairs. The color was high in her cheeks as she embraced Cassandra. "I'm going to my nephew. On Green Street. Call on me there if you need me." Within an hour, she was gone.

CHAPTER 39

Crispin returned home at half-past four and much earlier than was his custom but his aunt's arrival had changed things. Seeing her on his doorstep the night before was certainly unexpected. She'd been so upset and uncharacteristically disheveled, with her auburn hair falling from its chignon and the whites of her eyes, a web of red. Crispin felt it was too much to press her for the details of the evening that had ended in her leaving Grosvenor Square. He knew she would tell him in her own time. So, Nora had settled her into one of the three guest bedrooms, and master and maid decided together that they would let their new arrival sleep.

"You're early today." Nora curtsied quickly and rushed over to Crispin, her voice a hushed whisper. "On account of your Aunt, I think."

"How is she?"

"Well, I brought her a tray at 10 this morning, and then she didn't come out of her room until 2 o'clock. She looks right pale, poor thing. It must have been really terrible for her to escape in the dark of night! She's in the library having tea at present." In her usual fashion, Nora went about mothering everyone who entered the house. "I think she might be ready to talk."

"Well, we'll see about that."

Crispin entered the library to find Emma nestled into the cushioned sofa with a steaming cup of tea. She stared at the enormous fire that Nora had built up.

"There you are, Aunt Emma! You look well."

"Yes, Crispin. I am feeling much better." She rose to greet him. "You are so kind to let me stay . . ."

"No thank you necessary. Please. My home is yours." Crispin looked at the plate of biscuits Nora had left and began munching on one as he sat down next to his aunt on the sofa.

"Alright, I won't thank you, but I do think I owe you an explanation. It's not often, I suspect, that you have a distant relative show up on your doorstep late at night."

"You don't have to tell me anything. And I don't think of you as distant." He didn't want to pry, but he couldn't imagine what had driven her to leave her home of ten years, to leave Lord Drayton and Cassandra.

"I think I've had enough of privacy and discretion." She shifted uncomfortably in her seat, gathering her courage, then looked her nephew straight in the eye with determination.

"You may have guessed this already, but my relationship with Lord Drayton is . . . complicated."

"Aunt Emma, you don't need to continue . . ." He moved awkwardly in his seat as he remembered that autumn afternoon in the barn all those years ago and willed himself not to blush by nibbling the edge of a biscuit.

"I am sure that it has been rather obvious." She flushed a deep pink.

Recovering his composure, Crispin said, "I have had a sense of it for some time. I know it was your influence over Lord Drayton that saved me from far greater ramifications. And while you gave me a new life, you never left Drayton Manor. It must have been hard for you to leave him last night."

"It was." Tears gathered in her eyes. "But I cannot sit by and watch James *sell* Cassandra to Anthony Forsythe for the mortgage on Drayton Manor."

Crispin rose and paced the room, turning what she had just said over in his head. A month had passed since he had last seen Cassandra, and the dreadful wedding plans still marched forward toward their dismal end. Crispin shook his head. Though he was not surprised, Emma's words confirmed and clarified what was required to save Cassandra: the mortgage for Drayton Manor. It was a high price, one that he could not afford. Though

Crispin had risen substantially in life; he was comfortable, but not rich, at least not in the way required to pay for an estate like that.

"That was their settlement in the end?"

"Yes! In a month's time, Cassandra will marry that man so her father can have his manor back. I could see James doing the calculations in his head at dinner. Forsythe would give him a few hundred thousand pounds, and I'm sure he would have paid twice that for Cassandra. He's been eyeing her since she was a child." Emma hissed in disgust.

Crispin stood in front of the fireplace, his hand on the mantle as if to steady himself. "Forsythe is repulsive. I've begged her to change her mind, but she won't."

"She told you?"

Oh no, Crispin thought, as he sucked in his breath. Of course, Cassandra hadn't told Emma about her late-night visit to his house. And that was something he did not want to share with his aunt.

"You two have become close, haven't you?"

Crispin flushed under her intense stare. "In a way, yes. But I can't compete with 100,000 pounds, let alone multiple hundreds. I can't give her Drayton Manor back. A nice life, yes, but not that."

"And have you proposed then?" She looked at him expectantly.

"No, I haven't. When we last spoke, it seemed impossible for both of us. But I've since learned that . . . well, there is no point in getting into the details. My engagement is broken."

"Your engagement is broken? What happened?"

"It doesn't matter, Cassandra still won't have me."

"But Crispin, do you believe she cares for you in that way?" The question tumbled around in his head for a few moments. He was fairly certain he knew the answer, though it made him feel all the more helpless.

"I think she cares for me, yes. And I think she would consider my suit despite my social standing if . . ."

"Social standing! These last few months have taught me how empty those words are. James put her into this position and now he expects her to get him out of it. You are a respectable businessman. You have a fine house and the means to purchase an even larger one. And your friends are well connected. That is more than enough for a happy life."

"True, but I don't have the means to buy Drayton Manor. And she seems to think that is the only way out of this mess."

Emma moved to the fire and clasped her hands in Crispin's. "We will find a solution, Crispin, you and I. Cassie will not be sacrificed for James' pride."

For the first time, Crispin felt he had pierced that impenetrable aloofness that had kept his aunt apart from him all these years.

"Crispin," Archie swept into the library at Green Street and poured two large tumblers of scotch with unusual exuberance. "Old Drayton is coming to his senses."

"What are you talking about?"

"I called on him yesterday to see if I could stop this runaway train."

"What? But you barely speak to him."

"I may be a cad, but I'm not going to let such a peach of a girl be swallowed whole by that python Forsythe. Not when you're waiting in the wings. You know as well as I that Forsythe will ruin her life. She thinks she's being noble and is trying to make her father whole again. You said it yourself, it's too high a price to pay."

Crispin stared at Archie in disbelief.

"You don't mean to tell me that you thought you could do this on your own?" Archie continued. "You're just like her. You have grandiose notions that the world rests entirely on your shoulders. Listen, Crispin, we all have our limits. Even you."

Stunned into silence, Crispin picked up his scotch and glugged down the whole glass, trying to think of nothing but the scorching in his throat. Archie was right, Crispin had wanted to be the savior. He hadn't yet figured out how he was going to do it, but it fueled his every waking thought, and most of his sleeping ones too. Obsessively, he played out conversations he would have with Lord Drayton, with Cassandra, even with Lady Gray. He rehearsed his rhetoric, his tone, his gestures. Sadly, each fanciful scenario seemed more flawed than the one before it.

"What did you say to him?"

"I can't say I was subtle. I came right out and said that given what I knew about Forsythe, I could not, in good conscience keep silent, not when my sister's dearest friend's honor and future were at stake."

"When he asked what I was talking about, I admitted that Forsythe was a shrewd man of business and that he is tolerated in the male sphere and even seen as indispensable by some. But I told Lord Drayton that it ends there. 'Forsythe,' I said, 'is a necessary evil, and will never be accepted into intimate social circles. It's not just a matter of his parentage or upbringing. While his family will always be on the fringes of society, his flaws run far deeper.'

"At first Lord Drayton did not comprehend my meaning. He's awfully slow with any sort of innuendo, apparently. So, I told him about the brothel on Norfolk Street and included a few details that I'm sure chilled his blood . . . or boiled it. I can tell you it was an awkward exchange. We stood in silence for more than a few seconds." Archie grinned like a Cheshire cat, reveling in the memory of his success.

"He looked angry and flummoxed in turns. I almost thought he was going to ask me to leave. Before he had a chance to do so, I told him that if he had been spending more time at Brooks of late, he would know what I was referring to. 'For some time now,' I said, 'Forsythe's private affairs and proclivities have become rather public, and people have been talking.'" Imagining the exchange, Crispin's jaw dropped to his chin.

"What did Drayton say to that?"

"I let the words linger. When I could see my meaning had registered, I tossed one more log onto the fire. My mother. I mentioned that stories about Forsythe had trickled down to her and her friends. These women who quietly control our society, I reminded him, would never include Forsythe at their dinner tables or in their drawing rooms. I think that is when it sunk in. It really is treasonous to allow that man into our inner circle."

"You're an unmitigated snob," Crispin said with near giddiness.

"Yes, I am. And aren't you glad?" Archie kicked out his legs in front of him, crossing them while he leaned back on the couch and dramatically lifted his chin to the ceiling.

"But would *I* be allowed into your *inner circle?*"

"Of course. We're a dying breed and most of us know it. If we have any hope, any hope at all, it's because we can and do introduce men like you into the anointed ranks. You can work, you can roll up your sleeves. How else can we afford these crumbling, frigid estates and our archaic traditions? They all cost money, and a damn lot of it. But we must draw the line somewhere."

Archie leaned toward his friend, swirling the scotch in his glass meaningfully. "Crispin." He took a deep breath. "I'm as serious as I've ever been. I told Drayton that he was a fool to put his money on the Trojan horse. And that's when I told him about you."

"You did? What did you say about me? He must have been appalled. I was the lowliest person in his household."

"I didn't name you but indicated there was a man of breeding, intelligence, and wealth, a friend of mine, who had taken an interest in Cassandra. And, that both he and his daughter would lose out on a future worth having if he did not intervene in haste. This race is yours to win, Crispin. Don't let me down." Archie beamed at Crispin.

Crispin's hopes, which until now had felt like floating, unreachable clouds, had suddenly grown roots in solid soil.

"I won't."

"To your happiness." They clinked glasses.

An afterthought came to Archie as they sauntered down the stairs. "I almost forgot; Mama's on the case as well. She had Eugenia over for tea. I have no doubt it was an *enlightening* conversation for 'Lady Superior.'"

Then Archie left, Crispin's jaw still sweeping the floor. "The Dowager Countess has spoken on my behalf?" He murmured to himself in disbelief. He had been released by Middleton, and now the Douglas family was pleading his case.

Crispin paced his library. Fourteen steps from the fireplace to the window and fourteen back. It seemed unreal. In some ways, he was more comfortable when the odds were stacked against him. That was the situation he was accustomed to, and the idea of a life with Cassandra had always been a dream, just a dream. As time marched on, he had pulled himself up, but he had been reminded time and again that no amount of hard work on his part would breach the entrenched social divides that dictated the Draytons' world. The closer he got to that world, the better he understood which doors would open and which would remain firmly shut. Yet, now the knob turned, the hinges creaked. *Remember,* his father had said, *you're a gentleman's son.* A gentleman's son would be worthy of Cassandra's hand, but Crispin had not felt his father's words were true until that very moment.

CHAPTER 40

Hoping to escape to her bedroom unnoticed by anyone, Cassandra tiptoed past the drawing room door, which was ajar.

"I don't understand James. What are you suggesting?"

It was Forsythe's voice, at an unusually high pitch, that made her stop. Cassandra crept past the door holding her skirt so that it would not rustle.

"I am suggesting that there will be no wedding."

"Excuse me?"

"At first, I was, and I still am to some degree, heartened by your desire to help my family, but I cannot accept your generosity, nor can I let my daughter enter a marriage with you, who would surely make her miserable. In more ways than one. For some time now, I have been isolated. I have no one to blame but myself; I withdrew from society, but recently my eyes were opened, forcibly so."

"I still don't understand you."

"That surprises me, Forsythe. Though, I suppose, nothing should. I will be more direct then. I have heard stories of late, stories that reveal your character. I won't repeat them."

"I don't know what you mean, James."

"I think you do. And there is no point in discussing it further."

"Your sister will be very disappointed." Forsythe hissed warningly. "I think she was rather looking forward to rejoining society."

"My sister, if you must know, is among those who have opened my eyes." He sounded even more resolved and harder-edged. "You see, Lady Douglas, who does not think all that highly of you, has told Eugenia some unflattering rumors." The edge grew sharper. "I rather think her odds of being included in society are better without an attachment to the Forsythe name."

It was true. Aunt Eugenia had "come to her senses about Forsythe." Cassandra heard her speak to her father the night before with a mixture of reticence and contriteness in her voice, as well as a dash of derision—she was after all the same person. Eugenia had spoken in a low voice to keep Cassandra from hearing, but her young ears perked at Forsythe's name, followed in quick succession by Miss Fairfax's.

"It seems your governess was right about him. Lady Douglas told me . . ." Eugenia would not go into details; decorum would not allow a Lady to discuss certain matters. "Suffice it to say Cassandra is better off a maid . . . if it comes to that." Cassandra was surprised by Eugenia's change of heart but stood by the window pretending to be lost in thought. "But she's such a dear and so beautiful, I don't think it will. And, neither does Lady Douglas."

Once again, Cassandra was eavesdropping. That seemed her lot—to be constantly behind the wings of the curtain as the theater of life played out. She listened closely and placed her eye against the sliver of an opening at the hinges of the door.

Lord Drayton seemed to lift his shoulders at the memory of Aunt Eugenia's words and rang the bell. Braxton, who must have been listening in just as Cassandra was, appeared in the instant.

Forsythe's face twisted as he tried to process how the ground had so suddenly shifted beneath his feet.

"Braxton, Mr. Forsythe would like his coat and hat. He is leaving."

"James, is this how you do business? You go back on your word?"

"I suppose. As we both know, I have worse flaws." Lord Drayton grimaced. "Here is your investment. The check is good, as I have decided to sell Drayton Manor. I think that will conclude our business."

The hammer fell on Forsythe. Cassandra couldn't fathom what his reaction would be. What does one do when an opponent forfeits the one card that would win the game? Surely, Forsythe would start yelling, though she didn't think he would resort to violence. Cassandra stared transfixed as

Forsythe looked at the check, an empty ace in his hand. He didn't move. A strange silence filled the hall, and, for a while, there was no movement outside or inside the room. The two men stared at each other, waiting for the other to make a move. Braxton's eyes darted between them as though he were watching a boxing match.

Cassandra could almost hear her heart beat. Finally, the door flung open with a burst of energy and noise, and Forsythe, hat in hand, coattail curling up behind his legs, scurried out. He had not seen Cassandra, or if he had, he had pretended not to.

She slipped the heavy betrothal ring off her finger and walked into the drawing room. Her hand had never felt so light.

Lord Drayton sat at his desk, a determined, steadfast expression on his face. He did not look up to face his daughter, but said to her, "I can live with selling Drayton Manor, but I could not live with selling you to a man like him."

Cassandra rushed to his side, tears in her eyes, and knelt so her face was level with his.

"But father, what will happen to us now?"

He smoothed his daughter's hair and for the first time in months looked her in the eye. "You will be free to do as you choose, and I will face the consequences of my actions."

He swallowed and straightened his shoulders; like a man who had peeled off artifice and self-deception and finally saw with clarity what had been before him all along. "Cassandra, you are wiser and stronger than I have ever given you credit for. You tried to warn me, and I dismissed you as a child. My words to you then still echo in my mind. 'Don't instruct me on my investments.' Do you remember when I said that? I feel the sting of those words like a sharp rebuke."

Cassandra winced to hear her father so chastened.

"Father you are too hard on yourself. You couldn't have known. No one could have—"

"No. In that one thing, you are wrong—I am not hard enough." He clutched his daughter's arms. "I, who tried to protect you from everything, who for so long kept you from the world, even kept you from riding a horse, I am the one who gambled away your future. And rather than protect you from my disgrace, I used you as a shield to hide behind without regard to the consequences for you. It's time I own up to what I've done, to all I've done."

"But Father, you will lose everything you worked so hard to rebuild. I can help. I *will* help. I would do anything for you." A tear trickled down her cheek.

"I know. But you don't have to." He kissed his daughter's forehead and wiped away the tear with his thumb.

CHAPTER 41

Crispin took the stairs two at time, energized at the prospect before him. It loomed large, like the full harvest moon, and each step somehow seemed a rung on the ladder to his dreams. He had been climbing for some time, but the summit was finally within reach, and it thrilled and terrified him.

He knocked heavily on the door of 37 Grosvenor Square and was greeted by Braxton. The butler's hair was now salt and pepper gray, and the crow's feet that stretched from the corners of his eyes were longer and deeper. Softened by time, he looked even kindlier than when Crispin had first met him.

"Braxton, I doubt you'll remember me. It's Crispin St. John."

"Of course. Crispin! I mean Mr. St. John. It is a pleasure to see you."

"Braxton, is Lord Drayton home? I need to see him." Crispin blurted out.

"Why yes. In his study. Is he expecting you?"

"No. But could you tell him I'm here?"

"Certainly." Sensing Crispin's urgency, Braxton quickly ascended the stairs, leaving Crispin fidgety and agitated in the foyer. It suddenly occurred to him that Lord Drayton might refuse to see him. He might still despise the guttersnipe responsible for his daughter's near-death fall. In fact, it was likely that looking back through the telescope of time, his paltry crimes had grown larger in Lord Drayton's view. Or perhaps Drayton would refuse to see him for different reasons, after all, he was a stranger barging in uninvited at an inopportune time. Or maybe Lord

Drayton wouldn't even remember him. A scruffy stable boy surely did not occupy his thoughts for long.

"Wait," Crispin called after Braxton, who did not hear him. He shifted from foot to foot and decided to follow the butler. When Braxton opened the door to Lord Drayton's study, Crispin was just a few feet away.

"M'Lord. Mr. Crispin St. John is here to see you."

"Hello, My Lord," Crispin said haltingly as he moved into the doorframe and gave a short bow. Braxton raised his eyebrows but took a step backward to let Crispin pass.

James Drayton looked ashen in the harsh afternoon light that streamed in through the curtains. Crispin hardly recognized the man. He hardly recognized himself. The first time he had been in a room with Lord Drayton, Crispin was an awestruck, frightened boy, meeting the master of the house. Above the man had hung a famous painting, not that Crispin knew at the time, of a chestnut mare and red-coated rider that so resembled Lord James Drayton, Crispin had thought it was a portrait. It now hung in Crispin's library. Ten years had passed, and that same man stood before the former stable boy, older, grayer, damaged; he no longer embodied the enthusiasm for the hunt, the vivacity of the rider and the horse. His face was placid; his expression still; the wall behind him empty.

"Lord Drayton," Crispin began, searching for the words. "I know I may not be the man you would have sought . . ." He stumbled.

"You're Crispin. St. John."

"Yes."

"The stable boy."

"Yes, I was."

"I have heard . . . good things. From your aunt and others." Lord Drayton sounded regretful. "I am not the man I once was, and I suspect that you are not the same boy."

"I should hope not." Crispin had a vague recollection of Lord Drayton's face, violet with anger as he tried to choke him so many years ago. He seemed so powerful then. But the world had shifted and now Crispin navigated the landscape more surefooted.

"I have rehearsed a hundred speeches in my mind," Crispin summoned his courage, "but all of them only amount to one thing—Lord Drayton, I love your daughter. She is everything to me, and I would like to ask for her hand in marriage."

Crispin waited for a response. Half-seconds seemed like hours.

Lord Drayton's eyes widened, and the corner of his lip moved as if to curl upward. Finally, he said, with slow deliberation,

"I'm no expert when it comes to love. In fact, truth be told, I'm a failure at it." His piercing honesty took Crispin by surprise, but the Lord did not seem entirely defeated. "My daughter is much more educated in matters of the heart. I trust her. If she'll have you . . ." he drifted off.

"If she'll have me, I'll do all that is humanly possible to deserve her. I promise."

Lord Drayton reached his hand across the room and took Crispin's, gripping it tightly.

Buoyed higher than the clouds, Crispin bound for the door. He needed to get a ring. He needed to write Cassandra a letter, a long letter filled with love and sentiment. He needed to purchase a bouquet of flowers as big as a bushel. The list of needs scrolled so thunderously, that he almost didn't hear her feet on the landing above. But he did.

Dressed in a blue gown, the same color as the one she had worn that day she marched into the stables, her face was soft, framed by long curls that hung unpinned beneath her shoulders. She was no better and no worse than in his dreams. Exactly the same.

Cassandra smiled, a happy tear drifting down her cheek, and Crispin rushed up the stairs to catch it.

CHAPTER 42

October 1874

"Do you really want to go?" Crispin asked with gravity.

"Yes." Cassandra tucked her arm deeper into the crook of his and burrowed her cheek into the curve of his neck.

The memory of their summer honeymoon hung on Crispin and Cassandra like perfume. They had been to so many places. Paris, Florence, Prague. They had long picnics in the Swiss Alps and meandered without hurry through the canals of Venice. They had lingered over dinners and talked deep into the night while the stars blinked through their windows. In the wee hours of the mornings, Cassandra woke in quiet awe at the way their bodies fit together. She would weave her fingers into Crispin's, and he would gently squeeze his hand around hers to make a shared fist, awake but asleep. Cassandra felt certain of the world in a way that reminded her of childhood, but a knowing childhood.

"I need to say goodbye," Cassandra said, and Crispin's arms tightened lovingly.

"Johnson, we'll go up to the house."

"Yes, sir."

Johnson, their coachman, turned the horses toward the long drive that led to the house. He paused and stepped off his perch to open the heavy gates. They moved like old men, tired from long years of service. Cassandra wondered if the new owners would replace them. It would be logical. The wrought iron D, a relic of her father's proud embellishments, would be meaningless to a new owner.

The smell of the Dorset autumn filled their carriage. The last of the viburnum and the first of the crab apple mingled in the crisp air. The carriage climbed the slow-sloping hill, each turn revealing a familiar sight: the little chapel buried among the tall pines, a knot of red and yellow trees beyond the first pasture, a bank of sleepy summer lavender. Another turn and Cassandra could see in the distance the outline of their gardens. Hedges once manicured in straight, upright lines now grew reckless and fat. The swaying fountain grass crossed paths with the pop of aster and purple heather. Ivy crept over the stone walkways and fences and spiraled around the winter jasmine trees.

Crispin looked at Cassandra with understanding. He did not ask what thoughts coursed through her brain. He did not need telling that this was Cassandra's last pilgrimage to a sacred place.

It had only been a year and one month since Cassandra had left and yet it felt much longer. The house seemed to have aged, as if it was conscious of the year's hardships. Maids and footmen no longer came to the door to greet the carriage. They had all been dismissed, along with the head gardener, the groundskeepers, the groomsman, the stable boys. The Joneses were all that remained of the old Drayton Manor staff, along with Eleanor, who had once been an assistant cook. The head cook had been given an outstanding reference so that she could find an equally fine house for her elaborate meals.

Jones greeted them.

"Miss Cassandra, I mean, Mrs. St. John. Mr. St. John." He bowed deferentially, but the corners of his mouth curved up revealing that he was amused. Cassandra was fairly certain it was at Crispin's change in circumstance, rather than hers. Jones was not a mean sort.

"Jones, it is good to see you." Crispin's hand shot out for a proper shake. As always, Cassandra was impressed with the easy way he swung between two worlds—between the stiff-lipped crustiness of Aunt Eugenia and the comfortable manners and cockney tongues of the workingman's circle.

"Cassandra wants a good look around the place. It may take some time."

"Of course. Eleanor is preparing tea. What room will you take it in?" A final domestic decision to make at Drayton Manor.

"What rooms are open?"

"Most are still closed mum, but I'm 'appy to open whichever you would like."

"No need. We'll take tea in the garden. Under the pagoda."

They walked slowly through the house, Crispin always a few steps behind Cassandra. Each room was shrouded in white sheets to keep the dust off the exquisite furniture and relics. Cassandra lifted a sheet off the grand piano and pressed a single low note, which echoed sadly through the house.

Drayton Manor was filled with the ghosts of memory. Midway up the stairs, she stopped on the landing to look out the window at the stables and the untamed gardens. There, that hedgerow, was where she had first spotted Crispin and wondered, *who is that shaggy-haired lad about her age?* Cassandra could feel his adult self behind her, his broad shoulders framing her back. Crispin reached his arms around Cassandra's stomach and rested his chin lightly in the crook of her neck.

For a moment, before time went hurtling forward as it always does, Cassandra was ten again, with soft yellow curls, swinging her feet under her chair as she and Lord Drayton played chess. She was thirteen, riding up Bryanston hill, craving freedom. She was twenty-two watching her father's crestfallen face as they handed the title to his Landau, among other cherished items, over to the auctioneer. She was standing at the altar, her mother's lace veil framing her face, Crispin staring back at her.

"We have been lucky," Crispin whispered in Cassandra's ear. Dizzying nostalgia spun around her, so she kissed him to steady herself, a long slow kiss.

EPILOGUE

October 1875

Emma threw her arms around Cassandra, giddy as she hugged her. She drew back and held out Cassandra's arms, staring at her waistline to see if it had changed, but the mother-to-be wasn't showing yet.

"And when does the doctor say the baby will arrive?" Emma drew Cassandra to the sofa, fussing over her as they sat down. They were in the parlor at Green Street, formerly Crispin's home which he continued to let for his Aunt.

"In the spring, April he thinks. I'm so excited and Crispin is beside himself. You should see how he worries about what I eat and what I carry. He reminds me of you when I was a child." Cassandra chuckled at the thought. Crispin had been thrilled when she'd told him about the baby. He couldn't stop planning, thinking about the baby's room, getting a nurse, schooling. Her head was spinning with his plans.

"I'm sure he is, he loves you so." Emma smiled wistfully, and Cassandra wondered if she was thinking of her father. They'd barely spoken to each other since the wedding, and Cassandra thought perhaps Emma wanted it that way.

"And how are you, Emma? I feel like we spend all of our time talking about me, never about you."

"Well, there isn't much to say. I love this house and I've even begun to entertain a bit; just a few ladies but it's nice to have that freedom. I find I enjoy my independence." She did seem genuinely happy.

"Do you ever think of my father?" Cassandra wasn't sure she should have asked, but now with the baby coming, they would inevitably see each other more often, and selfishly she yearned for them to make peace.

Emma walked to the window looking out at Hyde Park in the distance, with its dusky green canopy of maples, elms, and copper beech trees. The bottom sash was slightly open, letting in the crisp bite of autumn.

"I do." She stroked the velvet curtains with the back of her hand absentmindedly. "And more so now that he's written to me." She retrieved the letter from a mahogany box on the mantle and handed it to Cassandra.

"He's written to you? After all this time?" James Drayton had kept his own counsel, especially where Emma was concerned. Since Cassandra and Crispin's wedding, he had been more subdued, spending much time at home and only rarely going out socially. His days of scheming and investing were long gone. Cassandra read his familiar scrawl.

> *Dearest Emma,*
>
> *For the first time in my life, I am unfettered by ambition and the tricks my hopes played on the truth. I was driven by childish desires. I wanted to be loved. I wanted to be the center of attention. I wanted to have everything. Without an adult's sense of prudence and pragmatism, I wanted to be a hero, and to restore the Drayton name and fortune, and when I failed, I wanted someone else to dig me out of the hole in which I had buried myself. In short, I wanted all of the glory, but none of the responsibility or the blame.*
>
> *If the Northern Pacific Railway had delivered its fruits, I wonder, would I have been any better off? Financially, of course, yes. But perhaps I would have lost you anyway. You must have been getting tired of my self-indulgent ways. Cassie, would she have grown to despise me as I led her down a disenchanting path? Would she have awoken to an empty life, bitter and malcontent? I was well on my way to sacrificing the very person I love most in all this world.*
>
> *I write to thank you for stopping me. You tried to teach me in your gentle way to be cautious. But I did not take heed. I was always a terrible student. Forever in trouble, testing the limits without paying attention. Even as a child my governess had warned me against the habit. "You want to gallop before you*

can trot," she would scold. She was a different sort of governess than you—her face freckled with age and her hair always divided with a pin-straight part. She was far more severe and strict, but she loved me as deeply as you do Emma.

When you could not get me to see reason . . . Well, I see now that even your leaving me was an act of selfless devotion. You were trying to stop me from betraying my daughter.

I have so much I want to say to you, I wonder if we might meet. The place and time of your choosing. Not as we had before, but as friends and equals.

Emma, you are in my every thought.

Yours,

James

Cassandra was speechless at the depth of her father's feelings for Emma, at hearing them for the first time in his own words. Emma had returned to the window, her expression inscrutable.

"Have you responded? Will you meet him?"

"How could I not?" Emma asked rhetorically, acknowledging the power James Drayton held over her. He had always drawn her in like waves to the shore. "I've loved him ever since you were a young girl." Her tone was solemn, but her countenance was bright. Cassandra's heart warmed at the thought of her happiness; she hoped her father would be worthy of Emma Fairfax. She rose to join her, clasping her hands in Emma's.

"Miss Fairfax? You have a visitor." Nora surprised them both as she entered the parlor with a shallow curtsy and an expectant gaze.

"Yes, Nora. Who is it?" Emma squeezed Cassandra's hands in return.

"It's Lord Drayton ma'am. Lord Drayton is calling."

ACKNOWLEDGMENTS

This book has been in equal parts a labor of love, a needed distraction, and a team effort. We couldn't have done it without the following:

Alison Bardeen and Ron Faris, who read our first (terrible) draft. First, sorry! Second, thank you for not laughing at us, but rather pointing us in the right direction and giving us the confidence to keep going.

Anges Turner for connecting us with all the right people to start our literary journey.

Ali Tancred and Zibby Owens, who answered our calls, texts, and emails at every step in the process and gave us invaluable insight into the literary world. Thank you for not blocking us—you would have been justified. We have no idea what we would have done without you.

Liz Van Hoose for her smart critique and needed advice. We tried to listen!

Jennifer Haskin and the TouchPoint Press Team. Thank you for taking a chance on us and for shepherding us through the process.

Danielle Faris—a.k.a. "The other Danielle"—who at a moment's notice built our website, sharing our story with the world, and making us realize this was real!

Kimberly Brower, the best agent two girls could have. You believed in us. You were both a coach and a cheerleader.

Our families: our parents, siblings, children, nieces, nephews, and godchildren, who are the center of our world.

And, especially our husbands, Nic and Craig. They were, in turns, locked out of rooms so that we could write and read in private and then forced to listen to us yammer on about the book. Thank you for being our champions.

ABOUT THE AUTHORS

Photo credit: Kimberly Butler

The Last Season is a collaboration between Jenny Judson and Danielle Mahfood, who met in high school and shared a mutual love of historical fiction and romance novels. Instead of passing notes in class, Jenny and Danielle would write short excerpts from imaginary novels that featured themselves and their classmates as characters caught up in tales of romance and adventure. Many years later, after cheering for opposite teams at Harvard-Yale games, they came together in New York City to begin writing *The Last Season,* inspired both by the Victorian period and the financial crisis of 2008.

daniandjenny.com